PRAISE FOR
LORD OF WINTER

"If you tell me a story is epic, there needs to be some serious 'swept me away' going on. Exactly what happened when I read Lord of Winter. This one's a keeper, my friends."

—JAMES L. RUBART,
CHRISTY HALL OF FAME AUTHOR

"As a long-time fan of Williamson's Blood of Kings trilogy, I loved being back in a familiar story world with a brand-new tale. And what a tale it is! Lord of Winter is an expertly woven, unforgettable story of courage, sacrifice, and real, true love."

—S.D. GRIMM,
AUTHOR OF THE CHILDREN OF THE BLOOD MOON TRILOGY
AND BENEATH FALSE STARS

"A beautifully woven tale of love, sacrifice, and resilience, set against a backdrop of intrigue and betrayal, where duty and desire collide in a fight for the future."

—J.J. JOHNSON,
AWARD WINNING AUTHOR OF THE IGGY & OZ SERIES

LORD OF WINTER

←BLOOD OF KINGS: LEGENDS→

LORD OF WINTER

◄Blood of Kings: Legends►

Andrew Swearingen

Jill Williamson

Lord of Winter
Blood of Kings: Legends Book 2
Copyright © 2025 Sunrise Media Group LLC

Print ISBN: 978-1-963372-60-1

This book is a work of fiction. Names, characters, places, and incidents are either products of the author's imagination or used fictitiously. Any similarity to actual people, organizations, and/or events is purely coincidental.
All Scripture quotations, unless otherwise indicated, are taken from the King James Version.

For more information about Jill Williamson please access the author's website at www.jillwilliamson.com.

Published in the United States of America.
Cover Design: Emilie Haney, eahcreative.com

Blood of Kings: Legends

Squire of Truth
Lord of Winter
Lady of Shadows
Heir of Light

Blood of Kings

By Darkness Hid
To Darkness Fled
From Darkness Won

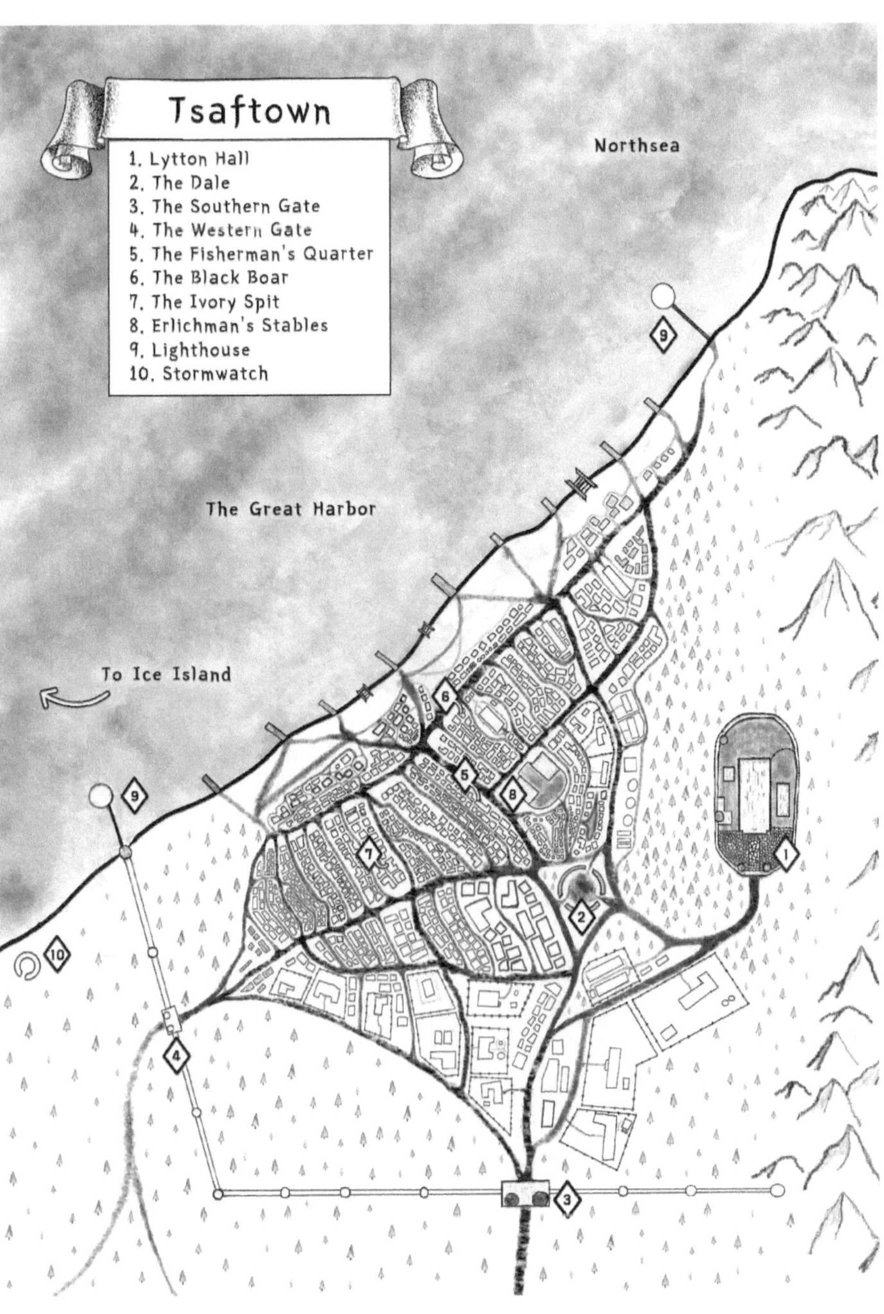

Tsaftown
1. Lytton Hall
2. The Dale
3. The Southern Gate
4. The Western Gate
5. The Fisherman's Quarter
6. The Black Boar
7. The Ivory Spit
8. Erlichman's Stables
9. Lighthouse
10. Stormwatch
Northsea
The Great Harbor
To Ice Island

To Dad.
I think you would have loved this book.

CHAPTER ONE
ERIC

SOMETHING WASN'T RIGHT.

A knot soured Lord Eric Livna's gut as he rode his stallion, Guffey, in the column just behind the advance guard. This same knot had warned him of looming dangers on the eve of battle, but there was no such battle waiting at the end of this journey. The war was over. Gidon Hadar, the true king, sat on the throne and had turned back the literal Darkness that had covered half of Er'Rets for the past ten years.

Instead of battle cries, the men of the Tsaftown army laughed with one another. A gleeful bard sang the chorus of "The Pawn Our King" and had entertained them with many other anthems as they traveled the long road home.

Their route currently wove through a snowy valley in the foothills of the northern Chowmah Mountains. The noon sun cast silvery light over the frosted patchwork of trees that had once been the mighty northern forest Eric had hunted in as a youth. Darkness had marred its beauty these past ten years, but the stark whiteness revealed signs of renewal. Oak and maple trees stood tall beneath icy mantles, their trunks shedding remnants of lichen and moss.

Even brittle grass peeked timidly through patches where the snow had thinned, a fragile promise of life beneath the wintry shroud.

The land was healing at last.

"Something on your mind, my lord?" Whiffs of vanilla-scented smoke tickled Eric's nose as his grey-bearded valet rode up alongside. Apparently, the pleasant weather had inspired the typically reserved Walter Blackburn to relax a bit and savor his pipe.

"Home is the only thing on my mind," Eric said. "A warm hearth, a proper meal, and a soft bed."

"And a nice pair of dry boots," Walter added, puffing on his pipe.

Eric chuckled. "If that is your wish. You may use your downtime however you see fit."

Walter leaned in toward Eric. "I hadn't wanted to say so, but your squire appears to be getting a head start on his downtime."

Eric traced Walter's gaze back toward where Derby Wenk, Eric's young squire, followed on his own horse. He was supposed to be serving as Eric's back rider, but the lad had drifted several horse lengths and was listening to one of the soldiers weave a longtale.

Not just any soldier, Eric noted. Kurtz Chazir. One of the king's men. Originally from Tsaftown, he had long ago earned a reputation for indulging in drink and female company. He had been involved in King Gidon's now legendary escape from the Ice Island prison and had served at the king's side faithfully throughout the war, sometimes heroically, other times making blunders worthy of a Captain's Row.

Apparently, there had been some falling out between the king, his former squire Cole Tanniyn, and Kurtz in the weeks following the war. The king himself had asked Eric to let the two men ride north with the Fighting Five Hundred to seek out some new endeavor.

Derby cackled as Kurtz's tale reached its climax. The lad was clearly enjoying himself at the expense of his duty. While on campaign, such a lapse in discipline would have been met with harsh rebuke. Yet with the army but two days from home after months of battling their way down and back up the length of Er'Rets, perhaps such valiant service had earned the lad a bit of latitude.

On the other hand, Eric didn't want his squire getting accustomed to being lax in his duty.

"Master Wenk!" Eric barked. "On your post."

Surprise shone in Derby's eyes as he turned away from Kurtz. The lad prodded his horse and quickly resumed his position behind Eric.

"I'm sorry, my lord."

"Chin up," Eric said. "If you hope to make the Fighting Fifteen one day, you can start by keeping vigilant. And you can't do that while staring at your boots. You'll have plenty of time to trade stories with your comrades once we reach home."

Derby forced his head up, making proper eye contact. "Of course, my lord."

Eric internally squirmed at Derby's repetition of the words "my lord." Not merely the words themselves—he'd heard them plenty over the past few months—but the reverence Derby often put in them. The title still didn't seem to fit. Like an overly snug shirt, tugging at his shoulders. Like he was borrowing the title from his father.

A sharp ache spiked in Eric's chest.

Four months ago, Esek Nathak, the false prince, had run the elder Lord Livna through with the sword. Eric's father, killed on the whim of a bloodthirsty tyrant.

There had been precious little time to grieve. Soon after, Eric and the Tsaftown army had marched south to war with the then Crown Prince Gidon Hadar. This left Eric's grieving mother and his wife, Viola, to tend to the needs of the city in his absence. Eric had no doubt they were up to the task, but he hated that he had been pried away from his family when they no doubt had needed him most.

The bard ended his performance of "The Pawn Our King" with a playful flourish which earned a round of laughter from the men. He segued seamlessly into "The Sparrow that Was a She," a new song first sung at the king's wedding that chronicled the adventures of Lady Averella as she traveled through Darkness with the then Crown Prince.

Queen Averella now. It would take some time for Eric to get used to addressing his younger cousin by such a title.

A sharp whistle echoed from the front of the column, signaling a halt. Hooves and armor clattered as the line came to a lumbering stop. Eric pulled Guffey out of formation and galloped toward the head of the column with Walter and Derby riding close behind.

At the front of the line, Eric reined Guffey to a halt beside Captain Roxburg Demry, the commander of the army. A large clearing on the side of the road exposed the burned-out husk of a house. Beyond lay a snowy field, stretching far into the distance. Dark scorch marks marred a stone half wall that formed a large rectangle around the perimeter of what had once been the manor house. The only structure left standing was a dilapidated shed on the back corner of the property.

"By the Three," Walter muttered. "This was Glodwood Manor."

Eric's chest tightened.

Glodwood Manor had long been a landmark for travelers of the King's Road. It wouldn't have rivaled the beautiful structures in Carmine or Armonguard, yet such an elegant home stood out in the North where most houses were built to be functional. But where the beautiful log home and barn once stood, only scorched timbers and a collapsed chimney remained. A swath of snow blanketed everything. The tragedy must have transpired months ago.

Could it have been an accident? Such an explanation didn't satisfy Eric. He eyed a strange mass covering a section of the cobblestone walkway in front of what used to be the door. A closer look, and Eric noticed that the lump wore boots.

A body.

Eric slid from Guffey's saddle and gave his squire a pat on the leg. "Come along, Derby. Get your shield and let us take a closer look."

Derby grabbed his shield off his saddlebag as he dismounted, and the pair strode through the snow toward the iron gate.

Captain Demry called after them, "My lord, what is it you mean to do?"

Eric looked back. "I merely wish to see the scene for myself."

Captain Demry's eyes narrowed. "I can send soldiers, if you want to investigate."

Eric smiled to himself. Captain Demry was a fantastic commander, but he could be paranoid when it came to Eric's safety. "Your concern is touching, but unnecessary. I'll take a quick peek, then we can carry on."

The iron hinges of the gate creaked as Eric and Derby entered the front yard. A faint stench of death touched Eric's nostrils. The fire might have been months ago, but the poor soul lying prone on the walkway couldn't have been dead for more than a week.

Eric knelt by the remains and used his gloved hand to brush a fine layer of snow off the body. The man was dressed in traveling clothes with a black sash running over one shoulder to his opposite hip. He had been run through multiple times and pinned to the ground with a series of stakes and ropes. A steel badge bearing the likeness of a wolf had been fastened to the sash, right above his heart.

"What do you make of this?" Eric asked.

Derby crouched beside Eric and gestured at the corpse. "Why'd they pin him to the ground?"

Eric traced the length of the rope with his gaze. Something about this seemed familiar, but he couldn't say exactly what.

"Here's another one." Derby pointed at a second thin rope tied across the corpse's waist. He hooked his fingers around it and gave a tug.

"Stop!" Eric seized Derby's wrist as a sudden realization came over him.

Poroo raiders.

Derby glanced at Eric, rope still in hand. "My lord, what—?"

"Take care, lad. It appears you've stumbled across a trap."

Derby's eyes went wide.

Eric had seen a snare like this years ago while hunting with his father. He reached around Derby and slipped the shield from the lad's shoulder. "Hold tight. You've only engaged the first part of the snare, but if you let go, it will fire." The trap would have been invisible in Darkness, but daylight had exposed a line of footprints trailing away from the body through the snow and into a cluster of trees some ten paces away.

"Captain Demry!" Eric called. "Have archers ready."

Demry hollered out the order, arming his bow along with the others.

Eric slid Derby's shield in front of them. In their crouched position, it might be enough to save them. "Remain absolutely still."

"I'm sorry, my lord. I didn't—"

"None of that now. Do as I say, and we'll all come through this." Eric's eyes darted to the nearby trees. The patches of underbrush that edged close to the stone wall. The run-down shed in back. Anywhere the Poroo might be hiding. Scurrying motion in the woods caught his eye.

"On my right, Captain," Eric said.

More movement. Glimpses of pale skin and furs shuffling through the underbrush. Were there four? No, five.

"More on the left," called Walter.

Eric glanced quickly to the left and counted at least three Poroo behind a snowbank. He couldn't worry about them. The bigger threat was on the right, so he'd have to trust Walter to watch their backs.

All chatter among the men had ceased. Only the creaking of

the gate, buffeted by a soft wind, could be heard in the otherwise silent scene.

Eric slowly turned on the balls of his feet toward the expected direction of the strike. "Captain Demry, I'm going to spring the trap." He hunched his shoulders, making himself as small of a target as possible. "Duck your head, Derby. Then let go of the snare."

Derby's dark eyebrows shot up.

"Now!" Eric said.

The squire swallowed, lowered his head, and let go.

There was the sound of stretching leather. Then a sharp wooden snap.

As the rip cord snapped back, snow flew up from the ground and flung a wooden projectile into Eric's shield. The impact rattled his teeth and knocked him and Derby to the ground.

A chorus of angry war whoops shot up on the fringes of the forest. Footsteps scampered over the ground as a war party of fur-clad Poroo warriors charged out of the woods on Eric's left and right.

Twice as many as he had first counted.

"Loose!" Captain Demry yelled.

A collective flutter of fletchings preceded the arrival of the first volley of Tsaftown's bowmen. Several arrows met their targets, and three of the charging raiders fell.

Eric leaped to a defensive position and drew his sword. The embedded spear threw off the shield's balance, but it was far better than nothing.

Two of the raiders vaulted the stone half wall and sprinted toward Eric and Derby. One took an arrow to the chest and fell. The other swung a massive club at Eric, who sidestepped and sliced his sword deep into the man's thigh. The Poroo stumbled and was swiftly finished off by a barrage of arrows from the bowmen.

"More beyond the sheds!" Captain Demry's voice roared over the battlefield, calling out the order. "Wroxton! Get your men to Lord Livna."

Wroxton leaped off his horse, followed by Torin Oxbow and Gunnar Gedmund. Kurtz Chazir also drew his sword and charged into the fray.

Derby still knelt on the ground, pawing at the snow. What was he doing?

"On your feet!" Eric yelled.

"I—I'm trapped!"

Eric took a closer look. The rope from the snare had cinched Derby's wrist to the ground. Eric stepped between the helpless squire and the oncoming attackers.

"Cut yourself free. Quickly." Eric slammed his shield into the next Poroo, breaking off the remnant of the wooden spear against the attacker's breastbone. The man crumpled, and Eric ended him with a swift stroke.

Wroxton and the other soldiers barreled over the half wall and joined Eric at his side.

A cry from Derby distracted Eric. The loop pulled tighter and tighter around Derby's wrist. Poroo trickery. The trap kept twisting. Derby tried to cut himself free, but now he risked slashing his wrist open in the process.

Eric traced the line of the snare to its source. The rope led into the burned timbers of the house. He slashed with his sword. The line snapped and retracted completely into the house. Finally free, Derby fell onto his backside.

"Up, and make haste!" Eric yelled.

Derby got to his feet, drew his sword, and joined the fight. The six men stood in a loose circle, ready for the next onslaught.

Horse hooves rumbled, and Jol Quimby led a trio of riders around the outer edge of the wall. The Poroo in the open scrambled away from the charge, but arrows flew from the underbrush and from behind snowdrifts in the field. Three riders in a disorganized charge were simply not enough to deter the attackers.

"Form ranks. Prepare your spears!" Captain Demry bellowed.

Yet more Poroo tore out of the woods. How many more were there?

The army could have handled the raiders easily if they were prepped for battle, but the ambush had caught them completely flat-footed. And the Poroo's evasive tactics meant that Captain Demry's men had no target to engage. The bowmen provided support at a distance, but they couldn't easily get past the fence to charge into the fray without exposing their flank.

Eric and his group would have to hold their own until Captain Demry's men could form a proper cavalry charge.

A trio of Poroo climbed over the stone wall and charged Eric's position. The tallest bore down on them with a great ax. Swift arrows slowed the two smaller attackers, but the first man charged forward, ax already swinging. Eric raised his shield and caught the ax in the wood. He wrenched the shield to the left and slashed into the man's unguarded left arm, nearly severing the limb at the elbow.

The Poroo dropped the ax. Eric swung at the raider's neck. Somehow, the one-armed man caught the killing stroke, wrapping his meaty fingers around the blade and pushing it back. He glared with bloodshot eyes and howled an ear-splitting war cry in Eric's face.

A sword strike came down on the Poroo's collarbone. Derby Wenk landed the final blow. The Poroo's grip slipped from Eric's sword. Derby slammed his shoulder into the man and knocked him to the ground. The squire quickly pivoted to stand shoulder to shoulder with Eric, and they braced for another onslaught.

"Northlanders, ho!" Captain Demry's voice called out over the din of the skirmish.

The thunder of a dozen sets of hooves shook the ground as Captain Demry rode his red warhorse at the head of a properly organized column around the outside of the stone wall. Even Walter had joined the charge, firing his bow into the heaviest group of Poroo. Quimby's trio followed in Captain Demry's wake, wielding their swords like men in a blood rage. More arrows zipped past as the cavalry charge swiftly wheeled around the back of the homestead and picked off the raiders one at a time.

Eric gazed across the battlefield. The skirmish had turned into a full retreat as the surviving Poroo made for the safety of the woods. Or at least most of them.

A solitary figure stood in the burned remains of the barn, lingering far longer than any of his compatriots. A great deal older than the majority of the Poroo who had fought today, this man leaned on a large staff adorned with bear claws and glared at Eric across the battlefield. Was that hatred in his expression? Contempt?

Eric took a measured step toward the Poroo and raised his sword in a silent challenge.

The lone Poroo retreated from the barn and disappeared amidst the snowy trees.

Eric met Derby's gaze for a moment and clapped the young man's shoulder. "Well done, Derby. Keep that up and Captain Demry will have no choice but to appoint you to the Fighting Fifteen."

Captain Demry brought his mount to a halt at the gate in front of Eric. The rest of the riders secured the perimeter of the homestead, ensuring no Poroo stragglers lingered.

"Are we clear, Captain?" Eric called.

Captain Demry tucked his bow over his shoulder. "All clear, my lord. We took a few wounds from the Poroo hiding in the trees. Nothing life-threatening. No doubt they expected a wagon train of peddlers, not the leading edge of the Fighting Five Hundred."

Eric and Derby withdrew through the gate and rejoined the scattered column.

"Are you quite satisfied with your investigation, my lord?" Walter asked.

Eric chuckled. "I believe so."

"Well, look who stumbled into a spot of bother," Wroxton said as he handed Derby the reins to his horse. "Wenkling was determined to fight the Poroo *single-handedly*."

"Consider yourself lucky you didn't step in a cham trap, eh, Wenkling?" Kurtz added. "That would've shortened your step in a hurry, it would."

The men laughed, and Derby's overlarge ears reddened as he climbed up on his horse again.

"But did you see the way he tackled the big brute?" Quimby said, his voice filled with admiration. "Wenkling may have stumbled into that trap, but he sure knows how to wield a blade. Saved his lordship's hide, he did."

Derby sat a little higher in the saddle after that comment.

Eric mounted Guffey and took one last look at what had once been Glodwood Manor. The fight had only left him with more questions. Too many to feel at ease.

Poroo weren't known to conduct raids this far north. Perhaps the end of Darkness had changed their hunting patterns? But why burn the farmhouse? Why mutilate a body and set a trap in the ruins? And all this happening so close to Eric's home. Too close for comfort.

"Onward!" Eric called. "To home."

The column resumed their procession toward Tsaftown. There he intended to find answers to his lingering questions.

Something wasn't right.

CHAPTER TWO
VIOLA

A WOMAN COULD ATTAIN ANYTHING in life if she dressed appropriately for the pursuit.

"The violet gown will do for tonight," Lady Viola said as her lady's maid, De'Lana, worked to cinch her corset.

"But the gold is much prettier," De'Lana said. "And with the beaded black fringe, it matches Tsaftown's colors perfectly."

A gown Viola had strategically commissioned, but not one appropriate for this occasion. "The attention tonight should not be on me, but on my husband, the new lord, returned home a war hero. And on Nevandra, his heir. Only they should be dressed to match."

"My lady?" Arne's breathless voice called through the door from the hallway. "Are you in there?"

Lady Viola rolled her eyes to the coffered ceiling of her bedchamber. Though the interruption was inopportune, she took advantage of the reprieve from her ever-tightening corset and sucked in a deep breath.

Again the door rattled. "My lady?"

Arne must have known that Viola would be dressing at this time and wouldn't interrupt without a good reason.

"One moment," Viola called. "De'Lana, my robe?"

De'Lana fetched the blue chenille and draped it over Viola's shoulders. With her modesty protected, Viola nodded to De'Lana, who opened the door.

Arne, House Livna's chief servant, stepped slowly into the room. The curled wisps of hair that encircled his otherwise bald head were damp with sweat. Certainly no surprise given the amount of work ahead of him for tonight's feast.

"Forgive the intrusion, my lady." Arne dipped his head ever so slightly. "Lady Revada wishes to see you in the great hall."

Viola might have guessed. There were few people in Lytton Hall who could force Arne from his duties on such a busy day. The recently widowed matriarch of House Livna was certainly one of them.

"You couldn't have sent one of the serving girls?" De'Lana asked.

Arne's cheeks reddened. "Lady Revada insisted I relay the message myself."

Viola offered Arne a gentle smile. "Thank you for telling me. I will come as soon as I am dressed. You may continue with your preparations. I am sure that the hall will be in wondrous condition for the evening's festivities."

Arne dabbed at his forehead with his handkerchief. "Indeed it shall, my lady." With that, he departed.

De'Lana closed the door and loosed an elaborate sigh as Viola shrugged off her robe and handed it over. "Goatheaded woman. Busiest day of our year, and she's going to drag you out to meet with her?"

Viola shook her head. "Please don't call my mother-in-law *goatheaded*. It's unbecoming."

And the insult was common Jaelport slang. Nobody in Tsaftown needed any more reminders of Viola's Jaelportian heritage.

"I'm sorry, my lady," De'Lana said. "But she treats you as if you were a servant. Not the lady of a noble house."

Viola ran her hand over her head, taming several strands of stray hair. "Lady Revada has been the mistress here for the past two decades. She is still entitled to being heard. Plus, Eric and I need both her and Lady Merris's support if we are to run this house properly."

"Well, it won't be them that folks will be looking at tonight. If I've anything to say, you'll have all eyes on you. Once you're dressed, I'll see to making sure your hair is properly braided." De'Lana finished tightening the corset. "You'll be an absolute delight to look upon. Especially for that husband of yours." She punctuated her statement with a cheeky wink.

Viola sighed, running a finger along her brow and down to her temple. She cared little for how she looked to Eric. It was how Nevandra was perceived that truly mattered.

"Let us save the hair for later," Viola said, tucking a stray strand behind her ear. "We mustn't keep Lady Revada waiting."

Lytton Hall had never felt like home to Viola. Individual elements of the manor house were charming enough. She rather liked the library and her own bedchamber. And as she made her way down the stairs toward the great hall, the pleasant smell of woodsmoke clung to the timbers.

But it was not a home.

None of this lessened her responsibilities. As wife of the new city lord, it befitted her status to make sure that Eric and his soldiers received a grand homecoming.

Down in the kitchens, the cooks would be roasting venison, dicing endless quantities of vegetables, and preparing the ovens to bake dozens of loaves of bread. And Viola had taken special care in the great hall.

As she entered the cavernous room, the sounds of preparation echoed up to the high ceiling. Servants and staff scurried about, arranging tables and hanging freshly ironed black-and-gold banners.

The narrow room could seat as many as two hundred individuals. It had been built of unfinished logs and used to be filled with the preserved trophy heads and antlers of Sir Edik's hunting expeditions. Viola had asked that they be put away for this special occasion so that the hall might have a more majestic feel, rather than a rustic haven for soldiers to carouse.

As per Viola's request, Arne had polished the carved dagfish on the wall behind the high table and washed and pressed the black-and-gold checkered tablecloth. She had also commissioned a new gold runner for the center aisle to replace the one that had been soiled in her father-in-law's blood.

Everything was coming together nicely. This evening, the hall would see all the city council, tradesmen, clergy, and other leaders filling nearly every corner of the towering room, with the ruling members of House Livna sitting at the high table down front.

At the moment, there was only one individual in the great hall requiring Viola's attention.

No. Not one, Viola realized. Two. They were both here.

In the center of the aisle stood Lady Revada, dressed all in black, including her mourning veil which hid her eyes and nose but left her mouth visible. Next to her, at one of the tables, sat Lady Merris, Eric's grandmother. The dowager tapped a finger impatiently on the top of her ornate cane as Viola reached them.

An encounter with Lady Revada was one matter. But facing them both at once? Viola pressed her palms against her belly, flattening invisible wrinkles in her violet dress, and approached the two matriarchs of House Livna.

"Ladies, I apologize for the delay," Viola said. "I was told you wished to speak with me."

"Viola, darling." Lady Revada gripped Viola's elbow and kissed her on the cheek. "The hall is resplendent. I cannot remember a time when it looked better."

Viola smiled politely. "Very kind of you to say so. I could only build on its inherent grandeur."

"The servants moved my son's stuffed animal heads," Lady Merris interjected.

Viola clasped her hands together. "Sir Edik's trophies were moved to create space for more banners. Once the banquet is concluded, they'll be put back in their proper places."

Lady Merris clicked her tongue. "Leave them in a closet, I say. Dreadful to look at those beastly things at every meal."

"Nevertheless"—Lady Revada took Viola's hand in her own—"it takes a unique vision and a keen mind to pull together something like this."

Viola sensed a "however" coming. Lady Revada would not have summoned her simply to pay her a compliment.

"I do wish," Revada said, "that I had been consulted on some of the changes in the regular arrangements to the hall."

"There's a space for Mistress Nevandra at the head table," Lady Merris said, fixing Viola with a crooked eyebrow. "Was that your doing?"

"Yes, that is Nevandra's seat," Viola said. "She is Eric's firstborn, so it seemed fitting to give her a place at the table. Unless that will be a problem?" Viola held her arms out to either side, gently inviting further discussion.

"Children ought to be seen and not heard." Lady Merris tapped her cane on the wooden floor.

Viola struggled to keep her expression passive. She would not allow the woman to rile her.

Lady Revada patted Viola's hand. "There are simply concerns

about having a child so young at the banquet. It is a celebration, yes. But it is also an important function for the city. The council will be paying their respects to Eric tonight for the first time. Do you really trust that Nevandra will be able to behave for the entirety of the evening?"

A sharp prickle ran down Viola's neck. "Has House Livna not had children sit at such functions before? I know that the standard age is twelve, but exceptions have been made. I was told that Eric joined in on feast evenings at age seven."

"Nevandra is much younger than that," Lady Revada said. "And Eric was a firstborn son, not a daughter. We both know such things are weighed differently. There will be many eyes on her. And a lady must always make the right first impression. Even a very young one."

"This isn't Jaelport," Lady Merris added. "The rabble who attend this banquet will be less forgiving of a daughter's presence."

Tempest's mercy. The old dowager was in no mood to mince words.

Viola politely held up a hand. "I know the temperament of my own daughter. Nevandra is—"

"Mama!"

Tiny footsteps pattered toward them.

Oh dear. What perfect timing for Nevandra to make an appearance.

Loose dark hair fluttered behind the girl dashing down the aisle toward Viola, clutching a stuffed rabbit by the ears. Back at the front doors, Sabrea, Nevandra's nanny, speed-walked into the hall.

The three-year-old threw herself against Viola's legs, wrapping her knees in a hug.

"Nevandra." Viola gently pried the little hands off, knelt, and gave her daughter a proper hug. "What have I told you about running away from Sabrea?"

An impish smile creased Nevandra's rosy cheeks, and she shook her stuffed rabbit. "Bunny is dancing!"

Viola arched an eyebrow at her daughter. "Nevandra...what have I told you?"

The girl huffed, holding the bunny close to her chest. "No running away."

Sabrea finally reached them, gaze fixed on the floor. Her pale face had flushed pink, either from exertion or embarrassment. Knowing Sabrea, it was likely both.

"I'm sorry, milady," Sabrea said. "She got away from me."

"Precisely our concern," Lady Merris mumbled.

Viola rose, straightening her back and adopting the proper posture of a noble. "All is well." She gave Sabrea a gentle nod. "Perhaps play time in the garden will be helpful. Just be certain that she has enough time to rest and clean up for the banquet."

"Yes, milady," Sabrea said.

Viola laid her hand on Nevandra's head. "And we are going to do a better job listening to Sabrea, aren't we, young lady?"

Nevandra nodded obediently. "Yes, Mama."

Viola smiled. No doubt Nevandra's adventurous spirit would overtake her obedience, but such was the way of things.

Before letting them go, Viola laid a firm hand on Sabrea's shoulder. "She cannot get away from you again," Viola whispered. "Understood?"

Sabrea shrank under Viola's words. "Yes, milady. I can handle her. My apologies."

"I know what you're capable of at your best," Viola said. "Please strive for that."

"Yes, milady." The nanny nodded, took Nevandra's hand, and they exited the hall.

Viola steeled herself and turned back to the two matriarchs, who were watching her with raised eyebrows. "I assure you," Viola said. "Nevandra is capable of sitting still for the amount of time this evening will require."

Lady Merris said, "After what we saw—"

"But if it would make you feel more at ease," Viola said, "I can have Sabrea tend to her during dinner." She suppressed a mental image of the nanny chasing Nevandra through a crowd of distinguished guests.

"Pah," Lady Merris said. "A servant sitting at the high table? Unfitting of a noble house."

Did Lady Merris have a snide rebuttal to everything?

"I do beg your pardon, Viola," Lady Revada said, "but I'm not sure this particular nanny is up to the task."

Viola steeled herself against the opposition. "It will be fine. Once the men begin feasting and drinking, no one will notice if one child begins to act out of sorts."

Lady Revada pressed her lips into a thin line. "I merely advise caution. 'A people must respect their noble lord and love their noble lady.' This evening must be the starting point of that for you and Eric."

"When Eric has a proper heir, it will be a different matter altogether," Lady Merris said. "As for Nevandra, how she is seen tonight will impact her reputation. If she causes a scene, she will be remembered as a rowdy hellion, even as she grows into a woman. Could even sour her marriage prospects."

A proper heir. Viola bit back a retort. Grandmother Merris only saw Nevandra as fodder for some future noble marriage. The dowager had orchestrated numerous political unions over the years, including Eric's little sister Tara's marriage mere months ago. Almost none of those matches had resulted in happy marriages.

Viola swept aside the unpleasant thoughts. "You speak of respect for Eric and House Livna. That is part of my hope in seating Nevandra at the high table. To retain the proud legacy of House Livna. After all the pain that has been suffered, it is more important than ever for people to have hope for the future. What better way to do that than to let them see four generations of Livnas seated at the high table, ushering in a new era under Eric's leadership?"

Lady Revada tapped her chin. "Perhaps Lathia could be seated by Nevandra. The two of them get along nicely, and it might help redirect some of Nevandra's energy."

Viola fought off a smile. Such an arrangement would also help to keep Lady Lathia out of trouble. Eric's young cousin was very sweet, but was a shameless flirt. Some responsibility would help keep her in line as well.

"Splendid," Viola said. "I will have Arne adjust the seating arrangement immediately. And I will keep the nanny on standby in case an early bedtime is in order."

Lady Merris stood from her seat, tapping her cane. "I've heard worse plans."

"Thank you, Viola," Lady Revada said.

The pair made their way out of the great hall. Once alone, Viola allowed herself a slow sigh of relief.

Lady Revada had accepted the idea of seating Nevandra at the high table. Lady Merris, too, in the end. Doubtless neither woman was fully convinced of the idea's merit, but they had accepted it.

Viola whirled and exited the hall. There was still much to do before Eric returned. Grandmother Merris was right about one thing. Tonight would impact how the people saw Nevandra.

This would be Eric's first time appearing before the people not as a dutiful knight and heir, but as their lord. And next to him, they would see his firstborn child. Perhaps more than a firstborn, if Viola's other plans fell into place.

This banquet needed to be a significant moment. For Eric. For Nevandra. For all of House Livna.

CHAPTER THREE
ERIC

SMOKE. DID THAT MEAN ANOTHER FIRE? Tsaftown wasn't in view, but they were close enough that Eric could expect to smell the home fires burning. But the aroma only conjured images of the torched ruins of Glodwood Manor and the mutilated body left by the Poroo.

Eric swallowed hard. He wouldn't breathe easy until he looked upon his home with his own eyes.

"Something wrong, my lord?" Walter said, riding alongside him. "We're so close to the city, yet you seem less at ease with each passing minute."

Eric shook off thoughts of smoke and fire. "Simply remaining vigilant, Walter. What's Mother's old adage? 'Most misfortune happens close to home?'"

Walter ran his hand gently down his horse's mane. "Doesn't the thought of seeing your wife and daughter lighten your heart?"

Slight heat burned Eric's neck. "Of course. I'm eager to see my entire family."

Walter stroked his grey beard. "Your reply is positively *neutral*, my lord."

"Tell me, were you always this inquisitive with my father?"

"Oh, I was often much more persistent with him. He once threatened to have me sleep in the stables with the horses for not minding my own business."

"That sounds about right," Eric said. "What was that nickname he had for you? Drowned rat?"

Walter twisted one end of his grey mustache. "The name was muskrat, my lord. But only when he was particularly annoyed with me."

Eric chuckled. "Well, if you are going to remain on as my valet, then perhaps I shall have to continue the muskrat legacy."

"As you wish, my lord."

They surmounted the last of the great hills, and a large valley opened in front of them, presenting an expansive view of a snow-covered city built of logs around a massive harbor which played host to hundreds of sailing ships. Brilliant sunlight gleamed off the water and the ice floes in the harbor, which glistened with a layer of melt in the sunshine.

Tsaftown. Eric allowed himself an easy breath as he looked upon his home in the light of day for the first time since the end of Darkness.

The last few switchbacks went swiftly, and soon the army was approaching the city gates. A group of seven armored soldiers rode out to greet them, led by a bear of a man, whose mere presence caused the advance guard to part. Eric quickly recognized the burly rider with his thick black hair and beard as Lovell Dunn, a close friend and one of the soldiers who served House Livna.

Dunn handled his horse masterfully through the crowded street. One never would have guessed that the man had sustained several near life-threatening wounds mere months earlier.

Eric beamed, relieved to see Dunn looking his hearty self again.

"My lord," Dunn said, as he brought his horse in line with Eric's. "Welcome home."

"Dunn!" Eric said. "Good to see you up and about. Seems you're well on the mend. And then some."

Dunn sat higher in his saddle. "Aye. Both the arrow to my arm and the spear to my leg stung plenty. Barely felt the crack to my skull though. My old man always said I was so thickheaded that I didn't need a helmet."

Eric winced internally. Dunn had been attacked by the same vile men that had killed Eric's father. They had been kinder to Dunn, but barely so. "Thank you for keeping an eye on the city in my absence, especially when it's no longer your duty."

Dunn dipped his head, his usual swagger subdued. "You're welcome, my lord. Not that either of us had a choice in the matter." The man's deep voice resounded with intensity, and his green eyes gleamed with unspoken understanding. "I bring a message from Lady Viola. All of House Livna and the ruling council have gathered in the courtyard to receive you before tonight's banquet."

A banquet? Now there was something for Eric to look forward to. Even if he had to rub elbows with the stiff-necked men on the city's ruling council.

"Let's not keep them waiting," Eric said.

Dunn and his riders formed up on either of Eric's flanks, and the column continued toward the main gate of the city wall. A pair of unfamiliar soldiers in well-worn leather armor greeted Eric and his company as they passed through the gates. A closer glance revealed braids of long hair tied to their belts and at their shoulders. Câan's mercy, were they wearing scalps? One wore a pair of painted bear claws on a necklace, displayed next to a hound-shaped pendant on his chest. The same pendant that had been on the body at the Glodwood Manor.

Who were these men? It wasn't simply their strange trappings. They looked apprehensive at the arrival of the army. Perhaps Eric imagined it, but some of them seemed to glare directly at him.

As Eric and his men passed through the gate, more guards leered over the icy parapet. Each wore the same hound-shaped pendant prominently on their chest.

"Dunn," Eric said, "where did all these guards come from?"

The soldier clinched his jaw. "Sellswords, my lord. They're called the Howlers. Ruling council hired them to deal with the Poroo."

Mercenaries. That explained their unusual accessories. No doubt they were trophies from their skirmishes with the raiders.

"The Poroo attacks have been that bad?" Eric asked.

"Bad enough," Dunn said. "They haven't been bold enough to attack Tsaftown directly. Been raiding in the country and on the King's Road ever since Darkness left. We didn't have the soldiers to pursue them without leaving the city vulnerable."

Cinders. Eric loathed that his city had needed defending while he'd been absent.

"These Howlers," Walter said. "Are they competent soldiers?"

"More brawlers than soldiers. Seem to like violence. Word around town is that some of them are escaped prisoners from Ice Island."

Mercenaries weren't uncommon in the North. While Tsaftown had traditionally maintained a high standard for their fighting men, these last few months had been anything but typical.

Before Eric could think on the matter further, he caught sight of a large bonfire up ahead in the city's center. The smoke in the distance had been a celebration, not an attack. The sounds of music and laughter carried through the city, beckoning the soldiers forward.

Citizens of Tsaftown filled the streets, cheering as the army proceeded through the city. Several children ran up and offered sprigs of pine to the soldiers. Familiar and friendly faces came forward to greet the army. Some even danced in the slushy street, clearly having imbibed generous amounts of spirits.

The tightness in Eric's shoulders slowly melted away. He could breathe properly for the first time in months.

The advance guard neared the Dale, a gathering space located halfway between Lytton Hall and the Fisherman's Quarter by the harbor. The procession slowed as the crowd grew thicker. Many families had gathered, awaiting the return of their loved ones. Captain Demry's typically stern demeanor melted ever so slightly at the sight of his wife and daughter standing in the crowd.

Eric stopped Guffey and faced his men. The army stretched back nearly to the city gate. The men held ranks, but the expressions on their faces testified to their eagerness to reunite with family and friends.

"These men have valiantly performed their duty," Eric said. "Wouldn't you say so, Captain?"

Captain Demry's expression softened. "Indeed they have, my lord."

Eric wheeled Guffey around and found himself looking on the remainder of his bowmen and the first two formations of infantry.

"Northlanders!" he yelled. "You have journeyed far and served well. Now you have but one duty left to perform." Eric paused, letting his words hang for a moment. "You are to report to your homes! Kiss your wives. Hug your children. And eat a hearty meal. You've certainly earned it."

"What if we've got no wife?" Jol Quimby yelled from several rows back.

"Then go find one, you rapscallion," Eric hollered.

The men roared with laughter then cheered as they swiftly broke ranks and parted into the crowd. Soldiers reunited with wives, children, parents, and friends. All with much joy.

Not all, Eric realized. Master Ruk Haldor watched for his son, Shen. The young man had been a fiend with his bow, but he had fallen in the Battle of Mahanaim. Young Shen was one of many who had not returned home. Of the original Fighting Five Hundred who had marched south with the king, ninety-three had fallen.

Too many. Câan's mercy, too many hadn't come home.

Derby took his leave of Eric and was quickly embraced by his mother and two sisters. The sight warmed Eric's heart. It couldn't make up for the loss of so many men. But seeing a loving family reunited? That was worth something. Hopefully Derby's father, Captain Wenk, would return home safely aboard the sailing ship *Williwaw*.

Dunn brought his horse up alongside Eric's. "My lord, if you desire, I can take my leave from House Livna's service now. My wounds have healed, but my vision still betrays me in the dark."

"Nonsense," Eric said. "You're one of the best men we have."

"Yet Lytton Hall cannot have a blind watchman, my lord."

"This is the North, Dunn." Eric put his fist over his heart. "I won't reward your faithful service by leaving you without a role."

Dunn put his hand over his own heart. "You honor me, my lord. I will remain in your service as long as you will have me."

Walter, Dunn, and the remaining soldiers stayed with Eric as they continued down the street toward the amphitheater at the center of the Dale. A trio of singers sat on a large stage, playing a jaunty tune. The performers weren't the apex of talent, but the highly lubricated crowd didn't seem to mind.

As Eric rode past the grandstands, a new sound entered the fray. The clanging of steel echoed across the open air.

Two armored combatants dueled in a six-sided ring next to the stage. The musicians, Eric now realized, were providing background music for the duel.

Eric steered Guffey toward the ring. He always enjoyed watching a good fight.

"My lord?" Walter called after him. "Are we not expected at Lytton Hall?"

Eric winked at Walter. "A quick stop. I'm curious about the festivities."

The company followed Eric's lead toward the amphitheater. He stopped Guffey with Walter on his left and Dunn on his right.

A tall man with a steel helmet and well-oiled black-and-green leather armor battled a stout man in a bronze helm and breastplate. The tall man's armor was etched with the wolf's head emblem over his heart. Yet another Howler.

The Howler forced his opponent back into the rails. The smaller man squirmed away, clearly overmatched.

Spectators in the back of the crowd parted as Eric and his retinue drew closer. Many cheered the return of the soldiers, while others remained focused on the fight. As they pressed into the crowd, an odd chill worked its way down Eric's spine. He felt someone's gaze on him. His soldierly instincts were honed to find threats, but what threats could be found among a gathering of his own people?

Eric surveyed the spectators, and his gaze settled on an old man on the other side of the ring who wore a cloth band over his eyes and held a long walking stick in one hand. Was he blind? There was something familiar about him. Eric had seen his face. But where?

A dozen or so men standing next to the blind man also turned their attention Eric's way. All bore the Howler's insignia. Cinders, how many of these Howlers were there? One of the men, a muscular brute with a shaved head and knotted black beard, cracked his knuckles while glaring at Eric. This man wore more Poroo scalps than anyone and had them draped over both shoulders like epaulets on a uniform.

"Dunn," Eric said. "Who's the big Howler by the edge of the ring?"

"His name's Ikârd," Dunn said. "He's the enforcer of the group. Used to work as a guard at Ice Island, before the warden fired him for being too brutal to the prisoners."

Ikârd's eyes remained fixed on Eric. What sort of horrors could a man commit that were too harsh for Ice Island? The Poroo scalps on Ikârd's shoulders indicated that he had not given up his penchant for cruelty.

Eric rested his hand on his sword hilt and continued to watch the duel unfold. The Howler took a wild swing at his shorter opponent and struck one of the ring posts. The maneuver exposed the Howler's right side. The shorter fighter moved quickly and jabbed at the Howler's ribs. A blunted *thwack* echoed through the arena as the strike landed. Stunned cries rose up from the crowd.

The success was short-lived.

The tall man reset his feet and launched into his opponent with a furious set of strikes. The two locked their swords together. Then the Howler kicked his opponent hard in the knee.

A horrible pop drew gasps from the spectators.

The wounded fighter dropped his sword and stumbled backward, clutching at his knee.

The Howler smashed his cross guard on the downed man's head, knocking his helmet off.

"Not exactly sporting, is he?" Walter mused.

"He's a beast is what he is," Dunn said.

Eric agreed. But the violence had invigorated the crowd.

The Howler raised his sword high above his head, eliciting cheers from the spectators.

The blare of a conch shell horn echoed over the arena as the barker entered the ring and raised the victorious fighter's hand. "Ladies and gentlemen, your winner, Sir Fenris Yarden!"

A cold tingle shot up Eric's spine.

"By the Three," Walter muttered. "Sir Fredrick's son?"

The Howler pulled off his helmet, confirming his identity. A mess of curly blond hair tumbled down past his shoulders as he pressed into the crowd and rejoined the other Howlers. The group embarked en masse toward the exit, straight toward Eric and his riders.

Fenris's jade green eyes met Eric's through the crowd. He grinned with one side of his mouth and stroked his bearded chin. The wild glint in his eyes dragged Eric back to his childhood. The man's face and expression were exactly as they had been when they were boys. Only weathered and pockmarked by twenty years in prison.

"Fenris?" Eric asked.

"Cousin!" Fenris said. "Or rather...*my lord*?" Fenris offered a theatrical bow, letting his hair flop toward the ground.

Eric clenched his jaw. "Why are you here?"

Fenris stood back to his full height. "I'm here in my capacity as the host of these festivities." He extended his arms, gesturing toward the raucous crowd. "Darkness has fallen. A new king sits in Armonguard. We have much to celebrate."

Fenris seized a turkey leg from one onlooker. The man grabbed for his stolen meal, but a fierce glare from Ikârd made him relent. Fenris sank his teeth deep and ripped out a mouthful of meat and charred skin. Then he turned back toward the crowd, raising the turkey leg skyward.

"Long live the king!" Fenris yelled through a mouthful of food.

The crowd cheered, echoing his praise for the young King Gidon.

Fenris tossed the turkey leg to its original owner, who sighed and shuffled off into the crowd. Fenris faced Eric again, slowly chewing his mouthful of meat.

"Why are you *here*?" Eric growled. "And where is your father? Why are you both not in your cells in Ice Island?"

Fenris's gleeful expression broke. "My father gained his freedom ten years ago when his heart gave out. Our fellow inmates celebrated his passing by heaving his corpse down into the privy pit." Fenris brushed a wild strand of hair out of his eyes. "As for me, my sentence has been commuted and my crimes absolved."

"Absolved? By whom?" Eric asked.

A wicked grin crossed Fenris's face. "Why, by who else? King Gidon Hadar himself."

Heat swelled in Eric's chest. "You've met the king?"

Fenris set his hands on his hips. "Indirectly. The king offered full pardons to all the former residents of the Pit."

This much was true. The Prodotez, also called the Pit, was an especially awful place in the Ice Island prison for keeping the king's worst offenders. The young king had gone into the Prodotez himself to rescue Sir Eagan and Kurtz Chazir, while Sir Gavin had freed over two hundred other Kingsguard soldiers who had been unfairly imprisoned on Ice Island. Those men had formed the backbone of King Gidon's army during the war.

"You were pardoned, but you didn't see fit to serve in the king's army?" Eric asked.

Fenris shrugged. "Not when my Howlers and I were needed here to help the good people of Tsaftown."

His Howlers. Eric regarded the pack of ruffians standing behind Fenris. Not simply comrades in arms. More like loyal followers.

"You've been fighting the Poroo?" Eric asked.

Fenris's oversized canine teeth gleamed with his grin. "I'm glad to see our exploits have reached your ears so quickly."

Eric narrowed his eyes. "You plan on staying in the city, then?"

"I'll stay as long as I'm needed." Fenris tilted his head slowly to one side. "Unless it displeases *my lord* for me to live here?"

Eric rubbed the back of his right ear. Old memories of Fenris and Uncle Fredrick drawing swords against Eric's father stirred in Eric's mind. His gaze fell to the Howlers standing behind Fenris. The man who had betrayed his family had returned. With a host of soldiers at his beck and call.

The heat in Eric's chest smoldered. He had his own soldiers. Hundreds of them. What could this gang of mercenaries do against the fabled Fighting Five Hundred?

But...absolution.

The word circled in Eric's mind. No matter what evils Fenris was capable of, his cousin had been freed. By a royal decree.

Eric's hand found Guffey's reigns. "Your sentence has been commuted," he said. "You're welcome to stay. See to it that I'm not given reason to throw you back in Ice Island."

"Thank you, my gracious lord." Fenris genuflected as Eric rode past. "I'll see you at the homecoming banquet this evening."

Eric halted Guffey. "The banquet?"

"Why, yes," Fenris said. "I received an invitation. From Lady Viola herself."

The hair on Eric's neck stood on end. What in the depths was Viola doing talking to this wretched man?

Walter rode up between Eric and Fenris, breaking Eric's eye contact with his cousin. "Let us return home, my lord."

Eric exhaled sharply and urged Guffey forward, leaving Fenris and the rest of the revelers behind. He stared straight ahead, but saw nothing. Not the people. Not the road. Not Lytton Hall.

The sour feeling in his gut had taken shape and been given a name. Fenris Yarden.

CHAPTER FOUR
VIOLA

WHERE WAS ERIC? VIOLA COULD forgive him being late, but the council would be less patient, even for their lord.

The members of House Livna and the city's ruling council had assembled in the courtyard of Lytton Hall, ready to receive Eric upon his arrival. Though the longer they waited in the cold, the less formal the attitude of the group became.

The army had been seen approaching over an hour ago, and Viola had immediately dispatched Master Dunn to inform Eric about the reception. So what in all Er'Rets could be delaying him?

Nevandra's focus had not lasted long, but Lady Lathia, one of Eric's many cousins, had made a game of piling sticks into neat little piles on the front steps of Lytton Hall. Hopefully the distraction would last.

With her sandy blonde curls, elegant demeanor, and youth, Lathia was the spitting image of Lady Tara. Viola wished Tara were here now. She missed her a great deal.

The murmuring of those assembled grew steadily louder. Most

of the chatter was pleasant enough, though Viola did hear several whispered complaints about how long they'd been made to wait.

"His father never was especially prompt either, was he?" a voice said over Viola's shoulder. Councilor Joonas Erlichman, the head of Tsaftown's ruling council, offered a gentle smile as he ran one of his manicured hands over his pointed beard.

Viola smiled back. "If Sir Edik was late, it was typically because you or your father had gone off on some hunting excursion with him."

Councilor Erlichman held out his palms, jostling the silver tassels of his robe. "The late Lord Livna could be very focused while on the hunt."

"Perhaps he stopped off at the Dale to enjoy some of the festivities," rumbled another voice. "I hear Sir Fenris is dueling there today." The speaker was Councilor Rathskellar, a heavy man who both sat on the council and held the title Chief Priest of the Temple of Thalassa.

The clacking of hooves echoed on the cobblestone as—*finally!*—Eric rode into the courtyard, followed by his retinue of soldiers.

Viola took a deep breath and slowly exhaled the worries that had lingered in her mind for months. She had heard that Eric had survived the war without any major wounds, but part of her heart had refused to relax until she'd seen him with her own eyes. Eric cut a striking profile with his dark beard and hair, which had been allowed to grow out after months of travel. He looked every bit a victorious lord, like a hero from a longtale. For whatever he lacked in refinement, her husband certainly was a handsome fellow to behold.

She shut the thought away. Now wasn't the time. There was work to do.

Eric dismounted his horse and approached the gathered assembly. Seeing him up close, Viola noticed the hardened mud on his boots and cloak. Flecks of dirt dappled his face and clothes. His gait was stiff, likely sore from months of travel.

Viola would typically forgive his disheveled appearance. But today? The whole point of sending out Master Dunn was to give Eric time to make himself presentable for the reception. The rugged appearance of a warrior was fine in front of his soldiers, but the members of the ruling council needed to see him as their lord.

Yet he was here now, muddy boots and all. It would have to do.

Viola retrieved Nevandra, and the pair of them walked forward to greet Eric.

"Welcome home, husband." She offered him her hand.

Eric's gaze was distant. Not simply fatigue. Had something angered him?

Walter Blackburn, Sir Edik's ever-mindful valet, had dismounted his own horse and now cleared his throat. Eric snapped to the present. His dark eyes met hers, and she could have sworn he almost smiled. His rough hand wrapped around Viola's fingers, and he kissed the back of her knuckles. His coarse beard prickled her skin and gooseflesh erupted on her arm. She fought the impulse to pull her hand free. It was important that she play the part of the devoted wife.

"It's good to be home," Eric said, then crouched and regarded Nevandra. "Hello, Nevie. My, but you've grown since I've been away."

The little girl's big brown eyes bulged as she looked at Eric. He extended a hand, but instead of greeting him, Nevandra hid behind Viola's skirts.

"Nevandra, say hello to your father," Viola said, but the girl only withdrew further. Heat seeped into Viola's cheeks. This was exactly the sort of thing her mother-in-law had tried to warn her about.

Eric offered a half-hearted smile. "It's all right. We'll have time to converse later."

Eric and Viola, with Nevandra in tow, stepped toward the gathered assembly.

Lady Revada glided forward and wrapped her arms around Eric's neck. "Welcome home, son."

"How long has he been back?" Eric rumbled in a low growl.

"Fenris?" Lady Revada whispered.

A grimace twisted Eric's features.

Viola's stomach fluttered. She knew Sir Fenris and his father had been the cause of a rift between House Livna and House Yarden, but every member of House Livna seemed to tell a different version of the events. Viola had never gotten a clear picture of what had started the feud. From Eric's reaction, that rift was far from healed. She would have to take steps to ensure that Sir Fenris's presence in the city wouldn't become an even greater distraction for Eric.

Viola laid her hand gently on Eric's forearm. "Perhaps these are matters that can be discussed later? After formal greetings have concluded." She gestured to the line of council members waiting to receive Eric.

Eric furrowed his brow. "Very well."

He brushed bits of dust off his shirt and trousers, though dirt still lingered in his fingernails and the creases of his palms. Viola cringed internally as each of the councilors sized up their new lord at what was clearly less than his best.

Viola sent Nevandra back over to Lathia, where they resumed their stick game. She then accompanied Eric to greet the council members.

Councilor Joonas Erlichman met him first. "Welcome home, my lord. When things calm down, I have some fine boar in the woods, the kind of brutes that make for a true hunt. When you're ready, I'd be glad to see you take one down."

"Certainly," Eric said.

He moved on to Councilor Okerlund, a square-jawed man with a sour countenance. The councilor clamped down on Eric's hand.

"My lord, the Thusk Shipping Exchange is inflating their prices for their trade caravans. They claim the route is too dangerous with the current Poroo threat."

Renshaw Thusk, another councilor and part owner of the Thusk Shipping Exchange, narrowed his already beady eyes at Councilor Okerlund. This feud had been brewing for some time. "My fellow councilman exaggerates," Councilor Thusk said, speaking out of one side of his mouth. "Every shipping and import business has had to increase their prices. Such is common in time of war."

Eric glanced between the two councilmen. "I shall look into it." He attempted to move down the line, but Okerlund maintained his firm grip.

"It's a grift. Plain and simple," the man said. "They mean to bleed us dry before my fishing boats can have a full season on the sea—"

"I said I shall handle it, Councilor." Eric ripped his hand away from Councilor Okerlund's grasp and moved down the line. He'd been so eager to withdraw from Okerlund that he failed to shake Councilor Thusk's hand. In the space of a breath, Eric had managed to offend two members of the council.

He didn't appear to notice his multiple faux pas, but from the myriad of glances exchanged among the assembly, many had taken note.

Eric passed down the rest of the receiving line without incident. The other councilors offered little beyond a simple greeting. If scaring them into silence had been Eric's plan, that simply wouldn't do. Like them or not, they needed to work with these men to run the city effectively.

Eric lumbered up the steps toward the large oak doors of Lytton Hall. Voices murmured as the rest of House Livna followed.

"How the lord of Tsaftown has distinguished himself today," grumbled Councilor Rathskellar.

Viola bit her lip. The vision of a grand homecoming for Eric and his men was off to a rocky start.

ERIC

Would this day simply never end?

A warm bath had eased the aches in Eric's joints. All he wished to do was lie down in his own bed and sleep for a week. Instead, Walter now dressed him in a fine ensemble for the banquet.

"You will need to make some sort of apology, my lord."

"Apologize? To Councilor Okerlund? I had not even reached the front steps of my home and the man was badgering me about a trade dispute."

Walter fastened the last of the buttons on Eric's dark wool doublet. "Certainly Okerlund's ego will require some assuaging, but your primary concern should be your wife."

"Viola?" Eric replayed the short interchange he'd had with his wife. How could he have wronged her?

"She went to great pains to pull together that reception. You could have handled yourself with a bit more decorum."

Eric lifted his chin, allowing Walter to secure the buttons of his collar. "I wasn't exactly in the mood for such formalities."

"Is that what you will tell your people during an unexpected crisis? That their lord is not *in the mood* to deal with such things?"

Eric bit back a sharp retort. Wrangling the council would, of course, be part of his responsibilities now, but he had not expected to be thrown into the politicking so immediately. Despite his annoyance with Councilor Okerlund or the other members of the council, Viola *had* made an effort to see that Eric was properly received as their lord. She deserved an apology.

Walter draped a black half cape that bore gold embroidering over Eric's ensemble. "There we are." He brushed Eric's shoulders. "Now we shall show the people of Tsaftown how a lord can properly dress."

"The collar is rather tight."

Walter fixed Eric with a look. "You are a noble, my lord. You are no stranger to formal attire."

Indeed. Life on campaign had not been easy, but at least his clothing had been chosen based on functionality, not high fashion.

Walter secured the final button. "Take comfort in knowing that a lady's beauty regimen is even less forgiving."

They departed Eric's chambers and took the stairs down to the main floor.

Viola waited just outside the doors to the great hall, illuminated by the light of torches in the hallway. A pair of guards, dressed in formal uniforms, stood on either side of the door. Sounds of revelry could already be heard inside. No doubt drinks had been served as the assembly awaited Eric and Viola's entrance.

Viola wore the same violet dress from the reception, now topped with a black fur shawl and a silver pendant around her neck. Her dark hair had been bound up into a crown-like braid that wrapped around her head. The entire ensemble accentuated every ounce of her natural beauty.

"I'll see you inside, my lord." Walter headed for the side entrance.

Viola looked Eric over and offered a gentle nod. "You've cleaned up nicely. Master Blackburn's taste in clothes is impeccable, as always."

Eric held out his arms to either side to give her a better view. "Walter can indeed do miracles. I suppose I have need of a valet now."

"Of course you do. And there's no one better than Walter." Viola offered a faint smile. Was the expression genuine or a simple pleasantry? Five years they'd been married, and still this woman was an enigma to him much of the time. Their first year of marriage had been filled with long periods of adjustment. Viola had needed to transition to life in a new place after leaving her home. Then Nevandra had come. Then war. All under the shroud of Darkness.

Torchlight danced in Viola's eyes, and Eric's heart stirred at her radiant beauty. Perhaps, with Darkness gone and the war over, now was the time for a fresh start.

"I'm sorry about before." Eric stepped closer to Viola to keep the guards from overhearing their conversation. "Councilor Okerlund's demands took me by surprise. I could have handled it better."

"Thank you." Viola steepled her fingers in front of her waist. "But if you truly wish to make things right, then you ought to smooth matters over with Councilor Okerlund. His quarrel with Councilor Thusk's company has been brewing for months. It will require your involvement one way or another."

Eric tightened his jaw as he stared at the door to the great hall. "Why must I mediate their squabbles?"

Heat simmered in Viola's eyes, but instead of lashing out, she stepped closer and ran her hand along the black fur of his cloak. "The council members are not soldiers. They won't always do what you ask simply because you are their lord. They must be *properly* motivated."

Viola's touch was so distracting that Eric had to concentrate to digest her words. "Can I not simply throw them into the stockade? Would that not motivate them to get along?" He grinned.

Viola's expression narrowed, and she folded her arms, clearly unimpressed with his attempt at humor.

"Very well." Eric held his hands up in a conciliatory fashion. "Who else must I make amends to?"

Viola's expression softened as she considered his question. "Obviously the members of the council. Plus, Elder Rathskellar. And...I'm also concerned about your feelings toward Sir Fenris."

Eric's right ear began to burn. *Sir* Fenris. What a mockery of the title. "What have I done to wrong *him*?"

Viola gave a thin smile. "Whatever problems there are between him and House Livna, they are best left in the past. He's established a presence here since his return. Not simply with the dueling tournaments. Many people are grateful to him and his men for protecting the city from the Poroo."

Eric scratched at his ear. Certainly he was thankful someone had defended the city while he and the majority of the fighting men had been gone. If it could have been anyone else... "No matter what he's done since his return, he's a threat to House Livna. That will never change."

Viola laid her hand on Eric's shoulder, which disrupted the tide of anger growing in his heart. He looked deeply into her eyes.

"I can see that this is difficult," Viola said. "I do not know all of what transpired in the past with Sir Fenris. He may be a scoundrel, but no more so than half of the other city leaders. And we manage to work with them."

Eric clenched his hand into a fist, then opened it up again. "I can be civil with him," he said. "For tonight, at least."

Viola dipped her head softly. "That's all I ask."

Eric offered his arm, and Viola took hold.

"And if that doesn't work," Viola said, "then you can make use of stockade diplomacy."

Eric grinned, and together they turned to face the doors that led into the great hall.

The older of the two guards bowed to them as they approached. "Lord Livna. Lady Viola," he said, his voice a rich baritone. "It's an honor to announce your entrance tonight."

"The honor is ours, Master Ambrose," Eric said. "Your continued presence in my family's home is always welcome."

Ambrose's well-groomed grey sideburns framed his bright smile. One would never guess this kind-faced man once had been a member of the Fighting Fifteen, serving under Eric's father.

A moment later, the doors swung open, and the couple stepped forward into the great hall.

"Lord Eric Livna and Lady Viola!" Ambrose bellowed.

The men of the Fighting Fifteen and a dozen more soldiers roared mighty praise for their lord as Eric led Viola down the aisle. Even Kurtz Chazir stood and cheered with the king's former squire beside him. Eric's chest swelled at the adoration from his men and the joy on their faces.

Members of the ruling council had been seated near the front along with several fishing boat captains and local clergy. They applauded and even smiled, but there was little mirth in their expressions.

Despite the cheers, an ache filled Eric's chest. He was painfully aware that he currently followed the same path his father had walked on many similar occasions, the last of which had resulted in his murder.

Eric shivered as he passed over the spot where the vile false prince had run a sword through his father's heart. His gaze flicked forward to the lattice panel that ran along the front skirt of the dais—the place he had hidden and watched helplessly as his father's blood spilled out on the golden carpet.

Eric pushed away the grim memory and glanced up. At the head table stood his mother, his cousin Lathia, and Grandmother Merris. Nevandra was there too, sandwiched between his mother and cousin, so short he almost missed her. The little girl craned her neck to see better. Eric could just make out the elegant braid in his daughter's hair as well as her black dress with gold accents. She looked very much like a proper young lady.

Eric escorted Viola along the front of the dais and up the small set of steps to the dining table. He helped his wife to her seat, then kissed his mother on the cheek, holding her hand for a moment before he knelt and kissed Nevandra's hand. His daughter's cheeks reddened, and she hid her face in Lady Revada's skirts. Her shyness toward him tugged at his heart. Could she not even smile at him?

Eric's mother ushered Nevandra to a chair between herself and cousin Lathia. Eric then took his own seat with Viola at his left.

No sooner had they sat down than Arne and the rest of House Livna's servants brought forth trays of hot food from the kitchens. Aromas of fresh bread and roasted meats stirred Eric's stomach. Generous helpings of fish, venison, stewed potatoes, roasted carrots, and dark loaves of rye bread were set out on the tables. Certainly the right kind of meal to satisfy the bottomless hunger of men who had been traveling for months.

Eric ate in silence, savoring every morsel. It was the first proper meal he'd enjoyed since Gidon and Averella's wedding feast. The ache of hunger slowly subsided, and he found himself scanning the faces in the room. Councilors. Trade guild masters. Clergy. Would they respect him as their lord? Or would they try to cajole him into fulfilling their own personal agendas?

"The garlic is rather strong in the potatoes," Lady Merris said on Eric's right. "All in attendance shall have foul breath after this."

Viola leaned forward, speaking past Eric. "The dessert tarts have been made with mentha leaf. That should offset any lingering aromas from the feast."

"Pah." Lady Merris retorted. "I should hope so."

Eric returned his focus to his own dinner. Grandmother could always find something to nitpick.

Viola leaned toward Eric. "I see the garlic did not offend your sensibilities."

"Hmm?" Eric slowly pulled his mind back to the table. "Oh yes. Quite satisfying. Certainly after months of dried meat and hardtack."

"That was the hope," Viola said. "Do prepare yourself though. Soon your guests will begin presenting themselves to you. You'll be expected to acknowledge them and say something stately. And, of course, you'll need to lead the dance later on."

Cinders. Dancing? His father had entertained guests in such a way at many grand banquets, but his father had also been uniquely gifted for social gatherings. Such graces had skipped a generation when it came to Eric.

He cleared his throat, eager to steer the conversation away from any talk of dancing. "You said this feud with Thusk and Okerlund has been brewing for months. What can I say in one evening that can resolve it?"

Viola took a quick bite of cheese, chewing as she considered his question. "It's not your responsibility to resolve the matter out-right," she said. "Councilor Okerlund wants you to acknowledge his grievance publicly so he can leverage that against Thusk. In this instance, it might be prudent to give Okerlund what he wants."

Eric bristled at the thought. "I'll not be made a puppet by one of these men."

"And you needn't be," Viola said. "It's well-known that Thusk and his family have been price gouging for years. You're simply acknowledging a known fact. Then you can make it clear to both men that it's in their best interest to resolve their squabble. Oth-erwise they risk displeasing the lord of their city."

Intriguing. Viola's solution seemed almost too simple, yet Eric found no fault with it.

"I shall say as much to Okerlund when I see him," Eric said. "What other problem can you solve for me?"

Viola looked out across the banquet hall. "Unfortunately, I don't have a solution for all situations."

Eric followed her gaze to Lathia, who had apparently dismissed herself prematurely from the head table to speak with a roguish young man with blond hair tied into a loose ponytail. They stood in one of the aisles between the tables, making playful conversa-tion.

"Who's that fellow?" Eric asked.

Viola let out a bemused sigh. "I believe his name is Connor Clave. He was hired on by Sir Fenris's patrols a few months back."

Of all the young men in Tsaftown, Lathia had to get entangled with a Howler?

"Lathia's been stringing him along for some weeks now," Viola continued. "She broke the heart of the poor netmaker's son not long after you left. It seems she's moved along rather quickly."

Lathia had always been a wild card. Her father, Captain Chantry Livna, always left her in their care while he was away at sea. Perhaps Uncle Chantry had hoped that guidance from the women of House Livna might make a proper noblewoman of Lathia, but the teasing smiles she gave Master Clave hinted that such maturity still evaded her.

The banquet proceeded without incident. As expected, various guests soon made their way to the head table, offering their well wishes to Eric and House Livna. Eric managed to conjure something to say to each of them. He even handled his exchange with Councilor Okerlund gracefully, an achievement that brought a smile to Viola's face.

Then Eric's stomach sank upon seeing the next guest.

Fenris swaggered forward, shadowed by Ikârd's towering form. Eric locked eyes with his cousin.

"Lord Eric Livna." Fenris spoke slowly, his voice dripping with sweet flattery. He slowly dropped to one knee, holding his hands out to either side. "I am honored to feast here in this hallowed hall tonight and proud to defend the city in your absence. I hope that despite our troubled past, you can once again accept me as family."

In your absence. Eric chewed on Fenris's words. He knew the man was trying to get a rise out of him, but that knowledge did nothing to stifle the heat in Eric's chest.

Viola laid her hand on Eric's wrist. Her eyes pleaded with him not to lash out.

"Sir...Fenris," Eric said, measuring each syllable. "Thank you for your service to the city. Continue to make yourself of use, and *perhaps*, with time, the ties of family may be remade."

Fenris raised his eyebrows. "Well said, my lord. In the meantime, you and the lovely Lady Viola are welcome to join our festivities in the Dale. We always manage to have a splendid time."

Eric turned his chin up and looked down his nose ever so slightly. "Perhaps. If time allows."

Fenris nodded and left the table, with Ikârd's hulking form following in his wake.

"You handled that well," Viola whispered. "I do believe it would be a good idea to make an appearance at his festival."

Eric furrowed his brow. "Whatever for? To appease Fenris?"

"Not for him. For the people. It will do them good to see you there."

Eric tapped his fingers against the table. Viola's suggestion made sense. While he loathed the idea of being trotted out to a public festival, much less one hosted by Fenris, his father had made many such appearances over the years. Eric would no doubt be expected to do the same.

Something jostled the table. Viola and Eric exchange confused looks. Another thump, clearly from underneath.

"Young lady, back in your seat." On Viola's left, Eric's mother had leaned to one side and reached beneath the table, speaking in a tense whisper.

Eric moved aside the tablecloth and found a pair of wide eyes staring back at him. Nevandra on her hand and knees, her long braid hanging on the floor.

He stifled a laugh. "Oh my. There's a mouse under our table."

He slipped a piece of cheese off his trencher and offered it to Nevandra. She stared at him for a moment. Then a small smile crept across her face, and she snatched the morsel, quickly popping it in her mouth.

Eric's mother gently pulled Nevandra back to her seat and rather pointedly kept a hand on her shoulder. There was a short exchange of looks between Revada and Viola. Both women spoke volumes without uttering a syllable.

The sound of shattered glass disrupted the moment. Eric's head whirled in the direction of the crash as sounds of a struggle broke out.

"Let go of him!"

"You feckless oaf!"

A knot of men formed in the middle of the room.

Eric leaped from his chair and charged off the dais, down the steps, and toward the middle of the fracas. Startled screams echoed in the hall. Some guests hurried away, not wishing to be drawn into the fight. Councilor Okerlund stumbled on an overturned chair and fell backward onto the floor, disappearing amongst the mass of people. More men pushed into the circle, and Eric had to shove his way into the fray.

In the center of the fight was none other than Kurtz Chazir, locked in a rear choke hold by Fenris. Kurtz fought in vain to free himself as Fenris squeezed harder around his neck. Eric charged forward and gripped Fenris's arm.

"Enough! Enough!" Eric barked.

"Briny maggot!" Fenris fought out of Eric's grip and swung an elbow. Eric caught the blow and wrenched his arm back. Fenris's right eye twitched as he glared at Eric.

Kurtz, free from the choke hold, reared back to throw a punch. Lovell Dunn intervened, hooking his muscular arm around Kurtz's and dragging him out of the scuffle.

"Restrain him!" Eric said.

Torin Oxbow leaped to Dunn's aid and grabbed Kurtz by the shoulders. Fury lingered in Kurtz's eyes, but intervention of a noble lord appeared enough to quell his interest in continuing the fight.

Ikârd and the Howlers formed up behind Fenris, clearly ready to continue the brawl if their master wished.

Eric stared Fenris down. "Enough."

Fenris licked his lips and wiped spittle out of his beard. "My apologies. I'm a bit rusty on my decorum. Perhaps my men and I won't be staying for dessert."

"I believe that would be best," Eric said through gritted teeth.

Fenris sneered. "Come on, boys. Seems we've overstayed our welcome." He and his men backed away slowly and turned for the door.

Eric exhaled slowly. Countless sets of eyes fixed on him. Priests and councilors and family members, all staring at the aftermath of the fight. Councilor Okerlund, now back on his feet, dusted himself off and scowled at Eric.

In a moment, what had been a peaceful banquet had turned into a scene of chaos. Punches thrown. Guests dismayed. Pottery shattered. Eric's gaze settled on Viola, still seated at the high table. Her face remained composed, but even from across the room, Eric saw the sadness reflected in her eyes.

CHAPTER FIVE
ERIC

DUNN, OXBOW, AND GUNNAR GEDmund had dealt with Kurtz more crudely than Eric would have preferred, roughly depositing the man into a chair in the study.

Eric had been tempted to have Kurtz removed from Lytton Hall altogether, but the man had fought for the king in Armonguard and helped defend against the Poroo at the ruins of Glodwood Manor, which earned him just enough credibility to not be heaved into the night like a common drunkard. Instead, a stern questioning in his father's study would suffice.

No. It was Eric's study now. He ought to start thinking of it that way.

Dunn's intimidating presence would be enough to keep Kurtz in line. Eric dismissed Oxbow and Gedmund and stood behind his desk.

"Explain yourself, Master Chazir," he said.

Kurtz folded his hands in his lap and avoided eye contact. "That was Fenris's fault, it was. He got in my face and said I didn't belong at such a fancy gathering. Tried ignoring him, I did, but he kept pushing."

"You know Fenris Yarden?" Eric asked.

"Aye. He was in the Prodotez with me and the rest. Right foul blackguard, he is."

Eric didn't disagree with Kurtz's assessment, but neither was he going to let Kurtz off the hook quite so easily. "You two weren't friends in Ice Island?"

A shadow passed over Kurtz's expression. "No one is friends in the Pit. Except me and Eagan. But Fenris was a biter, eh?"

The mention of Fenris's time on Ice Island piqued Eric's interest. He was tempted to push for more details, but this was neither the time nor the place.

"Which of you threw the first punch?" Eric asked.

Again, Kurtz's gaze shifted to the side. "I...ah...that was me. But only because he wouldn't let it go. Kept insulting my honor, he did. Acting like he was all high society, when he and his friends spent more time in Ice Island than I did—and I was falsely imprisoned!"

Eric steepled his fingers. No doubt there was some truth to Kurtz's words. And no doubt Fenris would have a different telling of the events from the banquet. The truth was likely somewhere in between.

"What brings you to my city in the first place?" Eric asked.

Kurtz rubbed his hands together. "Well...ah. The long and short of it would be that the king isn't needing my services anymore. Came north looking for a fresh start in my old stomping grounds, eh?"

Eric fixed Kurtz with a stare. "Do you intend to pick a fight with someone in every establishment you enter?"

"Not at all, my lord," Kurtz said. "Trying to stay on the straight and narrow, I am."

Eric suppressed a laugh. "Straight and narrow? You have been in this city for not even a full day and you've started a brawl in my home."

He let the statement hang for a long moment. Kurtz wrung his hands together as the thick silence surrounded him.

"If you were any other man, such behavior would see you tossed into the dungeon. However, as you were a loyal servant to King Gidon, I'm inclined to let you go free."

Kurtz lowered his head. "Very kind of you, my lord, that is."

"Stay out of trouble, Master Chazir. Understood?"

Kurtz nodded vigorously.

Eric gestured to Dunn, who set about escorting Kurtz from the room. Hopefully Kurtz understood the full extent of his error. As well as the consequences if he stepped out of line again.

And yet a stray thought still gnawed at the back of Eric's mind.

"One last thing," Eric said.

Kurtz winced as he turned back to face Eric.

"You mentioned Fenris's Ice Island friends," Eric said. "What did you mean by that?"

"All those men he's got with him. His Howlers. Prisoners from Ice Island, they are."

"You're sure? You knew these men?" Eric asked.

"I don't know the men themselves, but they have that look about them, they do."

True. Parolees of Ice Island often came through Tsaftown. And many of the Howlers had the hardened, withered appearance that often accompanied time in the frozen prison. Even Kurtz still carried the burden in his expression.

The tale of King Gidon's escape from the Prodotez had grown into a proper legend over the last several months. Many of the escaped prisoners had traveled south with the army to wage war against the false prince, but there was speculation that some of the fugitives had deserted and gone into hiding.

And who better to hire a brace of escaped prisoners than a pardoned nobleman like *Sir* Fenris Yarden?

Dunn escorted Kurtz from the study. Eric heaved a sigh toward the ceiling. What was he supposed to do about this? Hopes of an easy solution to the Fenris problem dwindled. Perhaps tonight merely had been a singular occurrence brought on by running into Kurtz, but Eric doubted it would be that simple.

He exited the study and was surprised to find Viola waiting for him in the adjoining hall.

"I see you chose to err on the side of leniency," she said.

"Master Chazir and I have reached an understanding," Eric said. "He'll not be a problem any further."

Viola's lips wrinkled. "A man assaults one of your guests and you let him walk free?"

"That's not what happened. At least not entirely," Eric said. "And Fenris Yarden never should have set foot in this hall."

Viola narrowed her eyes. "There are many who respect him in this city, despite the legacy of his father. Inviting him was simply a matter of appeasing certain factions."

Appeasement? If people were going to side with an enemy of House Livna, then Eric didn't want their support.

"Husband?" Viola said.

Eric realized his mind had drifted. He refocused on Viola.

"I have dealt with him these past months while you have been gone," Viola said. "Leave Sir Fenris to me. I know how to handle him."

Eric tapped his fingers against his thigh. "Enough games. I can tell when you're working an angle. Do you have some sort of plan with Fenris?"

Viola laid her hand against her chest. "My only agenda is the success of House Livna. If you wish to call that an angle, then so be it. There is nothing wrong with having a plan in place."

Eric crossed his arms, unsatisfied with her answer. "Plans and strategies are one thing, but I can't say I always appreciate your methods. Let's not forget when De'Lana's husband was arrested and the city watch miraculously released him the next day without pressing charges."

"One drunken night ought not ruin a man's livelihood, should it?"

"Or my father's tobacco store that molded from a mysteriously placed raspberry?"

"Your father was fond of raspberries. How is it my fault he dropped one in his tobacco store?"

Eric raised his eyebrows. "Mother gave you up on that one."

"Fine. But if you ask Lady Revada, she will support me. Any healer can tell you pipe smoke leads to weak lungs."

"And what about Miss Laone? Our nanny who mysteriously disappeared one night only to be replaced by Sabrea the very next morn?"

Viola folded her arms. "Say what you will about my methods, but my aim is only ever to benefit House Livna. When it comes to Sir Fenris, a degree of caution benefits us all, but if you claim treachery at his every step, then you'll not be ready if any real treachery presents itself."

Eric wanted to find fault with her logic, but he saw none. "I suppose you're going to say I should make amends by attending his tournament?"

The corner of Viola's lips turned up in a half smile. "I believe it would help settle any rustled feathers."

They walked together to Viola's bedchamber, and she gave Eric a detailed account of the rest of the evening. At the very least, dealing with Kurtz had saved him having to set foot on the dance floor.

"If it will help make amends," Eric said, "then we can attend Fenris's festival tomorrow." Though Eric loathed dignifying his wretched cousin's proceedings, there was no denying that it would be good to be seen out and amongst the people.

"Wonderful! I shall arrange a private box for us at the amphitheater." Viola smiled, and her expression seemed to brighten the entire hallway.

Eric returned the smile, grateful that the scuffle hadn't entirely ruined his wife's evening.

They reached her bedchamber, and he kissed her hand. "Would you like me to join you?"

Viola tilted her head.

Did she think he was trying to force his way into her bed? That hadn't been his intention. Proper intimacy had always been rare in their marriage. A new urgency stirred in his chest. Not simply physical urges, but a desire to be close to her. So many men had not returned to their families after the war. Eric and Viola shouldn't take any moment together for granted.

"Another time," Viola said. "It has been a long day. For us both. We could do with some rest."

The desire in Eric's chest scattered like snow on the wind. "Very well, then." He released her hand and bowed his head, trying to hide any disappointment in his face. Such things would only make matters more complicated.

"Good evening, husband." Viola turned and slipped inside her room.

Eric lingered in the silence of the empty hallway. He laid his hand on the door to Viola's room and ran it across the rough grain. "Goodnight."

The joyous echoes of songs and laughter led Eric back to the great hall. Most of the guests had departed, but a group of soldiers, including most of the Fighting Fifteen, had gathered in a half circle by the hearth and showed no signs of departing. One of the bards who had traveled north with the army sat in the middle of the group, strumming a quiet medley on his lute.

On the opposite end of the gathering, Dunn straddled a bench, gesturing wildly as he spun a yarn for the group. "And then I looked at her and said, 'Wait, if you're here, then where is Lady Brandilyn?'" He leaned toward his audience. "And the lass says, 'Well, she's still back at the outhouse!'"

The men erupted with braying laughter, and Dunn took a hearty swig from his tankard.

"Where's that bard?" Jol Quimby asked. "We need another song!"

"The name is Jeffrey. The same as it has been all evening, Master Quimby," the bard said, not looking up from his lute. "I thought you men of Tsaftown were all rugged fighters and hunters, yet here you all are singing and dancing."

"Bah," Dunn said. "This is the North, where we fight hard and celebrate harder."

"The North!" Jol Quimby smacked his tankard against Dunn's.

"Be that as it may," Jeffrey said. "While my talent may be a free gift from Arman"—he plucked out a saucy chord on his lute—"my performances are not. If I am to continue playing into the night—"

"Then it's time you pay the man." Eric strode into the circle. He pulled a gold coin out of his belt pouch and flipped it to the bard.

The men followed suit, and several more coins made their way to the musician.

Jeffrey swept his new bounty into his long, pointed cap, firelight twinkling in his eyes. "Well, I did take the time to learn one of your local tunes. Are you familiar with 'The Tragedy of Lady Katine'?"

He rose and paced in front of the fire, strumming the strings of his lute. The swift rhythm brought a cheer from the men.

"'Tis a tale of romance and heartbreak about a mad sorceress," Jeffrey said. "A mysterious woman, driven out of her mind. Perhaps by greed. Perhaps by her own potions. Or maybe…by the ghost of her dead husband. A cautionary tale, meant to warn young men against falling for the charms of Jaelportian women."

Lysander Thane guffawed. "Be careful, bard. Our lord's wife is from Jaelport."

Jeffrey's eyebrows shot up, and he glanced over to Eric. "I see. Well, if the song offends..."

"Carry on," Eric said. "My wife was born in Zerah Rock. It's her mother who is of Jaelport. And while she is no crazy Katine either, I do know that to underestimate Jaelportian women is to do so at your own peril."

Jeffrey bowed. "Very well, then. Master Wroxton, would you mind playing the harmony? In a minor chord, please."

Wroxton retrieved his own lute and followed Jeffrey's lead as the bard worked the lute strings, then sang:

"Lady Katine, with her mind on a string
And a birthmark on her thigh.
When her husband was dead, she took a squire in his stead,
And she gobbled him up like a fly."

As the tale grew more and more bawdy, the men roared with laughter. Eric sighed contentedly, pleased to see his men in such good spirits. Many of them would disband after this night, returning to their farms, fishing boats, and other trades. The original members of the Fighting Fifteen would retain their positions, but for the rest, this was their last night as part of the Fighting Five Hundred who had served valiantly during the war. It was a night worth celebrating.

Eric found Walter sitting alone on the fringe of the gathering, cleaning out his pipe. He joined him, and they both watched as the men continued their revelry.

"My lord," Walter said, "you don't wish to join in the merriment?"

Eric smiled. "The men can enjoy their song and dance. I'm surprised you're not over there with the rest of the soldiers."

"Oh, I've not been one of the soldiers for quite some time. I picked up my sword again to serve you on the war front. Now that we've returned home, I am content to hang up my armor and return to the life of a humble valet."

Eric leaned back against the table, breathing easy for the first time in weeks.

"If you're not in the mood for revels, then perhaps a game?" Walter set his pipe aside and retrieved from the end of the table a circular game board, speckled with red and black segments in concentric circles. "It's been some time since our last citadel match. I might even take it easy on you."

Eric turned to face the game board. "Don't you dare. When I beat you, it will be a proper win."

Walter retrieved the wooden game pieces out of a small bag, then he and Eric set them around the perimeter of the board. Eric set the red pieces on his side, while Walter took the black. There were fancier game boards than this one. Some with finely crafted stone or even glass pieces, but Eric liked the feel of the wood and the smell of the maroon stain.

They played in silence. Eric quickly moved his baron pieces to secure the citadel in the center of the circular board.

Walter stroked the end of his grey beard. "I was rather surprised to see you return from your wife's bedchamber so early."

Eric flinched and knocked over his own baron. "I beg your pardon?"

"I don't mean to pry, my lord," Walter said. "But one might have assumed you would spend your first evening back enjoying the company of your wife."

Eric exhaled a protracted sigh. "Tonight was not the night for such company."

Walter moved his rogue piece several spaces sideways. "Is that disappointment I hear in your tone?"

The brazenness of this man. Trusted right hand of his father or not, this line of questioning pressed well into Eric's comfort zone. "Is this what you call not prying?"

Walter chuckled. "There's no shame in wanting to be with the woman you love."

Jeffrey's song continued. The tune had started with a playful rhythm, but now slowed, evoking a sense of melancholy. Layers of worry and concerns that had insulated Eric's heart for months began to peel away.

"Walter, you know full well that love is not the cornerstone of our marriage," he said. "It was a match arranged by our families. Nothing more, nothing less."

Eric moved his barbarian forward several spaces, hoping to ward off Walter's pesky rogue.

"Is there no affection between you and your wife?" Walter asked.

The memory of Viola in the hallway sprang to mind. Her elegant dress. The way her copper skin glowed in the warm torchlight.

"I do care for her," Eric said quietly. "Our marriage is not a grand romantic tale like that of King Gidon and Queen Averella, but it works."

Walter lifted his eyes from the game board. "Perhaps. But are you content with that?"

The shadows from the fire continued to dance to the bard's music as the song swelled to an emotional finish.

Eric rubbed his temples. "There has been much loss in these last months. I find myself wanting to hold tight to the things...to the people I care for."

And yet even as Eric said this, his heart was duty bound to serve and protect Tsaftown above all else. Duty had always come first in his life. To love truly, he would need to be vulnerable. And he couldn't afford such liabilities.

"Many minstrel songs say that a man falls desperately in love with a woman and marries her," Walter said. "But it's also right to learn how to love the one you marry. That's a noble labor."

Noble, indeed. But not for Eric. Not for the lord of Tsaftown.

Walter moved his rogue in another side-to-side pattern, scooting past the barbarian and into the first ring of the inner circle. The first step toward establishing his citadel.

The match was far from finished, but Walter's swift maneuvering didn't bode well for Eric's chances. As the game unfolded, Eric's thoughts drifted over Walter's words. Could his and Viola's marriage of convenience become a truly loving one? Or were such hopes best left in storybooks? And even if such hope was viable in his own heart, would he be able to open the door to Viola's heart as well?

VIOLA

Cernell Crow.

A dull pressure settled in Viola's temples. Motherless goat. That wretched bloodvoicer's attempts to speak into Viola's mind always unsettled her. Why did just the sound of the man speaking his name make her skin crawl?

She shook off the gooseflesh and continued down the hall. Mother had taught her all about bloodvoicing, the strange magic that allowed certain individuals to speak into others' minds or look through their eyes. Viola's half-brother Eagan had the ability, and while Viola had no magic of her own, Mother had insisted she learn to shield against it. She'd once thought the woman paranoid but was grateful now that Crow had invaded her life.

Viola cupped her hand before the small candle she carried, protecting the delicate flame. She reached the door and slipped inside as quietly as possible. Moonlight filled one corner of the room, providing enough light to gently illuminate the tiny figure lying asleep in bed.

Viola took several measured steps into the room and gazed down on Nevandra.

The girl slept in contented bliss, undisturbed by Viola's presence. It had been a long day, and Nevandra had thoroughly worn herself out. A smile crept across Viola's face. There were so few precious moments such as this, where title and duty and expectations melted away, and Viola could simply be a mother watching her daughter sleep.

Cernell Crow

A sharp pulse accompanied the magical knock, a side effect of shielding. Viola pressed a hand to her temple, quieting the echo of his voice inside her head. Crow couldn't speak more into her mind unless she allowed him in, and for that she was grateful. Though it might be just as well to answer him. At least then she could tell him off for reaching out to her this late at night.

Nevandra turned over in her bed, nuzzling her stuffed rabbit.

No. Viola had nothing to say to Crow tonight. He could throw a fit if he wanted. But after reaching out with his magic at this hour? The man deserved silence.

Viola bent down and kissed Nevandra on the cheek. "Mama loves you, little one," she said, risking the quietest of whispers.

Though she loathed having to associate with men like Crow, it would all be worthwhile if Nevandra's future could be protected. Viola exhaled, then stepped carefully back into the hall with the guttering candle and made her way through the shadows.

CHAPTER SIX
VIOLA

A PERFECT DAY. NOT MERELY FOR AT-tending a festival but for Eric to interact with the people of Tsaftown, something Viola knew that he—as their lord—needed to do more often.

She sat beside her husband, Nevandra on her lap, in a private box in the lower gallery of the amphitheater in the Dale, where citizens could stop and offer blessings or concerns to their lord. Walter had dressed Eric in a black ensemble with gold trim. The outfit was beautifully tailored, outlining his chest and powerful shoulders handsomely.

Hundreds of Tsaftown's residents had taken advantage of the pleasant weather and ventured out to Sir Fenris's festival. The smell of cooked meats wafted in the air. Another day of duels and other entertainment had been scheduled, which had brought the people out in droves.

Derby Wenk stood at the entrance to their box, handing out freshly baked sweet bread rolls to anyone who stopped by. Lathia had also joined them and was supposed to be helping hand out bread, though she often sidetracked herself with conversation, leaving Derby to do most of the work.

"Aye, the fishin' has been decent," said a hunched man in a loose tunic, who had struck up a conversation with Eric. "But not near what 'twas before Darkness."

The fisherman's wife nodded in agreement.

"No doubt a proper summer will warm the waters and bring the fish back to their old feeding ground," Eric said. "Of course, there's always the adventure of ice fishing to look forward to."

The hunched man smiled, revealing several missing teeth. "Well said, my lord."

Viola marveled at Eric's natural ability to carry on a conversation with anyone and make them feel heard. Likely because he spent so much time interacting with soldiers, most of whom were lowborn. Unfortunately, he still lacked the social graces needed for dealing with the upper crust of the city, but that was something he could work on with time.

The fisherman's wife presented Eric with a rare bundle of winter flowers. "For your lovely wife and daughter, my lord. And we pray for the day when Arman will bless you with a son and heir. It will be a glorious day for Tsaftown."

The woman's words were kindly meant, but they stung Viola's heart. Everyone in Tsaftown so eagerly awaited the arrival of a male child, as if she and Eric could produce an heir simply by looking at each other. No one in the city or House Livna paid any regard to Nevandra. She was seen as an adorable little lady but never thought of as the future of their house.

The couple received their sweet bread rolls from Derby and meandered back into the crowd.

Eric handed the flowers to Viola. "For you. I don't know much about flowers, but they look pretty."

Viola set the flowers across her lap, while using one hand to balance Nevandra, who was now standing so she could see the festivities.

"They are wonderful," Viola said. Even these simple blooms of phlox and asters had been impossible to find during Darkness. They slightly eased Viola's discomfort from the fisherman's wife's words.

Eric slipped one of the flowers out of the bundle, broke off half the stem, and tucked the blossom behind Nevandra's ear.

Their daughter beamed. "A pwetty flower, Mama."

There was at least one other person in Tsaftown who could appreciate sweet Nevandra.

Lathia turned up her nose at the old fisherman, who had moved out of earshot. "Why must all these people smell so sour?"

"Lathia, that's unkind," Viola said.

"No, truly," Lathia continued. "It would make sense if they smelled like fish or sea salt. But they all have that sour smell that always burns my nose."

"It's vinegar," Eric said. "To preserve the fish for winter or for shipping."

Lathia seemingly found something new to complain about every minute. The girl might be seventeen, but she continually acted the part of a spoiled child. It was staggering to think that Lathia and Queen Averella were the same age.

The *tap tap tap* of a walking stick echoed on the gallery floor. A gaunt man in well-worn clothes approached. His bristly grey hair hung down to his shoulders, but most noticeable was the long strip of cloth that covered his eyes.

"My lord, have you any alms for an old blind man?" he asked.

A cold finger traced Viola's spine. She held Nevandra closer to her chest. That voice was unmistakable. The same as the bloodvoice that had reached out to her the night before.

"We have several baskets of sweet breads," Eric said. "You're welcome to one of them."

"Much obliged, your lordship," the blind man said.

"What is your name, friend?" Tension hung in Eric's tone. Something had triggered her husband's defensive instincts.

"Cernell Crow, my lord. But most call me Crow."

Eric crossed his arms. "I thought I recognized you. I saw you at the dueling ring yesterday. You're a bloodvoicer, correct?"

"Aye," Crow said.

"You're also a thief," Eric said flatly. "I remember you being thrown into Ice Island for using your bloodvoice to coerce people to give you coin."

Crow's already surly demeanor soured. "'Twas a long time ago, my lord. I did my time in Ice Island. Surely you'll not hold such things against an old man forever?"

"I can be forgiving, but I'm no fool," Eric said. "If I hear that you're up to your old tricks again, you'll face stiff consequences."

"Bah," Crow said. "You needn't worry of that. The magic betrays me now. I can still voice, but it pains me awfully. Makes my head spin. Not much use these days."

Bloodvoicing caused him pain? Crow had never let on to such a thing. His employer must pay him decently to use his gift.

Eric eyed Crow and tapped his finger against the arm of his chair. "Regardless of your past, you are a citizen of the city. And I will serve your needs as best as I can."

Crow shuffled along and received one of the rolls from Derby. He put it up to his nose and inhaled slowly, then sank his yellow teeth deep into the soft white bread.

Cernell Crow.

The voice startled Viola. She turned her head to the side, pretending to adjust the silver clip in her hair.

What do you want? She had gotten better at focusing her thoughts and responding to Crow without speaking aloud.

Sir Fenris sends his regards, Crow voiced. *And his apologies for the fight at the banquet last night.*

This is why you've interrupted my time with my family? An apology? First, he messages her in the middle of the night, and now this? Crow, or perhaps Sir Fenris, had to be trying to get a rise out of her.

She risked a sidelong glance at Crow. He had already wolfed down half of the roll.

You'd have had your privacy if you'd answered last night. Crow grimaced as he moved away from them. Perhaps a headache brought on by use of his bloodvoice.

Also, Crow continued, *Sir Fenris says he's nearly completed the task you've assigned him. He'll expect payment upon completion.*

Sir Fenris could have relayed this news any number of ways, none of which involved bloodvoicing. Perhaps he simply enjoyed using Crow to show off that he had a bloodvoicer in his entourage.

I will hold up my end of our bargain if Sir Fenris can, Viola thought. The sooner the better. *He needn't come try to shake me down.*

Crow offered no reply. He simply ambled off, feeling his way down the steps with his walking stick. Viola exhaled slowly and distracted herself from the encounter by focusing on the festivities in the arena.

The duels concluded and were immediately followed by the arrival of a troupe of actors performing a skit about a group of travelers. The caravan was beset upon by a tribe of Poroo, played by actors made up in grey face paint and dressed in ragged clothes.

The performance quickly devolved into a hijinks-laden chase around the arena, with the Poroo almost catching the travelers several times yet always being thwarted through more and more ridiculous means. One of the Poroo performers tripped and took what appeared to be a very real fall to the ground. This earned raucous laughter from the crowd. The actor jumped back up and continued the chase while hobbling on one foot.

"He fell down!" Nevandra cackled.

The Poroo finally encircled the helpless travelers. Right as they were about to meet their fate, a figure appeared on the opposite side of the stage, wielding a wooden sword and donning a lumpy blond wig on his head.

"It's Sir Fenris!" one of the travelers declared. "Praise the gods, we're saved!"

"Hooray for Sir Fenris!" cheered the rest of the troupe.

Next to her, Eric groaned.

The actor playing Sir Fenris charged forward, ousting the Poroo one by one with his wooden weapon. This left the travelers with nothing to do but fawn over their newfound savior.

"He has funny hair," Nevandra said.

Eric chuckled in amusement. "Funny hair indeed."

The actors took a bow and exited, receiving a smattering of applause. A group of minstrels climbed up on the stage and began tuning their instruments.

"Fantastic performance, isn't it?" Councilor Erlichman ascended the steps toward the Livnas. "I hear they're opening in Carmine next month."

Viola let out a genuine laugh. "It was truly one of a kind."

Erlichman reached their box and leaned forward on the railing. "My lord, I wonder if you'd be interested in seeing some horses I've just acquired from a trader down in Nahar. I've got them saddled and waiting in a corral on the opposite side of the dueling rings. They're of very fine stock."

Councilor Erlichman's family typically raised and sold boar and other similar livestock for hunting. Apparently, his business interests had expanded.

Eric slid to the edge of his seat. "Nahar?" he said. "Do you have any festriers?"

Erlichman nodded with pride. "Five of them."

A gleam appeared in Eric's eyes. The massive war horses were the animal of choice among the giants in the South. But they were rare this far north. And expensive. How had Erlichman gotten ahold of five of the animals?

Eric's father had owned one for many years until Eric had given it to the Crown Prince after the elder Lord Livna was killed. Eric had said it was the eve of war and, therefore, an appropriate gift for the future king.

"Horsies?" Nevandra chirped. "Can we see the horsies?" The girl tugged at Viola's arm, her large brown eyes pleading sweetly.

Viola glanced up at Eric, who had more than taken his turn with Nevandra already today. He likely didn't want a little girl in tow.

Eric stroked his beard. "That's a wonderful idea, Nevandra. We can go see them together."

Viola thought on it for a moment. "It's fine if you want to take her, but perhaps I should stay here to receive any who stop by."

"Do you want to come see the horses?" Eric reached for Nevandra.

Nevandra hesitated, showing the same bashfulness around Eric as the night before. The wonder that had bloomed in her eyes at the mention of horses had dimmed slightly.

"I bet Councilor Erlichman has horses that are taller than me." Eric bulged his eyes playfully and reached for her.

A tiny smile raised the girl's cheeks. She gently placed her tiny hand in Eric's and crawled into his lap. Now, this was different. Not only Eric's playfulness but Nevandra's desire to go along with it.

Eric picked up Nevandra and followed Erlichman down the steps. Viola tracked their progress through the crowd. Eric's new affection for Nevandra was unexpected but not unwelcome. So many in House Livna had been openly disappointed when they discovered that Eric's long-awaited firstborn child was a daughter, not a son. That dissatisfaction had affected Eric as well. But now, just one day since his return, Eric had gone out of his way several times to give extra attention to their daughter. Even being playful with her. Like he wanted to turn over a new leaf as a father.

Viola could use that.

Storms. She dismissed the intruding thought. That echo of her mother's voice. Her mother's calculating nature had its place, but Viola would not use her daughter as a pawn.

Lathia hmphed. "Well, if Eric is going to leave, then I think I shall go *mingle*."

"Lathia, please," Viola said.

"It's fine." Lathia slipped her hand around Derby's elbow. "Winch is doing a fine job handing out the bread. I would only be in the way if I stayed."

Young Master Wenk stayed silent, not correcting Lathia on his name. The lad appeared unsure how to handle himself with a beautiful noblewoman on his arm.

"You're not going to mingle with that Clave boy, are you?" Viola asked.

Lathia untangled her arm from Derby's and slipped out of the box. "If Connor wishes to find me, then he shall. Unless you plan to arrest me for talking to a boy?"

"Speak with whomever you wish," Viola said. "But know that your choices have consequences. Doubly so as woman of noble status."

"Thank you for reminding me of things every adult has told me since I was a child. It is so very enlightening and not at all condescending." Lathia flounced past the guardrail and down the steps.

Merciful tempest, how had that girl developed such a snooty attitude? She could hold her own amongst the noblewomen of Jaelport.

Bu-doom!

Drums. Not from the minstrels on the stage, but from farther away. Derby tilted his head and looked off in the direction of the noise.

Bu-doom! Bu-doom!

A horn blared in the distance. Understanding quickly dawned on Viola. It was a warning call from the city walls.

"Lady Viola!" Derby said. "The city is under attack. You must get to safety."

The squire ushered her out of the private box. Viola tripped slightly and knocked over one of the bread baskets, sending its contents bouncing down the steps.

Panicked voices filled the air. The minstrels dashed off the stage. Spectators abandoned their seats and headed toward the stairs.

Viola and Derby caught up with Lathia, who had paused in the middle of the chaos. Derby grabbed her by the arm and dragged her with them.

"Don't push me!" Lathia whined.

The three continued down the steps. Clarity focused Viola's mind. Only one thing mattered. She needed to find Nevandra.

ERIC

Thunder. A fitting name for such a majestic creature.

Eric stood outside the paddock, inspecting a white festrier. The horse stood a full five hands taller than Eric. Even taller than his father's war horse, Dove. Nevandra had climbed on the outside of the fence to watch, her feet on a lower slat, her arms folded over the top. She reached out with one hand to pet the animal, and Eric rested a hand against her back to help support her.

Erlichman stood inside the paddock, showing off the other festriers to another set of onlookers. It seemed Erlichman, ever the businessman, was ready to make a deal of some kind to any who expressed interest in the war horses.

Bu-doom! Bu-doom!

Eric turned swiftly, keeping one hand on Nevandra. The sound of those drums wasn't familiar. Another one of Fenris's special performances? How far away could they be?

The blasting of horns rose over the noise. *That* sound Eric knew well. The southern wall was sounding the alarm.

Nevandra looked up from Thunder and watched as the onlookers began to scurry away, heading for safety.

"Papa? Where they going?" Nevandra asked.

Eric needed to move. Get to the gate as soon as possible. "Councilor, I will require one of your horses."

"Certainly, my lord." Erlichman summoned a pair of stable boys who quickly brought a mounting block to Thunder's side.

What of Nevandra? Perhaps Eric could send her with Erlichman to find Viola and get back home. He wasn't dressed for battle, but he would have to sort that out after he reached the gate.

Nevandra turned to face Eric, fear growing in her large brown eyes. "Papa?" Her bottom lip quivered.

No. Eric would not hand his child off to another like a duffle roll. Nevandra was his to protect.

"Let's go for a ride, Nevie." He lifted her to his hip and carried her to the mounting block. The stable boy helped Eric up the wooden steps.

"My lord, I must protest," Erlichman said. "This horse is far too big for the child."

Eric hoisted his daughter up in front of Thunder's saddle. "Hold on to the saddle horn. Grab it tight. That-a girl!"

Those big brown eyes glossed over with tears, and Nevie began to whimper. Eric had clearly terrified the poor child. But he had little time for gentleness. They needed to move.

"I've got to get her to her mother," he said. Unable to use the saddle horn now that Nevie had hold of it, Eric reached across Thunder's back and gripped the opposite edge of the leather saddle. He tucked his boot into the stirrup and jumped, grateful to feel Erlichman give him a boost. He settled into the saddle and tucked Nevie close to his body, a bit uneasy himself as he adjusted to Thunder's great height. Thankfully, the well-trained animal barely moved.

"Please be careful, my lord." Erlichman tugged the reins from where they'd been coiled around the saddle horn and Nevandra's fists and passed them to Eric, who took them in his right hand.

"Thank you, Councilor," Eric said as he steered the horse out of the paddock.

Nevandra trembled in his arms, so Eric squeezed her close. "It will be all right, little one," he sang. "Let's find Mama." He nudged Thunder into a trot as he surveyed the Dale. Waves of frightened citizens scurried away from the festival grounds, and Eric had to steer Thunder carefully to avoid trampling anyone. The amphitheater had emptied, including the private boxes.

Viola could be anywhere.

Eric wheeled Thunder around, which made Nevie squeal and tighten her grip on Eric's arm. The horse snorted anxiously, and they made their way through the panicked throng.

"It's okay," Eric said, both to Nevie and the horse. "We're doing just fine."

Sitting high on Thunder, Eric quickly surveyed the crowd. A glimpse of black hair caught his eye. Then a flash of silver shimmered in the sun. Viola's hairpin. Derby stood at her side along with Lathia. The three moved slowly, fighting to stay together in the chaos.

"Viola!" Eric called.

She whirled and quickly steered the others toward him and Nevandra.

Eric urged Thunder forward until they met in the midst of the mob.

Viola reached up and grabbed Eric's leg, holding tight like a drowning woman to a piece of driftwood. She said something to Nevandra, though Eric couldn't hear her over the din of the crowd.

On Eric's right, Erlichman rode up beside him on a majestic black festrier with rippling muscles. The positions of the two horses made a pocket of safety for Viola, Lathia, and Derby in the midst of the relentless buffeting of the throng.

Eric handed Nevandra down to Viola, and the child swiftly wrapped her arms around her mother's neck.

"All of you, go with Councilor Erlichman," Eric said. "Derby, as soon as they are safe, meet me at the southern wall."

"Aye, my lord," Derby said.

Viola's brow tensed. "You're not coming?"

"I must lead the men," Eric said.

"Eric, please don't put yourself in danger needlessly," Viola said. "Your men need a lord more than they need a commander right now."

"Today I must be both," Eric said. "There's no time. Now go."

He wheeled Thunder around toward the southern gate, then threaded the horse carefully yet swiftly through the bustling people. He prayed Arman would protect his family and that Câan would give him strength for whatever clash lay ahead.

Finally finding an open path, Eric urged the animal into a gallop. His teeth rattled as Thunder reached full speed. The gate came into view. Debris was strewn across the road. No soldiers.

Eric slowed upon a scene of broken spearheads and splintered wood from the remains of a caravan. One wagon lay abandoned. The other sat in the archway of the entrance, pinned by the massive oak doors of the gate. Someone must have closed the gates while the caravan was still passing through, nearly crushing the wagon and leaving the gate unable to close. The guardhouse itself had been closed up. Arrows and impact strikes marred the front siding, as if the building had been through a siege.

The hairs on Eric's neck tingled as he caught sight of several bodies lying motionless on the ground. Most looked to be members of the wagon caravan. Closer to the guardhouse lay one of the

Howlers. Arrows and broken spear tips protruded from his torso, but he had been picked apart by the Poroo, his limbs a bloody tapestry on the ground.

The man hadn't simply been killed. He'd been mutilated.

Why kill the Howler so brutally and not the rest of the people from the caravan?

A groan caught Eric's attention. A young man lay on the ground behind the overturned wagon, trying to push himself up. He had taken an arrow to his shoulder and sported a nasty gash on his forehead.

Eric dismounted Thunder, landing hard from the height, and knelt by the man. "What happened here?"

"Poroo attacked just after we passed inside the guardhouse." He tried to say more, but winced and expelled a shuddering breath.

"Stay still," Eric said. "Help is on the way."

A heavy metallic thump startled Eric. He looked the scene over, but saw no movement, Poroo or otherwise.

Another thump, followed by murmuring, coming from the guardhouse.

Eric reached to his hip only to remember he had no sword. Curse his thoughtless self. He grabbed a broken spear from the ground and walked slowly toward the guardhouse, listening carefully to the sound of muffled voices inside.

Eric yelled the password "Juniper Thornspire!" as he pounded on the door.

"Hello?" a man asked. "Who's there?"

"Shut it, Taggert!" This second voice was deep, raspy.

These men hadn't recognized the security password, but they clearly weren't Poroo. Could be they were merchants?

Eric beat on the door again. "The danger is over. Come out. Slowly."

The guardhouse door opened, and two Howlers stepped out. The first, a lean man with stringy hair, carried a Poroo dagger in his belt. The second Howler was brawny with a long black-and-silver beard.

"What happened here?" Eric asked.

The bearded man sneered and crossed his arms. "Respectfully, we report to Sir Fenris." His raspy voice told Eric that the scrawny fellow must be Taggert.

"The city has been attacked!" Eric yelled. "Men have been killed. Do you think I care who you work for?"

The Howler's black-and-silver beard quivered. "Gonna make somethin' of it?" He took a step forward, close enough that Eric caught a whiff of his foul breath.

Eric gripped the spear handle tighter. Was this fool truly going to fight him?

The scrawny man, Taggert, stepped in front of the angry Howler. "Easy, Skunk."

Eric took note of the big man's silver-streaked beard, his sour breath. Fitting nickname.

Taggert caressed the hilt of his dagger. "It all 'appened so quick like. We was checkin' in the three wagons. Collecting a..." He trailed off, glanced at Skunk. "A donation."

Cinders. A bribe? Such a racket was not uncommon at guard posts, though Eric loathed to learn it happened in Tsaftown. He would have to deal with that bit of petty crime later.

"Go on," Eric said.

Taggert shrugged. "Outta nowhere come them pale devils. Screamin' like demons, they was."

Three wagons, but there were only two left in the road. The Poroo were infamous for their ability to disappear into the woods on foot. But they couldn't hide a wagon so easily, which meant they could be tracked. But only if Eric moved quickly.

"One of you, I need a sword," Eric said.

Skunk's forehead wrinkled. "What? Why?"

"A sword, man!" Eric barked. There wasn't time to waste. Every second meant the Poroo were farther and farther away from the city.

Skunk shuffled into the guardhouse and returned with scabbard and belt. It wasn't the same quality of blade as Eric was used to, but it was better than coming at the Poroo with a broken spear. Eric wrapped the belt around his waist.

A group of riders approached the guardhouse, led by Captain Demry. With him were Dunn, Derby, and several of the Fighting Fifteen. They slowed to a stop and circled around Eric while Skunk and Taggert shuffled back toward the guardhouse.

"The city is secure, my lord," Captain Demry said.

"And your family is safe," Dunn added. "All accounted for inside Lytton Hall."

Eric inhaled a swift breath of relief. "Poroo attacked a caravan and seized one of the wagons. Gedmund, choose two men to post here with you at the guardhouse. Tend to the wounded until a healer can arrive, and take care of the dead."

"Yes, sir," Gedmund said.

Derby retrieved Thunder and led the towering animal back to Eric.

"The rest of you are with me." Eric took his horse's reigns. "We can overtake them if we ride hard. Grab whatever weapons you need from the guardhouse. We're going hunting."

CHAPTER SEVEN
ERIC

THE HUNTERS HAD BECOME THE HUNTED. Days after being ambushed on the King's Road, now it was Eric and his men lurking in the woods, waiting to attack the Poroo. In less than an hour, they had nearly caught up as the raiders entered the foothills of Craven's Hook Canyon. Instead of simply charging from behind, Eric sent a detachment of four archers with Captain Demry up a path along the high bluffs, then he took the other eight men along an old hunting trail that ran parallel to the King's Road until it eventually hooked back around.

They should be ahead of the Poroo now. Eric sent Alden Wroxton and Torin Oxbow to scout on foot while he and the other riders waited in silence in a hollow in the woods as the late afternoon sun glimmered through the trees. Eric squinted through the tattered forest canopy, trying to catch a glimpse of Captain Demry's group on the high ridge, but saw nothing. He had to trust that they would be in position.

"What's taking them so long?" There was an eagerness in Derby's tone.

Eric recognized it in the faces of the other men. The nervous anticipation before battle. "Patience," he said. "We wait for Captain Demry's signal."

Deterrence was their aim. Retribution not vengeance. A swift surprise strike would make the Poroo think twice before attacking Tsaftown again.

Soft footfalls through the brush caught Eric's attention. Wroxton and Oxbow scurried into view and quickly rejoined the group.

"They're almost here," Wroxton whispered. "Right around the corner."

"Counted eighteen," Oxbow added.

The two scouts quickly remounted their horses.

Eighteen was large for a raiding party and gave the Poroo the advantage, but Eric's men were on horseback. Plus Demry's men had high ground, and the Northlanders had the element of surprise.

Eric tried to get a glimpse of the raiders, but the woods and rock face made it impossible to see anything. The same cover that hid Eric and his men also blinded them to the enemy's advance.

A shrill whistle echoed through the canyon. Captain Demry's signal.

Eric drew his blade. "Slowly. We keep our distance until Captain Demry's team engages them."

On Eric's signal, the riders eased out of the underbrush and onto the King's Road. As they slowly rounded a bend in the road, the Poroo came into view. Most were on foot but for those riding in the stolen wagon.

Eric signaled the group to halt, creating a standoff in the middle of the trail.

A tall Poroo warrior who had been driving the wagon stood up and raised a war club over his head. "*Itam Poroo! Aqni!*" he screamed, distorting the red war paint on his nose and brow.

The man's words were lost on Eric, but his meaning was clear.

A sharp crack echoed overhead, disrupting the face-off. Several large boulders tumbled down the edge of the bluff toward the

Poroo and the stolen wagon. The raiders dodged out of the way, though some were hit and pinned by the fallen rocks. One of the boulders crashed directly into the wagon, cracking one wheel in half and leaving it completely immobile.

Eric and his riders charged forward, swiftly forming an arrowhead formation. Eric steered the column to the right, into the majority of the raiders. The Poroo fled the oncoming charge, all but the red-painted warrior, who remained standing on the wagon. He hurled his spear, and the weapon whistled as it cut through the air.

Eric veered Thunder to one side, narrowly evading the projectile. The Poroo warrior crouched and picked up an abandoned spear, but before he could launch another attack, a falling boulder bashed him in the forehead and knocked him off the wagon.

On the ground, some of the Poroo came back with weapons in hand. One raised an ax at Eric, who knocked it away with his sword.

Fletchings sang their deadly song as Captain Demry's bowmen rained down arrows from the bluff, scattering the few Poroo who had stood their ground. The remaining raiders scrambled into the trees or clambered up the sides of the bluff.

Eric and his horsemen circled the end of the wagon for another attack but found no enemy to engage. Some Poroo lay fallen on the ground, but the survivors had escaped into the trees.

Eric could order a pursuit, but diving into the woods blindly would only put his men at risk. Retribution had been carried out. There was no need to push further.

"Secure the wagon!" Eric said.

Dunn led the rest of the riders back to the wrecked wagon, circling up and forming a perimeter. Eric held back, taking in the entirety of the scene. Captain Demry and his men stood on the edge of the bluff.

"Well done, Captain Demry!" Eric called. "Your men have excellent aim with both arrow and rock."

This was met with laughter from Captain Demry's group. Then they drew back to find their horses and the trail down off the bluff.

A ghastly feeling crept over Eric as a figure appeared in his peripheral vision. He looked upward to an elder Poroo hunched on the far rock face. The wrinkled grey man held a tall staff adorned with animal claws and glared down at Eric.

Recognition dawned. Eric had seen this Poroo man before. After the attack at the ruins of Glodwood Manor. He gripped his sword tighter. What was this strange wizard up to?

The elder Poroo stepped back and disappeared into the trees, gone like a wisp of smoke.

"My lord!" Dunn's voice came over his shoulder.

Eric turned and urged Thunder over to the wreckage of the wagon.

Dunn knelt over a fallen Poroo. The red-painted warrior. "My lord, this one is still alive."

Quimby stood alongside Dunn with his sword at the ready. A trickle of blood ran down the raider's forehead and mingled with the red war paint on his face. He stirred and mumbled something incoherent, clearly dazed from the rock impact.

The Poroo had been formidable in battle, but looking at him now, Eric only saw a wounded youth. Barely older than Derby.

"Bind him," Eric said. "We'll take him back to the city."

Dunn and Quimby exchanged looks.

"My lord," Dunn said, "he wouldn't hesitate to finish you off if he were in your position."

"Then I shall be thankful that our positions are not reversed," Eric said. "Câan blessed us in battle, but that does not give us the right to murder a helpless prisoner."

"As you wish, my lord," Dunn said. He and Quimby bound the Poroo warrior's hands before leading him to one of the horses.

"Make sure you gag him too," Dunn warned. "The Poroo are biters."

Laughter erupted from the opposite side of the caravan.

"He's a hungry little one, isn't he?" Some happy commotion had broken out amongst the men.

Eric rounded the corner of the wagon and found Derby and Wroxton huddled around a hollow in the rock. A small, fuzzy muzzle poked outward. Wroxton tossed a bit of dried fruit toward the opening. The animal came out of its hiding place to investigate the tiny morsel, then seized the fruit in its paw.

Eric's chest tightened as he recognized the animal. A cham cub.

The chubby little bear plopped itself down on its rump and began feasting on the fruit.

"My lord! I believe we've found a mascot for the Fighting Fifteen," Wroxton said.

"Aye," Derby added. "He's a fierce one indeed."

The men laughed, but a prickle shot up Eric's neck. He performed a swift survey of the surrounding underbrush.

"Best let your new pet go, gentlemen. Cham bears are nothing to be trifled with. Even a miniature one."

Derby offered another bit of dried fruit to the cub.

An earth-splitting growl erupted from the trees. All activity stopped. Derby's eyes went wide, and he dropped the food.

Another horrifying growl thundered. Câan's wrath. How could they have been so foolish?

"Back away!" Eric barked.

"My lord! Above you!" Dunn yelled.

On a higher ridge, nearly striking distance from Eric, stood a massive, fully grown cham bear. Mama had arrived.

Smoke erupted from the mother cham's nostrils, and she charged down the rock face.

Derby dashed away, but Wroxton stumbled in his attempt to escape the cub. The she-bear swiped her massive paw, tore into Wroxton's shoulder, and knocked him prone.

The cub scurried to take refuge behind its mother. She loomed over Wroxton and loosed a mighty roar.

"Get him out of there!" Eric seized a spear from the ground and heaved it at the mother cham. The spear stuck in her side, provoking a howl from the beast. Derby grabbed Wroxton under the arms and dragged him to the other side of the wagon. The cham swiped at air, but did not pursue.

Then she turned toward Eric and unleashed a stream of fire in a wild arc. Eric dove to ground. The flames singed the back of his hair and caught the fringes of his riding cloak on fire. He rolled, stifling the flames. Charred debris fluttered around him.

Arrows flew from the bowmen. Some struck the she-bear while others bounced off her thick hide. Still, she charged toward Eric.

He scrambled on hands and knees across the rough ground toward the cover of the wagon. Rocks and branches stabbed at his palms and forearms. He reached the wagon, grabbed the underside, and curled up to a half sitting position as he pulled his body between the wheels.

He had almost made it when a terrible force slammed down on his still exposed right leg, ripping into the side of his shin.

Blasted ashes! Eric howled as the mama cham sank her mighty claws deeper into his leg and pulled him toward her. He fought to maintain focus and clamped down on the underside of the wagon, desperately holding on against the force of the cham.

The bear's grip slipped, and Eric pulled his legs completely under the wagon. He twisted back to his front and tried to crawl out the other side, but his wounded leg hindered his mobility. He glanced back. The bear was still here. She reached her paw after him, slashing blindly.

The wagon rocked with each swinging grab. The cham let out another burst of flame, and Eric pressed himself to the ground. The heat above him ignited the wagon. Flames licked the back of Eric's neck and embers fell around him. His clothing protected him from the embers, but they would do nothing against another fireball.

The bear pawed the ground, trying to reach her trapped quarry. Eric pulled his dagger and sank it deep into the bear's meaty paw.

The bear retracted her paw with a sharp roar, leaving a crimson streak on the ground. Eric gripped his knife again, ready for another attack, when strong hands seized him from behind.

"I have you, my lord." Dunn's massive arms wrapped around Eric's chest, pulling him to his feet. Eric leaned on Dunn for support as the soldier led him to a safe distance.

Eric's head rushed. That had been too close.

"My lord, do you wish to pursue?" Captain Demry asked.

Eric wiped sweat off his face, shaking off a bout of dizziness.

"Pursue?" Eric said, catching his breath. The mother cham, backside laden with arrows, was retreating with her cub into the woods. "Not at all. I've seen quite enough of that bear for one day."

He took a step, testing his wounded leg. Sharp pain shot up his leg. The cham had gotten him worse than he'd thought. Again the dizziness seized him, and he leaned harder on Dunn.

"My lord?" the soldier asked.

Eric glanced down. Blood flowed freely from his wounded leg, leaving a trail of crimson in the snow.

Shadows crept into the corners of Eric's vision.

"My lord, do you need help?" Dunn asked.

Eric heard Dunn, but could offer no reply. The forest began to spin, and darkness consumed his sight.

CHAPTER EIGHT
VIOLA

ERIC COULDN'T DIE. VIOLA SIMPLY couldn't let that happen.

Rumors had spread through the manor house after the men returned from their mission. De'Lana said Eric had been rushed to his chambers on a gurney and that Captain Demry had sent for the healer.

If Eric were gravely wounded, or dying, what would become of Nevandra? As it stood currently, succession would pass to Leif Livna, Eric's younger brother, who was currently serving on his uncle's ship, The Brierstar. Would Nevandra become yet another noblewoman doomed to be shipped off and married to some wretched lord like Tara had been?

That could not happen.

Viola reached Eric's chambers and halted. A horrid image of his handsome face covered in blood sprung into her mind. Did that horrific sight await her on the other side of the doors?

Tempest's mercy, why was she hesitating? She had sworn a vow to tend to Eric's needs, no matter what he may require. She pushed the door open and strode in gracefully.

"Out! I am with my patient!" The hoarse voice belonged to Rubart, Lytton Hall's healer. The stubby old man leaned over one of Eric's legs. He glanced up and raised one of his bushy white eyebrows at her.

"It's fine, Rubart," Eric said.

Eric sat upright on the bed, dressed in a dirtied undershirt, with a blanket draped over his lap, his legs exposed. He was coherent enough. Perhaps Rubart's presence was simply a precaution?

Then Viola saw the bloody gashes that stretched the length of his shin. A thick blanket, stained with blood, lay under Eric's leg.

Viola looked up at Eric, hiding her aversion to the grim scene. She rounded the bed and sat down at his side. "Is he all right, Master Rubart? Will there be...permanent damage?"

"Bah." Rubart wiped his hands on the towel. "It'll scar, but the leg will heal. Provided you keep it clean. Disinfect with alcohol and fresh bandages every day. And keep an eye on him. Wouldn't want his lordship to faint again."

"Faint?" Viola looked to Eric.

He cleared his throat. "Battle fatigue. It's not uncommon after the rush of combat has passed."

"Could call it swooning, if you prefer," Rubart added.

Eric's brow narrowed and his cheeks blushed ever so slightly.

Viola let out a small laugh, muffling a relieved sigh. Eric would live. Wounded, but on the mend. "Perhaps one day people will tell the legend of Lord Eric the Brave, lying spent after fighting a cham bear. I could commission one of the minstrels to write a ballad to immortalize the tale in song."

Eric pursed his lips. "I'd be truly honored."

"Cracking lucky is what you are, my lord." Rubart straightened and twisted one of the ends of his wiry mustache. "When I served your father in the army, we had a man go hunting for a cham. Said he was gonna get a full set of cham claws. All we ever found of him was a boot."

Eric chuckled. "I'm thankful that neither I nor my boots ended up as some cautionary tale."

"Thankful indeed." Viola rested her hand on Eric's shoulder. "I suppose you gave the cham equally harsh injuries?"

Eric placed his hand on hers and squeezed. "Not as such. Several spear and arrow wounds, but the mama cham was quite resilient." His strong touch took her by surprise. She hadn't meant her touch to be quite so affectionate, but she wasn't going to pull away in this moment.

"My lady, if you wish to be of use, would you mind fetching a mug of water?" Rubart asked. "I need to mix a tonic."

Viola wrinkled her nose. Be of use?

"I suppose I'm your nurse now," Viola said. "Aren't I?"

Eric stifled a smile. "Only if it suits you."

She stood up and filled a tankard at the sideboard. If Queen Averella could serve as a battlefield healer, Viola could at least offer Rubart assistance.

She carried the water to the old physician and held it while he stirred in a generous spoonful of yellow powder.

Rubart nodded to Eric. "Please do drink all of it."

Viola kept the tankard steady and gently held it to Eric's lips. He drank generously. And nearly spat the tonic back out.

"It's...rather chalky." Eric wiped yellow clumps out of his hairy upper lip.

"It is not meant to be enjoyed. It is meant to take the edge of the pain," Rubart said as he wrapped Eric's leg in a fresh bandage. "That will be good for the day. More than that and you lose your senses."

"I don't think I'll be tempted to overindulge," Eric said before choking down the rest of the tonic.

Rubart gathered his tools into his healer kit. "Rest your leg and keep the wound clean. If you smell rotting flesh, let me know. I've not had to amputate a limb in some time, and I would rather keep it that way."

"Rested and cleaned," Eric said. "Understood."

As Rubart reached the exit, the door suddenly swung open.

In strode Lady Revada, barreling past Rubart, her black mourning veil tight against her face.

"A cham bear?" she asked.

Walter and Lady Merris followed Lady Revada inside. The valet gave Eric a sheepish glance.

"I do apologize, my lord," Walter said. "Your mother...insisted."

Rubart wrinkled his nose at the arrival of the new interlopers. The healer sidestepped Lady Revada and scowled at Walter. "I leave it to you to handle this rabble," he said to Walter before stepping out the door.

Revada's dark blue dress billowed as she marched up to Eric's bed. "A wretched cham?"

Eric sighed. "In fairness, Mother, our target was the Poroo. The cham became involved later. I did manage to cut off one of its claws."

"Pah," Lady Merris muttered. "Makes for a poor trophy."

Lady Revada drew her shoulders back. Her dismay showed on her face even through her mourning veil. "This family has experienced enough tragedy. We'll not have more of it because a headstrong lord throws himself into harm's way."

Eric leaned back against his headboard. Viola took private satisfaction in seeing Eric taken down a notch. She had made the same point to him before he'd ridden off.

"Mother," Eric said, "I'm sorry if I frightened you. It was a quickly evolving situation. Perhaps I wasn't as careful as I should have been."

Lady Revada sighed and stepped up to Eric's bed. She lifted her mourning veil slightly and kissed Eric's forehead. "Perhaps not," she whispered.

"Better hope that leg heals properly," added Lady Merris. "Otherwise you'll never be able to lead the celebration dances correctly. You've got two left feet as it is."

Eric muffled an amused grunt, clearly unbothered at the thought of sitting out the dancing portion of any future events.

"Was your little crusade at least successful?" Walter asked.

Eric shifted in his bed. "It would seem so. They'll think twice before attacking the city again. And we took one of them prisoner. Captain Demry will have taken him to the dungeon by now."

"You brought a wild Poroo into our home?" Lady Revada asked.

"Pah." Lady Merris tapped her cane on the wooden floor. "Distasteful."

"He's contained," Eric said. "These raids have been going on for months, and they show no sign of stopping. We need to try a new strategy."

"You intend to question the prisoner and find out why they're attacking us?" Viola asked.

Eric turned toward Viola. "That would be helpful. Do you know someone who speaks Poroo?"

"Not exactly." Viola shifted off the bed to stand. "But King Trevn's journals include numerous accounts of his interactions with various peoples across the continent. He mostly wrote about their customs, but there are many references to language as well. Likely enough for me to start a conversation with our guest in the dungeon."

A contented expression crept across Eric's face. "Beauty and wisdom. All wrapped together," he said.

Viola's cheeks warmed. Surely that was the tonic speaking. His words were kind, but to say them in front of his mother?

"And how do you know that the prisoner will have any interest in talking?" Walter asked.

Eric shifted in his sheets. "We have to try. This engagement was a success, but if our people are to be safe, then we must stop these attacks. We need a more permanent way to deal with the problem."

Lady Revada gave a quiet sigh. "If speaking with the Poroo means he'll be out of our home sooner, then all the better."

"I know it's a difficult proposition," Eric said to Viola, "but even the slightest bits of information could be helpful."

His eyes softened as he said this. Like he was asking for her help but wouldn't make it an order.

Viola smiled and offered a slow nod. "Well then. I suppose I shall have to brush up on my Poroo."

What a wretched space this dungeon was. Several days spent reading up on the Poroo, and the pages of parchment she now carried, made Viola confident she could communicate with the prisoner. But nothing had readied her for the putrid smells creeping out of the stairwell that led to the subterranean jail cells.

"Do watch your step, my lady," the guard said, holding a torch high. "And be sure to stay to the right side of the hall. Our charming guest tried to take a bite outta me earlier." He unlocked the gate.

"I'll take it from here." Eric took the torch from the guard and led the way down the tunnel. Walter had suggested sending one of the Fighting Fifteen to escort Viola to speak with the prisoner, but Eric had insisted on being there himself despite his wounded leg.

Viola ran her thumb along the parchment in her hands. It was now or never, it seemed. She took a deep breath and followed Eric down the dark stairs.

Clingy dampness joined the horrid aroma as they continued downward. Eric progressed slowly down the narrow steps. Very slowly.

"Do you need a hand?" Viola asked.

"I'll be fine." Eric took another ginger step forward. "The steps are slick. That's all."

Did he have to be so goatheaded? "Storms, Eric, will it upset your pride to have your wife assist you down some stairs?"

"I'll not be a burden," Eric grumbled.

"And if you fall? Would you rather I try to drag you out or would you prefer I summon the Fighting Fifteen to render aid?"

Eric gave a long-suffering look to Viola. "Very well."

He reached around Viola's shoulders and leaned on her for balance. The pair proceeded down the remainder of the steps together.

They reached a long hallway which led to the jail cells. A row of torches lined the hall but provided only minimal light. Thick shadows swallowed the passageway, and it was like they were back in Darkness.

A furious cry came from the far end of the hall. The clanging of iron echoed off the damp walls. The prisoner had taken note of their arrival.

Anxiety welled up in Viola's throat, and she fought to swallow it.

Eric squeezed her shoulder. "It's all right," he said. "The cells may appear haphazard, but they're reinforced iron. Our guest can beat on them all he likes, and they'll still hold."

Breath came easier to Viola's lungs, comforted by Eric's presence.

Each of the cells contained a bench, but the prisoner had broken his apart and was rapping one of the broken legs against the bars of his cell.

As Eric and Viola approached, the pale warrior halted his screaming and backed away from the bars.

Eric stepped forward, putting himself between Viola and the prisoner. "Good morning," he said.

The Poroo bared his teeth at Eric. A splash of crimson war paint speckled the prisoner's brow. Along with stitches from a nasty head wound.

"*Tsot nu, malassi!*" the man growled.

Eric raised an eyebrow to Viola. "Did you catch any of that?"

Viola unfurled the notes she'd taken from the various journals on the Poroo. Some of the words rang familiar, but the tone was so much more guttural than she had imagined while reading the words.

"I need to hear him speak more." She spoke directly to the Poroo. "Talk…more. I need you to talk." She did her best to pantomime words coming out of her mouth.

The prisoner eyed Viola's movements. He seemed as vexed by her language as she and Eric were by his.

"*Pakova malassi. Himu um lavati? Tsot nu, taa!*"

Viola scratched her head. "He said something about unclean people. Perhaps that means us? And then something else having to do with speech. Perhaps he's saying he won't talk. Or that he wants us to talk?"

"Well, give it a try," Eric said. "Ask him why they attacked the city?"

Viola read from a list of questions she had translated beforehand. "*Hinoq Poroo tsuuwan ituum suuwa?*" The words felt ridiculous as she said them, but opening a dialogue with the Poroo was important. Even if she had to play the part of the fool to make it happen.

The man tilted his head, then sneered and muttered something again.

Viola read the sentence again, trying to emulate the guttural tones of the Poroo's speaking voice.

This time, he looked startled, and his mouth hung slack for a moment. "*Malassi lavati wutaga?*"

Again, unclean people and speaking, but now it sounded like he was asking a question. Perhaps she was getting through to him.

Viola again asked why the Poroo had attacked the city.

The prisoner growled and rattled off an angry reply. His words flowed too quickly, and Viola struggled to catch anything. The words *malassi*, which she felt certain meant "unclean." *Lavati* was the word for speak. And then *aaso*, which meant "truth" or "true."

"I believe he is saying that they came north following animal herds for hunting. That they don't want to fight *unclean people*. Or the dog men."

"We're the dogs?" Eric said. "Is that it?"

"Patience, please." Viola had managed to catch one other word: *makto*. She flipped through the pages of the journal. "*Makto* means 'attack'. I thought *tsuuwan* meant 'attack.'"

"Attack who?" Eric asked.

"It's strange," Viola said. "The words are aggressive, but his tone is not. He's speaking matter-of-factly, as if reporting. I just wish I knew what he was reporting."

Eric put a hand on her shoulder. "You're doing excellent work."

She turned to another page, puzzling over the details. Then something clicked into place.

"That's it," she said. "They have different words for different types of attacks. *Tsuuwan* means 'battle.' *Niina* means 'murder.' They use *maawi* for 'steal' or 'raid.' And *makto* means 'revenge.' Eric, I believe he's saying it wasn't a raiding attack but one of retribution."

Eric stroked his beard. "Retribution. For what though? They've always attacked first."

Viola strained to see her notes in the poor light. Curse this darkness. Clear communication was essential for a meeting like this, but there was no way she could master the intricacies of the Poroo language in so short a time. She needed to boil her thoughts down to the simplest terms possible.

Perhaps she could say *The men of Tsaftown did not attack*? But that left no room for further dialogue. She settled on some version of "Who attacked you?"

"*Tsa tuyi. Pokoo taaqa makto. Niina ituum waqatsi. Wekna ituum waqatsi. Itam maawi vataa,*" the prisoner said.

Viola translated again. "Something along the lines of, 'The dog men attacked. Killed them. And the Poroo took revenge.' But this time he also used the phrase *wekna kachi*. I don't know *wekna*, but *kachi* is a word for their spirit god." She flipped through the pages until she found a clue. "*Koh kachi* means to worship idols, or so King Trevn put it."

"They were killed for worshipping idols?" Eric guessed.

Viola tapped her finger against her lip. "Dog men" had come up multiple times. It had to mean something. Perhaps not dog but wolf? But wolf men didn't make any more sense than dog men.

"*Pokoo taaqa*," the Poroo said again. He rubbed two fingers across the filthy floor and smeared the dirt on his chest, drawing a right angle over his heart. "*Pokoo taaqa*."

The placement was intentional. Like a tattoo. Or…a badge. She looked at the symbol again. It was far from a perfect rendering, but it was close enough to convey the idea. The side profile of a dog.

Her stomach sank as understanding dawned in her mind.

"Viola?" Eric asked. "What did he say?"

She wanted to hold back. Tell Eric something else. Deal with this on her own. But that would never work. For better or for worse, Eric needed to know.

"The *dog men* are the Howlers," Viola whispered. "He's saying Sir Fenris's men attacked the Poroo first."

CHAPTER NINE
VIOLA

VIOLA'S MOTHER OFTEN SAID THE BEST way to keep a secret between three people was to bribe one and kill the other. She didn't know if that was a common phrase in Jaelport or if her mother had made it up. But it rang true.

So what would her mother say of keeping a secret between the four people gathered in Eric's study?

"I have no reason to believe the prisoner is lying," Eric said, sitting against the edge of his desk. "And even if the claims are merely exaggerated, they are worth investigating."

Viola sat to one side, watching the faces of Captain Demry and Walter as Eric relayed what they'd learned from the Poroo prisoner. Captain Demry's expression remained stoic throughout, while Walter stroked his beard as his gaze drifted toward the fireplace.

"What do you suggest we do next, my lord?" Captain Demry asked.

Eric paced to his chair and leaned on the tall back. He should be resting his leg, not roaming all over the study. The man truly could not sit still to save his own life.

"We need to know more about the encounters between the Poroo and the Howlers," he said.

"The Howlers seem quite proud of their battle trophies," Walter said, looking away from the hearth. "Perhaps it might be easy to get one of them talking."

"Especially if they're getting liquored up at the Black Boar," Captain Demry added.

It was true. The Howlers had established quite the reputation for drunken antics in the taverns of the Fisherman's Quarter.

Eric tapped his fingers on the back of the chair. "Could you send any of your men to the Black Boar? Have them buy the Howlers a couple rounds and see what they learn?"

Captain Demry grunted. "Let them drink on duty? They'd all volunteer for that."

Eric offered a bemused smile. "Pick your most sober-minded men. See what they can glean. But don't mention anything about the Howlers attacking first. Let's keep that to ourselves for now."

"As you wish, my lord," Captain Demry said.

"Also, we'll need to change the security password." Eric pushed off the chair and shuffled around the side of his desk and over to the sideboard. "I used the current one in front of the Howlers at the gate. We can't risk a breach of that kind if we're investigating Fenris's men."

Captain Demry nodded. "It will be updated immediately."

"What about the prisoner?" Walter asked. "Should he be questioned further?"

Eric turned, leaning against the sideboard, and looked to Viola. "Thoughts?"

Viola started. Was he asking her input on strategy? He'd asked for her thoughts on intellectual matters or in dealing with the household. This was completely new.

"I could learn more if there weren't such a language barrier," she said. "But as is, I don't think I'll learn more than we already have."

"Indeed." Eric stroked his bearded chin. "Perhaps it's better to use him as leverage with the Poroo."

"Use him as a bargaining chip?" Captain Demry asked.

Viola shook her head. "That won't get us much. The Poroo would only view that as a hostile act. But if we free him, it extends an olive branch. Gives us a chance for diplomacy."

Viola bit her lip, certain her suggestion wouldn't be well received. There had been too much blood shed for a pair of military men like Eric and Captain Demry to simply release a prisoner.

"I like it," Eric said, limping back to his desk. "Brilliant actually."

Viola's head spun. Was he really going along with it? She glanced at Captain Demry. The commander of the Fighting Fifteen furrowed his heavy brow.

"Sound thinking, my lady," he said.

"Indeed," Walter said. "The prisoner may be of more use to us out there with the Poroo than wasting away in our dungeon."

"Excellent." Eric sat on the edge of his desk. "As soon as I can ride, I'll return the prisoner myself. Captain Demry, please put together a group of riders. I'll want a dozen men to accompany me. And..." He trailed off, his gaze on Viola. "I'll need someone who can translate. Viola, you did exemplary work, but I don't want you in the middle of things if the Poroo decide to pick a fight."

"That's fine." Viola was humble enough to know she would be no good in a fight. Besides, the Poroo language had not come easily to her. Let someone else snort and grunt their way through a conversation.

"I'll assemble the men straight away, my lord," Captain Demry said.

"Thank you," Eric said. "You're dismissed."

Captain Demry departed. Eric sighed and leaned on the back of his chair again. He was wearing himself out and needed to rest.

Viola began to say something, but Walter held up a hand to her.

"Awfully kind of you to include me in your circle of trust, my lord," he said.

Eric eyed the man. "I can always use the insight of an old musk-rat."

The valet chuckled softly. What an odd relationship the two of them had formed.

"If you're so trusting of me, may I suggest you make use of the fireplace?" Walter gestured to the fireplace, where the citadel board sat with a game in progress. "You could rest your leg. And perhaps we could finish our game from the other day."

Eric's eyes narrowed at the hearth. "I believe you made the last move?"

"Indeed, my lord. Swept your paladin off the board rather succinctly, if I do say so myself."

"Yes, well, I'll have to make you pay for that." Eric walked gingerly over to the fireplace.

Viola smiled at the subtle strategy in Walter's suggestion. Eric would have refused to rest if he were simply told to do so, but Walter had cleverly enticed him into sitting for a bit.

Viola got up and helped Eric into his armchair. He groaned softly as he set his wounded leg up on an ottoman. As Eric settled in, Viola glanced at the citadel board. The board and pieces were both beautifully crafted, similar to the set her father and brothers had used. But what caught her eye was the game playing out between Eric and Walter. The match was still up for grabs, but she couldn't help noticing a glaring error in strategy on one side of the contest.

Viola stared at the board for a long moment, then cleared her throat. "Walter, before you sit down, would you mind fetching us a bit of food and something to drink?"

"Excellent idea, my lady." Walter departed, leaving Eric and Viola alone.

Viola quickly sat down across from Eric. "Do you want to

beat him?" Her voice had come out hushed—more so than she'd meant—and created an air of conspiracy between them.

Eric quirked an eyebrow. "Walter?"

"Yes," Viola said.

His gaze settled on the board again and he shrugged. "It's not hopeless yet, but the old man does have the upper hand. What do you suggest?"

"You're spread too thin." Viola tapped one of Walter's black pieces. A sword-shaped piece at the edge of the board. "Walter's using his barbarian to pull your pieces to the edge of the board and away from the citadel."

Eric steepled his fingers, tracking her movements with his eyes. "The barbarian is the strongest piece in the game. I need to deal with it."

"Strongest, yes. But not the most important. While the barbarian wreaks havoc on the fringes, Walter is moving his rogue and villager into the center of the board." She tapped these two pieces, shaped like a dagger and a pitchfork respectively. "Where they can be the first pieces of his citadel. Father used a similar strategy against my brother when they played."

Eric's eyes slowly moved back to the board. "Which brother? Eagan or Rigil?"

"Rigil," Viola said. "Losing to Father or Eagan always drove him mad. Took him years and a few broken citadel boards, but he finally mastered the game."

"So how would Rigil get out of a jam like this?" Eric asked.

Viola peered over the board, tapping her lips. "Leave your slowest pieces behind to keep the barbarian in check. Move your rogue and scout toward the center."

"Center of what?" Walter had entered silently, carrying a bottle of wine, two goblets, and a tray of bread and dried meat.

Viola adopted an innocent expression and offered the chair to Walter. "Merely keeping your seat warm."

"Indeed." Walter eyed both Eric and Viola, barely covering a smirk. He poured Eric and Viola some wine, and the game resumed.

Eric moved his rogue in a counterclockwise direction around the board, eventually capturing one of Walter's villagers. The attack didn't gain him much, but it forced Walter to move his paladin laterally to help guard the citadel. But two moves later, Eric swept into the gap left by Walter's paladin, decimating Walter's efforts to hold the citadel. All the while, Walter's barbarian had been trapped on the edge of the board and effectively neutralized.

Walter held out a valiant defense, but soon enough, Eric formed his own citadel in the center of the board and won the match.

"By the Three," Walter mumbled. "Very impressive, my lord. I don't think I'll let the two of you team up on me again. You work far too well together."

Eric raised his goblet and gave Viola a wink. "To working together."

Strange. Eric's demeanor had changed so much since he'd returned. He was kinder. Gentler. Even playful. And despite the echoes of her mother's voice warning against such warm feelings for one's spouse, this version of Eric wasn't unpleasant to be around.

Viola raised her own goblet. "To working together."

ERIC

Returning to Craven's Hook had felt like a risk at first. Eric and his men knew firsthand how easy it was for the Poroo to set an ambush up in the mountains, which was why he'd brought the entirety of the Fighting Fifteen with him this time.

Yet they had been waiting in the road for hours with no sign of the enemy. Derby and Gunnar occasionally tapped out a tribal war cadence on large drums in an effort to draw out the Poroo, but none appeared. Now the sun had dropped below the canyon walls, and snow flurries fluttered past on a cold wind.

If there had been another way to find the Poroo, Eric would have done so, but there was no way of knowing where they made their camp. They seemed to always have eyes on the King's Road leading south out of Tsaftown. The wrecked wagon had been picked clean of anything useful, so the Poroo had clearly been there again since the fight. So, Eric and his men waited.

The Fifteen kept their horses in a standard diamond-shaped formation with the prisoner sitting on a mule in the middle. Even as the hours passed and the frigid wind buffeted them, there was a minimal amount of grumbling.

Except for Jeffrey the bard, who Captain Demry had enlisted to serve as translator.

"Not especially punctual, these Poroo," Jeffrey said, vigorously rubbing his hands together. "Perhaps they're waiting for us all to freeze to death, then they can loot our bodies."

Eric chuckled. The bard must have gotten his fill of military action during the long march from Armonguard.

Eric peered past his riders at the prisoner. The Poroo man currently stared up into the trees, perhaps also wondering where his brethren were. His disposition had settled after the conversation in the dungeon, and he was no longer shouting or tugging at his bonds. Trust wasn't quite the right word, but at least Eric had confidence that the man wouldn't try to bite him if he got too close.

Eric stretched his bandaged leg. He knew it would be uncomfortable riding out with his wound, but the cold made his stitches itch more and more with every passing moment. At least he was back on Guffey, his own horse. Leaping up on Thunder with his wounded leg would have been quite the task. Though he had to admit, he had thoroughly enjoyed having such a powerful animal at his beck and call.

"Derby, give the drums another try," Eric said.

Derby nodded obediently. He and Gunnar gripped their wooden mallets and pounded on the tabor drums they'd hung on each of their saddles. The drumbeats echoed off the rock faces and through the trees. It wasn't a perfect imitation of the Poroo war drums, but it would have to do.

The prisoner grunted. "*Pakova komotawa. Hinoq um wala vosi?*"

Eric didn't understand the words, but the man's dismissive tone was plain to hear.

Jeffrey snickered. "I couldn't agree more, my friend. Those boys are doing it all wrong. Beating on those drumheads like a squirrel trying to crack open a nut."

Derby groaned. "Why does it matter how I hit a drum?"

"Why does it—" Jeffrey threw his arms up. "Certainly even a group of grunts like yourselves can appreciate the importance of playing an instrument well?"

"I dunno. We is but humble soldiers," Gedmund said, gleefully playing the part of the buffoon. "Can yeh show us yer mystical ways, oh great master?"

This was met with a chorus of laughter from the men.

Jeffrey grinned. "I thought you'd never ask." The bard slid off his horse and took Derby's mallet. "You're not swinging a hammer, Master Wenk," he said. "Hold it loosely in your thumb and forefinger, like so. You see?" He switched from a tightly fisted grip to using only two of his fingers.

"I see." Skepticism hung in Derby's tone, but the squire was too reserved to truly speak his mind.

Jeffrey twirled the mallet in his fingers, demonstrating remarkable dexterity considering the cold. "Now, don't pound with all your might. One is liable to break the drumhead if you do that." He ran the mallet over the drum in a circular pattern. "With a gentle flick of the wrist..." He gave a solitary tap of the mallet against the drumhead. Then another. Then a series of taps.

And suddenly, Jeffrey launched into a staccato rhythm, slapping his thigh to keep time. The sounds reverberated off the trees and up the bluffs, not with the same volume as Derby's and Gedmund's earlier strikes, but with something that sounded a bit more like music.

Jeffrey beat the drum faster and faster until he finished with a flourish. Some of the men applauded. Jeffrey offered the mallet back to Derby and turned to the ring of horsemen. "And that, gentlemen, is how it's—"

Bu-doom! Bu-doom!

"—done." Jeffrey's eyes bulged.

"*Ituum tuutskim ween*," the Poroo prisoner muttered.

Eric surveyed the woods, searching for the sources of the new drumbeats.

Bu-doom! Bu-doom!

He looked up along the ridge and finally saw them—three positioned on the eastern side of the bluff.

A pair of the Poroo each carried at their hip a wide-headed drum made of carved wood and hide.

"In the trees, my lord," Derby said.

The lad was right. More warriors stepped out of the woods on the west side of the trail.

"Hold!" Eric called. "Shields at the ready, but do not break formation."

Bu-doom! Bu-doom!

More Poroo appeared every moment. Sixteen of them? No. More than twenty now. But not the one he was looking for. Where was that old wizard?

Then Eric saw him. The hunched figure, carrying a staff adorned with claws. Not just any claws, Eric realized. Cham bear claws. Dozens of them.

Silence hung in the canyon for a long moment as the two parties sized each other up.

Eric urged Guffey forward and took center stage in the impromptu amphitheater that had been formed in the bluffs of Craven's Hook.

"Jeffrey, I believe it's time to earn your keep," Eric said.

"Wonderful." The bard moved forward to stand on the ground alongside Guffey.

The Poroo made no effort to hide their hostility. Each carried a spear or a blade of some kind. But they made no move to attack. Not yet.

"We are here to return a prisoner," Eric said. "And to seek a peaceful end to these violent skirmishes between our people." Eric kept his voice even but firm. If they couldn't understand his words, hopefully they'd understand his tone.

He nodded to Jeffrey, signaling the bard to offer a translation.

"Here goes nothing," Jeffrey muttered. He drew his shoulders back. "*Itam ween tsot nupkwa. Itam paqu suanta nat uuta Poroo nat komotawa makto.*"

Curious expressions fixed onto the Poroos' faces. The elder wrinkled his nose before opening his mouth wide and barking out a harsh guttural noise. The other Poroo joined in, echoing the noise.

Cinders. The Poroo were...laughing?

The elder slammed the butt end of his claw staff against the ground, partly silencing the mocking chorus of laughter. He then made a guttural exclamation, shaking his clawed staff as he spoke.

Eric recognized bits of the Poroo language from listening to Viola and the prisoner's conversation but could make no sense of it. He looked to Jeffrey. "Anything?"

Jeffrey gave Eric a long-suffering look. "Still piecing it together, my lord."

The elder spoke again. "*Aqni, malassi siskamaawi. Hinoq uma maawi ituum tawa? Tavia ituum tiyo nat aqni! Itam Poroo!*"

"*Itam Poroo!*" The surrounding warriors repeated the elder's words and banged their weapons on the ground for emphasis.

Eric's gut tightened as he awaited Jeffrey's translation.

Jeffrey cleared his throat. "I believe he said: Go away, dirty skin thieves. Why do you take...uh, dirt? Drop our child. We're the Poroo...Yes?"

Eric narrowed his gaze at Jeffrey. "Skin thieves?"

Jeffrey shrugged. "I'm not deciphering an Eben love song. It's a loose interpretation."

"I just don't recall my wife saying anything about dirt or skin," Eric said.

"Well, thankfully for both of us, I'm not your wife."

Eric turned his focus back to the Poroo. "We're here to return this prisoner to you. But the attacks on our city must cease."

Jeffrey swiftly offered his own translation.

The elder slammed his staff against the ground again. "*Naaka! Siskamaawi weeta kwa. Pokoo taaqa kyaami. Pukiw naaka.*"

The surrounding Poroo joined in, beating their weapons against the trees and rocks.

"He doesn't believe you," Jeffrey said. "He called you a liar and a dirty skin thief. And a *wolf man,* whatever that is."

Interesting. *Wolf man* could be a further reference to Fenris or the Howlers. Grim images of the Poroo scalps and braids hanging on the belts of several Howlers haunted Eric's mind. Who could blame the elder for not trusting anyone from Tsaftown?

"He doesn't seem interested in talking, my lord," Jeffrey said in a hushed tone. "I'm no diplomat, but I can tell a harsh crowd when I see one."

Eric could only agree with the bard. "Perhaps we need something stronger than words," he said. "Derby, go untie our prisoner."

Derby dismounted and quickly removed the sailor's knot that had been tied around the Poroo's wrists. The man hopped down from the mule, and Derby escorted him to the front of the formation.

Suspicion lingered in the prisoner's eyes as he moved out of the circle of horsemen and stepped out into the open. He offered Eric a meaningful look and thumped his fist against his chest. "*Kwaa uma wukoki.*"

As ever, the words were lost on Eric, but he got the impression that the warrior had paid him some special respect.

Eric tapped his chest with his fist and offered his own words of respect. "This is the North."

The Poroo cackled, then crossed the space between the two groups, rejoining the other Poroo.

The gathered warriors welcomed their tribesman, tapping him on the shoulder with their fists.

Eric straightened in his saddle. "Jeffrey, ask him if he trusts me now."

"Uh...*Um weeta nu taa?*" Jeffrey said.

The elder held his scowl, although it had softened. Freeing the prisoner had certainly gotten his attention, but something in his manner still appeared unsatisfied. He spoke again, with less bombast but still serious. "*Pokoo taaqa wekna weye. Maawi kachi. Niina ituum hura nat kotsu. Itam maawi vataa.*"

"Oh, mercy," Jeffrey muttered. "He claims the Howlers desecrated sacred ground and stole holy relics. And..." Jeffrey's shoulders sank. "And killed women and children in the process."

Eric clenched his teeth, furious that Fenris could have done something so vile. If what the elder said was true, then amends could not be made with a simple prisoner exchange. He remembered the mutilated Howlers, first at Glodwood Manor and later at the southern gatehouse. The macabre memories shed a new, haunting light on the Poroo attacks.

Eric waited a long moment. What could he say that would mean anything to these people? Maybe there weren't any words that could make matters right. Still, he needed to say something.

He set his fist over his chest, imitating the gesture the prisoner had made to him. "I can't return the lives taken, but I will right these wrongs against your people. Your relics will be returned to you. And the Howlers' spoils will be buried appropriately. I swear by my God Câan it will be done." Eric lifted his fist for emphasis. Content with his declaration, he glanced over to Jeffrey. "I know that's a lot to convey. Do your best."

"I will give it the proper weight, my lord." Jeffrey again spoke to the Poroo.

The elder stared and ran a finger across a massive cham claw as he listened to Jeffrey. Then he answered with a quiet menace in his voice. "*Pilavayi uum ungawa, siskamaawi! Makto haa Pokoo taaqa niina.*"

Eric had heard the Poroo speak enough that he understood bits and pieces of the elder's statement. Some key words stood out in his mind. "Skin thief." "Dog men." "And attack?"

The elder slammed his staff against the ground three times. Immediately all of the Poroo withdrew. Many vanished into the woods, and others scaled the bluff's face and disappeared over the ridge. Within moments, they were all gone.

Eric exhaled slowly. "I got the idea of what he said. We need to stop the Howlers?"

"Nearly." Jeffrey licked his lips. "He said that there will be no peace until all the Howlers...are dead."

CHAPTER TEN
VIOLA

IOLA RUBBED HER PALMS AGAINST her stomach as she and Eric approached the closed doors of the meeting chamber. The ruling council of Tsaftown had gathered behind those doors while Masters Dunn and Ambrose stood watch on the outside.

"You're certain you want me here for this?" Viola asked.

"Indeed, yes," Eric said. "The same as the last time you asked."

This was the first opportunity for Eric to preside over a meeting of the ruling council. A chance for him to make a strong impression. And Viola too, apparently.

Eric laid his hand on her shoulder. "Your insight on the Poroo culture and their language is sharper than mine. Not to mention your general skill with diplomacy."

Viola searched his eyes for some ulterior motive but saw none. It was true that she had privately wished to sit in on this council meeting and bolster Eric's position in any debate. Even if it meant that she had to run the gauntlet of stubborn old men.

"Shall we, then?" Viola asked.

Eric nodded and strode toward the guards. "Dunn, there's a

guest waiting in the front courtyard. I need you to fetch him and have him wait here until he is summoned."

"Aye, my lord." Master Dunn thumped his fist against his chest and departed.

Eric then gestured to Master Ambrose, who opened the door. Viola entered the meeting chamber with Eric, and they rounded the long table surrounded by council members. She felt their eyes on her as she took a seat at Eric's right hand. She had dealt with far more impressive individuals than the eight members of Tsaftown's ruling council, but now apprehension fluttered in her chest. Each man on the council was an esteemed member of the community. Joonas Erlichman was there, or course. Then there was Dorn Godfries, priest of Arman; Elder Rathskellar of the Temple of Thalassa; Valdemar Okerlund, who owned a fleet of fishing vessels; Renshaw Thusk of the Thusk Shipping Exchange; Haldor Deppner, a retired fishing boat captain; Knut Nemeth, who led a smithing guild; and Harland Steadroot, a retired captain of the City Watch.

Outside of House Livna, these were the most powerful individuals in Tsaftown. For better or for worse, Viola and Eric needed the cooperation of these men if they were going to run the city.

The only remotely friendly face on the council was Joonas Erlichman, but even he had his own interests to look out for. It was up to her and Eric to sell the council on their solution to the Poroo problem.

"Good afternoon, Councilors," Eric said. "Let us begin. As most of you no doubt know, last week my men and I successfully ambushed the Poroo who attacked the city."

"A word, my lord," Elder Rathskellar said. "Before we get started, perhaps Lady Viola might excuse herself?"

Some of the councilors murmured at Rathskellar's interruption.

"She is here at my request," Eric said sternly.

The priest sputtered in response. "But there's no protocol in the Northlander Charter for a lady in these proceedings. Noble or otherwise."

Councilor Erlichman stroked his pointed beard. "That's a long-held custom, but the charter itself says nothing for or against women in attendance. Would you ban Duchess Amal from the premises if she chose to grace us with her presence?"

Tense silence hung over the room as Eric glowered at Rathskellar. "My wife is here at my request," he said. "Do I need to tell you a third time?"

Rathskellar turned his gaze to the center of the table. "Of course not, my lord. Lady Viola is welcome to stay."

Viola disguised her smile, trying not to appear too pleased at watching Eric put the crude man back in his place.

"There has been a development in the Poroo situation," Eric said. "I've held negotiations of a sort with the elder of the local tribe."

The councilors exchanged looks and murmured among each other.

"Negotiations?" Councilman Erlichman asked. "The Poroo are uncivilized. They barely have a language of their own. You think they're capable of abiding by a treaty?"

"They're not brainless creatures," Eric replied. "They are men like us and capable of being reasoned with."

"They may be men, but they're certainly not men like us," Elder Rathskellar said.

This provoked laughter from some of the council members.

Viola straightened. "Simply because they don't speak Kinsman does not make them sub-human. Our people have learned their language and worked with them going back to the first kings of Er'Rets. And if these Poroo are settling here, then we must learn how to get along with them."

Rathskellar groaned in response, refusing to make eye contact with Viola.

"Why do we even need to bother with them?" Councilor Okerlund asked. "If the Poroo are nomads, won't they simply pass through?"

"We could certainly send out the Howlers to give them some encouragement to move on quickly," Councilor Thusk added.

"It's not that simple," Viola said. "They're following herds. Many local hunters have reported changes in the animals' travel patterns since Darkness ended. If this area is becoming a bountiful hunting ground, then the Poroo may be sticking around for a long while."

She had expected some kind of interruption, but none came but a few sour expressions. Eric's stern warning to Elder Rathskellar must have convinced the rest to hold their tongues.

"If the Poroo were content to hunt in the forest, then I say we let them," Councilor Erlichman said. "But they've attacked the caravans and farms. And now the city? What do they want from us?"

Eric leaned back in his chair and glanced to Viola, his expression silently asking a question. Was it time to bring him in?

Viola nodded slowly.

"For that, I will need to invite another person to these discussions." Eric's gaze turned to the far end of the room. "Master Ambrose, please send in Fenris Yarden."

Viola's stomach shifted as Master Ambrose opened the door and ushered in Sir Fenris. This would be the first time he and Eric would be in the same room since the banquet. With luck, Eric would be able to control his temper. And hopefully Sir Fenris wouldn't stir up any new trouble.

Sir Fenris swaggered forward, followed closely by the hulking form of Ikârd, and leaned against one of the chairbacks. He offered a wry smile and bowed his head forward slightly.

"Councilors. Lord Livna," he said. "You honor me with this invitation."

Eric's expression hardened. As much planning as had gone into this moment, it all hinged on Eric's ability to contain his contempt for Fenris.

"I'll not waste your time nor ours," Eric said. "You led your men in numerous skirmishes against the Poroo over the last several months, correct?"

Sir Fenris narrowed his gaze at Eric. The strength of Eric's words seemed to have drained some of the bombast out of him. "Yes, *my lord*. That's accurate," he said.

"And is it also true that not only did you and your men desecrate the bodies of dead Poroo, but you also stole their relics and idols as war trophies?"

Sir Fenris let out an uneasy guffaw. The mention of the idols seemed to have taken him off guard. The council members murmured amongst each other as each man reacted to the allegations.

"It was a battle." Sir Fenris shrugged. "We won and we took spoils. Such is common enough in war time."

"We are not at war with the Poroo," Eric said. "They say you attacked first, and the Howlers went out of their way to commit atrocities. Atrocities that enraged the Poroo and led them to seek retribution against the people of this city."

Sir Fenris glared at Eric. "And you take the word of a Poroo at face value?"

"You claim these events never took place?" Eric asked. "Even as your lieutenant wears Poroo scalps on his person?"

Sir Fenris whirled, locking his gaze on Ikârd, who stood against the wall. Indeed, a dozen locks of different lengths of hair hung from the man's shoulder. Sir Fenris sneered at his lieutenant. Ikârd merely shrugged his broad shoulders, clearly indifferent to the grim nature of his trophies.

"Fine," Sir Fenris growled. "I'll concede that my men were overzealous in their duties. It won't happen again."

"I'm afraid it's not as simple as that," Eric said. "Your actions have put the people of Tsaftown in peril, and for that, restitution must be made."

Again, the councilors murmured amongst themselves.

Sir Fenris merely glared at Eric. "Such as?" he asked.

"First, you and your men will remove your disgusting trophies and bury them. You will surrender the stolen relics so they can be rightfully returned to the Poroo. Additionally—"

"Return their worthless trinkets?" Sir Fenris scoffed. "For what? Are you trying to appease the Poroo or simply humiliate me and my men?"

Erlichman raised his hand. "Mind your tone, Sir Fenris. Lord Livna was not finished."

Acid burned in Sir Fenris's eyes at Erlichman's interjection, but he held his tongue.

"Thank you, Councilor Erlichman," Eric said. "Additionally, you will put an end to your attacks on the Poroo. Your contract to protect the city remains in place for now, but your men will only keep the peace within the walls of Tsaftown itself. Any Howler who goes against this will be arrested and thrown into my dungeon for judgment."

"Judgment? For protecting this city?" Sir Fenris said.

"The Poroo want your head for what you've done," Eric said. "I think you'll find my decision gentle by comparison."

Sir Fenris gripped the chairback in front of him. "Big words, Little Eric, but can you back them up?"

Silence hung in the room for a moment. This was the crux of the matter. Sir Fenris was trying to get under Eric's skin.

Eric leaned forward and folded his hands. "Test me, and you will see how far my authority extends." His voice was a quiet rumble, filling the silence of the room.

Sir Fenris sneered at Viola. "Have you anything to add to this, fair Lady Viola?"

His gaze still simmered, despite the warnings from Councilor

Erlichman to remain civil. Why had the louse called her out specifically? Was he working an angle? Or simply trying to get a rise out of Eric?

Viola drew her shoulders back and offered a kind smile. "Being arrested would likely harm your standing within Tsaftown. It would be wise to do as my husband says."

Sir Fenris gritted his teeth and pressed his eyes closed tightly. "Very well. I will do as you say, my lord."

Nevandra's laughter was exactly what Viola needed. The council meeting had been informative, but it had dragged on for several hours. The endless droning of the councilors' voices had left her with a headache.

Even the cold and smell of the stables were a welcome reprieve. Especially seeing Nevandra's excitement as Eric led the towering white festrier into the stables.

"I hope Councilor Erlichman gave you a fair price?" Viola shuddered to think how much a rare creature like a festrier might cost.

"I haggled him down a bit," Eric said.

"A bit?"

"Enough. A war horse like this is worth every last copper penny."

Viola smiled to cover her skepticism. She knew Eric would put the horse to good use, but she also knew how much of a smooth talker Councilor Erlichman could be when he had something to sell.

Eric walked Thunder down the center aisle and into one of the stalls. Guffey stood in the next one, contently munching on fresh hay, unaware of his recent demotion.

Nevandra tiptoed behind Eric, staring up at the festrier. "Is Dunder hungry?"

Eric patted Thunder's muzzle. "I believe he is."

He knelt beside a bag of oats and opened it for Nevandra. The girl grabbed a fistful and tossed them on the straw-covered ground. Thunder nickered, then lowered his head and gobbled up the feed. Nevandra cackled, watching Thunder sift through the straw, hunting for more.

This new bond between father and daughter was beautiful to behold, but how long would it last? If they had a son one day, would Eric lose interest in Nevandra and ignore her as so many noblemen did their daughters?

Regardless of how long it lasted, this new connection was a good thing. And furthermore, it genuinely warmed Viola's heart.

Nevandra was desperate for a ride with Eric, but neither Viola nor Eric had been able to take a proper meal all day. The three of them retired to the great hall, and Arne brought them a scrumptious spread of roast chicken, juicy apples and grapes, and warm bread.

Viola attempted to present herself properly during the meal, but the chicken made this task difficult. Eventually the savory aromas of roasted meat won out, and Viola took a generous slice from the tray. Juices dribbled down her chin as she took her first bite, but she paid it no mind and savored the cozy atmosphere of a lovely dinner.

Nevandra finished eating and was sent off with Sabrea to prepare for bed. Viola had been eager to return to her chambers, but the warmth of the fire kept her in place in her chair.

Eric joined Viola on her side of the table next to the hearth. "I really ought to find a way to thank you," he said.

What was the meaning of that? Eric's typically stern face had relaxed into a picture of contentment as he settled into his chair.

"Whatever do you mean, husband?"

"Today with the council. Your insight with the Poroo ways. I couldn't have done it without you."

Viola mulled over Eric's words as she fetched a small cluster of grapes from the table and picked them off their stems one by one.

"Matters with the Poroo aren't resolved yet. And the ruling council will always find some way to be a thorn in your side."

"Even so," Eric replied, "your work has been exemplary of late. It is to be commended."

Viola snickered softly, then popped another grape into her mouth. "Is that supposed to be a compliment?"

Eric scrunched up his face. "What in the depths do you mean?"

Viola steepled her fingers, contemplating her answer. She knew she had his attention and wanted to toy with him for a moment. "*Your work has been exemplary.* Kind words, but that's what you say to your soldiers." Viola leaned forward. "Hardly how a husband ought to thank his wife."

Eric chuckled again and smiled at her. "Fair enough. What should a husband say then?"

That smile. Where had that been all these years? There was a ruddy charm buried under her husband's rugged exterior. She inhaled Eric's natural smell mixed with the smoke of the fire.

Without thinking, Viola leaned forward and laid her hand on Eric's. "Well, husband, why don't you tell me?"

Eric's breath hitched. Then he leaned forward and kissed her.

His beard was soft. Not coarse against her face, but gentle enough to barely be noticed.

She hadn't expected this. Apparently, Eric had taken her words as an invitation. Or even a challenge. Should she withdraw? Her fingertips tingled as she interweaved her fingers with Eric's. Viola's hesitation quieted, and she wrapped her hand around the back of his neck, pulling herself closer. She rose up off her chair and sat on his lap, deepening the kiss. She ran her fingers through his hair and caressed his right ear, brushing past the scar. Eric flinched and pulled her hand away.

"Oh, Eric, I'm sorry," Viola said. Had she done something wrong?

He shook his head and smiled. "No worries, dear." He pulled

her close again and placed several slow kisses down her neck. His breath warmed her skin, and she ran her fingers through the soft curly hair at the nape of his neck.

The protective walls around her heart began to crumble. For once in her life, she wasn't a noblewoman. She was free to be a wife savoring the embrace of her husband.

Cernell Crow.

Tiny needles pricked her temples. Motherless wretch. Now?

Viola pulled away from the kiss.

Eric inclined his head. "Are you all right?"

She fought to catch her breath. Her head pounded, tossed to and fro by the waves of emotions and excitement.

Cernell Crow.

The dull pain his knock caused spread in waves that left her blinking. What accursed timing.

Eric reached out and grabbed her hand. "Viola, what's wrong?"

She stood, pulled free of his grip, and rubbed her temple. "I'm sorry. I—lost my head for a moment."

Eric tilted his head. "It's fine." He rose as well and put his hand on her waist. "If you need a moment, I understand."

Viola's stomach sank. She couldn't give him what he desired. Not until she could resolve matters with Crow. "I'm so sorry, Eric. I cannot continue."

Eric furrowed his brow. "Oh?"

"It's very silly." She pressed her hand to her head. "My month-blood has started just today, and I simply cannot go forward."

The lie tasted like poison on her tongue.

A frown deepened on Eric's face. Could she blame him? They had been drawing closer together. Stopping now, even with her excuse, felt like a refusal of him. Strangely, Viola had found herself wanting things to move forward. For Eric's sake and for her own.

"Of course," he finally said. "If I had known, I wouldn't have... We can simply enjoy the fire together."

The disappointment was plain on Eric's face. She loathed dismissing him this way, but it was necessary if Crow was going to continue reaching into her mind.

Eric moved her chair back in place, offering her a place to sit.

"Thank you," Viola said, taking her seat and setting her facade of calm firmly in place.

Eric straightened his tunic and stepped away to tend the fire. His expression was still pinched, but she could see he cared. Beneath the exterior of the rugged warrior lord, he was capable of such gentleness. He did not deserve the lies she was forced to tell him.

Cernell Crow.

The knock came more forcefully this time, and Viola barely masked a gasp at the band squeezing around her head.

Is there something you require, Master Crow? she thought.

Sir Fenris wishes to speak with you, Crow voiced.

How did his voice sound hoarse and gravely even while speaking only with his mind?

Viola fought to keep her thoughts as diplomatic as possible. There was no point in angering the man. *Inform your master that I cannot be summoned at his whims like some sort of butler.*

Nevertheless, Crow voiced, *he asks for your presence. He requires your approval on the document you requested.*

The amendment was ready? For anything else, she would make Sir Fenris wait, but it had taken him a very long time to hold up his end of their bargain. This couldn't be put off.

When and where? Viola asked.

Tonight. Behind the Black Boar Inn. At midnight, Master Crow voiced.

Eric rejoined Viola at the table. She poured them both some more wine, attempting to appear casual while doing so.

He took hold of her hand and rubbed his thumb over the back of her knuckles. "Is the fire warm enough for you?" he asked.

"Of course. Thank you," Viola said. Then, in the same breath, she thought to Crow. *I'll be there.*

Her prayer life had never been what one would consider robust, but in that moment, she found herself praying that Eric would one day understand what she had to do tonight.

CHAPTER ELEVEN
VIOLA

MIDNIGHT. TEMPEST'S MERCY! WHY did Sir Fenris want to meet at midnight?

Fierce winds blew in off the great harbor, knifing through Viola's cloak. Growing up on a different section of the northern coast, she'd thought the chilled wind and briny smells of Zerah Rock had been bad, but no matter how long she'd lived in Tsaftown, she could never fully adjust to the merciless cold of a northern night, the briny smell of the sea mixed with the sharp, oily tang of freshly caught fish being sold at the market. And, of course, the aroma of the fishermen themselves only added to the stomach-churning array of odors permeating the streets.

She approached the Black Boar Inn, a tavern in the heart of the Fisherman's Quarter. Coarse laughter and bawdy music echoed out into the streets. She stepped into the alleyway behind the tavern, and her foot found an unseen puddle and sank down to her ankle in freezing, slushy water. What rotten luck. She shook her foot and continued farther into the shadows of the alley.

Oh, if Viola's mother could see her now, what would she think? She steeled her mind. Lady Zora of Zerah Rock would understand. Viola was doing what was necessary to protect her family. To ensure the best possible future for her daughter.

She rounded the back of the building and beat her fist on a locked door tucked discreetly into an alcove. It swung open, revealing Crow, mouth scowling beneath the black cloth that covered his eyes.

"Master Crow," Viola said.

He sneered, shifted his weight to his walking stick, and ushered her inside. "Quickly, your ladyship," he said. "My feet are freezin'."

She stepped out of the cold and into the confines of a long narrow room faintly lit by a pair of lanterns along the long interior wall and a beaten-up chandelier, lit candles dripping wax on the floor. The space was sparsely furnished save for a trio of armchairs arranged in a triangle at the far end and a small table upon which sat several open bottles of alcohol. The rambunctious sounds of carousing from the inn carried through the wall. This room must share a wall with the main floor of the tavern.

Movement in back. Sure enough, in the far corner of the room, occupying two of the chairs, Sir Fenris and another figure sat obscured by shadow. She followed Crow toward them.

Dim lantern light flickered in Sir Fenris's eyes as he watched Viola approach. "My lady, come sit with us. There's much to discuss."

The other figure turned toward her.

Viola masked her surprise. "Councilor Erlichman," she said. She recalled that his family owned the Black Boar tavern, but what was he doing *here* with Sir Fenris? All her efforts to keep her meeting secret, and she came face-to-face with a member of the ruling council.

The councilor tugged at his conical beard. "My lady."

"Sir Fenris, I understood this was to be a private meeting," Viola said. "Not that your presence is unwanted, Councilor. Simply unexpected."

"My lady, the good councilor assisted me in this undertaking." Fenris patted the chair next to him. "Come sit."

She removed her hood and made her way toward the chair. How had Sir Fenris and Councilor Erlichman come to work together? They made such an odd pairing. Sir Fenris the mercenary and Councilor Erlichman the businessman-turned-politician.

Viola sat across from the two seated men in the remaining, well-worn armchair.

"Did you come alone as agreed?" Sir Fenris asked.

Viola tilted her head. "My husband is the lord of this city. Do you think I want anyone to know that I've ventured here in the middle of the night?"

Sir Fenris shook his head. "Alas, this is the Fisherman's Quarter. Trust is in short supply."

Viola sat straighter in her chair, trying to disguise her annoyance. Had Sir Fenris really dragged her out of her home simply to play some twisted game? "And what would gain your trust?" she asked.

Sir Fenris scratched his chin as Crow ambled up and took up a position by his employer.

"Master Crow could take a look inside that pretty head of yours." Sir Fenris said. "Make sure all is as you say it is?"

Being called pretty by Sir Fenris made Viola's stomach churn, but not as much as the thought of Crow peering into her thoughts. Could the man even do such a thing? It wasn't likely that he had hidden such a powerful ability, but that didn't mean it was impossible. Perhaps Sir Fenris's whole reason for suggesting Crow's bloodvoicing was to unsettle her.

"I've been paying you for months," Viola said. "Not only to serve as an intermediary, but to keep these matters discreet. Why would I spend that money only to see it wasted now by my own carelessness?"

Sir Fenris leaned forward, grabbed one of the bottles from the small table, and took a quick swig. He wiped a small dribble from his chin. "I suppose Crow's services won't be needed. After all, ours is a relationship built upon trust and mutual benefit. Isn't it?"

Viola chose not to reply—had no interest in prolonging this visit.

Sir Fenris pressed the neck of the bottle into Crow's hand. "Dismissed."

The blind man ambled away, bottle tucked under one arm, the other feeling his way with his walking stick. He reached a concealed door, opened it, and golden light spilled through along with the amplified sounds of the tavern. Crow passed into the tavern and shut the door behind him.

"Where do you find such charming employees?" Viola asked.

Sir Fenris snickered. "Crow is a salty old soul, isn't he? We helped each other on the way out of Ice Island. Figured I'd keep him around."

"Are all of your men escaped prisoners?" Viola asked.

Fenris brushed a wild strand of hair from his eyes. "You say that with such disdain. Do former convicts not deserve a second chance at life?"

"I don't mind men receiving second chances. As long as they do something with them," Viola said, refusing to rise to Fenris's bait. "Now, if you don't mind, I have risked my safety and reputation to come to this *lovely* place. I trust that means you have what I need?"

Sir Fenris gestured to Councilor Erlichman, who produced a rolled piece of parchment and handed it to Viola.

"As requested," he said, "a draft amendment to be submitted to the ruling council of Tsaftown."

Viola took the parchment but eyed the two men. "Sir Fenris, I assumed you would hire a solicitor to write this up," she said.

"And I have. The Erlichman family has run numerous successful businesses for decades. He was more than up to the task."

The floor felt uncertain beneath Viola, as if the new foundations she'd attempted to build were crumbling from under her. She needed to stay calm. She couldn't let Sir Fenris's games distract her. "I could have hired a solicitor myself," she said. "I needed discretion. And distance from Lytton Hall. This amendment cannot be connected back to me. Even when it's presented to the council." She turned her gaze to Erlichman. "House Livna appreciates your service, Councilor, but this is a deeply sensitive matter."

"I understand the need for discretion, my lady," Councilor Erlichman said. "Your anonymity will certainly be maintained. I can present the legislation, or it could be submitted by a citizen of the city. Such details can be ironed out as we proceed."

Viola gripped the arm of her chair to avoid wrinkling the parchment in her other hand. "And there is no conflict of interest? You'd be voting on legislation that you yourself wrote."

"It happens all the time on the council," Erlichman said. "Officially or unofficially, council members often have a hand in legislation before it's presented for a vote. I guarantee that everything will be aboveboard." He lifted his eyebrows and glanced at the parchment.

Viola simply crossed her arms.

"At least look at the amendment," Erlichman said. "Then you can suggest whatever changes you deem necessary."

Howling wind whistled through the cracks in the outer wall. Viola had come this far. Erlichman already knew she was the voice behind this proposal. There was no turning back.

She unfurled the parchment.

> *Be it known to all that we, the duly appointed ruling council of the sovereign city of Tsaftown, do hereby proclaim the following decree:*
> *In recognition of the noblewomen of our realm and their inherent autonomy and free will, we hereby grant them the right to refuse any marriage arrangement proposed*

*to them by their families or guardians. No noblewoman
shall be compelled to marry against her wishes, and she
shall have the right to choose her own spouse.*

The document went on to outline changes in inheritance laws and rites of succession. It was all quite dry reading, but still her pulse raced.

It was real. Ideas that had once simply been distant hopes were now written down and given structure. If the council approved it, this beautiful bit of parchment would mean that no woman in House Livna would ever be subject to an unwanted marriage ever again. It meant freedom for the young women of House Livna. For Nevandra.

Viola handed the parchment back to Councilor Erlichman. "What will the rest of the council say?"

He stroked his beard as he contemplated the question. "Rathskellar, Okerlund, and Steadroot will vote against it. They're all too stubborn to accept something so groundbreaking. Deppner and Nemeth will likely vote in favor of it. Godfries as well, with some convincing. And myself, of course. I'm not sure about Thusk. His vote is fairly pliable, but it may take some coaxing."

Sir Fenris yawned, apparently losing interest in the talk of politics.

Viola tapped her finger against her lips. Pliable was no doubt a polite way of saying Thusk could be bribed. Despite her initial trepidation, Erlichman was providing valuable insight. Now she simply needed to keep her own hands clean in the matter. She couldn't let herself get entangled more than she already was.

"Can you get his vote?" she asked.

Councilor Erlichman offered a diplomatic smile. "I can be very persuasive when needed."

Viola hoped so. In the event of a tie, Eric would have the final say. Perhaps he would vote in favor. Perhaps he wouldn't. There were more variables than she cared to consider.

She handed back the draft. "Please, Councilor, persuade him."

Erlichman rolled up the parchment. "I can make the necessary arrangements."

"Outstanding." Viola began to stand, but Sir Fenris waved a hand, ushering her to remain seated.

"A moment, Lady Viola," he said. "I have one other matter to discuss."

Councilor Erlichman took his leave of them, following the same path Crow had taken into the tavern.

Sir Fenris kept his eyes on Viola. Jubilant voices from the tavern echoed through the wall, filling the silence between them. Erlichman's presence had startled her when she'd arrived, but the feel of Sir Fenris's gaze on her now made her wish he were still here.

She finally broke the awkward silence. "You require something?" she asked.

"I hope I've proven myself useful to you, my lady," Sir Fenris said. "I may not be a wordsmith like Erlichman, but I gave you what you needed. Found the right person to write up your amendment. As you asked."

"Indeed," Viola said. "You've held up your end of the bargain. And been paid for your services. Your point?"

"I felt you and I had a solid foundation," Sir Fenris said. "Something that could be built upon. So you can imagine my surprise at being dragged before the ruling council to be excoriated by your husband. All while you sat there, prim and proper, at his right hand."

So this was it? The airing of grievances?

"Could it truly have been that much of a surprise given the trouble you've stirred up?" Viola asked.

"Trouble I stirred up?" Sir Fenris scoffed. "Did the Howlers raid those caravans? Attack the city gates? Burn down Glodwood Manor?"

"You were hired to protect the city," Viola said. "Not commit atrocities against the Poroo."

Sir Fenris waved his hand. "Don't question my methods. Question my results."

Viola set her jaw. What was he getting at? "Speak plainly, Sir Fenris. If there is something you need, then say so."

Sir Fenris folded his hands together and leaned forward. "I have a reputation to uphold in this community. I can't do that with Little Eric looming over me." He scratched at his neck. "There must be something you can do to get your husband off my back."

"If you feel trapped, then perhaps you need to reevaluate the conduct of your men," Viola said.

Sir Fenris tilted his head. "That's disappointing. I thought you of all people could appreciate how overbearing House Livna can be."

Viola wrinkled her nose in genuine surprise. "Why should I feel trapped by my own family?"

"I spent fourteen years in Ice Island," Fenris said. "I know a prison when I see one. You're not truly free within that beautiful manor house. Otherwise you wouldn't have come to me for help."

He was grasping at straws. Trying to find leverage against her. Certainly there were tensions in her relationships in House Livna, but that didn't constitute a trap.

Viola needed to end this conversation for so many reasons, but she doubted he would let this go if she simply said no.

"What is it between you two?" Viola asked. "Eric's always been stiff-necked, but he holds such ire for you."

Sir Fenris shifted in his chair and sighed. "You're part of House Livna. I'm sure you know the story."

"Your father's coup?" Viola asked.

"Attempted coup," Fenris corrected. "The Livnas have spent

years casting my father as the villain of that story, when in truth he was a fat fool whose ambition outreached his intelligence."

Viola leaned to one side, resting her elbow on the arm of the chair. "I know the events as told by the members of House Livna, but if I am to help you, I need to see the other side of what happened."

Sir Fenris narrowed his eyes at Viola. Then relaxed and blew out a sigh. "My father labored greatly to make sure I received my knighthood. A fact he was quick to remind me of at every opportunity. So when he told me his plan to storm Lytton Hall, I went along with it, not because of any animosity to House Livna, but because I owed my father a debt."

Sir Fenris's eyes seemed to gleam in the dim lantern light.

"For following my father's lead, old Lord Livna decided I was beyond saving and shipped me off to Ice Island to rot with my father. One would think such punishment would satisfy House Livna's thirst for retribution, but it seems that's not the case."

Again, Viola was left with a frustratingly broad retelling of the coup. It would simply have to do for now. "Do you desire peace with House Livna?" she asked

Sir Fenris offered a derisive snort. "Would *they* ever want peace with me?"

"Not likely," Viola admitted. "At least not right now. You spoke earlier of second chances. You've been given that. Prove you are worthy of the king's pardon, and perhaps one day these grudges can be set aside."

It was lofty talk, but it could be the start of something. If the man wanted to work alongside Viola, then she should at least try to reap something from that relationship.

Sir Fenris sat up from his slouched position. "I can't tend to my business with Eric's shadow looming behind me. Convince him to let my Howlers move freely in and out of the city. Promise me that, and I assure you that I shan't be a thorn in your side."

Promise. He wanted a guarantee of a thing she could not ensure. She could simply lie. Utter a pledge of cooperation without any intent of upholding it. But as a rule, she did not take the swearing of oaths lightly. Misdirection and withholding information was one thing, but an outright lie would easily become a snare.

"I will urge Eric to take a levelheaded approach to these matters. If you're able to keep your Howlers in check, then there shouldn't be any problem," Viola said.

Sir Fenris exhaled slowly. "Of course. I knew we could come to an understanding." He rose from his chair and crossed the long room to the tavern door. "Remain as long as you wish. I don't want to send you out into the cold."

He passed through the door. A chorus of cheers erupted from the tavern, doubtless revelers applauding Sir Fenris's arrival to the drunken festivities.

Viola leaned back in her chair, listening to the clamoring voices on the other side of the wall. For all his faults, Fenris had a magnetism that inspired a strange loyalty from men like Ikârd and Crow.

Had she been taken in by Sir Fenris's twisted charms as well?

A shiver crept up her spine. She jolted out of her seat and headed for the exit. Something inside her needed to get away from this place. She pulled her hood up over her head and retreated into the cold dark of night.

CHAPTER TWELVE
ERIC

ERIC'S FOOTWORK WAS OFF. EACH LAbored step across the courtyard put him farther out of step with where he wanted to be. He needed to move, wounded leg or not.

Derby's sword came in high. Eric sidestepped the attack easily but held back, not pressing his advantage yet.

"Don't be timid, Derby," Eric said.

His squire stood on the other side of the dueling ring. Captain Demry and the Fighting Fifteen formed a circle around them as they watched the practice duel unfold.

Derby nodded. His overlarge ears had turned red with exertion. "I'll try to do better, my lord," he said, catching his breath.

Eric twirled his sword. "Try?"

Derby clenched his teeth. "I *will* do better." A spark lit his voice, and he lunged forward and struck out at Eric's legs.

"Get him, Wenkling!" Alden Wroxton yelled. He still wore a sling after his encounter with the cham.

There was just enough chill in the midmorning air to truly get Eric's blood pumping. He'd always wondered why his father had insisted on rising early with the other fighting men to go through drills. Now that he was saddled with the responsibilities of leadership, Eric wouldn't trade these training sessions for anything. They gave him a reprieve from the burdens of his title.

His marriage, however, was a different matter. He could not escape the memory of Viola's strange behavior the night before. He understood that intimacy hadn't been possible, but why had she grown so cold? They'd had plenty of quarrels before, but for her to halt an affectionate moment without any conflict between them? That weighed on his heart differently.

The whole encounter left him deflated.

Derby stepped in close, swinging low at Eric's unguarded shins. Eric sidestepped the strike, but his distraction slowed his reaction time. He shuffled his feet, nearly tripping, but still evaded Derby's strike. A strike that left the young soldier overextended.

Eric pushed off on his good leg and swung down at his squire's helmet. Metal struck metal and rang out through the courtyard. It wasn't a vicious stroke, but certainly enough to rattle Derby's teeth.

Derby made a half-hearted swipe toward Eric, then lowered his weapon, conceding the duel.

"Come on Wenk," Jol Quimby said. "Wroxy's got one arm and he coulda done better."

Eric sheathed his sword and tucked an arm around Derby's shoulders. "You almost had me."

Derby chuckled in spite of himself. "I didn't think you'd be able to move like that with your wounded leg."

"It was only natural for you to take advantage of my leg," Eric said. "So I played up the limp. Knowing your enemy is important, but don't underestimate them."

Eric patted Derby on the shoulder and left the ring. Captain Demry ordered two more men to duel, and the sound of swords filled the courtyard again.

Eric glanced up at Viola's window. He should go talk to her.

Even if he didn't understand why she'd left, he could still try to make things right.

As if summoned by his thoughts, the door to the inner hall opened and out stepped Viola. She wore a dark blue woolen cloak over her dress, with the hood pulled up to cover her head. Their eyes met across the courtyard, and Eric immediately left the soldiers to greet his wife.

He took her hand and kissed it. "Good morning." Was that all he could think to say?

Viola gave a conciliatory smile. Snowflakes gathered in her eyelashes, softening the typically intense look in her fierce eyes.

"Good morning," she said, pulling the cloak tighter to protect against the snow. "I cannot believe your men are out dueling in this."

Eric chuckled, sending out a cloud of hot breath into the frigid morning air. "They must be ready to fight in all circumstances. Besides, the cold encourages them to work harder to stay warm."

Viola smiled and brushed snow off her brow. "I suppose so."

He *did* enjoy her smile. More and more, he could tell when her expressions were genuine and when she was hiding her feelings from the world.

"What brings you out on the cold morning, then?" Eric asked. "Surely not to spar with the men?"

Viola laughed gently. "Not today at least. No, I wished to apologize for..." She paused, not something she did often in conversation. "I'm sorry for putting a stop to our evening so suddenly. It was all very pleasant. I'm sorry if I upset you."

He held her hand to his chest. "Indeed, it was pleasant. I would appreciate doing it again. As often as possible."

Viola took hold of Eric's other hand. Her eyelashes fluttered, knocking snowflakes away. "That would be nice. Very nice." Such simple words, but her voice rose up, as if pleading with her to believe him.

"My lord!"

Alas, another short-lived exchange with his wife. Derby approached in Eric's peripheral vision, followed by Master Ambrose. Sweat clung to the old guard's typically cheerful face.

Derby bowed to the two of them. "I'm sorry to interrupt, but Master Ambrose said it was urgent."

"Lord Livna," Ambrose said. "The ruling council requires your presence for a vote."

Viola's eyes narrowed, but she said nothing.

"The council met yesterday," Eric said. "They're here again?"

Ambrose wheezed, still catching his breath. "Councilor Erlichman called a special session for an amendment to the city charter."

Viola's eyes bulged. "They're voting *today*?"

Cinders. What was going on? Eric didn't know everything the council did, but something as large as an amendment should have at least been mentioned yesterday. What fresh madness was this?

And why did he feel a knot twisting in his stomach?

Eric strode toward Lytton Hall. He bounded up the steps and through the front doors. A few paces past the foyer, he turned up the wooden stairs toward the council meeting chamber on the third floor. Each step seemed to echo louder.

"Eric, wait!" Viola was a whole flight of stairs behind, and Eric slowed to allow her to catch up.

"Think this through," she said. "There must be a reason for them to do this. It could be a simple matter of scheduling."

Eric tried to think as they continued up the stairs. Viola was right. There had to be a reason. But what? He halted at the third-floor landing. Derby and Ambrose caught up and waited several steps down from them.

"What do you suggest I do?" Eric asked.

Viola shook her head. "If you go charging in looking for a fight, then you'll find one." She set her hand against his chest. Trembling. "Whatever you hear in there, please...listen first."

This development had rattled her too.

Eric took her hand in his, and together, they strode down the hall to the council chambers. He still wore his leather armor from the dueling ring. Not exactly befitting a formal meeting, but it would have to do. Besides, if there *were* some foul plot afoot, then perhaps the presence of Eric's sword belt would remind any conspirators of his oath to defend his domain against all enemies. Foreign and domestic.

He pushed the doors open and interrupted a lively conversation among the council members. "I'm sorry for the delay..." He froze.

The eight members of the council sat in their typical spots around the table, but they had been joined by another.

"Fenris," Eric growled. What in the depths was he doing here?

Viola came up from behind and stood at his elbow. She audibly gasped. Why did she seem so rattled by all this?

Fenris rose from his seat on the opposite end of the room.

"Lord Livna," he said. "The council is voting on an amendment to the city charter. An amendment that I've chosen to sponsor."

Eric stormed forward and took his seat at the head of the table, keeping his eyes locked on Fenris. The chairs from the previous day's meeting remained, providing Viola a seat at Eric's right hand. Ambrose and Derby closed the door and took up sentry positions at the entrance.

"I would see this amendment," Eric said.

Erlichman handed him a rolled-up sheet of parchment. Viola leaned in close at his elbow as he read the text.

"Primarily," Erlichman said, "this amendment would allow noblewomen of marrying age the right of refusal to any proposal."

Eric read the document further. The amendment would entitle noblewomen those rights and more. Statutes against no-fault divorces would be dissolved. There were even provisions that would allow a noblewoman to inherit positions of authority. Including lordship of the city.

Councilor Rathskellar cleared his throat. "It's practically Jaelportian, my lord. It sets Tsaftown on a path toward becoming a matriarchy."

"You exaggerate," Councilor Nemeth said. "Simply because legislation defies your understanding does not mean it is a threat to tradition."

"I'll not stand for anything sponsored by Sir Fenris. Neither should you, my lord," Councilor Okerlund said.

"Enough," Eric said. The voices at the table halted. Eric glanced around the table, looking each man in the eye. "How does the vote stand?"

"Three and three," Erlichman said. "Councilors Godfries, Deppner, and Nemeth voted *yay*. Councilors Okerlund, Rathskellar, and Thusk vote *nay*. Councilor Steadroot is absent and sent no proxy."

"And your vote?" Eric asked.

Erlichman folded his hands. "I was contracted to pen this amendment. As such, I have a conflict of interest and must abstain."

Something wasn't right, but who was behind it? And to what end?

"I don't understand," Viola said. Her voice, typically calm, warbled as she spoke. "Councilor Erlichman, why is this vote being rushed? Surely such a matter demands further discussion."

While Godfries, Deppner, and Nemeth chimed in their agreement, Eric eyed his wife, concerned by the emotion in her tone. What had gotten her so off-kilter? Surely such a matter would interest her, but to this degree?

"It's merely a scheduling matter, my lady," Erlichman said. "The council will not be able to meet regularly over the next few months. We either vote on this now or delay it indefinitely."

"Why not delay it until spring?" Viola asked.

Erlichman shook his head. "Unfortunately, that's not feasible. We cannot have legislation lingering on our docket for months at a time."

Yet there was an odd gleam in Erlichman's smile, like he was holding on to a secret. He'd said he'd been commissioned to write the legislation. Did his involvement go further?

Eric shook off the thought and locked eyes with Fenris across the table. "And you?" he asked. "Why are you involved in this?"

"I had the opportunity to lend my voice to new legislation," Fenris said. "There was no reason *not* to get involved."

He was being evasive. "But why?" Eric demanded. "Why is this important to you?"

Fenris slowly tilted his chin up toward Eric. "I was asked to oversee the original drafting of the amendment. It seemed only natural that I sponsor the legislation when it was brought before the council."

Eric pressed harder. "Asked by *whom*?"

Fenris grinned wide. "Well, Lady Viola, of course."

Heat flooded Eric's chest.

Fenris was lying. She couldn't be involved. His own wife?

"Viola?" Eric muttered.

"She approached me about drafting this amendment months ago," Fenris said. "I'm surprised she didn't tell you."

There was an explanation. There had to be. Eric looked to Viola. Her skin had paled to a sickly olive color.

"This isn't what it looks like," she said.

"It isn't?" Eric said. "You're not working with Fenris?"

Eyes pleading, she reached out for his arm. "Please just listen," she said in a stressed whisper. "I'll explain everything."

As good as a confession. Unbelievable. Eric ripped his arm away and stood up, leaning on the table.

Voices murmured as the councilors reacted to Eric's outburst.

Okerlund crossed his arms and scowled at Eric and Viola while Fenris barely hid his amusement at the unfolding drama.

Viola gazed at him, her eyes silently begging for understanding. Eric could summon no sympathy. She had plotted in secret. Was she trying to push this through without his knowledge? Had she hoped he might die in the war so she could set herself to rule over Tsaftown? Could his own wife be so devious?

"You can table the amendment," Viola said softly. "Delay until spring. I can explain everything in detail, just"—her gaze flickered across the council members—"not here. You're being played for a fool."

Heat shot up Eric's spine, and he growled. "Indeed."

"Perhaps," Erlichman said, "the yays and nays can each appoint a speaker, then make their own case for or against the amendment and—"

"No," Eric said. There had been enough games. Enough manipulation. This was the North. He was the lord of his city. "I vote nay."

Silence hung over the room. Viola sighed mournfully and shrank back into her chair. Eric could offer her no kindness, no affection. He couldn't even look at her.

This amendment, and whatever trickery accompanied it, was dead.

VIOLA

If there had been a worse day in Viola's life, then she certainly couldn't remember. Betrayed by Sir Fenris and Councilor Erlichman. Humiliated in front of Eric and the ruling council. And worst of all, Nevandra's future was now at risk.

Viola followed on Eric's heels as he strode away from the council chambers. It wasn't yet midday. They'd met with the council for less than an hour. How had so much gone wrong in such a short period?

Viola blanched as she recalled Sir Fenris's delight at undermining her. How had she ever thought she could trust that wretched blackguard? Was this all part of some long-term stratagem? A ploy to sow chaos between her and Eric?

"My lord?" Walter hurried toward them from farther down the hallway. "I heard there was some commotion with the council. What has happened?"

Eric shook his head. "I'll not discuss it in the open."

"Very well, my lord." Walter reached them and turned to walk alongside Eric. "I had prepared the study for after your drills with the men. Perhaps it would provide a private space for conversation?"

Eric merely grunted.

The three of them walked in silence toward Eric's study.

If only Viola could calm Eric down and explain everything. The entire purpose of the amendment was to save Nevandra. If he could understand that, then she could convince him to take a stand against the council's treachery. There had to be a way to reach a positive outcome to all this.

So why wouldn't her accursed hands stop shaking?

They retreated into the study. True to his word, Walter had prepared a fire. He poured a cup of tea for Viola as she sat at the table. The smell of spiced apples tinged the air. Ordinarily it would have been perfect for a chilled day such as this. Now the aroma simply died in her nostrils.

Viola reached for the cup, but her hands continued to tremble, and she buried them in her lap.

Eric trudged over to the hearth and stared into the fire.

Walter wordlessly prepared a cup of tea for Eric and set it on the hearth in front of him. Eric made no move to reach for the drink.

"Eric, please hear me out," Viola said. If he would just listen, then they could still make things right.

Her husband exhaled slowly but did not look away from the fire.

"At least let me explain the reason behind my amendment. It was never meant as a means of stealing power. I only wanted to protect Nevandra."

Still, Eric said nothing. She had been prepared for his anger. For accusations. Or even threats.

But his silence?

"Eric, please."

"You say you can explain." Eric turned slowly away from the hearth and pinned Viola to her seat with his glare. "Do so."

She pressed her palms against her thighs. "Sir Fenris wasn't supposed to be here. He was simply a broker so I could have the amendment formally drawn up. Councilor Erlichman penned the amendment, but he rushed the vote. There was supposed to be time to present it properly."

"I don't care about Erlichman's motivations," Eric snapped. "You lied to me. What else are you hiding?"

"I never lied to you." The words were colder than Viola had intended, but she couldn't back down. "I did it for my daughter. To give her a better future. Surely you can understand that?"

She searched his eyes for some spark of understanding, but he simply gazed lifelessly ahead. The fire flickered behind him, making his silhouette loom threateningly.

"Were you simply going to tell me after it was enshrined into law?" Eric asked. "How many secret amendments have you craftily signed into law under my nose?"

"Enough accusations!" Viola had endured too much today. She would not sit by while her husband slandered her as well. "Is no answer good enough for you? How many ways must I say it? I wanted to protect House Livna. To protect Nevandra."

Eric's eyes darkened. "And instead of bringing your ideas to me, you took matters into your own hands, plotting behind my back with Fenris."

"You were gone to war! What if you had died in battle? What would have happened to our daughter? I couldn't simply have faith that you would return. So I took action."

"Always you work an angle," Eric said. "You always play your games. Isn't that just like—"

He bit off the end of the sentence, but Viola recognized the words that had been on the tip of his tongue. Venom rose up in her throat. She stood and took several slow steps toward him. "Just like what? Don't mince words on my account."

How many times had she heard the servants whispering? Or Eric's own family, for that matter. How many people were waiting for Viola to reveal her "true colors" and pledge her loyalty to the motherland.

"Like what?" she demanded. "Like a woman of Jaelport?"

Walter took several steps forward, putting himself between them. "My lord. My lady, please."

Eric grimaced and averted his eyes.

"Or maybe just like my mother?" Viola added.

Eric exhaled through his nose. "You always have a way to justify your schemes. If that's all you can offer, then I have nothing to say to you." Eric turned back to the fire.

That was it? Less than a day ago, they had been opening up to each other, growing closer. Now he refused to even look upon her.

"Very well then...*husband*." She pushed past Walter, shoved the door open, and retreated down the hallway. She hurried toward her private chambers, desperately fighting to keep the tears welling in her eyes from spilling out.

Chapter Thirteen

Eric

Eric needed to fight someone. Or something. Fenris. The council. Even another blasted cham. He was still wearing his armor from the dueling ring, and his fingers itched to grip his sword and lash out properly at an enemy.

Viola had given answers but no satisfactory explanation for what had happened in the council chambers today. Fine. He would just have to handle this himself.

The room was too blasted hot. Eric turned away from the fire, peeled off his leather armor, and tossed it on the floor.

Walter stood quietly in the corner by the door, but the empty chair where Viola had been sitting stared back at him.

Eric had lashed out at Viola. Not heard her out fairly. He could go to her now. Try to make things right before they got worse. Would she even listen? Or just evade and deny any wrongdoing?

No. Eric had a city to protect, and if Viola was going to plot behind his back, then he would deal with matters without her.

"Walter, fetch me the records of the ruling council's meetings from the last several months," Eric said. "After my father died but before I returned. Perhaps we—I can use those to glean some of

Councilor Erlichman's broader intentions. See if Fenris has interfered before."

Walter folded his hands in front of himself. "No, my lord. I'll not be doing that."

Eric eyed Walter. "I beg your pardon?"

Walter remained where he stood. "You heard me, my lord."

The valet's words were edged. From anyone else, they would register as mild annoyance, but such a tone coming from Walter? It was the angriest Eric had ever seen him.

"What is the meaning of this?" Eric said. "Will no one follow my instructions today?"

"I have no intention of helping you with anything until you apologize to your wife."

Eric's stomach churned. What in all Er'Rets was happening? "I don't have time for this," Eric growled. "Fenris—"

"Fenris can wait," Walter said. "If you wish to preserve your marriage, it is essential that you speak to your wife without delay."

Eric shook his head. "There are more pressing matters at hand."

"There will always be pressing matters, but if you push aside the needs of your family at every crisis, then one day you will push so hard they will not come back to you."

Eric bit the inside of his cheek. "I am the lord of this city. I must sacrifice my own desires for the sake of those who follow me."

Walter's gaze softened, and he sat down at the table. "You must lead your family first. Otherwise, all of House Livna will collapse beneath you."

Eric blew out an angry breath. "And if my wife is a traitor?"

"Do you truly believe that?" Walter asked. "That she aimed to betray you?"

The old valet's persistent gaze pierced Eric's resolve, but the anger felt good. Eric wanted to let it burn, despite Walter's efforts to subdue him.

"She suffered no lapse in judgment," Eric said. "This was strategic. How can I ever trust her, knowing that she lied to me?"

Walter stroked his bearded chin. "You've never trusted easily. And I cannot say that I blame you, given some of your history. Perhaps it's time you share some of that with Lady Viola. Particularly regarding Fenris."

Eric quirked an eyebrow. "The coup? She knows about that."

"Not your family's past. Yours." Walter tapped his right ear.

Eric's ear burned as he surmised Walter's meaning. "I see no reason to share that with anyone."

"Lady Viola is not just anyone. Not to you."

Eric paced, rubbing the scarring on his ear.

"I would not ask you to revisit such a painful memory without good reason," Walter said softly.

Eric crossed his arms. "What's the use of telling her about that?"

"Are you going to withhold trust from your wife unless she behaves perfectly at all times? If so, you've set a bar that no living person can reach. Keep it up, and you'll find yourself with no one standing by your side."

Eric shook his head. "I am not just some man. I rule this city. And right now, I'm surrounded by enemies. I can't afford to have such liabilities."

Walter huffed. "Lady Viola is not a liability. She's your wife. You must allow yourself to be vulnerable with her. Otherwise your heart will die. And so will hers."

"What gain is there in vulnerability?" Eric asked.

A gentle smile touched the corners of Walter's mouth. "So much. If you allow it. Husbands are called to love their wives as Arman loves His people. That means service. Sacrifice. To the point of death, if necessary. That's a reflection of Câan's love for His people. Not always a perfect reflection, but it points to the perfect love that Arman offers."

Silence stretched out as Eric mulled over Walter's words. For generations, House Livna had followed Arman, the mysterious God that was one and also three. Such confounding mysteries bothered Eric. He understood Câan. The warrior god who sacrificed himself for the greater good, but Arman was more concerned with matters of the heart. Holy men spoke of Arman's people being the "bride of Câan," which had never made sense to Eric.

There was so much he didn't understand.

"What am I to do?" Eric asked.

Walter rose and crossed back to the hearth. "Pray. Call out to Arman." Walter smirked. "I know prayer does not come easily to the men of your family. It seems a bit too much like asking for help, but it's necessary."

Eric's mouth twisted, a faint frown creasing his brow. "I'm more comfortable praying to Câan."

"Indeed you are." Walter retrieved Eric's tea from the hearth and set it down on the table in front of him. "Yet if you believe only Câan's justice, but not his mercy, then you have missed the whole of Him."

Such faith didn't come naturally to Eric, yet he had witnessed the king's faith push back the curse of Darkness. "What must I do to reach out to Him?" he asked. "Temple Arman in Mitspah is too far to travel. Must I go to the Armanite temple?"

"Arman does not require you seek him by pilgrimages or in the mighty works of man." Walter gently tapped Eric across his heart. "His true temple is here."

The urge to ride out and fight a battle tugged at Eric's heart. To prove his worth to Arman by some great deed. It was a fool's instinct. This particular conflict was not of sword and armor but of the heart. Something he was less confident dealing with.

"I'll take my leave," Walter said, "give you space to think."

Eric sat by the fire for a long while. He meant to pray. Or at least try. But his thoughts soon became muddled, and he ended up merely staring at the citadel board. The fire flickered off the polished game pieces, animating their shadows into an endless back-and-forth battle.

Minutes drifted into hours. Surely there was something that needed his attention elsewhere, but the hypnotic dance of the fire held his focus. He mulled over all the events of the last weeks. Viola. Fenris. The Poroo. Stressors that had built in the back of his mind for weeks without relief.

Walter returned with a tray of food but left quickly. Apparently, it was already dinner time. What would the citizens of Tsaftown think if they knew their lord had locked himself away in his study all afternoon?

But it still wasn't Eric's study. Not really.

The strikingly lifelike portrait of King Axel Hadar above the hearth had been a royal gift to House Livna upon the late king's coronation. The books and scrolls had been gathered by his father and grandfather over decades. Eric had little idea what words were on their pages. All these things had been collected by the lord of Tsaftown. Lord *Edik* Livna.

This was Father's study. Even though Eric had been using the space for weeks, he felt out of place. The patterns in the wood grain of the desk. The lingering odor of tobacco. Everything in this space was deeply connected to his father. It was as if Eric were simply waiting for his father to return home from some great hunt.

Eric stared at his father's empty chair behind the desk. "What would you do?" he demanded.

No answer came. And it never would.

Eric exited the study. Too many ghosts haunted that space today. He walked down the hall and found the setting sun pouring through the windows. Glorious. For too long, Darkness had held Tsaftown in stasis. The shorter days were a sign that balance was returning.

Arne, the chief servant, approached. Eric's shoulders tensed. He had no mind for dealing with household tasks at the moment.

Or ever, really. Yet Arne greeted Eric with a kind "my lord," and continued on down the hallway. No doubt the man had his own tasks to handle.

Playful giggles carried from farther down the hall. Eric smiled. He knew that laugh. He reached the door to the nursery, which had been left slightly open. Inside, Nevandra and Sabrea played on a thick rug with an assortment of wooden toys. Nevie sat on her knees with her dress splayed out around her as she made a wooden horse jump back and forth across the nanny's lap. Sabrea, usually so quiet, played along with the game, whinnying.

Eric knocked on the door frame. "Good afternoon," he said.

The knock startled Sabrea, and the young woman let out a small squeak.

Nevie hopped up off the rug and ran over to Eric. "Papa! It's a horse!" She held up the wooden animal for Eric to see. "It's Dunder."

Eric beamed. "Thunder? Well, you must be careful. Thunder is a strong horse."

The girl nodded vigorously, then ran back to her other toys.

"My lord!" Sabrea tried to shift to her feet and stand. "I—do you require something?"

"As you were. Just wanted to see Nevie." Eric knelt on the rug.

Sabrea studied the floor. "I can go, milord."

"Not at all," Eric said. "You're clearly having fun."

The nanny shook her head. "But I was told I ought not be alone with you, milord."

What in the depths? This was the first Eric had heard of such a policy. "Who told you that?"

"Mistress De'Lana said so." Sabrea's voice was rigid. "She said the old nanny was too familiar with you, and it made Lady Viola uneasy."

The old nanny. Miss Laone? Eric had always wondered why the woman had been dismissed so unceremoniously. She'd been competent and pleasant to talk to, but Eric had thought nothing of it. Apparently, Viola had felt Miss Laone's friendliness had gone too far.

Sabrea's face paled, as if she realized she'd said too much.

Eric chuckled and waved his hand. "For the moment, that policy can be suspended. So says the lord of Tsaftown."

The three sat on the floor, Nevie giving and taking different toys to each of them. Though the girl's enthusiasm persisted, her steps grew sluggish. The hour was growing late, and Nevie would need to sleep soon.

She crawled into Eric's lap to show him her stuffed rabbit. He recognized it as one of Tara's creations. Eric thought of his baby sister, so far away in Meribah Corner. He had hated watching her wed Lord Gershom, even if her marriage had benefited Tsaftown.

He held Nevie tighter in his arms. She nestled deep into his chest and looked up with her beautiful brown eyes.

"Tell me a story, Papa," Nevie said.

Eric shifted, getting comfortable under Nevie's weight pressing on his lap. "A story?" He made an effort to sound whimsical. "What kind of story?"

"A silly one," Nevie said.

Eric scratched his chin. "Sabrea, I only know long stories. Perhaps this would be a good chance for you to take a break. I am sure there is some hot tea in the kitchens."

"Thank you, milord." Sabrea rose from the floor on wobbly knees and quickly departed.

"Now," Eric said. "You want a silly story?"

Nevie nodded.

Eric carried her to an oak rocking chair and settled down with her on his lap. "Well, what about Sir Balen Treskillard. Do you know about him?"

Nevie shook her head.

"Oh, you should. He was a great hero from Tsaftown. He fought many battles and defeated many enemies. But the greatest enemy he ever fought...were the Terrible Turkeys."

Nevie's eyes went wide, and she cackled with glee. "Turkeys?"

"That's right." Eric tapped her gently on the nose. "Many years ago, at the start of spring, a boundless horde of hungry turkeys crossed all of the Northland regions, from Meribah to Tsaftown and all the way to Zerah Rock. And everywhere they went, they ate and ate and ate. Gobbling up all the crops across the land. No lord or soldier or farmer could figure out how to stop them. So they called on the hero of the North, Sir Balen."

There were many different versions of this tale, and like most of Sir Balen's tales, the fantastical feats grew more grandiose with each telling. But such details made the legend that much more fun to tell.

Nevie snuggled deeper into Eric's arms as he continued the story. Right as Sir Balen had explained his grand plan to the townspeople, Nevie's head lolled into the crook of Eric's elbow, her breathing heavy.

Eric rocked the chair back and forth. Had he ever seen anything so beautiful in all his life?

He could lay her down in her bed and fetch Sabrea. There were certainly many things that needed his attention. Yet even with all his troubles, there was nothing in the world more important than letting his precious girl sleep.

Could there be something of Arman's love in this moment? Perhaps a reflection of such things, like what Walter had mentioned earlier?

"Show me more, Arman," Eric whispered. "Perhaps I've not always been the best son, but could you teach me to be a better father?"

A better husband...

Eric closed his eyes, taking in the silence. He wasn't sure how praying was even supposed to work. His father hadn't been a praying man, and whenever his mother or grandmother had tried to cajole Eric to temple, Lord Edik had always put his foot down. *Arman has elected the Livna men to be men of battle who stand in the gap against our enemies,* his father had said. *We've no time to sit in a temple and pray.*

Had his father been wrong? And what good was prayer if Arman didn't answer back? It was said that only the king could hear Arman's voice audibly. So where did that leave men like Eric? Was he to just speak aloud into the air?

"Arman, are you there?" he muttered. "The troubles in front of me are too great for one man to handle. If there is a path out of this mess, it is hidden from me."

He closed his eyes, taking in the stillness of the room. "I do wish I could hear from you. Is there no way you can speak to me?"

Prince Oren Hadar.

What? Who? Eric jolted, opening his eyes to find...no one?

Nevie stirred in her sleep. Eric's muscles remained tense, and he surveyed the room for the source of that invisible voice.

Arman?

"Hello?" Eric whispered. "Who's there?"

Prince Oren Hadar.

Cinders. He was being bloodvoiced. And by a member of the royal family. The prince was trying to speak to his mind. Eric had been around many bloodvoicers during the war, but he rarely experienced their special gifts firsthand.

He took a slow breath, began rocking the chair again, and tried to open his mind.

"Your Highness," Eric said. "I am here."

Lord Livna, Prince Oren voiced. *I hope I am not interrupting anything.*

"Not at all," Eric said aloud. Did he need to speak aloud? Or did the prince have access to his thoughts?

I do apologize for reaching out so unexpectedly, Prince Oren said.

But some informants of mine have presented me with intelligence that you may find useful.

Informants? Before the war, Prince Oren had maintained his network of Mârad spies and rebels to keep tabs on enemy movements, but they had always focused on activities in the southern half of the continent. What could have caught their attention this far north?

"I will certainly take whatever information you have, Your Highness," Eric said.

This involves a former prisoner of Ice Island, Prince Oren said. *I'm sure you are familiar with a Sir Fenris Yarden?*

CHAPTER FOURTEEN
ERIC

Eric carefully straightened in his rocking chair, not wanting to wake Nevie. He ought not to be too awestruck by speaking with a member of the royal family, but the mention of Fenris had taken him completely off guard. What information could the Mârad possibly have gathered on his cousin?

"Of course, Your Highness," Eric half whispered. "I...have the fortune, as it were, of being acquainted with Sir Fenris."

Prince Oren chuckled quietly. *Fortune indeed. I remember hearing word of his father's coup attempt all those years back. As for Sir Fenris himself, my informants in the North tell me he is up to some mischief in Tsaftown.*

"You could say as much, Your Highness," Eric whispered.

I do apologize. Some of this situation is a result of the amnesty the king granted to the occupants of the Prodotez. Unfortunately, that cannot be revoked. To single one man out in such a way would undercut the king's word.

"Of course, Your Highness. I understand completely." Eric had nurtured some small hope that the king could wipe away the Fenris problem with one swift stroke. "You mentioned that you had information regarding Fenris?"

Yes. There was a brief silence. *I'm told that a tribe of Poroo have migrated to your area and that they attacked and burned a manor house on the fringes of the city.*

Eric tapped his finger on the arm of the chair. "Yes, Glodwood Manor."

That's right, Prince Oren said. *My informants uncovered evidence suggesting that the Poroo did not attack Glodwood Manor at all, but that it was a planned raid by Sir Fenris himself.*

"What?" Eric said.

Nevie stirred in his arms. Blast it all. A crying child would not make this conversation any easier. He bounced her until she settled and pulled her little arms to her chest.

Eric kept his voice hushed as he replied to the prince. "You mean to say that Fenris raided Glodwood Manor and made it look like a Poroo attack?"

Indeed, Prince Oren voiced. *I'm told that the patriarch of the Glodwood family was an ally of Sir Fredrick Yarden and had been entrusted with a portion of Sir Fredrick's fortune before he was arrested.*

Could that have been after the coup? Eric didn't know for sure, but he remembered talk of a manhunt for Uncle Fredrick before his eventual arrest, and Father had seized both Uncle Fredrick's and Fenris's land and assets. Perhaps the elder Yarden had sought to keep some of his gold safe.

It seems that Sir Fenris sought out the Glodwoods after his escape from Ice Island. While the details are scant, it's possible they refused to give up the gold. Or had spent it all.

"So Fenris killed them." And made it look like a Poroo attack. The raids and atrocities of the last months had all started with Fenris. He'd hired his men with blood money taken from the Glodwoods and managed to get himself and his Howlers contracted to defend against the Poroo, who he had used as scapegoats for his own crimes.

"Could your informants testify to what they have seen?" Eric asked.

Unfortunately, that's not an option, Prince Oren said. *They must remain hidden for the time being. There are other tasks in the North that require their anonymity.*

"Other matters?" Eric's stomach lurched. What other fresh madness was unfolding under his nose?

Nothing you need concern yourself with at the moment, Prince Oren bloodvoiced.

A most unsatisfying answer. In principle, Eric trusted the prince, but he needed to know what was happening in his own city. "And how many of your *informants* are operating in Tsaftown?" he asked.

It isn't as ominous as all that, Prince Oren voiced. *I prefer to think of them as my ears.*

"How many *ears* are in my city, then?" Eric was pressing further than he ought, especially with royalty, but he didn't like the idea of dark-robed spies lurking in the shadows of Tsaftown.

I have ears where I need them, Prince Oren voiced. *I trust they have proven their loyalty by providing you with this information.*

Eric reluctantly conceded the point. "If I can't arrest Fenris based on this information alone, what do you recommend for a next step in my investigation?"

This is your city. You know the situation better than I do. If my sources glean any more information, I shall pass it along. Unfortunately, that's all I can do for now.

Eric sighed. "I am thankful for your help, Your Highness."

I'm happy to offer it. Until our next meeting, Arman be with you, Lord Livna.

Prince Oren's voice vanished from Eric's thoughts. At least he thought so. How could one ever be certain if a bloodvoicer was truly gone?

He continued gently rocking the chair. His arm had gone numb from where Nevie's head lay on his elbow.

Despite any misgivings about spies hiding in Tsaftown, the prince's information had been invaluable. It seemed another investigation of the Glodwood property was warranted.

And there was Viola.

Eric needed to tell her. Her insight in the Poroo situation had been priceless. How quickly he'd come to depend on her.

His stomach twisted. How could he have spoken to her so carelessly? Anger had consumed him, and he'd cut down his own wife without considering her side.

Eric's ear itched, and he scratched it with his free hand. He needed to make things right with Viola. Walter had told him to be truly open with her about everything. Perhaps it was time he told her about his past with Fenris.

er

Viola

Viola's chambers closed in around her. The prying eyes of the servants had followed her as she'd stormed out of Eric's study and up the stairs. What cruel words had they whispered behind her back?

She ached to explain what had happened. But to whom? She was too disgusted with Eric to speak with him. She had tried to explain, but he had accused her of being a traitor. Storms forbid he actually listen to her. It wasn't her fault if Eric was too goatheaded to understand she had been right. That was all that mattered…

Then why didn't she feel any peace?

Because her amendment had failed. Nevandra would be no safer than Tara had been.

She tried to distract her racing thoughts by reading, but the only books she had in her chambers were journals about the Poroo or a Book of Arman. The former made her think of Eric while the latter only reminded her of her many unanswered prayers. So she pulled on her coat and walked to the nursery where she had Sabrea bundle Nevandra for a visit to the stables.

This poured so much excitement into the child that Sabrea could barely manage to get her into her coat and mittens as she skipped to the door.

"I'll have her supper waiting when you return," Sabrea said.

Viola took Nevandra's hand. "Thank you, Sabrea."

"Dank you, 'Brea," Nevandra echoed.

The sun was low in the sky as they left the house. The frigid wind stung Viola's cheeks, but stepping into the stables brought an immediate and welcome reprieve from its biting chill.

They visited Guffey and Viola's chestnut mare, Ember, and finally Eric's new festrier.

"Dunder!" Nevandra jumped and waved with both hands at the giant horse.

Viola helped Nevandra feed and pet the horses, but when the girl found a pitchfork and tried to mimic the stable boy in mucking out a stall, Viola knew it was time to return to the house.

"I'm hungry," she said. "I bet Sabrea has dinner waiting."

Nevandra dropped the pitchfork and ran to Viola. "I want some cheese."

"Oh, yes, that would be tasty," Viola said. "Let's go see if there is cheese with dinner."

They returned to the nursery where, sure enough, Sabrea had prepared a tray that included a pile of small cheese squares. Nevandra ran toward the table and began climbing onto her chair.

"We must wash our hands first, Miss Nevandra," Sabrea said.

The child paused mid-climb, and her gaze found the nanny standing at a low shelf that held a basin of water. Nevandra pushed back to her feet and scurried over to make ready for the table.

Viola watched this routine with interest. Sabrea might be timid and reserved, but she was a capable nanny.

Soon Nevandra was seated at her table and working on her second piece of cheese. She glanced up at Viola, then at her lone tray of food. "You eat with Papa," she said.

Certainly not tonight, but Viola said, "Perhaps."

Nevandra blinked as she stuffed another square of cheese into an already full mouth. Her cheeks puffed up like a squirrel, yet she extended her hand for more.

Viola slid the tray out of reach and quoted her mother-in-law. "'One bite at a time, with poise and grace, will ensure a lady's steady pace.'"

Nevandra's brow wrinkled, and she glared at the tray while she chewed. Viola bit back a laugh and kissed her daughter on the top of the head.

"Goodnight, my sweet."

"Nighhh, Malmahh," Nevandra said over her full mouth.

Viola drew in a breath to correct the child but decided to leave it to Sabrea. She walked back to her chambers, annoyed by the instant gloom that settled upon her. Nevandra had been a lovely distraction, but the problems of the council, the amendment, and Eric's anger remained.

De'Lana had brought Viola a tray, and she picked at her cold dinner, not hungry. She caught sight of the inkwell on her desk and decided to write a letter to Tara. She took a seat, drew out a piece of parchment, and dipped her quill.

My dearest Tara, she wrote.

I do hope this letter finds you in the best of spirit. At least as best as you can manage.

Viola passed through the typical pleasantries of such a correspondence. Inquiring how Meribah Corner's shipping businesses faired. How the city was coping this winter with Darkness gone. The mundane process eased her troubled mind, if only slightly.

Everyone here misses you mightily. Nevandra asks after you at least once a week. And no doubt your mother's spirits would be lifted to see you again. I suspect even Eric would be happy—

Her hand froze, leaving the quill pressing into the parchment. The mere thought of that man wrecked her thoughts. How unfair that one person could influence her heart so much.

She continued writing.

—to see you again. Though I doubt he would say as much unprompted. I'm sure you know how stubborn your brother can be. How all men can be. It seems so impossible for them to admit what they feel.

If a familial visit is out of the question, then perhaps a diplomatic visit? I am certain I could arrange it.

Regardless of how or when, I do so look forward to seeing you again. I know matters have been bleak. Your husband is hardly the man that any would have chosen. Alas, it was the hand you have been dealt, and you mustn't despair. Even in your loveless marriage, I believe there is hope for a better future.

The words came faster. Her well-crafted handwriting frayed at the edges.

After all, if you lack hope for a brighter day, there will be nothing to carry you through the long, dark nights.

A stifled sob shook Viola's shoulders.

You are not as alone as you think you are. You are in our thoughts often, and even though we are separated by distance, we will do whatever is needed to help you. I have always found that there are often possibilities beyond what we can see in front of ourselves.

A tear dropped onto the parchment. The moisture soaked in, causing two sentences to bleed together.

Though you face dark times, you must not despair of hope.

Tears flowed freely like blood from a wound.

"Hope?" Viola muttered to herself. *"Hope?"*

She crumpled the parchment and swiped her arm across the

desk, knocking the letter, quill, and ink to the floor. The inkwell cracked, and thick black ink spilled out on the hardwood.

Viola slumped forward, putting her head in her hands, her shoulders now wracked with heavy sobs.

Hope? What a cruel lie.

She had allowed herself to believe she could have real love. Not just a marriage arrangement, but an actual family. Eric, Viola, and Nevandra. And maybe more one day. But Eric had shattered that hope. To him, loving her was a liability.

What hope was there for a woman like her?

She remained hunched over in her chair, staring at the fading sunset coming in through her window. She eventually examined her hands. The black ink had spread across her palms, staining her olive skin with black splotches.

She found a towel typically used for washing her face. She hated to ruin it with the ink, but that was preferable to ruining her dress or the bedding. She scrubbed the towel against her hands, removing most of the ink, but some had worked its way into the crevices of her palms. It would be impossible to clean her hands properly without hot water and soap.

Exasperated, she sighed and tossed the now soiled towel to the floor.

A gentle knock came from the door. Viola half jumped, her thoughts scattered by the sudden sound.

"Who is it?" she asked, fighting to keep her voice even.

No answer came. Had she been hearing things?

"Viola." Eric's voice. "It's me. I would like...to talk."

Ice flooded Viola's veins. Was he here to levy more accusations? Her heart trembled at the thought. She wanted to ignore him and shrink away behind her walls.

The knock came again. "Viola, please."

She drew in a breath.

No more hiding.

Though she loathed much of what her mother had taught her over the years, one lesson she had never wavered on was that true nobility was not simply in one's birth but one's actions. One did not avoid a problem simply because it was hard. Whether dealt with stealthily through cunning or challenged head-on, hiding was never an option. If Eric had more accusations to bring, then let him bring them. Viola would hear whatever he had to say and answer him in kind.

She stood, wrapped her fingers around the handle, took a mighty, deep breath, and opened the door.

Chapter Fifteen

Eric

SEVERAL DOORS DOWN FROM WHERE Eric stood, a maid was washing a window. If Viola chose to make a scene, would there be a witness to his humiliation?

The latch turned. No going back.

Eric was ready to apologize and make things right, but as the door swung open, his confidence wavered.

Viola's silhouette appeared on the threshold, outlined by candlelight. She took a step forward, hands clasped behind her back. "Yes, husband?" she asked.

Part of Eric bristled at being kept at arm's reach. He had come to apologize. Could she at least acknowledge that much?

But no. Such frustration would not help in this moment. *Love overlooks an offense,* Walter had said.

Eric set aside his bruised pride. "I want to speak with you. Please."

Viola shifted her piercing gaze to the floor. "Then by all means, do so."

Eric stared at the shadows that clouded her face. "Can we speak privately? Not in the hallway."

Still she wouldn't look at him, nor did she budge from the doorway. His vulnerability in this moment chafed. He had faced men and beasts in battle, yet he'd never felt as exposed as he did now.

He laid a hand on the doorframe. "I should never have spoken to you the way I did. I'm sorry for it all."

Viola pursed her lips. "You needn't apologize. A lord must protect his city. And if you have deemed me to be a threat—"

"You are no threat." Eric reached out and set his hand on Viola's shoulder. "Not to me. Not to the city. These last weeks of knowing you, of becoming a better husband and father, have been..."

Eric lost his words for a moment. The shadow that had lingered on Viola's cheek came into better light. It was no shadow at all.

"My goodness. What's that on your cheek?" He reached up and caressed the black mark on her face.

Viola wrinkled her nose and raised her hand, attempting to cover the stain. This only revealed splotches on her fingers and palm. The futility of her efforts quickly became clear to both of them, and she simply folded her hands in front of herself.

"Ink," Viola muttered. "I dropped a jar of ink. It's nothing, truly. I—"

"Nonsense." Eric turned down the hall and spotted the maid still working on the window. "Miss?" he called.

The maid paused and turned toward him. "Yes, my lord?"

"Please fetch us a basin of warm water. And soap," Eric said.

"As you wish, my lord." She immediately headed down the hall.

Eric turned back Viola. "May we retreat to your chamber?"

Viola considered this request for a moment and forced her eyes closed. She stepped back into her chamber, leaving the door open, and Eric entered.

The room was dark, shadowed, as the sun had nearly set. Viola lit a pair of oil lamps on either side of the chamber, chasing the darkness away. She then took a seat at her writing desk, faced Eric, and finally met his eyes.

Heavy silence hung between them. He hadn't considered what to do at this point. He needed to say something. But...what?

"Thank you for letting me in." Eric tucked his hands behind his back.

Viola shrugged. "You're welcome," she said. "I appreciate the warm water."

"It seemed only fair." Eric cleared his throat. "I've been far from kind today."

Viola's shoulders drew inward, and she pressed her eyes closed.

Eric knelt in front of her, being mindful of his sore leg, and took hold of her ink-stained hand. "I am dearly sorry, Viola," he said. "I should not have spoken to you that way."

She looked down at him. "You've already said as much."

"And I will say it over and over again. You mean more to me than I can say. More and more every day. Even when my anger betrays me, you are dear to me. Whatever you need, I will make it my goal to give you."

Viola sighed. "I don't need a grand gesture. I simply want my husband to hear me out."

"Yes," Eric said. "Your amendment?"

"You needn't call it *my* amendment."

"Fine," Eric said. "This legislation then. I trust it wasn't merely some power-grab like Rathskellar said. So what was your goal?"

Doubt lingered in her expression. The calculating stare he knew all too well was now focused on him. Perhaps trying to assess if he were a threat.

"It's for Nevandra."

When she said nothing more, Eric wanted to speak, but his gut warned him that she needed a moment.

"I needed to protect her," Viola finally said. "To save her from being shipped away as some wretched nobleman's wife."

Understanding dawned on Eric. "Like Tara."

"Like all women of our status," she snapped. "There's not a noblewoman in all Er'Rets who didn't come of age fearing that she would be married off to some heartless lord."

Heat sparked in Eric's chest. Was that what she thought of him? A cruel man like Lord Gershom?

Love overlooks an offense. Eric breathed in and out slowly, expelling his anger. "Is that who I am to you? Your heartless lord?"

"No, of course not." She sniffled. "You and I were old enough to understand what we were agreeing to when we married. But for every Queen Averella living out a grand romance, there are ten young women like Tara locked away in the fortress of some greedy nobleman." Her eyes moistened. "I did not want that for Nevandra."

It all made sense. Viola had been close to Tara. Sisters in spirit, as well as by law. And Tara loved being an aunt to Nevie. All that had ended when Tara had been sent off to Meribah Corner to marry the aged maniac, Lord Gershom.

Tara's marriage had benefited Tsaftown, but there was no way to view what had happened to Eric's sister as anything but tragic.

"If you were worried, why didn't you come to me?" Eric asked.

Viola shook her head. "You never showed an interest in Nevandra before."

"Not interested?" Eric said. "One of our greatest hopes has been to grow a family. And it happened. We've been blessed with a child."

"Children," Viola said. "The others may not have come to term, but they were, and are, ours."

Painful memories echoed in Eric's mind. He saw the same pain reflected in Viola's eyes.

"Our hope was to raise a family," he said. "And Nevandra is the fulfillment of that hope."

"How was I to know that? You were always off with the men, fighting or hunting. No time for our daughter. I believed you were waiting until I could bear you a son."

Eric's heart sank. There was truth in her words. Nevie's birth had confused him. Besides her not being his heir, Eric didn't know how to raise a daughter. What could he teach her?

A loud knock came at the door.

"Yes?" Eric and Viola said in unison.

"My lord?" the maid called. "I've brought the hot water."

Eric squeezed Viola's hand, then stood and crossed the room. His sore leg ached. He probably shouldn't have knelt for so long. He opened the door and took the water basin, soap, and cloth from the serving woman.

He set the items on the desk, then removed his vest and rolled up his shirtsleeves. He spotted a trunk at the foot of the bed and moved it beside the desk and Viola's chair. He sat on top, immersed the cloth into the water basin, and took one of Viola's hands, gently dabbing the cloth on her skin. Viola turned her palm upward, extending her fingers.

"I should have trusted you," Eric said. "We may not have always seen eye to eye, but you've never acted against this family."

Black stains formed on the pale cloth as Eric continued to gently scrub the ink off Viola's olive skin. He plunged their hands into the basin, and darkened suds sloughed off their skin and dispersed as they swirled in the warm water.

"I tried not to take it personally," Viola said. "You've always been quite guarded."

Too true. Trust had never come easily for Eric. Perhaps Walter was right, and it was time to tell Viola why.

"Did you ever meet Fenris? When you were younger?" he asked.

Viola shook her head. "I'm sure we were both at some tournament or at court at the same time, but we were never introduced."

Eric's jaw tightened. All for the better. "When I was a boy, he and his father, my uncle Fredrick, relocated to Tsaftown from Mitspah. Uncle Fredrick had a string of indiscretions with several young noblewomen that made him too much of a liability for the rest of House Yarden. Of course, I was too young to know any of this. I was simply excited that cousin Fenris was coming to live with us."

Viola tilted her head. "Excited?"

"Indeed." Eric ran the cloth over her fingers one at a time. "As the son of the city lord, I didn't have many boys my age to play with. Leif was Nevie's age, and Tara wasn't born yet. So, Fenris was my only friend. I looked up to him. There was even something enthralling about his devil-may-care attitude."

Memories seeped into Eric's thoughts. Echoes of warm spring days playing blind man's bluff with Fenris and the rest of their cousins.

"Even then, there were signs of who he would become," Eric said. "I suspect Uncle Fredrick took out his anger on Fenris—anger which Fenris then took out on others. After a while, he made friends with a group of boys. Mean boys. The sons of soldiers. Even then, Fenris liked having an audience."

Eric picked up the soap, submerged it in the water, and rubbed it against his hands to make a lather.

"Fenris and his cohort amused themselves with mischief of one kind or another. I tried to hold on to Fenris's friendship, but those boys enjoyed running off and leaving me behind. When they were feeling especially bold, they'd toss frozen horse dung at my head."

"Rowdy brutes," Viola said. "Surely your father put a stop to that."

"My father didn't know." Eric cleared away the last of the suds from Viola's left hand.

"One day, Father and the fighting men were off on some great hunt, which left us younger boys to our own devices. Fenris and his friends were entertaining themselves by throwing rocks at the side of the hall and into my mother's garden. I knew how much my mother cared for her flowers, so I told them to stop."

Eric forced himself to slow down, sensing that his grip on Viola's hand was growing too tight.

"Fenris cursed at me and threw a clod of dirt in my face." He winced, remembering the stinging pain of grit in his eyes. "The boys all laughed. Apparently, it was great fun. Anger took me in that moment. I charged at Fenris and punched him in the stomach."

Eric grabbed the soap and slowly lathered Viola's right hand.

"Fenris's friends were too scared to fight me. I was the lord's son, after all. But Fenris? He punched me in the mouth and knocked me down. I tried to get up, but he kicked me in the head. Over and over again. Split my ear open with his boot. He said, 'Listen up, Little Eric. Try to fight me and you'll lose every time. Never forget it.'"

He turned his head and touched the bubbled skin around his right ear. "Gave me this."

Viola's lips parted slightly, her gaze taking in his ear as if seeing the scar for the very first time. "I didn't know."

"No one knew," Eric muttered. "Or at least, I never told anyone."

He'd been too fearful of what type of reprisals he would have faced from Fenris had he confessed what had happened. "Except Walter. He came upon the end of it, ran off Fenris and his friends. I begged him not to tell. My father was a hunter and warrior. I was convinced that admitting to the beating would make him ashamed of me. I ran off, cleaned myself up as best as I could. But I couldn't hide my bloody lip and ear when I came down for dinner. There was a banquet scheduled that night to celebrate the great hunt."

Memories of standing outside the great hall haunted him, his mother's horrified expression followed by his father's quiet stare.

"Mother tried to get the truth from me, but I refused to tell. So they sent me upstairs to have dinner in my room. Punishment for fighting, I suppose. Or perhaps they didn't want their bloodied son to distract from the festivities."

Eric had spent that night alone, watching his supper grow cold while joyful songs and merrymaking echoed up from the great hall.

Moisture soaked into his sleeve, and he jumped. He'd been so lost in memory he'd dunked his hand into the water basin.

Viola took the cloth from him and dabbed at the side of her face, completely missing the ink that stained her cheek. "What happened after that?"

Eric took a deep breath and squeezed the excess water out of his sleeve. "Walter never told, but my parents came to the conclusion themselves. It could have been no one but Fenris. I remember a few intense conversations between Mother and Uncle Fredrick. Then he and Fenris relocated to a small estate on the fringes of town. I seldom saw him after that." He balled his hand into a fist. "I can still taste the blood and dirt in my mouth that day. Perhaps that's what drove me to practice my swordsmanship so vigorously. So I would never be caught off guard again."

Viola dropped her hands to her lap, fingers tracing along the edge of the cloth. "I understand why you can never trust Sir Fenris," she said. "But could you please trust me? Surely my mistake does not equal his?"

Eric's jaw clenched, and his fingers balled into a fist that tightened, released, then tightened again. Viola was not Fenris. He took the cloth from her and wiped away the last of the ink from her cheek.

"Part of me will always despise being vulnerable," he said. "Especially with the people I love. But if I let fear close me off completely, I'll never be able to love those people the way they deserve."

Eric wrung the water from the cloth and draped it over the side of the bowl. Then he took Viola's hands and squeezed them gently. "Viola, I'm sorry. I'm learning to trust you." He chuckled. "Though it appears I'm a slow learner."

Tears streaked down Viola's cheeks. She turned and brushed them away. "I...thank you. That means more than I can rightly say."

Eric took her by the chin and turned her face back toward his. Fresh tears ran down her cheeks. "Please don't hide your face from me." He ran his thumb along her jaw, capturing her tears.

Viola slid her fingers around his wrist and leaned close. Her gaze lifted slowly until her eyes met his. Her mouth parted, and her breath warmed his skin.

Eric leaned in and kissed her softly. Heat rose in his chest as her fingers intertwined with his. Being so close to her was simply intoxicating. Had he ever felt this way around her?

Every part of him yearned to prolong the kiss and pull her closer, but this was not the right time. She likely needed space, and he didn't want to ruin what had been mended here tonight.

Eric broke off the kiss and stood. "Sleep well, my dear." He stepped toward the door, trying to settle his thoughts.

Viola jumped up from her chair and grabbed his elbow, pulled him back. "Don't go," she whispered.

A wild lock of her dark hair fell across her lovely face. She reached up and caressed his beard. An ember sparked in his chest, threatening to ignite a blaze. He locked eyes with her, laid a hand on her hip, and kissed her again. She melted into his arms. How long had it been since his wife had kissed him like this? Had she ever? They had shared intimacy before, but this burning passion was something completely new.

"Stay with me," she murmured, breathless.

Eric's heart raced as he took in the meaning of her words. He slid his thumb over the petal-smooth skin of her face. "Are you sure?"

Viola took his hands in hers, her eyes glistening but stirring with something he hadn't seen for a very long time. "Yes," she whispered. "We have both been alone for far too long."

CHAPTER SIXTEEN
ERIC

ERIC OPENED HIS EYES TO UNFAMILIAR darkness. He slowly took in the room as moonlight highlighted the details of the space. A writing desk. A dressing screen. An ornate vanity set.

He was still in Viola's chambers. Memories of the night's events slowly returned to his mind. He felt the warmth of his wife lying next to him in the bed, sleeping soundly. How surprising that they slept so well together after such a prolonged period of time sleeping apart.

Viola shifted, rolling toward him, her head tucked on his arm. Eric smiled, savoring the feeling of her breath on his chest. Had they ever been so content lying together this way?

Hopefully, they had turned some sort of corner in their marriage. Not merely in terms of intimacy but in their trust of one another. With Arman's blessing, and maybe a little luck, this could be the beginning of something new for both of them.

A faint shadow moved under Viola's door. Someone out in the hallway, walking without the aid of a candle.

Something wasn't right.

Members of the household occasionally traipsed through the halls at night, either battling sleeplessness or simply to use the privy, but never without a light.

Ambrose and Dunn were on watch tonight, but those catfooted steps didn't belong to either of them.

Eric gently slid his arm out from under Viola and climbed out of bed. He pulled on his trousers but disregarded his boots and tunic, not wanting to waste time.

Instinct told him that whoever had passed by held hostile intent. He was painfully aware that his sword lay in his study down the hall, so he retrieved a brass fire poker from the hearth and moved to the door, silently listening.

The intruder had moved farther down the hall, toward Nevie's room. Eric's pulse quickened at the thought of someone harming his daughter.

Slowly, he unlatched the door, thanking Arman that the hinges did not squeak as it opened.

At first glance, the hallway appeared clear. Eric traced the shadows, bathed in moonlight. There. The slightest movement. The sound of weight shifting from one foot to the next.

Eric slipped into the hall, leaving the door open to ensure it didn't slam, and took several swift steps down the passageway, following the mystery figure. He reached a corner and peered around. A hooded figure skulked toward the staircase.

No time.

Eric dashed down the hall, his bare feet slapping the floor. He expected the intruder to bolt. Instead, he turned toward Eric, fists raised.

They swung at each other simultaneously, Eric with the poker and the intruder with his fist. Unfortunately, in the poor light, and with Eric's speed, he misjudged the distance and barreled into the intruder. Both sprawled onto the floor. The intruder expelled a low grunt.

"Indigo Emberfall!" Eric shouted.

If yelling the security password didn't get the guards' attention, then the sound of a fight would do it.

Eric and the intruder scrambled to their feet. Eric kept his hold on the poker and swung blindly. Metal impacted flesh and his opponent let out a pained grunt, staggered backward, out of Eric's reach. Voices echoed from farther down the hall. Someone had heard Eric's call for aid.

The intruder lowered his shoulder and threw himself at Eric. It was an impulsive attack and easy to see coming. Eric sidestepped and stuck out his leg. The man tripped, his momentum carried him forward, and his shoulder slammed into the wall. He yelped and slumped to the floor.

Eric jumped onto the man's chest and pinned his arms to the floor with his knees. His wounded leg throbbed, but he ignored it. He whipped the hood off the man's head, revealing a shock of long blond hair.

At first, Eric thought of Fenris, but this face was much younger. He scowled. "Hmph. Connor, isn't it? Connor Clave?" How had one of the Howlers snuck into Lytton Hall?

Clave struggled to free himself but to no avail.

Footsteps rounded the corner. Finally the guards—

"Nooo!" a woman cried.

Someone stuck Eric's shoulder. This woman was attacking him? Her "punches," if they could be called that, barely registered.

Eric held up his arm to fend off the slapping hands and caught sight of wavy blonde hair in his peripheral vision.

"Get off of him, Eric!"

He couldn't believe what he was hearing. "Lathia?"

His cousin continued her futile efforts to move him, now resorting to pushing and shoving. More voices filled the hallway. Ambrose trotted around the corner, followed by another guard.

The two men peeled Lathia away from Eric. She thrashed in

vain against the guards, screamed. If she kept this up, she would wake the entire house.

"Keep her quiet," Eric said.

Ambrose clamped his hand over Lathia's mouth, which only succeeded in drawing her wrath toward himself.

Eric returned his focus to the boy sprawled out on the floor. He pressed the fire poker up against Clave's windpipe. "What are you doing here?" he asked through gritted teeth.

The young man sneered up at Eric. "Let me go!"

Eric pressed harder against Clave's throat. "That's not how this works, boy. Your lord has asked you a question. Answer me or I'll toss you into my dungeon on charges of treason."

"Not *my* lord," Clave spat.

Eric's grip tightened. "Did Fenris send you?"

Clave scowled at Eric, mouth clenched.

"It was me," Lathia said, nearly in tears.

What? Eric turned slowly from Clave. "Say that again?"

Lathia clenched her hands together. "He was here to see me."

What in the depths? The guards exchanged bemused looks.

"How many times have you let him inside our walls?" Eric asked.

Lathia's words caught in her throat as she looked back and forth between Eric and Clave. She finally said, "I don't have to tell you anything."

Of all the...Eric turned back to Clave. "How many times, young man?"

Clave glanced toward Lathia, then back to Eric. "Two or three."

The lad's tough exterior seemed to fade under this new line of questioning. He looked less like a hardened rogue and more like a foolhardy boy caught in a compromising situation.

Eric removed the poker from Clave's neck and stood. "Let her go, Ambrose," he said.

The two men released Lathia, and she flung herself dramatically onto Clave, weeping into his chest.

Eric raised his eyebrows, stunned for a moment. Could there be any way this was a ruse of some kind? Lathia's tears could possibly be faked, but why would she help in a Howler's plot? The blush that covered the young man's face convinced Eric this was nothing more than youthful indiscretion.

Ambrose sidled over to Eric. "My lord, do you still want him taken to the dungeon?"

Eric's jaw clenched so tightly that a muscle twitched along his cheek. "More than ever."

VIOLA

Viola tried a proverb she'd often heard Lady Revada say to Lathia. "A lady's true strength lies not in her tears but in her ability to master them."

"Don't," was Lathia's reply.

Was this what it was like having sisters? Viola and Tara had gotten along wonderfully. Of course, Tara's personality was so bubbly that she could get along with nearly anyone. Lathia, however, was a handful on the best of days.

Viola had been startled awake by shouting in the hallway. She'd arrived just in time to find Lathia weeping as Eric and the guards dragged young Master Clave away to the dungeon.

Viola had mustered all her patience to calm the girl down and get her to Eric's study. It seemed as good a place as any for a private conversation, and Viola didn't know if Eric would want to speak with his cousin after dealing with Master Clave.

"At least tell me you understand why sneaking a boy into your family's home is a problem," Viola said.

They sat on either side of the fireplace. Viola had De'Lana bring some tea and a simple breakfast of boiled eggs and fresh bread in hopes that it might ease the dialogue.

"Hmph." Lathia crossed her arms, completely ignoring her tea. "I understand why you and everyone else thinks it's a problem."

The girl was unflappable. If she put this level of energy into anything other than young men, she'd be a force to be reckoned with.

"Your future depends on your choices now," Viola said. "Keep up this foolery, and you'll find yourself with fewer and fewer options."

"You sound like Grandmother Merris," Lathia said. "Always talking about my marriage prospects."

Tempest's wrath. Being compared to Lady Merris bothered Viola more than she'd expected.

"What kind of prospects would I have, anyway?" Lathia asked. "Some aged lord like Tara's husband? Or a fat knight from the South? Hmph. I'd rather marry the son of a fisherman, as long as he's handsome enough."

Viola suppressed a sigh. "There are many roads to a good marriage. You never know when you'll come upon the right one."

Lathia stuck out her bottom lip. "All the ladies say things like that. Usually when they're happily married. Or unhappily married and trying to spoil things. They talk like they were never young or had real feelings."

Viola tapped her finger against her lips. The girl wanted some honesty. Well, Viola had just the tale for her.

"Have you ever heard of Sir Joah Haddox? From Carmine?" Viola asked.

Lathia wrinkled her nose and shook her head.

"I wouldn't expect so. This was...fifteen years ago?" Viola stirred her tea. Had it truly been that long? "He was, according to some, the best man at the joust in the entire duchy. And everyone knew he was the most handsome."

Lathia reached for her tea, pulled it close, but didn't drink.

"I saw him in a tournament and later at court," Viola said. "He was a sight. Strong chin. Head full of dark hair. No woman, noble or otherwise, looked upon him without swooning just a little bit. Since I was a lord's daughter, I arranged a meeting with him. I've never been so smitten with a man in all my life."

"Did he like you?" Lathia's pout had vanished, replaced with a curious smile.

"He appreciated what he saw well enough," Viola said. "I may not have the curves of some other women, but I knew how to present myself to draw his attention. His wasn't the sharpest mind, but Sir Joah had a charming aura about him. So I spoke with Father about arranging a courtship."

Viola took a sip of her tea and looked at Lathia over the edge of her cup. "The first problem arose when my mother heard of my plans. Sir Joah was respected and had acclaim, but he lacked the pedigree that my mother preferred. She refused to go along with it."

Lathia leaned forward. "What happened?"

"I figured out how to get my way. My father had a soft spot for his only daughter. I went to him, and he allowed our courtship to continue. Mother was furious, but I didn't care. I had my knight. Or at least I did for a little bit."

Lathia took a drink. "You did what you had to."

Yes. Viola's gaze drifted to the fire. How did the memories of those days still ache? All these years later, married, with a daughter, and just thinking of Sir Joah's smile still saddled her with melancholy.

"We remained apart for a time," Viola said, "but wrote often. Made plans for me to go see him in Carm. His letters started to come less frequently. Then months went by, and I heard nothing. Finally one day, my father received a letter from Sir Joah's family stating that the engagement was off. They offered a kind apology and no explanation."

Viola set her tea down on the table, leaned back in her chair and folded her hands in front of herself. "A month later, I found out he had moved to Walden's Watch, married some buxom harlot, the daughter of a merchant."

Lathia gasped. "What an absolute barnacle of a man! How could he possibly—I mean, do you think he and that girl were…?"

Viola held up a hand. "I don't know. Perhaps. But perhaps I owe the pretty woman a favor."

Lathia's brows pinched together. "A favor? But she took your man."

"Lathia, this story is not a tragedy but a cautionary tale. The point is that Sir Joah was a fool. He gave up quite the opportunity to marry into a respected noble family. All because some pretty maiden batted her eyes at him."

"No offense," Lathia said, "but perhaps he fell in love with her."

Viola pressed her lips in a thin smile. "I thought that at first, and it broke my heart. Until I heard things, enough to help me realize that he wanted someone pretty and less intellectually intimidating. Easier for him to rule over and feel like a manly man. I was too… strong. Too opinionated."

Lathia rolled her eyes.

"After my feelings settled," Viola said, "I apologized to my mother. And admitted that she had been right."

Lathia groaned and slumped back into her chair. It seemed she enjoyed the salacious drama of Viola's tale but had no interest in the morals. "And then she told you to marry Eric."

"No, that was actually my own doing," Viola said. "Mother didn't love everything about me marrying a rugged Northlander, but she eventually conceded that the match made sense."

"So that's it? You made a good plan?" Lathia folded her arms. "Sounds to me like you don't really love your husband."

The comment took Viola off guard. Was there truth to it? Or had Lathia simply chosen words that would get under her skin? Viola loved Eric. Didn't she?

"I *care* for him deeply," Viola said. "In fact, the longer we're together, the more I find to appreciate about him."

ERIC

Eric took the stairs slowly, giving his healing leg a rest as he and Walter moved from the dungeon to the main floor of the hall. In the main corridor, he watched the midmorning sunshine cross the patterns in the hardwood floor as he tried to forge his disparate thoughts into a plan.

Eric had questioned Clave thoroughly. He had hoped such an interrogation, after being caught trespassing in a noble's house, would convince the young man to confess anything he might know about Fenris's dealings. Unfortunately, Clave either knew nothing or was unwilling to turn anything over.

A woman's scream from down the hall scattered Eric's thoughts. Was there a threat? Raised voices carried from the study. The door burst open, and out stormed Lathia.

"I'd still rather marry Sir Joah!" Lathia scowled at Eric and stomped past.

"By the Three," Walter muttered.

They entered the study, where Viola sat by the fireplace. She wore a simple green dress, and her hair hung over one shoulder in a loose braid. It was a much less formal look for his wife—likely brought on by the disruption and early morning—yet it took nothing away from her beauty.

"What did you say to her?" Eric asked.

Viola took a long breath through her nose. "Does it matter? She was a mess as soon as I sat down with her. I couldn't stave off her emotions to save my life."

Eric sighed. Lathia never needed help to heighten the drama

of a given situation. "I'm sure you tried your hardest." He gently patted Viola's hand and chuckled softly.

Viola narrowed her eyes, withdrawing her hand in what Eric hoped was mock anger. "Don't you patronize, Eric Livna. Next time I'll deal with the boy, and you can hold off Lathia's temper."

They locked eyes. Eric fought to keep his expression serious, but his resolve caved, and he chortled. Viola's stoic mask slipped, and she cracked a smile.

Walter laughed quietly to himself. The old valet was clearly happy to see that Eric and Viola had reconciled.

Eric took the other chair beside the fireplace. "My interrogation of young Master Clave revealed very little as well. He's wound up with misguided ideas of loyalty to Fenris."

"Patience, my lord," Walter said as he stoked the fire. "Perhaps the longer the boy sits in the dungeon, the more his resolve will weaken."

But did they have time to wait?

"He won't share what he knows, if he knows anything at all. I figure it would be best to let him stew in the dungeon for a day, then release him," Eric said.

"You don't think he needs to be punished more severely?" Walter asked.

Eric steepled his fingers. "He didn't break in. Lathia let him in. There's a difference."

There were several secret entrances to Lytton Hall. Most were only known by the members of House Livna and could only be accessed from the inside. Such a thing had never been a security risk until now. Lathia's skill for causing trouble never ceased to amaze Eric.

"Besides, there's something else we need to discuss." Amidst the conversation last night with Viola and the encounter with Clave, Eric had neglected to share the information from Prince Oren.

"I received word from a confidential source that there's evidence Fenris and the Howlers burned Glodwood Manor. Not the Poroo."

"Fenris? This *confidential* source told you that?" Viola's eyes implored Eric to explain further.

"I can't disclose my contact, but he is trustworthy," Eric said. "It seems that after the coup, Uncle Fredrick stashed away the lion's share of his fortune with the Glodwoods to keep it from being seized."

Calculations danced through Viola's eyes. "So Sir Fenris escapes from Ice Island and travels to Glodwood Manor, demanding his father's money. Then what? They refuse and the situation becomes violent?"

"Or they'd spent it all. It was a very nice home for a common family to have built," Eric said. "Either way, I'll dispatch Captain Demry to the ruins of Glodwood Manor. There may be evidence to be found."

"And if you find some?" Viola asked. "What do you intend to do?"

"I'm not sure," Eric said. "But if Fenris reclaimed some or all of his father's fortune, then he had no monetary reason to insert himself into the affairs of Tsaftown. Or ally himself with Erlichman. Unless he has some larger designs at work."

"Some plot against House Livna?" Walter asked.

Eric pursed his lips. "Something. Regardless, there's far too much we don't know."

Viola tapped her finger against her lips. "We don't need to know everything that happened to take action. Perhaps we can let him think we know more than we do."

"You look as though you're working out a plan in that beautiful head of yours," Eric said.

Viola fixed Eric with a mock-stern expression. The playful gesture warmed his heart. "You could meet with Sir Fenris on the pretense of negotiating for Master Clave's freedom and use that opportunity to apply some pressure to his plans."

Eric stroked his beard. "And if Fenris is willing to let Clave rot in our dungeon?"

"If Master Clave's predicament doesn't get his attention," Viola said, "then perhaps the promise of coin will pique his interest."

Eric's eyebrows raised. "Money?"

"Indeed." Viola crossed her arms. "To borrow a phrase from your mother, the love of money is a root of all kinds of evils. In this case, I believe we can use that."

CHAPTER SEVENTEEN

ERIC

THE TEMPERATURES DROPPED. THE meager flurries of snow from the past weeks became the roar of a giant, now blasting all of Tsaftown. Thick clouds lingered overhead, framing the setting sun with curtains of orange and violet. As Eric rode Thunder through the slushy streets of the Fisherman's Quarter—followed by Walter, Derby, and Dunn—the harsh Northern wind stung his eyes and rattled the doors and shutters of the rickety buildings.

Soon huts would pop up all over the frozen harbor and signal the start of the ice-fishing season. Fishermen and women would cut deep holes in the ice.

Eric had sent a messenger to Fenris at the Black Boar requesting a parlay to negotiate the release of Connor Clave. He also restated the demand that Fenris return the stolen Poroo relics, but this time offered a payment of five silver pieces each. This one-time offer came with a firm warning that in the future, such trophy hunting would be met with harsh punishments.

The Black Boar Inn had long held an especially unruly reputation, even among the many rough-and-tumble taverns of Tsaftown.

The severe weather had not deterred many denizens of the city from venturing out to engage in some hard-earned merrymaking.

Eric and his men stabled their horses and entered the tavern. Dunn and Walter took the lead, while Derby brought up the rear behind Eric. The squire carried a small satchel that held a pair of fur-lined boots—a gift for one of Fenris's men from Viola. More of her particular flavor of diplomacy.

The stuffed head of a large boar hung over the bar. The inspiration for the inn's title. A roaring hearth fire and several dozen lanterns provided just enough light to illuminate the crowded interior.

A trio of musicians played on a small stage in the far corner. The lead singer, a pretty red-haired woman, belted out her song over the din of the crowd. Behind her, a familiar young man with sandy brown hair played the lute beside a scruffy blond man pounding on a tabor drum.

Cinders. Kurtz Chazir? Which meant the lutist was the king's former squire. *This* was the fresh start Kurtz had mentioned? Leaving the service of the king...to start a band? The man was a soldier. And a bloodvoicer. He certainly must have had better prospects than this!

Eric shook his head. He could worry about the strange choices of Kurtz Chazir later.

The inn's patrons took up space at the tables, the bar, and any other available sitting space. Many sang along—mostly off-key—with the musicians, while occasionally harassing the serving women as they passed. Based on the levity of the crowd, many had been drinking for hours, despite the fact the sun was just now setting.

Across the room, Fenris slouched in a high-backed chair with his feet kicked up on a barrel. On his right stood Ikård. His shoulders appeared bare—the Poroo scalps now gone. He also seemed to be the only man in the establishment without a tankard and stood contentedly caressing the head of his ax while scowling at the crowd. On his left sat Cernell Crow, the blind bloodvoicer. It seemed there was at least one man in Tsaftown who would employ the old thief.

Eric and his men pressed into the crowd. A strange hush fell over the room as the people took note of the new arrivals. Skunk and Taggert, the two Howlers from the southern gate, stood at the bar. Neither man made any effort to hide his contempt at Eric's arrival.

Fenris spotted Eric's entourage and flashed a wolfish grin that burned Eric's ear. "My lord! Welcome, welcome!"

Eric stepped forward, and his men formed a loose wall behind him. He needed to keep control of his emotions. In this moment more than ever.

"Quite the crowd you've assembled here this evening," Eric said, attempting to keep his voice even.

Fenris took a long drink from his goblet. "Tsaftown's finest. The hardest-working men in all Er'Rets enjoying some well-earned comforts." He extended the goblet to Eric. "Join me for a drink, cousin? These men of yours seem like they could do with some rest and good company too."

Dunn scoffed. "Not likely to find either here."

Eric cleared his throat and hoped Dunn's loud opinions didn't get them into trouble. He crossed his arms. "You know why I'm here. What say we handle matters quickly so that you and your men can get back to your evening?"

The odd trio of singers concluded their performance, receiving appreciative applause from the crowd. Then an empty tankard flew from the throng and rattled across the platform. The band took this as a cue and quickly left the stage.

Fenris chuckled and swiftly downed the last of his ale. "Very well, then. Since the entertainment has left." He muffled a belch, then rose to his feet and gestured to a door along the back wall. "Let's talk in my office." Fenris sauntered toward the door.

Ikârd started after him. "Sir Fenris, I don't like you being alone with this man."

"Calm yourself." Fenris shoved his empty goblet into Ikârd's oversized hands. "This is merely a family meeting." He clapped his hand on Eric's shoulder.

Eric jolted and fought the urge to swing an elbow at Fenris.

"Stand guard at the door if it makes you feel better." Fenris shot Ikârd a look, then opened the door and disappeared inside.

Eric followed with Walter, which left Dunn and Derby to stand watch across from Ikârd.

The narrow space looked like a repurposed storage closet. Three chairs and a small, rickety table were all the furnishings the room afforded. The floorboards creaked as the three men approached the chairs. Harsh winds rattled an exterior door along the back wall.

Could an attacker sneak in that door from outside? Eric was a snow-blind fool for leaving Dunn and Derby in the tavern. If Fenris had chosen this place for an ambush, Eric and Walter would have to fend for themselves.

Fenris lit a pair of nearly melted candles on a table before slouching down in one of the three chairs.

Eric pushed a different armchair aside, breaking the triangle, and stood across from Fenris, looming over him and keeping both doors in his peripheral vision.

"I believe you've come for these?" Fenris reached under the table and produced a crate, which he set roughly on the tabletop. "Fifty-six Poroo trinkets. I counted them myself. For whatever good they are."

Eric took a step toward the crate to inspect its contents, but Walter laid a hand on his shoulder.

"Allow me, my lord." Walter opened the crate and inspected the contents. Cham claws. Bone necklaces. Ceremonial daggers and arrowheads. "All accounted for."

Eric pulled a small purse off his belt that already contained the proper coinage—nearly three hundred silver coins—and set it on the table. Walter slid the bag toward Fenris.

"That should suffice, then?" Eric asked.

Fenris chuckled. "Oh, more than suffice, I imagine."

"Very good," Eric said. "Take the crate outside, Walter. I'll be along in a moment."

Walter narrowed his eyes but hefted the heavy box and departed back into the tavern.

Fenris looked up at Eric quizzically. "So now, do I need to haggle the freedom of Master Clave? We all had a good chuckle when we heard that he'd been captured after canoodling with Lathia. I have half a mind to leave him in your care just for the fun of it."

Eric moved the chair again and sat directly across the table from Fenris. "That won't be necessary. You've given me what I need. I'll have him released as soon as I return to Lytton Hall."

Fenris's forehead wrinkled. "Just like that? You're letting him go?"

Eric shrugged. "It's hard to justify holding the boy when it was Lady Lathia who helped him enter in the first place."

Fenris sneered. "Careful, Eric. Such mercies will get a nobleman like yourself into trouble."

Strange. Fenris almost sounded like he was offering advice. What an odd thought. "Do you fear the city will be let down by my leniency?"

Fenris's lips parted into something like a smile. "What use do men like us have for charity or mercy? We are men of action. We can't let ourselves be held back by sentiment. Your father understood that."

Eric bristled at the mention of his father. Now *this* was the Fenris he knew. Trying to prove that all men were as self-serving as he was. Yet Eric also recognized a thread within the conversation that could be used to steer it the way he had hoped.

"Surely you've benefited from someone's charity at some point?" Eric asked. "Either on Ice Island or after you were freed?"

Fenris frowned. Perhaps he didn't enjoy the reminder of having ever been dependent. "I'm not without friends, but I'm no beggar," he said. "Everything I have now, I've built on my own."

Eric took a quick breath, hoping Prince Oren's information would pay off. "It must have been disappointing to find out that the Glodwoods had met such an unfortunate end."

Fenris scratched at his neck. "The Glodwoods?" He looked to the ceiling, as if searching his memory. "Farming family, right? Didn't they perish in a Poroo attack some months back?"

Eric nodded. "The same. Rather wealthy too, for farmers. I remember hearing that your father had some business with them."

"I wasn't privy to all of my father's dealings. Though I do remember old man Glodwood always looking down his crooked nose at me. Told me not to steal anything."

Eric laughed softly. "That's a shame, really. They could have taken you in. Is it true that your father stashed a considerable amount of coin with them for safekeeping?"

Fenris's eye twitched "Why is that any of your business?"

It was time to disclose the findings from Captain Demry's investigation. Eric pulled a cloth bundle out of his tunic. He unwrapped it and revealed a fist-sized chunk of melted gold. He tossed the sullied lump to Fenris.

"This was found in the ruins of Glodwood Manor. It seems they were still sitting on some of your father's gold when the fire took them. If that's the case, then I suppose that belongs to you."

Fenris hefted and examined the precious metal. "So they had some gold in their house. What does that mean?"

"It's unsurprising to find gold there. What's strange is that this was all that was left. The Glodwoods weren't shy about spending lavishly." Eric held Fenris's gaze. "It's as if their home had been plundered before the fire." He could have added that the fire had happened barely a week after Fenris's escape from Ice Island and not long before he'd started hosting tournaments, but he decided to let Fenris twist in the silence.

"Are you accusing me of something?" Fenris asked. "Or are you simply going to continue weaving wild histories of the dead?"

Eric shook his head. "There's no way to prove anything, but it does cast a suspicious light on you and your dealings. I don't know what larger plans you have in my city, but I suggest you reconsider them. Take whatever money you've hoarded for yourself and leave. Go south to Land's End or Jaelport. Somewhere your name doesn't carry the stain of your father's actions."

Fenris's eye twitched again. "You don't usually talk this much. You're generally much more stoic. I can't figure out which version of you I prefer."

"Then allow me to speak directly." Eric stood and allowed some menace to seep into his voice. "I'll be traveling tomorrow with a detachment of my soldiers to return these stolen items to the Poroo. It would be best for you to be gone by the time I return."

Fenris leaned back in his chair, chuckling softly to himself. "I shall take it under advisement."

Eric headed for the door, keeping Fenris in his peripheral vision as he went.

"Eric," Fenris called out, "please tell Viola I said hello."

Darkness filled Eric's vision. He was armed. He could draw his sword, be across the room in three steps, and end all of this in seconds. But those were the actions of a murderer. Not a lord. At least not the kind of lord he needed to be.

Eric continued to the door, having learned nothing of Fenris's aims. Perhaps he'd been foolish to think he would. There was still a chance Fenris would take Eric's warning to heart and leave the city, but with every step, he felt more certain than ever that the conflict with Fenris would not end without bloodshed.

Chapter Eighteen
Viola

Eric would come back. He had to. They had said their goodbyes, yet Viola lingered on the front steps of Lytton Hall, watching Eric and his men mount up for their rendezvous with the Poroo. He had assured her they simply needed to return the stolen relics to the tribe and would be back before sundown.

So why was it so hard for Viola to go inside?

Eric mounted his white horse then looked back and smiled at her. The wind tousled his hair. Viola smiled back and gave him a slow nod. Eric returned the nod, then with a loud, "Northlanders, ho!" led the riders out of the courtyard to the frozen wilds.

Viola remained for a moment, watching until the horses were out of sight, then retreated into Lytton Hall to give herself just a moment of privacy. Months earlier, she would have felt at peace with Eric gone, perhaps even relieved, but now she felt less like herself without him by her side. Her mother would have called it weakness. Perhaps it was. She had formed new bonds with Eric, but would such bonds become a noose?

As she made her way upstairs, Viola considered how she had

worn a mask for much of their marriage to protect herself. But the facade had slipped. She had allowed herself to be vulnerable with Eric and he with her. They had shared their pain with each other. And her heart had felt lighter ever since. Did that mean one day her mask would be unnecessary?

Was this what love was supposed to feel like?

Cernell Crow.

Viola winced at the twinge in her temples, and her shoulders sank. She had just reached her chambers, but apparently there would be no privacy.

She stepped inside her room and closed the door. "What do you need?"

Did you do this? Did you send him? Cernell's voice rang in her head.

"Send who? Please be more specific, Master Crow."

One of your soldiers, the skinny boy with the big ears. He gave me a sack with fur-lined boots. Did you tell him to do that?

Viola smiled, pleased to hear that young Master Wenk had carried out her errand while he and the other men were at the Black Boar.

"I sent them," she said. "You mentioned that your feet were cold. I thought you would appreciate the gift."

Crow had also mentioned a desire to get drunk, but Viola assumed he had his own ways to get ahold of ale.

What's the point of this hogwash? Crow asked.

"Well, they are very nice boots," Viola said. "I sent them as a peace offering of sorts. House Livna may not be on friendly terms with Sir Fenris, but there is no need to be unkind to you simply based on your employer."

Silence stretched out for a long moment.

You expect me to change my loyalties because of a pair of boots?

Viola tapped her fingers against the stone windowsill. "They're an offer of kindness. To show that we needn't be enemies." Clearly trying to press any harder would only result in souring the man's mood.

And if I refuse your kindness and simply keep the boots?

"Then you have warm toes. And I will have done a good deed."

Crow scoffed. *You Livnas are infuriating. Every single one of you.*

Viola chuckled. The comment could certainly have been taken as an insult, but she couldn't quite fight her own curiosity. "And what is it that is so infuriating about us?"

I'm sure you're well aware that your husband paid Sir Fenris a visit last evening, Crow bloodvoiced. *I don't know what he said, but Sir Fenris has been an unholy terror ever since. All sorts of irritable with his men and threatening to hang them up by their toenails.*

Interesting. Eric hadn't been certain if he had succeeded in rattling Sir Fenris in their conversation at the Black Boar. Clearly it had worked better than they'd expected.

"My apologies if my husband's visit made your working conditions less hospitable," Viola said. "I'm sure Sir Fenris has quite the temper."

He's found plenty of underlings to sink his teeth into. I do a fair enough job at staying out of his way. He has, however, asked that I relay a message to you.

To her? What threat would Sir Fenris levy against Viola now?

Sir Fenris wishes you to know that the ruling council will be holding a special session in the Dale this afternoon. He insists you be in attendance.

What trickery was the council brewing up now? And why in all Er'Rets were they holding it outdoors? Even the warmth of high sun wouldn't fend off the cold. It was all so odd.

"Sir Fenris insists, does he?" Viola asked. "What can I expect to find at this gathering?"

Silence hung in the air, and this time, no more came. Crow must have cut off their connection.

Viola sighed and rubbed her temples. How long would she be

bossed around by Sir Fenris? She wanted to ignore the request simply out of spite. Yet Eric was gone to meet with the Poroo, so someone from House Livna needed to see whatever plot Sir Fenris was unfolding next.

Viola pulled her hood over her head as she rode Ember out of the courtyard. The midday sun eased the chill, but icy gusts from the harbor still swept through the streets.

"Are you quite all right, my lady?" Walter asked as he rode beside her.

The valet had insisted Viola not venture out alone, even in daylight. How would the old man react if he knew she visited the Fisherman's Quarter by herself in the dead of night?

"I'm fine. Merely battling the cold, as ever."

Walter nodded, his own face tense against the winds.

The two proceeded from Lytton Hall toward the Dale. As they neared the circular gathering space, their path transitioned from crushed gravel to a snowy dirt road.

A modest crowd milled around the stage inside the amphitheater where a pair of musicians performed. Onlookers danced along with the tune or huddled around the stone firepits set up across the open yard. Behind the performers, the ruling council sat in a semicircle of chairs while a band of Sir Fenris's Howlers lined up along the front of the stage, scowling at the crowd.

"By the Three," Walter muttered. "The gall of these men. Turning a council gathering into some sort of performance. Filthy miscreants, each of them." He glanced at Viola. "Apologies for my language, my lady, but I cannot abide it."

Viola's lips quirked, and she dipped her head just enough to hide her smile. Walter's "rough language" was more refined than most dinner conversations she'd heard. She gave him a solemn nod, her voice steady. "No apologies needed, Walter. Your...choice of words was quite restrained, I assure you."

The singers finished their performance and departed the stage. Councilor Erlichman rose from his seat and took the spotlight.

"Ladies and gentlemen! I thank you all for braving the cold, but I assure you, we have saved the best for last." Erlichman's typically warm, susurrant voice sounded strained as he tried to project to the crowd. "I am honored to introduce your next speaker. A man of noble character. A cunning defender. And of course, he is our splendid host who has provided us with generous helpings of ale."

This last bit was met with enthusiasm from the gathering.

"I'm honored to present to you a true hero to the city, Sir Fenris Yarden!" Erlichman pumped a fist in the air.

As the audience applauded, Sir Fenris appeared on ground level and quickly strode up the stairs. He joined Erlichman at center stage where the two men shook hands. Erlichman whispered something into Sir Fenris's ear, then took his seat. This left Sir Fenris as the focus of the crowd's attention.

He had eschewed his typical sleeveless robe and working man's trousers for a fine red doublet and black breeches, topped off with a burgundy half cape. Whatever his plans were, he clearly intended to do so in style.

"My friends," he cried out over the crowd. "Our city has a problem. A horrible problem. It has lingered for months, and I can no longer remain silent on this matter." He paced across the stage. "For months now, the people of this city have been haunted by the lingering threat of the Poroo. They've burned homes. They've molested caravans. They've even attacked the city."

Angry murmurs rippled through the crowd.

"Kill 'em all!" someone cried out.

"And what does our so-called *noble lord* do?" Sir Fenris said. "He appeases them."

Some in the crowd hissed. Others hurled insults at House Livna.

Viola pressed her hands against her stomach.

"House Livna has lost its way." Sir Fenris thrust his arm in a wide, sweeping gesture in the direction of the manor house. "Eric Livna left our people defenseless to go fight in the South."

"No more King's Wars!" one man shouted.

But the crowd had quieted some and appeared split in their allegiance. Many near the front hung on to Sir Fenris's every word, while others listened in indifference. Councilmen Godfries and Okerlund shared troubled looks, and Erlichman leaned over and spoke to them. What lies or twisted truths was he telling to assuage their concerns?

Walter sidled his horse close and placed a firm hand on Viola's arm. His eyes darted back and forth over those assembled. "My lady, the crowd appears rather hostile."

Viola shook her head, refusing to take her attention off Sir Fenris. "I'll risk it. Eric is gone, and one of us needs to know what Sir Fenris is up to."

"My lady, I will happily report to you what goes on here, if you would merely seek safety in the hall."

Viola fixed him with a glare. "I'm not leaving. If you wish to see to my safety, remain by my side."

Walter grimaced but released her arm. "I live to serve, my lady."

Sir Fenris strode to the edge of the stage. "I was content to remain a private citizen, but I can stand the injustice no longer!" He raised his fist high above his head. "For too long, fools and traitors are allowed to remain in power, while the good people suffer. But we can do something about it. Councilor Erlichman, a true servant to this city, has informed me that it's written in the Northlander Charter that if a lord is found unfit for duty, the ruling council is allowed, required even, to take action to remove him!"

The mob closest to the stage cheered. Chants of "Fenris! Fenris!" broke out among the onlookers.

Tempest's mercy. They'd known Sir Fenris had some larger plan, but this? Had he been planning this all along? Or had Eric's confrontation pushed him to more drastic action? To think she had placed her trust in this man at one point. She cursed herself for being so blind.

Sir Fenris pointed toward where the eight councilmen were seated. "Knowing that there is action to be taken, I am calling upon the good men of the ruling council to enact a vote of no confidence against Eric Livna and the rest of his house, so that proper leadership can be set in place."

From Sir Fenris's finery and powerful posturing, it was clear to all in attendance who he thought would be a "proper leader" for the city.

Viola squeezed her eyes shut. This couldn't be happening. The entire council betraying House Livna? The people of Tsaftown cheering Eric's removal?

Someone hurled a snowball at the stage, just missing Sir Fenris. The icy fragments scattered across one corner of the platform.

"Go back to Ice Island, traitor!" someone yelled.

Hope lit in Viola's chest. Perhaps Sir Fenris had taken his delusions of grandeur a step too far.

The moment of opposition, however, was short-lived.

Those loyal to Sir Fenris hurled insults at the man who had spoken out. Angry words were thrown back and forth. Two Howlers shoved their way through the crowd and interjected themselves into the scuffle.

Viola strained to see what was happening as a full-out brawl threatened to break out. Walter seized her elbow again, this time refusing to let go.

"My lady, I fear you're not safe here," he said.

"Indeed not. To Lytton Hall. We need to update Eric as soon as he returns."

And figure out some sort of plan.

Viola hated to retreat. She wanted to stay and...do what? There would be no civil discourse here. And if a fight broke out, she would only be putting herself in harm's way.

The pair urged their horses up the hill toward Lytton Hall. Viola risked one last glance at the Dale. The Howlers had seized the lone supporter of House Livna by the shoulders and dragged him away to the chants of, "Fenris! Fenris!"

Sir Fenris stood, arms raised in a pose of victory, reveling in the adulation of his followers.

Chapter Nineteen
Eric

THUNDER'S HOOVES RATTLED TO A STOP as Eric and his men entered the courtyard. The meeting with the Poroo had gone without incident, but something had thrown the city into an uproar. There had been a large crowd gathered in the amphitheater, though Eric hadn't stopped to see what had drawn so many.

What in the depths was going on?

Viola stood on the front steps of the manor house, as if she hadn't moved since he'd left. One of the stable hands brought Eric a mounting block, and he quickly dismounted Thunder and ran to his wife.

"What's happened?" Eric asked.

A gust of wind kicked up, blowing a strand of Viola's dark hair in her face. "The council and Fenris have—" She swallowed hard. "They've called for a vote of no confidence against you. They're trying to remove you from lordship."

Cinders. Eric should have run Fenris and his Howlers out of town when he'd had the chance. Along with the whole blasted council.

As they walked into the house and toward the study, Viola explained everything she had seen in the Dale. Eric seethed, ready to charge down and answer Fenris's challenge with his fists.

Walter was already in the study, pulling various scrolls and tomes off the bookshelves.

"We've been looking at the laws, trying to find anything to refute them." Viola took a seat at the desk and began poring over the pages of the red leather-bound copy of the Northlander Charter.

Eric didn't want to read. He wanted to take Fenris down. "I'm gone for a few hours and the world falls apart. Where do we stand? Has he formally challenged me for lordship?"

Walter shook his head. "Not in so many words. He simply repeated the call for a no confidence vote. I imagine he's biding his time while Erlichman tries to get the other councilors behind the effort. I've sent Dunn to keep an eye on the proceedings."

Eric paced in front of the fireplace. Erlichman could do it. He had already proven himself capable of twisting the council's greed to his advantage.

Even if they found a legal way to unravel Fenris's plans, he had poisoned a vast segment of the people against House Livna. What in all Er'Rets could Eric do to defeat that?

He turned to Viola and asked, "What does the charter allow the council to do in a matter such as this?"

She ran her finger along the page. "Regrettably, it's within the council's purview. It's in a subsection about defending the city. The ruling council is entitled to hold an inquiry into the fitness of a lord if it's deemed he has failed in his duty. That bit says nothing about removing a lord from his position. However"—she flipped several pages—"in the older sections of the charter, conditions are laid out for the means of removing a noble family from their position. Councilor Erlichman is linking these two sections of law and presenting them forward as one."

Eric's stomach soured. He looked over Viola's shoulder and attempted to read the section for himself. "Does it give any information about what form such a challenge should take?"

Viola bit her lip. "Unfortunately not. The specifics are left up to the council to decide. Frankly, the details of the charter are not especially well ironed out. Zerah Rock has provisions to prevent frivolous inquisitions against the ruling family. I'm surprised someone hasn't tried something like this already."

Walter tutted. "The charter is a patchwork of Er'Retian royal law, maritime traditions, and Otherling tribal customs. It's three systems of law crammed into one document. In some areas, it's exceedingly specific, detailing how to settle disputes among noble family members or fair practices for the sale of fish. Yet in other areas, it's maddeningly ambiguous."

And with Erlichman's help, Fenris would use that ambiguity as a fog under which he could continue to strike at House Livna.

Eric tapped his finger on the table. "The ultimate point is that he can do it. The council can bring this matter to a vote to remove me and install Fenris. Am I to understand that properly?"

Viola furrowed her brow, flipping further through pages of the charter. "I'm not certain. There's no precedent for something like this. We would need to sift through the finer points of the charter to sort out how to combat the vote."

Getting mired in a protracted legal struggle was a losing proposition. They'd be fighting the battle on enemy terms.

"Fenris is no scholar, but he's no fool either," Eric said. "He and Erlichman wouldn't have laid this trap if there were an easy way to sidestep it. They've set this up so that it's in the council's hands. No doubt Fenris has confidence that he can sway enough council members to their side."

Then what could be done? If they couldn't use the law against Fenris or just arrest him, what options were there? Would Eric have to kill Fenris to truly be rid of him? The dark thought grew in his mind, calling for blood. The consequences were too far reaching for Eric to imagine.

He paced around the desk to take his mind off his growling stomach.

"Walter, would you mind fetching us a tray?" Viola asked. "Eric hasn't eaten since morning, and we may be here for a while."

"Of course, my lady," Walter said. "Would you like anything in particular, my lord?"

Eric took a moment to register the question, then shook his head. "Whatever is easiest will be fine."

Walter nodded, then departed.

Eric glanced at Viola. "How is it you knew I needed something to eat?"

"You pace a lot when you're hungry," she said.

"I always pace. It helps me think."

"It's different when you're hungry. You're more restless." Viola offered a playful smile that warmed Eric's heart. "You've got something else on your mind."

Eric stroked his beard. "I have a great many things on my mind." He circled the table and sat directly across from Viola. "We are beset by enemies. Every solution I can think of only leaves us with more problems."

Viola closed the book and looked up at Eric attentively. Something about her shift in focus relaxed his shoulders.

"If I battle him on legal grounds, Erlichman will try to tie my hands. If I have Fenris arrested, I risk making him even more of a hero to his followers than he is now. And if I..." The words drifted off. Something about saying them aloud changed everything, yet they needed to be said. "And if I simply kill him, then I'll be a murderer."

He could not live with that.

Viola wrinkled her brow but said nothing. The wind rattled

the shutters of the study. The cloud around Eric's mind cleared. Sharing his burden with Viola had eased his troubled thoughts.

"You say we have to contend with the legend Sir Fenris has built up around himself," Viola said. "Perhaps all we need to do is dispel the mystique around him. Tear down the legend of Sir Fenris. Then we needn't bother with the man."

Kill the legend. Intriguing. Fenris had made much of his pardon from King Gidon. He had crafted himself as a champion of the common man and bragged of his battles against the Poroo.

"What's the most important part of his story?" Eric asked. "Which thread could we pull that would unravel the entire tapestry?"

Viola steepled her fingers in front of her mouth. "He's quick to use his own knightly title and noble heritage, but he never brings up his family ties. Either to his father or to you."

Eric grunted. "Perhaps we should have Jeffrey write a song about Sir Fredrick. Tell the true story of Fenris's noble heritage."

Viola shook her head but couldn't fully suppress a smile. "It would certainly bother Sir Fenris to no end. Perhaps that alone would make the effort worth it."

They shared a laugh. Yet something else tugged at the back of Eric's mind. Some important detail, trying to work its way up to the surface. What was it? Eric strained his mind, desperately trying to unveil the pieces. Noble heritage. Family ties. House Livna.

"Eric?" Viola asked.

"One moment." He squeezed his eyes shut in an effort to clear the chaff from his thoughts. The answer flashed in his mind like sunlight on a pane of glass. Something Walter had said about the charter.

"The charter speaks about disputes among noble families, correct?" Eric asked.

Viola tilted her head. "It does..." Her eyes brightened in sudden understanding. "In fact, it has quite an extensive section on the matter." She reopened the tome, carefully turning the brittle pages.

Eric rose, circled the table, and sat beside Viola. Her finger ran down the pages, searching for a specific section.

"This? No, this. Contested inheritances." She tapped the page. "'In the event of a contested inheritance amongst a noble family, the primary named heir, upon being challenged, can determine the terms by which the challenge is resolved. The challenger can either accept the primary heir's terms or surrender his challenge.'"

Eric tried to follow, but her words flew so quickly. "Is there anything else?"

"We don't need anything else, Eric. You're Fenris's blood relative." A strange excitement had taken over her voice. "He's challenged you for a title you inherited. Which means you have the right to determine how to answer his challenge."

By the Three. Eric suddenly understood. "Will it really work that way?"

"It should. No, no it will. It will work." Viola turned more pages. "It's established law. We just need to make sure we have a firm grasp of the bylaws."

The door opened. In entered Walter, carrying a tray of food. Close on the valet's heels came Dunn, back from observing the council meeting.

"The council has adjourned for the day," Dunn said, unbuttoning his heavy overcoat. "Fenris and the Howlers have withdrawn to the Fisherman's Quarter. The council plans to meet again tomorrow at high sun."

Eric and Viola exchanged looks.

"You think that's when they'll try to cast their no confidence vote?" Eric asked.

"Likely," Viola said. "Or at least try to move their agenda further."

Eric's gaze settled on the text of the charter before them. "Then that's when we need to confront them."

Tomorrow. It felt like so little time, but it was all they had. One day to finalize their plan.

The sun had nearly reached its zenith. Eric and his group of riders waited on a small ridge on the fringe of the Dale, watching a crowd gather around the amphitheater. Derby and Jeffrey sat on horseback to Eric's right. Dunn and Alden Wroxton, who still wore his arm in a sling, were positioned on Eric's left. His men were loyal to House Livna, but how many of those going past had bought into Fenris's lies? Were they truly wicked or just misguided? He had sworn to protect this city, but what if the city had rejected him?

Eric banished the thoughts from his mind. Fear would do him no good. Not today. Not ever.

Most of the council had assembled on the stage. Conspicuously missing was Councilor Erlichman. The councilmembers did not appear happy about having been made to wait in the cold.

A crowd filled the amphitheater. The most fervent of Fenris's followers had packed the yard in front of the stage. This included a row of black-clad Howlers lined up before the stage. Other onlookers huddled on the arena floor or in the stands. Most gave no hint as to their loyalties, as if they were waiting to see which side of this power struggle would come out on top.

Like a game of citadel, the board was set. Now Eric waited to make his move.

Thunder nickered and stamped one of his massive hooves against the ground.

"Easy now, boy," Eric said. "We'll get moving soon." He ran his hand along the white hair of the horse's neck.

Jeffrey hummed. "*Soon* doesn't seem to be coming very quickly."

Movement in the crowd. A tuft of blond curls moved through the throng. "Here they come," Eric said.

Erlichman and Fenris walked side by side up the stairs and onto the stage. Fenris took a seat in line with the members of the council while Erlichman stepped forward to center stage and looked out at the crowd.

"I have an exciting update for all of you!" Erlichman cried.

Elder Rathskellar stood and made a show of raising his fists to the sky. Had the priest of Thalassa thrown his lot in with Fenris and Erlichman?

Some of the other councilors applauded, but Councilors Godfries, Deppner, and Okerlund looked upon the theatrics with stoic expressions. It appeared there were some on the council who weren't yet convinced of the allegations against House Livna.

"It's clear there is only one man in Tsaftown who can properly fulfill the role of lord and defender," Erlichman said.

A slow chant began from the ravenous crowd. Chanting one name over and over again.

"Fenris. Fenris. Fenris."

"We need a fighting man to be our lord. A man with the grit and gumption needed to face these challenges." Erlichman stretched his arms out wide. "And that man is Sir Fenris Yarden!"

Fenris's contingent cheered and chanted his name. Pockets of neutral observers looked on. No doubt some were curious about the strange spectacle unfolding before them. But it seemed those in the crowd who would fully support House Livna kept silent for fear of reprisals from the Howlers.

Fenris stood and stepped to center stage. He shook Erlichman and Rathskellar's hands. The whole exchange seemed very well rehearsed.

The two councilors withdrew to their seats, giving Fenris the entire stage. He lifted his eyes to the crowd, bathing in the adulation. "My friends, since my return to this city, I've never asked for special treatment or sought a position of power. At heart, I'm a simple man. But if I'm called to serve this city, then I will answer."

Fenris's words were met with cheers. Exactly what Eric had been waiting for.

"Jeffrey, I could do with some fanfare," he said.

"As you wish, my lord." Jeffrey whipped back his cloak and drew out a massive ox horn, polished to a gleam with a brass mouthpiece and intricate carvings spiraling down its length.

In unison, Derby, Gunnar, and Wroxton pulled out similar horns. The four riders hefted the instruments and blew. Powerful low tones resounded across the open air and cut through the noise of the crowd. The unwavering rich timbre demanded attention.

Eric urged Thunder forward, and the festrier advanced at a trot toward the amphitheater. His men followed, continuing to play their layered, lowing song. Swaths of people turned to see the disruption. Faces went wide-eyed as the lord of Tsaftown and his massive warhorse descended upon them. The crowd fell silent and parted to form a path up the middle.

Fenris's expression sagged as Eric approached. Perhaps he had expected some interruption from House Livna, but Eric hoped his arrival on a towering white steed took his cousin down a notch.

He steered Thunder right up to the stage and stopped directly in front of Fenris, where the two of them were nearly at eye level. Thunder snorted, spraying fine mist at one of the Howlers in front of the stage. The crowd pressed back and to the sides, away from the giant warhorse.

Jeffrey circled his arm, and the fanfare ended with three successive blasts.

A potent silence hung over the Dale. Eric felt the gaze of hundreds of people settle upon him. He looked from one council member to the next. Those who had cheered for Fenris earlier now averted their eyes. All except Erlichman. The traitor forced a smile, though there was no confidence behind it.

"Sir Fenris Yarden." Eric lifted his voice for all to hear. "You say that I and my family are unfit to lead. That House Livna no longer defends this city. You are entitled to that opinion, but I am of the opinion that those issuing this challenge are saltless cowards invoking archaic laws. Yet if that is your aim, I will meet your challenge with one of my own."

Confusion rippled across Erlichman's features. Voices murmured through the crowd.

"Fenris Yarden has challenged me for the seat of lordship," Eric said. "A title I inherited from my father. But this feud is deeper than politics. It's a matter of blood." He pointed at Fenris. "His and mine. Fenris Yarden is a member of my family, and because of that, his challenge falls under the inheritance laws enshrined in the Northlander Charter itself. This means I am allowed to choose how to answer his challenge."

Fenris wrinkled his brow.

"Therefore," Eric continued, "I demand that we settle this dispute...through combat."

"Combat?" Fenris swaggered up to the edge of the stage. "What are the terms?"

A lump stuck in Eric's throat. His next words could not be taken back. "According to the charter, victory in such a contest is awarded upon submission *or death*."

The corners of Fenris's lips turned up slowly. "Indeed? Well then—"

"Sir Fenris, wait." Erlichman's chair scraped as he scampered to Fenris's side. "This is outrageous. Surely this can be settled without bloodshed?"

"If you wish to use the old ways to undercut House Livna," Eric said, "then by Arman, I will invoke those same laws to protect my family's legacy. And my city."

Erlichman sputtered incredulously, trying to form words.

Eric turned back to Fenris. "What will it be, then, Fenris? Withdraw your challenge or answer mine." This was the crux of his and Viola's plan. Everything hinged upon how Fenris would answer.

"I have no qualms about fighting you, Eric," Fenris said. "But think of your family. Surely you've better things to do than jeopardize your life. Do not make me turn your little girl into an orphan."

The jab stung, but Eric had taken enough of Fenris's barbs to recognize it as bluster.

Erlichman grabbed Fenris's arm. "Can we not find some recourse that does not resort to violence?"

Eric couldn't let Erlichman talk Fenris into regrouping. He needed Fenris to withdraw his claim or officially accept the challenge. "Tell me, gentlemen," he said, "is this the North? Or are you afraid to lose?"

Murmurs rippled through the crowd, and a handful of men yelled, "This is the North!"

Councilor Okerlund leaned forward in his chair. Fenris looked across the crowd, then back to Eric. Understanding of the full weight of the challenge flickered in his eyes.

Fenris ripped his arm away from Erlichman. "I will not withdraw. And I will not lose. If you wish to die at my hand, then name the time and place."

Fire coursed through Eric's veins. "Here. Tomorrow. At high sun."

"Have your affairs in order," Fenris said. "I will take no surrender." He whirled and stormed off the stage.

Erlichman followed quickly behind. The remaining members of the council stared in bewilderment. Eric eyed each man again, then turned Thunder around and rode away with his men.

They exited the Dale and galloped back to Lytton Hall. The plan had worked. But Fenris's words lingered in Eric's thoughts. There would be no surrendering to Fenris. Eric pushed the worry from his mind and hoped he hadn't just signed his own death warrant.

CHAPTER TWENTY
ERIC

As Eric approached the study, he rubbed his hands together, working feeling back into his cold fingers. Ambrose had said both Viola and his mother were waiting there. He paused outside the door and braced himself for the onslaught that was sure to come his way.

No. There was no time to waste on such things.

Eric pushed the door open and entered the study.

Walter and Viola occupied the chairs in front of the desk, while Eric's mother stood by the hearth, staring into the fire.

Eric pulled off his heavy cloak and tossed it over the back of an empty chair. His arrival snapped his mother out of her trance. She crossed the room and intercepted him.

"Have you lost your mind? You challenged him to a duel?"

Eric had expected some response like this, just not so immediately. "I'm sorry you had to hear this way, Mother. There wasn't time to tell you before the council met."

And odds were that if Eric and Viola had told her, she would have protested the plan. Simpler to ask forgiveness after the fact.

Eric took his mother's arm and walked her back to the hearth where they both sat.

Walter rose from his seat and approached. "With all due respect, my lord, I cannot believe that you would go off and do something so foolhardy."

Eric narrowed his gaze at his valet. "Your respect sounds rather thin, Walter."

The valet cleared his throat. "I mean to say that there is much to be considered before so publicly issuing such a challenge. Many around you could have offered wise counsel."

"Quite right," Mother said. "You act as though you are the only member of this family with a say in the matter. By offering such a challenge, you have legitimized his claim. Now our entire family is at risk." She gestured across the room. "Viola, please talk some sense into him."

Viola glanced at Eric, then back to his mother. "I'm afraid I must stand with Eric in this. I helped him conceive the idea in the first place."

His mother's lips pursed, but she offered no reply.

"Mother, our family and our city are already at risk," Eric said. "By challenging him, I've given us a way to rid ourselves of him forever. If I beat him—and I *can* beat him—he will have no legal claim, and the adoration of his supporters will wither and fade away."

"Surely whatever archaic custom Erlichman has cited cannot trump royal law," Walter said. "Could an appeal not be made to Armonguard? Or to Duchess Amal in Carmine? You have high-ranking family members in both cities. Why not ask for their assistance?"

"There's no time," Viola said. "It would take weeks to reach either city on horseback, and we have no bloodvoicers to contact them remotely."

Viola had suggested tracking down Kurtz Chazir who was a

known bloodvoicer, but he'd last been seen at the Black Boar, and Eric had no interest in venturing into enemy territory.

"Plus, such an appeal to the southern cities would weaken our position," Eric said. "Our people would say 'It's not the Northlander way,' and they would be right. This *is* the North. For better or worse, I am expected to handle this on my own. Not lean on the influence of others."

"Then handle it," Mother said. "Arrest Fenris and his co-conspirators. Or exile them."

"If it were that simple, I would have done so," Eric said. "Fenris's actions are treacherous but not illegal. Arresting him would only aggravate his followers. The Howlers and the rest of his mob would be at our gate trying to free him. We have no peaceful options."

"Do not treat me like a fool," Mother said. "I may be a widowed dowager, but I know the charter, I know this city, and I know my own family—even Fenris—better than you, Eric."

"You think I don't know who I'm dealing with?" Eric's ear burned, but he took a breath to compose himself. He couldn't lose his temper at his own mother.

A subtle quiver shook Mother's bottom lip, but her resolve remained. She straightened in her chair and slowly pulled back her mourning veil, revealing her face to Eric for the first time in months. The lines had deepened in her months of grief, and her sky-blue eyes gleamed like ice reflecting the sun.

"Fenris is his father's son," Mother said. "You have to know this. Whatever you have been told about your uncle Fredrick, I assure you the truth of my brother was much worse. The night he stormed Lytton Hall, he put a knife to my throat and threatened to kill me unless your father ceded power to him." Her eyes grew moist. "You know the rest, Eric. Your father and his men surrounded Fredrick. He was distracted for a moment, and I managed to squirm out of his grip."

His mother paused, taking a breath. Eric wanted to cut in and stop her from reliving the horrible event, but he dared not placate the woman.

Finally, she went on. "After your uncle and Fenris were captured and arrested, I dared to go see Fredrick in the dungeon. To see if there was anything of my brother left. I looked in his eyes, and I saw madness that nothing would satisfy." She leaned forward in her chair. "And I saw the same thing in Fenris's eyes. Your father was only going to punish Fredrick, but I told him he needed to exact the same punishment on Fenris. We needed to snuff out the spark before it became a flame."

Eric's breath hitched. "You had Fenris sent to Ice Island?"

"No," Mother said. "I told your father to execute them both."

Silence hung thick in the room.

Eric struggled to understand. His mother, kind and gentle matriarch of House Livna, had demanded her brother and nephew be executed.

"Mother, I didn't know," Eric stammered.

She defiantly stuck out her chin. "I'm neither proud nor ashamed of it. It was necessary to protect House Livna from the poison of my brother. Your father met me halfway and sent them both to the king's prison. And we had peace. Until now."

Then why didn't she understand? "If anything," Eric said, "your insight into Fenris proves that we can't merely allow him to linger. Whether I break his spirit or kill him, he must be removed."

"It's not that simple," Mother said. "He will have some sort of trickery up his sleeve."

Eric shook his head. "It's not possible. The rules of the challenge forbid interference. It will be me and him alone."

"He'll use his bloodvoicer against you," Mother countered.

That gave Eric pause. He wasn't sure how one defended against a bloodvoicer, but he'd been taught to shield. He was certain he could handle it. He had to. "Crow is not some mage or black knight. His bloodvoice is weak. He'll not be a factor."

"Promise it, then," his mother said. "Promise you will win. We lost your father to a treacherous blade. We must not lose you too."

Grim memories of his father's murder materialized in Eric's mind. But this was different. He and Fenris would fight as equals in front of witnesses. He put his fist over his heart. "I swear, by Arman, I will defeat my enemy and return victorious."

Mother stared into Eric's eyes for a long moment. Then she leaned forward and kissed him on the forehead before settling back into her chair.

"What would you have us do, my lord?" Walter asked.

Eric rose from his seat. "We'll need additional guards for Lytton Hall. As many as can be spared. I'll not leave our home vulnerable to attack while I'm away."

Walter left to carry out the orders. Eric squeezed his mother's hand and kissed her cheek before leaving. There was much work still to be done.

VIOLA

Viola followed Eric into the hallway and watched him walk away. "Your mother is right about Crow," she said. "Sir Fenris will try to use him. Even just to distract you."

Eric kept going and said, "I can handle it."

She knew he *thought* he could handle it..."I'll be at the duel," she called after him. "My presence will bolster support for House Livna."

"No." Eric wheeled and walked back toward her. "The Howlers and Fenris's mob present too much danger. You'll be safe here."

Viola crossed her arms. "I know the danger full well. I'll not hide behind these doors while you risk your life."

Eric furrowed his brow. "I can't risk any harm coming to you.

If I fall, the city will not be safe. I'll need you here to ensure the hall is protected."

A cold hand grabbed Viola's heart and squeezed. *If he fell.* Nothing else Eric had said registered. The simple words brought the dire weight of the situation crashing down on her head.

"You will *not* fall." Viola fought the tremor that gripped her voice. Why was he pushing her out of this? Did he think so little of her efforts that he would cut her out? "I need to be there with you."

"Viola, no. Under other circumstances, it would be different, but Mother is absolutely right. Fenris will attempt to cheat. And if you attend the battle, it only makes you a target."

Viola balled her fists. "I will *not* be locked away in our hour of need. This isn't one of your games where you can move pieces around. I—"

He grabbed her by the elbows and kissed her. Viola froze, taken off guard by the sudden action. He pressed his hand gently against her cheek. The coarse hair from his mustache tickled her lip. Even so, her heart stirred despite the swirling storms around them.

Eric broke off the kiss and rested his forehead against hers. He slipped his free hand around the back of her neck and held her close for a long, quiet moment.

"You're right," he said. "This is no game. And I can't risk losing what matters most to me."

Viola wanted to protest. To argue against what Eric had said. But she saw the truth in his words. The crowd at the Dale had already been frenzied. How much more so would they be at the thought of bloodshed? And how easy for one of those horrible Howlers to distract Eric from his duel by grabbing her?

Viola made no effort to keep the grumble out of her voice when she answered. "You could have at least asked instead of making it an order."

Eric tipped back his head and narrowed his eyes. "What would you have said if I had?"

"I would have told you how much I hated the plan."

Eric laughed quietly. "I thought as much."

Viola reached up and took his hand from her face, her fingers tracing over the strength and roughness from years of training. He was strong enough to defeat Fenris. This man could do anything.

"When I return," Eric said, "I'd like to see your amendment. Your version of it, not Erlichman's trumped-up nonsense."

Viola drew in a sharp breath, blinked. "You—you mean that? You'll consider it?"

Eric nodded. "It's still a significant change, so the council will require some convincing. But if there's a way to protect our daughter, then I'm inclined to fight for it."

Viola threw her arms around Eric. "That would be wonderful! Thank you!"

He chuckled and hugged her back.

This man. This strong, brave, and truly gentle man continued to surprise her.

And he could die tomorrow.

The thought sucked away her joy. She stepped back, kept hold of one of his hands, squeezed.

Confusion wrinkled his brow. "Viola?"

No. She forced the best smile she could manage. She simply refused to consider that at this time tomorrow she might be a widow.

CHAPTER TWENTY-ONE
ERIC

ERIC WAITED WITH WALTER IN THE FOYER of Lytton Hall. Everything was unnaturally still. Master Ambrose stood guard at the large oak front doors, and even his cheerful disposition had hardened into a mask of stern determination.

Eric tugged at his armor. It felt too snug. Had the stitching shrunk? Had his body grown stouter as he'd aged? Or were his wits simply failing him?

The leather armor was not meant to cover Eric from head to toe. Instead, it favored mobility, protecting his chest, shoulders, and thighs. The only steel armor he wore was his gauntlets to cover his hands along with a pair of sabatons and greaves to shield his feet and lower legs.

Eric ran his fingers over the dagfish emblem emblazoned on his chest. Walter had oiled and polished the leather to the point of gleaming. His valet stood alongside him, holding Eric's maroon leather helm.

Sourness churned in Eric's belly. Every other battle he had entered had been at the head of an army and in a far-off city. Today he stood alone, with nothing less than the fate of his home and family at stake.

Tiny footsteps approached from behind, and a small hand grasped his finger.

"Papa?"

Eric's heart leaped at the sound of Nevie's voice. He smiled down at her. Movement in the hall behind her caught Eric's eye. Viola had arrived with Sabrea and his mother, whose mourning veil was back in place.

Eric knelt and kissed Nevie's forehead. She grinned and ran her finger across the dagfish emblem. "Is a pretty fish."

Eric laid his hand over hers. "That's right. It's the dagfish."

"Dog fish?" Nevie's brow pinched, making her look very much like her mother. The resemblance warmed his heart.

Viola watched, her hands pressed against her belly. Mother laid her hand on Viola's shoulder.

Through the windows that edged the front doors, Eric could see midday was fast approaching. Darkness had covered the land for so many years, but today the sun's ascent had become a herald of death. Eric's or Fenris's.

Nevandra's fingers traveled up Eric's armored chest and into his beard. He growled playfully as she tickled his chin.

She giggled and said, "Let's play cham bear."

Eric swept her up and stood. Kissed her cheek. "Not today, Nevie." He handed her off to Sabrea and approached his mother.

She embraced him. "I cannot lose you too," she whispered. "Not you too."

"I know, Mother." She didn't deserve to go through this. Not so soon after Father's death.

"My lord." Walter stood at Eric's elbow. "It's time."

Eric released his mother and faced the doors. Walter gave him a final once-over, produced a handkerchief from his breast pocket, and began buffing Eric's breastplate.

"Your daughter has left some fingerprints," he said. "I shall have them out in a moment."

Eric sighed. "Should I fret about getting my trousers dirty? Like a prancing dandy?"

Walter grunted and tucked his handkerchief back into his pocket. "No one in their right mind would ever confuse you for a prancing dandy, my lord, but the people of Tsaftown will come to see their lord. You must look the part."

And how many of those in attendance would come hoping to see Eric fall?

He presented himself to Viola. "Well, dearest, do I look the part of a lord?"

"Every bit." Viola smiled bitterly.

Eric embraced his wife. It was so natural for her to nestle in at his side, as if it were where she belonged. "Watch over our home." He forced himself to pull away. "I'll see you when I return."

"I'll be waiting for you." Viola's noble posture remained, even as the corners of her eyes moistened with tears.

Eric faced the exit and signaled to Ambrose. "You'll keep the hall secure while I'm gone, Master Ambrose?" he asked.

"Aye, my lord," Ambrose put his fist over his heart. "This is the North."

"This is the North." Eric set his fist over his own heart. "Let's be on our way, then."

Ambrose pushed open the towering oak doors.

"Northlanders! Present arms!" Captain Demry's sharp voice rang out.

"Guard, ready!" A chorus of voices called out in a response that echoed off the cobblestones.

Eric took several slow steps down into the courtyard and was taken aback by the display in front of him.

A formation of soldiers lined the front walkway of the court-yard. Captain Demry. Derby. Dunn. Quimby. Torin Oxbow and the rest of the Fighting Fifteen. Wroxton stood tall, a tabor drum slung over his good shoulder. Jeffrey waited beside him with a flute in hand. And dozens more men, many of whom had been proud members of the Fighting Five Hundred during the war, formed ranks behind the first row of soldiers.

Eric's chest swelled with pride.

"Your men are with you, my lord," Walter said from behind. "Fenris has his devotees, but not all of the city has fallen under his spell."

Eric marched down to the path. His armored shoes clacked on the stone path with each step. He held up his gauntleted fist and bellowed, "Northlanders, ho!"

"Ho!" the men responded.

"Many of you served my father with honor," Eric said, his words echoing off the courtyard walls. "He was proud of your strength. And your fighting spirit. You honored him with your service to House Livna. Though you can't enter the duel with me, I am strengthened by your loyalty."

"Long live House Livna!" Derby yelled.

"Long live House Livna!" the rest of the men called.

Eric made eye contact with each man as he approached the gates. When he reached them, he glanced back and saw that the soldiers had assembled behind him in a column, four abreast.

Wroxton's drum echoed in the open air, and Jeffrey's flute came to life, playing an energetic anthem. Gravel crackled underfoot as the entire assembly marched along the path toward the Dale.

VIOLA

Time was short. Viola secured her satchel and pulled the grey wool cloak over her shoulders. She had but a brief moment in the commotion of Eric's departure to slip past the guards.

Eric had asked her to stay in Lytton Hall, but Viola could not shake the certainty that Fenris would use Crow and his bloodvoice against Eric in the duel. If Viola was going to help, she had to sneak out of her own home.

And that was Lytton Hall. For so long, she'd felt like a stranger in these walls. But now? Nevandra had taken her first steps in the nursery. Her marriage had, against all odds, grown into a truly loving partnership here.

But now she needed to escape.

She turned a corner, eying the door to the study. No guard had been posted. She straightened, briskly entered the study, and froze.

"Viola." Lady Revada sat in one of the armchairs, casually reading. A cup of hot tea sat on the table in front of her.

Viola attempted to appear nonchalant, but something in Lady Revada's eyes told her that her mother-in-law already suspected what she was up to.

"I'm merely looking for a scroll. Something that might shed more light on the charter." The lie came too quickly.

"Merely?" Revada asked.

"Indeed," Viola said.

"It is a good idea. Eric can use all the help we can offer." Lady Revada's eyes narrowed, and she set her book down on the table. "I didn't have the chance to help my husband before he was killed. Do you know what I would have done?"

Viola lingered in the silence.

"I would have gone to any length to save him, even endangering my own life."

Viola nodded slowly. "As would I for Eric."

A weak smile curled Revada's mouth. "You look cold. I shall see to it that the fireplace here is restocked." She stood and crossed the room. When she reached Viola, she stopped and placed her hands gently on Viola's shoulders. "I left a tonic for you on the table. I understand it's quite helpful for calming one's thoughts."

Viola nodded slowly, uncertain. "I will keep that in mind."

Revada released her and continued to the door. "One more thing. A lady knows the value of a discreet exit. Please make sure you're not seen." With that, she departed and closed the door firmly on her way out.

Viola moved to the table and inspected the tonic. She popped the cork, wafted the glass bottle under her nose, and instantly recoiled at the unmistakable smell.

Âleh. The compound had only one purpose. To dull the minds of bloodvoicers.

Where had Revada gotten this?

It didn't matter. Clearly, she suspected the same thing as Viola. That Crow would attack Eric and had to be dealt with. One way or another.

Viola tucked the bottle in her satchel and quickly found the hidden lever on the bookshelf. The false wall opened, revealing a stone tunnel. The secret passage led outside, past the manor house's protective walls. Viola pressed her eyes shut for a moment. There would be no turning back once she left. She would have only her wits to protect herself. But it was necessary. For Eric. For Nevandra.

She disappeared down the passageway.

ERIC

Tiny flecks of snow flew into Eric's eyes as he approached the Dale. Hundreds had already assembled, despite the frigid weather, and Eric felt the weight of the crowd's gaze. The amphitheater was completely full, and countless more spectators stood in the yard. Several firepits had been lit on ground level, and many of the attendees clustered around them for warmth.

It appeared as though the entire city had turned out for the event.

The crowd parted for Eric and his honor guard, and they made their way toward the dueling rings. Low murmuring surrounded him as he passed through. Some bowed their heads respectfully and offered short encouragements.

The last of the crowd parted, giving Eric his first view of his battlefield: one of the six-sided fighting rings Fenris had used for his tournaments. The space was far from a proper dueling arena, marred with bare patches of uneven ground.

Spectators applauded as Eric stepped into the hexagon. On the opposite side of the ring, the eight members of the council sat on the same elevated platform they had occupied the day before. The Howlers, too, had resumed their position in front of the stage. Eric caught sight of Skunk's bulky form. The big, bearded man leaned on a tall war club next to Taggert.

Walter and the other members of Eric's honor guard filled in along the opposite edge of the hexagon, as if forming up for a pitched battle against Fenris's men.

Barking cheers rang out from the Howlers, who parted to let Fenris approach. He wore his black-and-green leather armor from the tournaments, but the most prominent piece of the ensemble was the large wolf pelt draped over his shoulders and head.

Fenris punched his fists into the air and marched around his end of the ring. Large sections of the crowd cheered and stamped their feet, no doubt expecting a good show like at Fenris's tournaments.

Fenris removed the wolf pelt and retrieved his helmet from one of the Howlers. Only then did Eric realize that neither Ikârd nor Cernell Crow were among the faces in the crowd. Perhaps Fenris assumed that the blind man would be of no use during the duel. But Ikârd? He had virtually been Fenris's shadow for months. What could possibly have taken him away from this moment?

Eric gripped the hilt of his sword. There was no point in distracting himself. Fenris was his focus. Nothing else.

The snowfall grew heavier. Brisk flurries swirled around the large circular structure. Many in the crowd huddled together or drew closer to the fires. But no one in the amphitheater moved to leave. It seemed that everyone, both combatant and spectator, were committed to seeing the contest through to the end.

Erlichman stepped to the center of the stage. He wore an over-large robe woven with blue and gold thread that was even more ostentatious than his typical attire. He raised his hands above his head, a posture that was perhaps meant to mimic Fenris's bravado but fell short.

"Good people of Tsaftown!" he cried over the sound of the wind. "We are gathered in this place to witness a great contest. But this is no mere exhibition. This is a formal duel to settle a dispute between two noblemen, dictated by the oldest customs of the Northlander Charter. Let the two competitors step forward!"

Eric took a deep breath, laced with smoke from the fires, and stepped into the center of the ring. Fenris sauntered forward slowly. Restrained rage smoldered behind his eyes as he stared Eric down in the center of the ring. Would the blackguard charge and try to take Eric down right then and there?

"As the rules of the charter state," Erlichman said, "each man is allowed one weapon. The duel shall be settled when one man yields—or is killed. Outside interference of any kind will not be tolerated and will result in an automatic forfeit."

Fenris grinned wildly. "Hear that, Little Eric? It's just you and me. Last chance to back out."

Flecks of snow landed on Eric's face, just below his eye, but he kept his expression stoic, as he had seen Viola do when someone tried to get a rise out of her.

"Think of little Nevandra," Fenris said. "Do her a favor and yield right now before this gets messy."

Eric touched the dagfish on his chest where Nevie had smudged his armor. How he hated hearing his daughter's name in Fenris's foul mouth.

Steel raked across wood as Eric pulled his sword from its scabbard. "I will hear nothing you have to say until you yield the fight." He planted his feet and set his sword at midguard.

Fenris chuckled and licked the inside of his cheek. "So be it." He drew his own blade, which was a narrower sword meant for slashing. He'd likely use swift strikes to counter Eric's power attacks.

The two withdrew, taking the traditional ten paces back from one another. Walter stepped into the arena with Eric's helmet and secured it over his head.

The valet clapped a hand on Eric's shoulder. "Arman be with you."

Eric turned back to the interior of the ring as Fenris donned his own helmet, streaked with crude lines of blood. A hush hung over the crowd as Eric and Fenris took their positions.

A page stepped up on the stage and presented Erlichman with a conch shell that had been carved into a ceremonial horn. He hefted the conch to his lips.

Snow blanketed the ground. Eric shifted his feet, searching for sound footing. Across the ring, Fenris whirled his blade a few times, then sank into position.

Eric clenched his teeth.

The conch blew.

Chapter Twenty-Two
Eric

MOVE. NO TIME TO WASTE.

Eric stormed to the center of the ring, taking the fight to Fenris.

Fenris withdrew, moving back and to Eric's left. Eric maintained his pursuit, measuring his steps. He'd expected Fenris to target his legs, but his cousin kept his distance, likely trying to bait Eric into overreaching.

So Eric stepped forward and feigned a strong attack, leaving his legs vulnerable. Fenris, eager to seize the opening, swung toward Eric's unguarded thigh.

Eric altered the angle of his blade and deflected the strike. Fenris stumbled forward, leaving his flank wide open. Eric's sword wasn't in a position for an attack, so he launched a powerful kick and caught Fenris in the ribs.

Fenris staggered sideways, barely keeping himself from tumbling on the ground. Eric pressed his advantage and swung his sword down at Fenris's back. Again Fenris skittered out of Eric's reach. He'd failed to capitalize on Fenris's stumble, but so far Eric had control of the fight.

He made a steady pursuit, shifting his sword to low guard, and slashed at Fenris's ankle.

A knife of ice stabbed into Eric's temple.

His blade went off course and dug into the frozen ground. Chunks of ice and dirt showered Fenris's back as he darted away. The impact reverberated up the blade and stung Eric's cold fingers. Instinct alone kept the hilt in his hand.

Câan's mercy. Had he been hit? The pain subsided to a dull throb. Eric pulled his focus back to the fight, and not a moment too soon. Fenris had regrouped and came in with a high strike at Eric's head.

Eric got his sword up in time to block, but the attack caught him off guard and pushed him back onto his heels. Fenris's blade pressed closer, nearly into Eric's chin. The pressure threatened to double Eric over backward. He felt Fenris turning his blade, attempting to wrench Eric's sword out of his hands.

He twisted his own blade, locking the two swords at the cross guards. It was a contest of strength, except Eric's feet were out of position. He started to slip backward on the snowy ground. Fenris's hot breath warmed his face as they pressed harder, trying to overpower each other.

In desperation, Eric gripped the pommel of his sword with his left hand and shoved hard. The swift movement broke the sword lock.

Fenris's momentum threw him past Eric, and he sprawled onto the ground. The crowd gasped. Eric regained his footing. Fenris's flank was open, so Eric raised his sword and—again, cold fire stabbed his temple.

He stumbled to one knee. His position was death if he stayed there. His head throbbed with a relentless pulse, but Eric forced himself back up to his feet.

Cinders. This must be that accursed bloodvoicer. It could be no one else. Mother and Viola had been right. Crow was attacking his mind. Eric thought the old thief would be too weak to harm him, but the throbbing ache in his temples testified to the contrary.

Fenris rose back to his feet and wagged his finger. "Tsk, tsk, Little Eric. Mind your manners."

Eric gritted his teeth and tried to ignore the bloodvoicer's attack. The cold air stung his lungs as he tried to catch his breath. He needed to keep his wits about him, but the fight had changed. With the bloodvoicer's attacks pecking away at Eric's mind, a prolonged fight would favor Fenris. He could simply wait until Crow's mental jabs sapped Eric's strength, then finish him off.

Eric needed to press the attack against Fenris. Get in a swift strike before Crow could stop him.

Fenris stood twenty paces away and twirled his blade. "Shall we continue?"

Stray snowflakes blew into Eric's face, stinging his cheeks. He exhaled, blowing a cloud of warm mist into the air.

"Arman give me strength," he muttered. Then he charged Fenris once again.

VIOLA

"Cernell Crow!" Viola rapped her knuckles against the back door of the Black Boar Inn. Her tone was unladylike, but she would make enough racket to be heard.

The latch shifted from the inside. The door swung open, revealing the blind bloodvoicer wrapped in a shabby cloak that hung loosely from his gaunt frame.

"Is that you, your ladyship?" Master Crow asked.

Viola stood straighter. "I would speak to you."

"Bah." Crow's scowl deepened. "I'm occupied."

Snow collected on Viola's shoulders, and she pulled her cloak tighter. "And what if I had use of your services at this moment?"

"Cut the pretense, my lady," Crow said. "I'll not help your husband in his duel. My loyalty is not so easily bought."

"If not your loyalty, then just your time." Viola pulled a bottle of ale out of her satchel and pressed it into Crow's hand. His clammy skin was unsettling to touch.

Crow uncorked the bottle. His nose wrinkled upon inhaling the liquor's potent aroma, but then something like a smile stretched across his face. "Ahh." He took a quick swig from the bottle. "Very nice, I must say. I'd guess that's made in Meribah? Aged ten years?"

"Berland. Thirty years," Viola said. "Distilled before Darkness."

Crow took another generous drink and recoiled. No wonder. Berland whiskey was one of the most potent spirits available in this part of Er'Rets.

"Ah-ha. That's worth somethin'." Crow cackled and stepped back into the room.

Viola followed the man inside. Somehow the space looked no less bleak during the day than it had in the black of night. No candles lit the windowless room, but what use would Crow have for them? Daylight leaked in through cracks in the wall, providing only the faintest semblance of proper light.

Crow tapped his way over to the chairs with his walking stick and slumped down. Viola sat across from him. She felt the urge to rush. To convince him quickly. But she knew well that hurrying a man like Crow would be a futile effort. She needed to keep him talking and drinking. That would at least distract him from the duel.

"You spoke of loyalty." Viola settled her satchel on the small table between them. "What has Sir Fenris done to earn your steadfast devotion? Surely his ale cannot taste that sweet."

Crow sipped at the bottle. "Freeing me from Ice Island was not enough?"

"How long does that one favor bind you to him?" Viola asked.

"You clearly enjoy his ale and coin, but he cannot be an easy man to serve."

Master Crow grunted. "Indeed. Men like Sir Fenris don't take kindly to people leavin' their service. His favors are lavish, but his anger...equally so."

"Then how can I convince you to leave this alone?" Viola said. "Make it a fair fight."

Master Crow cackled. "Fair? Unfairness is the only constant for anyone. All the world is..." He trailed off, as if lost in thought.

Viola reached out and gripped his arm. "You're fighting Eric now, aren't you?"

The bloodvoicer jerked back and rubbed his temple as his focus returned to the conversation at hand. "Hmm? Not exactly fighting. A little mental jab here or there."

The cloud over Viola's mind darkened. Eric was fighting for his life at that very moment, and here was proof that Crow was helping him lose.

"Who benefits from Sir Fenris becoming lord of Tsaftown?" Viola asked. "Sir Fenris, of course. And his closest lieutenants. Anyone else?"

"Why should that concern me?" Crow asked.

"Because many people in this city are still struggling from the years in Darkness. House Livna has taken efforts to fix those problems. Do you honestly think Sir Fenris Yarden, as lord of this city, would help anyone but himself?"

Crow adjusted the band that covered his eyes. "That's between Fenris and the gods. If he wishes to dirty his soul further, I say let him."

"And what of your soul?" Viola added. "'If anyone knows the good he ought to do and doesn't do it, he trespasses against Arman.' If you help Sir Fenris, his every foul act will hang on your shoulders. Every starving child. Every woman taken advantage of by those wretched Howlers. You will have played a part in it all."

Crow set the bottle on the table and slouched into his chair. His anger seemed to have broken, like a fever burning itself out.

"Many claim to sympathize with the less fortunate," he muttered. "Yet none have ever risked anything meaningful for my sake. Why should I risk Sir Fenris's rage for a bunch of strangers?"

Viola could imagine the hardships Master Crow had suffered in life, but that didn't give the man leave to harm others. "You say no one has done anything to help you, yet here you sit unwilling to inconvenience yourself for the sake of others. If you cannot see the hypocrisy in that, then your blindness has clearly spread from your eyes to your heart."

Crow's face tensed. Was he thinking about her words? Or interfering in the duel? Again, Viola forced down thoughts of the tragic outcomes of the battle.

"Why not simply kill me?" Crow asked. "If you suspected I might be working against your husband, the easiest way to deal with me would be to poison the whiskey. So why didn't you?"

Viola reached into the satchel and produced the bottle left for her by Lady Revada. "I will admit I considered some devious tactics." She uncorked the bottle and handed it to Crow. "I believe you're familiar with this potion?"

Crow sniffed the bottle and blanched. "Wretched âleh. Why didn't you use it?"

Viola had weighed that exact question on her entire journey to the inn. "Treachery often has unintended consequences. I wanted to treat you like a man and not a problem to be fixed." She leaned in closer, laying her hands on the small table. "I came here with the hope that I might be able to convince a man to do what he knew to be right all along."

Crow weighed her words and set the bottle on the table. "Yet you want me to betray my employer. What would Arman think of such a thing?"

The poison had faded from Crow's voice, leaving a trace of bitter humor that softened his words.

"Depends on the employer, I suppose," Viola said. "Perhaps you are due for a new one."

ERIC

Every sword strike took its toll on Eric, but he didn't let his guard down for a moment. Victory was in reach if he held on a little longer.

Fenris's blade came in high and from the right. Eric sidestepped to keep Fenris in front of him, but each step was a struggle, as if he carried lead in his boots.

Steel met steel. Eric's bones rattled as he blocked a pair of swift strikes. The two locked swords again. Eric broke away and swung at Fenris's exposed side. His blade struck true, catching Fenris's armored torso and knocking him backward.

Eric tried to reset his feet, but his boot snagged on a clump of frozen ground, and he stumbled into the railing and the line of Howlers. Rough hands seized him and pulled at his armor.

"Sir Fenris is gonna gut you," a harsh voice said.

A thick hand wrapped around his neck and twisted his helmet.

Eric swung his arm wildly. His steel gauntlet cracked against the man's head. The Howler cried out and Eric escaped his grip. His twisted helmet blocked his vision. With gauntlets on his hands, he couldn't fix it, so he ripped it off. This left his head exposed, but he couldn't fight if he couldn't see.

Fenris barreled toward him and slashed his blade through the air. Eric blocked the wild strike. Then another that came at his neck. Then another. And another. All aimed at Eric's head. Persistent. And predictable. Eric moved as fast as he could, knowing the bloodvoicer could attack again at any moment.

As Fenris came in with yet another high swing, Eric ducked and swung at his cousin's armored thigh. His sword cut into the leather cuisse. Fenris sank into a crouch and grabbed his leg. Eric lunged forward, raising his sword to strike again, but Fenris whirled and threw a fistful of snow into Eric's face.

The snow stung his eyes. He frantically brushed it out of his face while swinging blindly to keep Fenris from charging in and finishing him off.

Eric forced open one eye against the grit and melted snow just in time to parry a cut toward his neck. Fenris pressed forward. Eric managed to meet every strike but gradually gave up ground to the onslaught.

Yet even as the clash continued, Eric sensed a change. His vision cleared, and he saw where each strike would come a moment before it landed, giving him ample time to block. Fenris made no effort to change his attack pattern. The blade came at Eric's head. Then his right arm. Then his left arm. Then his chest. And the sequence repeated.

Fenris was a savage warrior. He'd no doubt had to defend himself on Ice Island but never had need to fight with swords and armor. Even during his tournament duels, he had chosen smaller, weaker opponents, all for show. Fenris was dangerous, but he had no endurance.

Eric wove a defensive tapestry with his blade. And waited.

The next time Fenris aimed for Eric's chest, he blocked the strike, then stepped forward, twisted his blade, and shoved the pommel of his sword toward Fenris's neck. The cross guard slid through the gap in Fenris's armor and slammed into his clavicle.

Fenris backpedaled, clutching at his throat. Eric forced his weary legs into a lumbering charge. Fenris failed to get his sword up in time, and Eric slammed his shoulder into his cousin's chest.

The collision echoed through the arena. Fenris crumpled into the snow. Pain racked Eric's shoulder, and he fell to one knee.

The spectators held their collective breath, stunned into silence.

Swirling lights danced across Eric's vision, and his hands shook as the adrenaline in his body burned against the frigid air.

Fenris lay sprawled on his back, gasping for breath. His sword lay in the snow several paces away.

Eric needed to get up. His joints screamed as he stood to his full height. The tang of iron hit his tongue, and he felt blood in the corner of his mouth.

But he stood. Sword in his hand.

Fenris rolled over and reached for his blade.

Eric stalked toward him. One swift strike to the neck and it would all end.

Mercy.

The thought brought Eric up short. As a soldier, there was no question what to do. Even as a lord, he was entitled to deliver swift judgment for Fenris's actions. Yet as he looked down on his cousin, Eric only saw a broken man lying defenseless on the ground.

Eric stopped a pace away. "It's over, Fenris. Yield."

Fenris pushed up to his hands and knees and crawled toward his sword.

Someone in the crowd cried out, "Finish him!"

Cold air stung the sweat on Eric's exposed neck. He prodded Fenris's side with his blade. "I said yield."

Fenris continued his desperate crawl toward his blade.

Eric sighed. He marched forward and kicked Fenris's sword even farther out of reach. Then he stomped on the man's outstretched hand.

Fenris yelped as the armored foot crushed his fingers.

Eric laid his sword gently at the nape of his cousin's neck. "It's over, Fenris."

Chapter Twenty-Three
Eric

"Erlichman!" Fenris yelled. "Do something, you fool!" He tried in vain to pull his hand out from under Eric's foot.

Eric glared across the arena at Erlichman, whose eyes bulged.

"The fight cannot be stopped," Councilor Okerlund cried out. "It continues until death or yielding."

Eric looked down on Fenris. "Yield. You have lost."

Fenris went rigid for a moment, then growled, "Very well." He relaxed the hand beneath Eric's boot. "Would you at least give me the honor of standing?"

Eric held his blade against Fenris's neck. "You can yield from where you are."

Fenris groaned and spat blood into the snow. "I yield the duel."

"Louder. So they can hear you."

Fenris growled again, then took a deep breath. "I yield!"

Cheers erupted around the arena. In Eric's peripheral vision, his men still stood ready. Fenris's word alone wasn't enough to convince the Fighting Fifteen to stand down.

A shocked expression clung to Erlichman's face. "Sir Fenris

Yarden has yielded the duel." His voice had lost its previous showmanship.

Eric expelled a slow breath and took half a step back, allowing Fenris to push up to one knee.

Fenris removed his helmet, and his tangled mess of blond curls tumbled down his shoulders. He looked up at Eric with a sidelong glare. "But...it's not over yet."

A flash of steel shone in the daylight. Fenris whipped a small, curved dagger at Eric. The strike scraped off Eric's armored shin, and he scrambled away, raising his sword again.

Blast it all. Of course Fenris wouldn't simply accept defeat.

Fenris cursed and staggered toward the pack of Howlers in the front of the stage. "Kill him!" he yelled.

Seeing their hero defeated had not quelled the Howlers' loyalty to him.

Skunk raised his club above his head. "Charge!"

The rest of the Howlers drew weapons and hopped the barricade into the ring.

Eric raised his sword. He wouldn't last long against such a mob, but he could take a few out with him.

Instead of leading the charge, Fenris slipped away from the fight. Taggert charged forward, fisting his stolen Poroo dagger. Apparently, the Howlers hadn't surrendered all their trophies. Eric set his feet as best he could and prepared for the onslaught.

The sound of footsteps crunching through the snow came from behind. A shock of grey hair flashed in front of Eric. Walter swung the flat of his blade at Taggert, catching the man in the shoulder and knocking him to the ground.

The rest of the Howlers advanced. Walter blocked a strike from an ax. Eric stepped up and covered Walter's flank.

"Northlanders, ho!" Captain Demry called.

"Ho!" came the old rallying cry.

Captain Demry broke into the melee. Lovell Dunn and Derby

leaped to Eric's side. Jol Quimby charged forward. Even Wroxton entered the fray, carrying a shield to protect Captain Demry's flank. Tsaftown's Fighting Fifteen powered ahead, engaging Fenris's Howlers.

Cries filled the air as the gathered crowd fled the skirmish. The sound of punches, club blows, and sword strikes clashed around the tangled knot of fighters. Just as quickly as it had started, it became clear that Fenris's men were outmatched. One Howler after another hit the ground, beaten and bruised.

The tide quickly turned in the Northlanders' favor. Skunk stood at the center of the fight, delivering blow after blow with his war club. The big man seemed convinced he could take on the entirety of the Fighting Fifteen single-handedly.

Skunk swung his club in wide errant arcs. "For Sir Fenris!"

Captain Demry advanced on Skunk, and the two men traded blows.

Derby got around Skunk's flank and cut into the large man's thigh. The brute groaned and stumbled to the ground, clutching his wounded leg.

Eric smiled, proud of the progress the young soldier had shown.

"Down with House Livna!" a man yelled.

Taggert lunged, his knife arching straight for Eric's neck.

Someone knocked into Eric from the side. His gelatinous legs buckled under the impact, and he fell. His head spun. Had he been stabbed? He felt no new pain.

Oxbow and Quimby had knocked over the would-be assassin and pinned him to the ground.

"My lord." Walter stood over Eric, stretching out his hand.

Eric accepted and pulled himself up, but Walter stumbled. Suddenly Eric was supporting the weight of his valet. Only then did he see the red stains blossoming on Walter's tunic below where Taggert's knife stuck out from his side.

"Walter, you old fool." Eric held his friend tight and knelt, lowered him gently to the ground.

Walter gripped Eric's shoulder, leaving a bloody handprint. "My lord, I appear to have stained your armor."

Câan's mercy. How had this happened?

"Blast it, he got Walter," Dunn said as he knelt beside Eric. "Don't remove the knife. He'll only bleed out faster."

"Rubart!" Captain Demry bellowed over the ruckus of the crowd.

"Just hold on," Eric said to Walter. "Hold on."

Arman, please. Just let him hold on.

Walter coughed, a horrible gurgling sound, and thrashed. Eric and Dunn fought to keep him still.

"My lord…" The valet wheezed with each breath. Bloody spittle formed at the corners of his mouth.

"Don't try to speak, Walter," Eric said. "Lie still."

But Walter persisted. He took a slow, labored breath. "My…my lord…are…are you…"

"Speak to him, my lord," Dunn said. "It will help."

Eric nodded. "I'm fine, Walter. You stopped him." He needed to say more. But what? "Not bad for an old muskrat."

Shadows shifted on the ground. The grey clouds had parted, and a ray of sunshine fell upon the arena. The new light bathed Walter's grey hair and beard with a golden hue. His chest raised as his lungs filled with air again.

"Muskrat…your father called me…" Walter's head lolled back, settling onto the snowy ground.

"No." Eric's voice sounded hollow in his own head. This couldn't be happening. Blasted ashes, no one was supposed to die today. "Arman," Eric prayed through gritted teeth. "Arman, please. Do something."

"My lord," Captain Demry whispered in Eric's ear. "Rubart is here."

Eric nodded and dragged himself to his feet.

The squat old healer pushed his way into the circle that had formed around Walter.

"He's still breathing," Dunn said. "He's just gone still."

"Help him, Rubart. Please." Eric hadn't meant to sound so desperate, but at this moment, he didn't care.

"I'll get him fixed up properly, my lord." The old healer sounded more sincere than his typical crotchety self.

Eric stepped away from them. The Howlers had been rounded up into a circle and made to kneel in the snow. A dozen members of the Fighting Fifteen trained their weapons on them.

A small crowd of onlookers remained, observing the scene that had unfolded in the Dale. On the stage, the council members stood watching as well. All except Erlichman, who seemed to have vanished in the chaos.

Eric's pulse quickened. He scanned the ring of prisoners again. Then the crowd. He examined each and every face, yet he couldn't find the one man he was searching for.

"Where is he?" Eric muttered. "Where is Fenris?"

VIOLA

Eric was alive. Crow had bloodvoiced Viola that much about the conclusion of the duel before he'd severed his connection. She could barely contain her relief.

Ember's hooves clacked on the courtyard stone as Viola returned to Lytton Hall. She had contemplated riding to the Dale, but Eric had been right. It was not safe there. Though her heart ached to see her husband, the best place to await his return was at home.

As she neared the stables, panicked voices echoed across the courtyard. The front doors to Lytton Hall hung open.

A tingle shot up Viola's spine. She urged Ember toward the doors where she dismounted haphazardly, raced up the front steps, and gasped.

Someone lay limp in the front foyer. Master Ambrose. Crimson splotches from a series of chest wounds stained his shirt and sideburns. Viola thought to help him, but he was clearly gone. The kind man's beautiful baritone voice had been silenced forever.

Lytton Hall had been attacked.

Nevandra.

Viola ran into the house and up the stairs. She nearly tripped on her skirts, but she dared not slow her pace.

She stormed into the nursery, saw Sabrea sitting on the floor, bawling into her hands. A shelf had been knocked over, and odd puffs of cotton covered the floor.

Viola's heart lurched, and a cold sweat broke across her brow as her eyes darted frantically around the room. "Where is she? Where is my daughter?"

Sabrea looked up. A fresh bruise had purpled her cheek. "I tried...I tried to stop them, milady, but I...I couldn't."

A hollow ache settled in Viola's chest. "Where is Nevandra?"

Sabrea covered her face with her hands and sobbed.

Viola wanted to grab Sabrea and shake her, but the woman was already traumatized.

"I'm so sorry." Lathia's voice came from behind her.

Viola whirled around. Lathia stood in the doorway, clutching her chest. No. Clutching a scrap of fabric.

"Connor said he had something to tell me." Lathia's voice came so softly she was difficult to hear. "So I opened the secret door in the study and waited for him to arrive. But he didn't come alone. They all pushed in, and Connor...he shoved me down."

Howlers? Viola's face tingled. It couldn't be true. It simply couldn't.

Lathia reached out and handed Viola the fabric she'd been holding.

Nevandra's stuffed rabbit.

The belly had been slashed and all the filling ripped out.

A tear streaked down Lathia's cheek. "They have Nevandra."

Chapter Twenty-Four
Viola

THE COLD DIDN'T MATTER. NOR DID the dwindling daylight. Viola would ride across the entirety of Er'Rets to get her daughter back.

The setting sun stretched the shadows of the trees as Viola and Lathia followed the trail Sir Fenris's men had taken through the forest. Branches and underbrush crunched under their horses' hooves, but they made no attempt to muffle the sounds of their approach. This was no surprise attack. It was a desperate attempt to negotiate with a madman for Nevandra's life.

Lathia had wanted to find a solider to escort them, but there was no time. Every moment that Nevandra spent in Sir Fenris's clutches was a moment too long.

The trail grew narrow and harder to follow. Just as Viola felt hope slipping away, she spotted distant firelight flickering through the labyrinth of trees. That had to be Sir Fenris's camp. Before she could decide how to proceed, two men approached on foot, both wielding spears.

"Who goes there?" one of them barked.

Viola straightened her back, fighting to keep herself from shaking in the cold. "Ladies Viola and Lathia Livna of Tsaftown. We're here to negotiate."

The man took a step closer and pointed the tip of his weapon at Viola's chest. "And no one else, my lady?"

Viola dismounted. "This is no trap," she said. "If my husband were here, you both would have been cut into stew meat by now. Take us to Sir Fenris this instant."

The men led them forward through a tangle of trees that forced Lathia to dismount as well. They finally emerged into a small hollow in the trees. The Howlers had made a fire and set out a few crates of supplies, but they appeared to have brought little with them besides their horses and weapons.

Viola and Lathia tied their horses to the trunks of two sturdy pine trees and followed the spearmen toward the fire. The other men leered at them as they approached. Some had fresh cuts and bruises on their faces and hands. Had there been a skirmish after the duel?

Viola now felt the absence of an escort. She should have tried to find Eric and formulate a plan, but there hadn't been time.

Besides, she already had a plan. One that Eric would have locked her away for even considering. But it was, as far as Viola could tell, the best way to get her daughter home safely.

She glimpsed Sir Fenris's golden hair in the midst of his men, next to the fire. His heavily bandaged hand and blood-stained beard testified to the brutality of the duel.

What wounds had Eric received in that fight?

Focus. Eric was alive. That was all she needed to know for now. The task at hand required her full focus.

The firelight revealed more faces behind Sir Fenris. Ikârd and Connor Clave lurked in the shadows. And Councilor Erlichman, the spineless snake, sat on a fallen log next to the fire looking quite out of place amongst the Howlers.

Viola took Lathia's hand. "Stay quiet and let me handle this," she whispered. "We're here for Nevandra. No matter what happens to me, get her and fly like a nor'easter back to Tsaftown. You understand?"

Lathia nodded.

Viola approached the campfire.

Sir Fenris met her eyes and bowed. "Greetings, my lady. Come join me. It seems we have many things to discuss."

"Mama!"

Viola's heart leaped. Across from Councilor Erlichman, Nevandra sat on a log, her hands and feet bound. Dirt covered her face, and long streaks trailed down her cheeks where tears had fallen. A Howler sat beside her, his hand firmly gripping the back of her neck. If these animals had hurt her...

Viola took a slow breath. Calm. She must stay calm. "It's okay, sweetheart," she said. "Mama is here to get you."

"Don't hurt her," Lathia cried. "Please don't."

Viola fixed Lathia with a stare and placed a finger over her lips. This situation was fraught enough without her bringing emotion into it.

Sir Fenris stepped around the fire and stopped in front of Viola. "I have no intention of hurting the girl, nor will I simply let her go. Not without the proper incentive."

"What do you want?" Viola asked.

Sir Fenris stroked his beard. "What are you prepared to give up?"

What was the point of this? Surely he and his men had better things to do than play mind games with her in the middle of nowhere.

"Name your price," Viola said. Nevandra's life was in the balance. Nothing was off the table, and she saw no point in feigning otherwise.

"How deeply a mother's love runs," Sir Fenris said. "Love drives us toward much. One could say it opens many doors. Wouldn't you agree, Lady Lathia?"

He chuckled and his men joined in. One man gave Connor Clave a jubilant shove.

The lad shoved back. "Step off, dung heaps."

Lathia covered her face with her hands. All their careful planning to protect House Livna undone by one girl's foolish heart. Seeing Lathia get her comeuppance might have been amusing under other circumstances, but they were beyond that now.

"Enough," Viola said. "State your demands."

"Very well, my lady," Sir Fenris said. "I hold the life of your daughter in my hands. If you and Eric want her back, then he must abdicate and leave his title of lordship to me."

The demand was laughable. Lordship of a city was not a bargaining chip that could simply be traded. Except Viola knew Sir Fenris. The validity of his demand didn't matter. He would do anything, even harm Nevandra, to get what he wanted.

Councilor Erlichman stood up from his seat on the log and grabbed Sir Fenris's shoulder. "This is madness. She cannot make that sort of deal. And now that Eric Livna defeated you publicly, the people of the city wouldn't accept—"

Sir Fenris seized Erlichman's throat. "Respectfully, Councilor, we tried it your way. I sat by while you schemed and played your political games. But you failed. Miserably."

Councilor Erlichman's eyes bulged as he gasped for breath.

"From now on, I'm in charge," Sir Fenris said. "Understand?"

The councilor croaked out a whispered, "Yes."

The pathetic reply seemed to satisfy Sir Fenris, who shoved Councilor Erlichman backward and chuckled darkly as the man scurried back to the safety of his perch on the log.

"Now, my wonderful Lady Viola," Sir Fenris said, "can you give me what I want?"

May Eric forgive her for what she had to do. "Let her go. Lathia can take her back to Tsaftown." She lowered her voice, speaking in a conspiratorial whisper. "We both know that I'm a far greater prize to you."

Shock shone in Sir Fenris's eyes. Her veiled proposition appeared to have taken him completely off guard. He chuckled softly, licking the inside of his cheek. "Well, my lady, I'll admit that's an enticing notion. You are a prize, indeed." His thoughts seemed to drift, then he shook his head. "However, it's simply not good enough. An innocent child makes a better hostage."

Viola's heart raced. Was she about to lose everything so quickly? This was her family. She must hold nothing back.

She took a slow step until she was but an arm's length from Sir Fenris. "I can provide that as well."

Sir Fenris's brow wrinkled. "What?"

Viola swallowed slowly, praying her bluff would work. "Right now, you hold my daughter. Eric's firstborn. Take me instead"—Viola slid her hand over her belly—"and you will have his heir."

A long moment hung between them. Sir Fenris's gaze darted down to Viola's abdomen, then back up as understanding slowly bloomed on his face.

"Viola!" Lathia gasped. "You're—" She covered her mouth, cutting herself off.

"A son?" Sir Fenris asked.

Viola nodded slowly. "Recently conceived."

Some of the Howlers murmured at this revelation.

"And you *know* it's a boy?" Doubt clung to Sir Fenris's voice.

Viola conjured an air of brazen confidence, reminiscent of an expression her mother wore often. "I'm a woman of Jaelport. We understand such things."

Sir Fenris stroked his beard. "Why would you give me your heir?"

"You said yourself, a mother's love is a potent type of incentive, especially where her daughter is concerned." Viola hated the poisonous words as she said them. "But the fate of a male child will matter more to Eric."

Sir Fenris's eyes bored into her as he contemplated the proposal. "No tricks?" he asked, with a note of intrigue in his voice. "No plotting with your feminine wiles?"

Viola held her hands out, wrists pressed against each other to pantomime bindings. "I'm at your mercy, Sir Fenris."

A twisted smile crossed his lips. "Mercy?" Then he roared with a mad cackle that carried through the barren trees.

Had he lost some of his senses? Not even Sir Fenris's entourage seemed to understand what had caused this sudden outburst.

He sighed contentedly. "Mercy indeed, my lady. I find this arrangement satisfactory."

He gave a quick nod, and Ikârd rounded the fire. The brute pressed a gag against Viola's mouth. The tang of stale sweat filled her senses as Ikârd wrapped the cloth roughly around the back of her head. She had known she was putting herself in danger by surrendering to Sir Fenris. Suddenly the peril felt much more real.

Sir Fenris smirked with twisted self-satisfaction. "Lady Lathia, take the girl and go. Tell Eric that I have his bride and his heir and that if he wishes to see either of them again, he will surrender the city to me by sundown tomorrow. Otherwise, I shall send his bride back to him in pieces."

He spun and marched past the fire. "Break camp. We make for the lodge at Lake Choshek. Move!"

The Howlers scurried to gather their supplies. The man holding Nevandra cut her bonds and hauled her roughly over to Lathia. Nevandra wrapped her arms and legs around Lathia, but her eyes searched the camp until she found Viola.

"Mama?" She reached an arm toward her.

Viola's heart shattered. She wanted to tell Nevandra to be brave, but the gag in her mouth kept her silent.

Sir Fenris stepped between them, blocking Viola's view. He tied her wrists with coarse rope and cinched it so tightly that Viola fought not to betray her pain.

He ran his finger under her chin. "Come along, my dear," he said. "I have the most charming little place up in the mountains. It's not as comfortable as Lytton Hall, but it's pleasant enough. Perhaps your husband will even see fit to join us."

Sir Fenris dragged Viola away, causing her to stumble over the snowy terrain. Nevandra's cries followed her into the shadows.

CHAPTER TWENTY-FIVE
ERIC

THE TASTE OF BLOOD LINGERED IN ERic's mouth, but not enough to be worried. Not now. Lytton Hall had been attacked, one of House Livna's guards had been murdered, and Viola, Lathia, and Nevie were all missing.

Eric lumbered into the great hall. Captain Demry's men stood guard, ready to protect the manor house, inside and out. Even some of the veteran soldiers from the Fighting Five Hundred had assembled to help.

Eric's mother sat at the head table. Even from this distance, he could see the shock plain on her face. Lytton Hall had been breached for the second time in her life.

Eric clenched his fist. He ought to go comfort her, but now wasn't the time. He had to know where his wife, daughter, and cousin had been taken.

Captain Demry stood at one of the tables speaking with Sabrea and De'Lana. The nanny held her head in her hands. De'Lana ran her hand down Sabrea's back in a comforting motion.

Eric marched up and stopped beside Captain Demry. "What happened?" he asked.

Sabrea cowered and kept her eyes on the table. "I'm sorry, mi-lord." Her words were barely a whimper.

"She says the Howlers charged in during the duel," Captain Demry said in a hushed tone. "They took Mistress Nevandra and fought their way out. Your wife and Lady Lathia left soon after."

So only Nevandra had been taken. "Did anyone else see anything?" Eric asked.

Captain Demry shook his head. "Sabrea was the only one with your daughter in the nursery when it happened."

Eric pounded on the table across from Sabrea. "Think! Did Viola say where they were heading?"

Sabrea glanced up and shrank away from Eric. Tears streaked down her flushed cheeks. "I don't know. I just—" Her voice broke, and she buried her face in her hands.

Not good enough. She had to know something. "Did you at least see—?"

Captain Demry grabbed Eric's shoulder and squeezed. "My lord, I've spoken with her. She's said everything she's able to tell us."

There was a softness in Captain Demry's voice. The care of a father. Demry's daughter was only a few years younger than Sabrea, and he no doubt had a clearer head than Eric at the moment.

Cinders. How much of a fool was Eric? Sabrea had been through a terrifying ordeal. What good could possibly come from yelling at the poor girl?

Eric stood up straight. "I'm sorry, Sabrea. I shouldn't have raised my voice. De'Lana, why don't you take her to rest?"

De'Lana nodded and helped Sabrea up from the table.

Eric faced Captain Demry. "Thank you, Captain. I have much on my mind at the moment."

"Of course, my lord." Captain Demry's stoic demeanor was firmly back in place.

But where did that leave them? Their one lead for finding the women had gone immediately cold.

"My lord." Captain Demry pointed to the door.

Torin Oxbow entered the hall, leading a woman—no. Leading Lathia, who carried Nevie.

The crowd of men parted as Eric crossed the hall as quickly as his limp would allow. He pulled his daughter away from Lathia and into his own arms. Nevie hugged Eric's neck and buried her face in his chest.

"Papa," Nevie cried.

"It's okay, sweetheart." He ran his hand slowly down her back. "Papa is here. Papa is right here."

Eric comforted her until his mother came up beside him and laid a hand on Nevie's shoulder. The hall and people fell away from his mind. He needed to make sure his family was safe.

But his family wasn't all here.

Eric shifted Nevie to his other arm and turned his attention on Lathia. "Where is my wife?" he demanded.

Lathia, typically full of bluster, merely stared at the floor. "I didn't mean for this to happen."

"Lathia..." Eric groaned. The Howlers had used one of the secret passages to break into Lytton Hall, and Eric hadn't seen Clave at the duel. He had little doubt that the young man had been part of the group that had attacked the hall. Lathia might not have wanted this disaster to happen, but she had certainly played a part in it.

"It wasn't..." She paused, her tears choking her, and cleared her throat. "She went to Fenris. Traded herself and her baby for Nevandra."

Eric's mother gasped.

Viola had gone without him. Made a deal with Fenris without him. And now...

"Baby?" Eric asked. That was impossible, wasn't it?

There was the feeling of everyone else in the hall, soldiers and serving staff alike, saying nothing in a very definite way.

Eric cleared his mind. This revelation, if it were true, didn't change what he needed to do. He tried to soften his voice when he asked, "Where are they?"

"In the mountains," Lathia said, whimpering. "Lake Choshek, I think. He said he would only release her if you surrender lordship to Fenris."

Cinders. Fenris's demand was utter folly. Except he had Viola. His twisted cousin was a desperate man, ready to take desperate measures.

Those mountain passes were treacherous under the best conditions. Much less after a snowstorm. Fenris's father had once owned a hunting lodge that sat on the lake with a view of the mountains. Hardly a fortress, but even with half of the Howlers arrested, Fenris and his men could easily defend the pass.

Before Eric had a chance to strategize further, Rubart entered the hall. Streaks of blood stained his apron. The healer had been tending to Walter. Eric and his mother both crossed the room and met him.

"Walter's stable. Resting in his room," Rubart said. "He needs time to mend, but if you wish to speak with him, you may."

"Praise Arman," Mother said.

Praise Him indeed. Eric desired nothing more than to go see his friend, but he needed to make a plan to rescue Viola. And he couldn't leave Nevie alone. Not after what she'd been through.

"My lord, you should go see him," Captain Demry said. "The men have the hall well protected. I can speak with Lathia and devise a plan for taking the mountain." He leaned in closer and lowered his voice. "And you're exhausted. Please take some rest. We can reconvene in the morning."

Eric met his mother's gaze. She smiled bitterly and nodded. Protests bubbled up in his throat. He itched to leave as soon as possible. There was no time to waste. Yet he also knew full well that only a fool would charge into the snowy mountains at night. Plus, the men would need to rest if they were to venture the mountain trails.

And if Captain Demry, rigid man that he was, had broken protocol to tell his lord to go to bed? Then Eric must look truly exhausted.

He needed to see Walter.

Eric kissed Nevie on the head and reluctantly handed her off to his mother.

He followed Rubart upstairs to Walter's bedchamber and entered quietly. Walter lay with his arms at his sides, breathing in a slow rhythm.

Rubart departed to retrieve fresh supplies, leaving Eric alone with Walter. He took a seat in a chair at the valet's bedside. It was the first time he'd sat down since that morning. So much had happened. And all so quickly.

"He has Viola," Eric said softly. "I've been given an ultimatum. Her life for the city. I know I can't make that exchange. Even if it were in my power to simply gift him lordship over the city, he would ruin so many lives."

Eric leaned forward, resting his weight on the bedpost by Walter's pillow. "Yet how could I live with myself knowing that I let Viola's life slip through my hands? And possibly another baby? If Lathia's version of events is to be believed."

Eric sighed. Could it be? After years of hoping for another child.

"I'm trying to find another way," he said. "Yet I see no path forward that doesn't endanger Viola. I can't allow that. What would be the point of any of this if I lost her?"

Walter seemed to twitch. Had his lip moved? Or had it merely been a trick of the candlelight?

"What is it you're always so fond of saying? 'In a multitude of counselors, there is safety.' I've always seen the wisdom of that, but right now I'd settle for just your wise counsel."

Rubart returned with his healer's kit and a bowl of fresh water. Eric paused, as if he had been caught talking to himself.

"You needn't halt your conversation on my account," Rubart said as he began mixing some sort of salve.

Eric settled forward, keeping his gaze on Walter. "Do you think he can hear us?"

"Eh?" Rubart looked up from his work.

"Walter. Do you think he can hear me even if he's not conscious?"

The healer scrunched up his face and scratched the back of his ear. "My lord, you are aware he's awake, yes? He was speaking with me just before I went down to get you."

Eric whipped his gaze back to Walter in time to see a smirk creep onto the corners of his lips.

His eyes opened ever so slightly. "I can hear you quite well, my lord."

"You rascal," Eric said, incredulous. "Muskrat, indeed."

The smirk on Walter's lips spread to a proper smile. "Is it such a crime for an old man to rest his eyes after a long day?"

"Just how long were you going to keep up your little charade?" Eric asked.

"As long as necessary, my lord," Walter said. "It seemed as though you needed a moment to speak your mind freely. I was content to listen."

Eric laughed, and warm relief filled his chest. Walter chuckled softly, then coughed. He pressed his hand gingerly to his chest before his breathing evened out again.

"Listen is all you'd better do," Rubart interjected. "The more you talk, the more likely you'll rip one of those stitches."

"I'm hardly in a position to argue." Walter closed his eyes and took several more breaths. "Viola claims she's with child. Is that even *feasible*?"

Eric cleared his throat. Typically, it wouldn't be anyone's business what was or wasn't feasible in such matters, but the stakes were high, and this was no time to be bashful about pertinent information.

"Possible," Eric admitted. "But not likely."

There was much Eric didn't understand about such miracles, but he didn't believe enough time had passed for Viola to be certain of such a thing. Knowing his wife, it could have been part of some ploy to trick Fenris. Yet if she really *were* expecting...

In the end, this only affirmed what they needed to do. Viola was in danger, and they must find a way to rescue her, one way or another.

Eric stood. He wished he were able to sit in vigil over Walter all night, but there wasn't time. "I must leave you in the care of the good healer," he said. "Feel free to rest those old eyes of yours. We will speak again tomorrow."

"Eric." Walter reached out. They clasped hands. "You're strong and courageous, but your heart...that's where your real strength is. Follow that."

Eric considered that, nodded. "Doesn't the Book of Arman say that the heart is deceitful above all else?"

Walter gave Eric a long-suffering look. "By the Three, boy, I'm a valet, not a theologian. Arman has given you a good heart. That's what makes you fit to lead." Another cough overtook the valet, and he drew his hand back to his mouth.

Eric cringed. He hated seeing the man in such a state. "Thank you, Walter. Please get some rest."

Walter's breathing settled and he nodded.

Eric ventured out into the hall, desperately hoping, and perhaps praying, that Arman would indeed share some light on the path he needed to take.

He ought to have gone to his own chambers to rest, as Captain Demry had recommended, but instead he was drawn to the nursery.

Nevie lay asleep in her small bed. Eric's mother sat sleeping in the rocking chair next to the bed. She must have brought the girl up after Eric had left the hall. It was some wonder Nevie could sleep at all after the trauma of the day. Thank Arman for that small mercy.

Eric knelt at the foot of his daughter's bed, haunted by thoughts of what must happen tomorrow. Viola had been willing to sacrifice her life for Nevie's safety. What sacrifice was Eric ready to make to get his wife back?

Dawn broke. Eric had fallen asleep on the nursery floor. He'd had a fitful night's sleep, but at least he had slept. He rose, feeling stiff, and took one last lingering gaze at Nevandra, kissed her brow. He would bring Viola back. Today.

He cast a long look at his mother, still asleep in the rocking chair, then retreated to his chambers. He changed into fresh clothes, then added a heavy fur coat, hat, and gloves that would protect against the harsh cold of the mountain.

Eric was headed down the hallway to find his men when quiet footsteps came up from behind. He turned gingerly, feeling a fresh pang of pain in his sore shoulder as his mother approached carrying Nevie.

"She woke asking to see you," Mother said.

"Of course." Eric hoped he hadn't awakened her when he left. He reached out and took Nevie into his arms. She nestled close, pressing her head against his coat.

"Where's Mama?" Nevie's tiny voice was muffled by the thick fur.

Eric sighed deeply. According to Lathia, Nevie had seen her mother bound by Ikârd. How could any child truly understand what had transpired in Fenris's camp?

He whispered softly in Nevie's ear, "Mama is away right now, but I'm going to go fetch her, and we'll all be together again."

"Did the bad man take her?" Nevie asked.

Eric winced. He knew there was nothing he could have done to prevent Viola's capture, yet he was a husband and father. He was supposed to make sure such things never happened.

"Mama is very brave," Eric said. "She gave herself up to protect you."

And soon he would have to put himself at risk to somehow get Viola back. Though how he planned to do such a thing was another matter altogether.

He glanced at his mother. "Have you spoken to Lathia?"

Mother loosed a protracted sigh that was almost answer enough. "As it is said, 'Flirtation's folly ends in melancholy.' Lathia is currently meditating upon that lesson."

Well, at least Lathia will have learned something from all this.

The three of them stood in silence for a long moment. Eric took several deep breaths, knowing that every moment delayed Viola's rescue.

"Mother—"

"I know." She reached out to take Nevie, but the girl clung to Eric's neck.

"Don't go, Papa."

Eric pried Nevie's hands away, though it broke his heart to do so. He kissed his daughter and handed her off.

"Noooo!" Nevie wailed and reached out her tiny hand to Eric.

"I'll be back, Nevie," he said. "And I'll bring Mama home."

He grabbed and kissed her hand, then turned away. Her wailing pleas followed Eric all the way down the hall and into the cold morning.

CHAPTER TWENTY-SIX
VIOLA

CURSE THESE ROPES, THE RICKETY chair, the drafty lodge.

Viola shifted her arms, trying to relieve the stiffness in her back and the pain of the rope cutting into her wrists. Last night, when they'd arrived at the snow-bound lodge, the Howlers had tied her to a chair in the main room and left her with no food and only a threadbare blanket draped over her knees to fight off the cold. She had gone nearly a full day without anything to eat, and her stomach ached.

It was horrible treatment for any prisoner, much less a supposedly pregnant woman.

The interior of the lodge had heavy log walls; a steeply pitched roof with narrow, high-set windows; and a sturdy stone fireplace that had nearly burned cold. A narrow staircase hugged the back wall and must lead to a loft. A wooden railing overlooked the open space where she sat.

It might once have been a pleasant space, but years without proper upkeep had left its logs weathered and cracked. The staircase and floors creaked ominously. Cobwebs filled the corners and covered the window shutters like faded curtains. Dust coated every surface, and the air hung thick with the stale scent of neglect.

Even under a full day of sun, the structure proved inadequate against the cold wind that swirled across the frozen lake. Viola had sat shivering through the better part of the day, and now the shadows in the room had stretched, hinting at the late afternoon hour.

The lodge had clearly not been properly stocked. Sir Fenris's men had even started breaking up furniture for firewood. She'd be happy to see her own chair chopped up and thrown into the fire.

The door opened, letting in a rush of cold air. A group of Howlers entered the cabin, carelessly tracking snow on the floor. They carried hammers, axes, and saws. What sort of project had they been working on?

"You there!" Viola called. "Have you any food?" Her voice sounded so pathetic, but her hunger would not let her stay silent. At least she might glean something about what work had kept them occupied outside.

"Bah," one of the Howlers scoffed. "Little enough food here as is, your ladyship. Best go fishin'."

They trudged over to the fireplace, leaving Viola to her solitude.

She hadn't considered what would happen after she surrendered to the Howlers. She had assumed Sir Fenris would be decent enough to give basic care to his prized hostage. Clearly she had been wrong.

No matter what else happened, Viola had saved her daughter.

Footsteps came her way. The hulking form of Ikârd emerged from the shadows and loomed over her, knife in hand.

"Don't move." The brute quickly cut Viola's bonds and forced her out of her chair.

"Where are you taking me?" she asked.

Ikârd seized her by the wrist, and she winced as his meaty fingers dug into her rope burns. He dragged her up the narrow staircase to the loft.

Upstairs, a pair of torches lit the space and revealed two Howlers leaning against the railing that overlooked the first floor. There was also a messy bed and an armchair in the corner. Councilor Erlichman sat there. His normally pointed beard had begun to fray at the ends, and his typical confidence appeared completely drained, leaving him an ashen husk of his former self.

Ikârd roughly shoved Viola into the center of the small space, and it was then that she spotted Sir Fenris, looking out of one of the unshuttered windows that was barely larger than an arrow loop.

"What do you think of your accommodations, my lady?" He kept his gazed fixed outside.

Viola straightened the front of her dress as best she could with her hands still bound. "It's certainly rustic. Could use a good cleaning."

Sir Fenris huffed and leaned forward on his toes, continuing his vigil.

"Was this cabin in your family, Sir Fenris?" Viola asked. When no answer came, she turned to the corner where Erlichman sat. "Or is this your humble abode, Councilor?"

Erlichman stood up and walked toward her. "Not everyone grows up with a second home, your ladyship. Despite my family's financial success and my years on the council, true power always lies in the noble houses."

Viola raised an eyebrow. "You betrayed House Livna because you didn't grow up with a hunting lodge?"

Councilor Erlichman jabbed a finger in Viola's face. "Mind your tongue, woman! We aren't in the protected confines of Lytton Hall."

Sir Fenris whirled and smacked Erlichman in the back of the head. "Don't try to sound menacing, Joonas. It doesn't suit you."

Erlichman whimpered and withdrew to his chair.

"She's here to speak to me," Sir Fenris said as he returned his gaze out the window. "My lady, I wish to give you a chance to make amends."

"Amends?" What in all Er'Rets could he be talking about?

Sir Fenris inhaled deeply. "You are a practical woman. Surely you understand that this situation does not have to end poorly for you."

Viola's stomach turned. "What do you mean by that?"

Sir Fenris shrugged. "When I rule Tsaftown, I'll need a bride. And you already make a fetching lady of the city."

The gall of this creature. He was honestly proposing marriage? After kidnapping her?

"You seem quite certain of your future position," Viola said.

"I've all the reason in the world for confidence," Sir Fenris said. "Little Eric won't leave you here. He'll charge up the mountain in some brash rescue attempt. He knows no other way. I have seen this coming and made preparations. When he makes his valiant effort, we shall be ready for him. And when he dies, your best option will be to ally with me."

What preparation could Sir Fenris have possibly made to this oversized shack that could sabotage Eric's life?

"You're suggesting I betray House Livna? My own family?" Viola asked.

Sir Fenris tilted his head, turned, and laid his hand on Viola's shoulder, almost as if consoling her. "The Livnas aren't your true family any more than they are mine. Is loyalty to them worth risking your own neck? Or your daughter's?"

The threat in Sir Fenris's voice was plain as day. Even so, he was opening up to her. Perhaps this was an opportunity.

"I'm a practical woman," Viola said. "Some have even called me coldly logical. You mentioned preparations you have made for Eric. Whatever do you mean by that?" She added a ring of curious innocence to her voice, hoping she might get him to boast, even a little about his plans.

Sir Fenris stared at her for a moment. "What would a woman care about such things?"

Viola shrugged. "If I'm to trust my future to you, I need to know that your superior tactics aren't merely empty boasts."

A pensive look lingered in Sir Fenris's eyes. He reached out and caressed Viola's chin with his bandaged hand. "In due time, my lady. In due time." He withdrew his hand. "Open the main window."

Ikârd balked. "Sir Fenris, it is freezing outside."

Sir Fenris bared his teeth "Do it, you fat oaf. Or I shall have you pushed off the cliff's edge."

Ikârd's eyes flared, then he stepped obediently to a much larger window and began working the rusty latches that opened the shutters.

"I wish for you to see outside, my lady," Sir Fenris said. "I do believe we have visitors coming this way."

ERIC

Eric's body felt full of rock and broken glass. A forced trek up the mountain on horseback so soon after his battle with Fenris left him in shambles. But there was no choice. He would not consider his own pain. Or even his own life. Not until Viola was safe.

The horses trudged up the last switchback in the mountain trail. The snowfall had ceased, but the snowpack had grown steadily deeper as Eric and his riders approached the summit. Derby and Gunnar Gedmund rode on either of Eric's flanks, while Dunn, Torin Oxbow, and Wroxton took positions in the rear. Eric had elected to take as few men with him as possible, sending the rest of the Fighting Fifteen with Captain Demry.

The deep snow made swift travel up to the lodge at Lake Choshek impossible. One bad slip and both horse and rider would tumble down the rugged terrain of the mountainside. Because of this, they had been forced to sacrifice a speedy ascent in the name of caution.

But at last, Eric saw the dim outline of the hunting lodge atop the highest point of the trail. A sheer cliff face arose on their left. On their right lay a rocky slope covered by a dense copse of pine trees. The landscape created the perfect pinch point for an ambush. Thankfully, none of snow showed signs of disruption, and Eric doubted that the Howlers had the resolve to lay in wait in the freezing snow for an entire day.

Derby raised a white flag of truce. Even a man like Fenris should honor the flag and come to negotiate terms. If he wouldn't, then it would come to violence.

How far would Eric go to free his wife from captivity? How many men's lives would be traded for hers? And what about his own life? Would he be required to give it to save hers?

Husbands, love your wives as Arman loves his people. Eric wanted nothing more than to protect Viola, but was he ready to lay down his life for her? Or would his character be found wanting?

Eric steeled his mind as the group worked their way up the snow-laden path. Doubt would only hinder him. He prayed that his courage would not fail.

They had neared the end of the trail, less than a quarter mile away from the lodge, when a solitary rider came out to meet them, his horse struggling down the snowy incline. Eric halted his men, and they waited. Shaggy blond hair shook as the rider neared. Fenris? Had he actually come out alone?

No. Details cleared, and Eric recognized that mop of hair, tinged orange by the setting sun.

"Master Clave," he said as the rider halted in front of them.

The young man brushed a lock of hair out of his eyes. "Livna." The boy seemed to take a special pride in refusing to acknowledge Eric's title.

Eric dismounted Thunder and just managed to avoid slipping

as he jumped off the giant animal into several feet of snow. He trudged toward Clave. "Where is your master?"

Clave scowled and dismounted his own horse. "Sir Fenris entrusted me with negotiating. Have you come to fetch your captured woman?"

Something wasn't right. Why in all Er'Rets would Fenris send this young man to negotiate? There were much better choices. Erlichman or even Ikârd.

It was feasible that Fenris had sent Clave as an insult, yet that didn't sit right either. It wasn't how Fenris worked.

Clave gestured to the setting sun, barely visible over the tips of the trees. "Cutting it a bit close. Sir Fenris said to come by sunset."

The lad had adopted a facade of roguish confidence, much like what he'd tried to portray during their encounter in Lytton Hall.

"Lathia is rather upset with you, young man," Eric said. "She may have broken her share of young men's hearts, but she is far from forgiving to those who do the same to her."

Clave's expression dropped for a moment. He made a show of gritting his teeth, but something in his eyes betrayed youthful heartache. Cinders, did the boy actually care for Lathia?

"Rubbish." Clave waved his hand. "What do I care about her feelings? She always acted like she was too good for me. Like all you nobles do."

"I'm not here to argue politics with you," Eric said. "Tell your master that he has one chance to return my wife. Otherwise, none of you shall leave this mountain alive."

Clave crossed his arms. "Sir Fenris's demands are still the same. Lordship of Tsaftown in exchange for your lady."

A rustling—like footsteps—on the ridge above drew Eric's attention.

"My lord, do you hear that?" Dunn asked.

Eric nodded and scanned the ridge, looking for signs of an

ambush. "Wroxton, looks like it's time. Signal Captain Demry's group."

"Aye, my lord," Wroxton said.

"Are you listening, Livna?" Clave spat.

Wroxton withdrew a drum mallet from his belt and rattled out a quick three-beat signal on the drum attached to the side of his saddle. The sound carried through the mountain air.

As if in response, a sharp metal clack echoed down from the ridge. Then another.

Eric drew his sword and turned his gaze to Clave. "You best surrender now, son. Whatever trap Fenris has set, you'll not survive it."

Genuine bewilderment shone in Clave's eye. "Trap? There's no trap."

By the depths. Either the boy was the finest actor in the North or he hadn't been let in on Fenris's plans.

A great crack shook the trail. Atop the ridge, Eric could just make out something like a net giving way.

Clave gasped. "What?"

The rumble continued. A clump of snow splattered on Eric's shoulder. A massive log tumbled down the cliffside. Then another. And another.

"Avalanche!" Dunn cried.

Each falling log knocked loose large sections of snow and boulders, which tumbled toward the men in a wave of frozen death.

Clave tried to move, but he lost his footing and tripped in the snow.

"To the trees!" Eric yelled.

His riders wheeled, turning their mounts into the wooded area next to the trail. The steep rocky ground was treacherous, but the trees offered at least some cover from the debris.

Clave's horse bolted, leaving the young man petrified in the trail.

Eric dashed forward, seized the boy by the coat, and dragged him into the trees.

Eric managed to get them both behind a towering pine just as the wave reached them. A powerful force knocked Eric sideways. He tumbled down the hill as his entire vision went white.

CHAPTER TWENTY-SEVEN
VIOLA

VIOLA'S WORLD ENDED.

The thundering avalanche shook the walls of the lodge. The distant view of Eric's parlay was hidden from her as a wave of powdery snow and debris swallowed the section of trail where her husband had been standing. That had been the great task that had occupied the Howlers. Assembling a deadly log trap along the upper ridge of the lake.

Viola's heart shriveled, and she stared intently, hoping against hope that Eric would emerge from the disaster. She saw only a white cloud of debris and death. Had her husband climbed a mountain to save her only to be crushed by treachery?

Her focus was disrupted by a harsh cackle. "Well, that worked better than expected, didn't it?" Sir Fenris said, grinning with self-satisfaction.

"You monster." Hot tears ran down Viola's cheeks.

Sir Fenris scowled and seized a fistful of her hair. He yanked her back and pinned her against the wall. "Now, since I have proven myself a better man, perhaps this is as good a time as any to reconsider my offer."

He leaned in, and his foul breath drifted over her like a deadly fog. Viola pressed her bound hands against Sir Fenris's jaw. He pushed his face past them and latched his other hand around her throat.

In the distance, something echoed. Drums? They repeated over and over again.

Sir Fenris paid the noise no mind. He opened his mouth and tried to kiss her. Viola dug her nails into his cheeks and raked them across his pockmarked skin.

He drew back and snarled.

Bu-doom! Bu-doom!

The drums finally captured Sir Fenris's attention. He shoved Viola away and stepped to the window as thin beads of blood formed along the welts on his face. Quick footsteps thumped overhead. Was someone on the roof?

A series of arrows shot through the open window. One took a Howler in the chest, and the man crumpled to the floor.

"Poroo!" Ikârd yelled as he drew his ax.

The shutters broke inward, and pale arms reached through the windows. Two Poroo hunters scrambled into the loft. The Howlers at the railing ran toward the first, and Ikârd swung his axe at the second. The Poroo struck Ikârd's hand with a club, and the ax fell from his fingers. Unarmed, he tackled the Poroo to the floor, and a desperate struggle ensued.

As angry cries and violent strikes filled the close quarters of the loft, Viola slipped to the corner opposite Councilor Erlichman's chair and sank down, trying to stay out of the fray. More yelling came from the first floor. Were more Poroo breaking in downstairs?

Sir Fenris retrieved Ikârd's fallen ax and savagely dispatched one of the Poroo. More war cries echoed from outside.

"Northlanders, ho! Knock in the doors!"

"Tuutskim! Niika, siskamaawi!"

Different battle calls. The Poroo and the Fighting Fifteen, working together?

Sir Fenris looked feverishly back and forth from the window to the door downstairs. His confident veneer melted, and panic filled his face like a wild animal caught in a hunter's trap.

"Horses! Now! We'll escape over the lake." Sir Fenris dashed down the stairs.

Councilor Erlichman followed. They were running like motherless cowards.

And leaving her behind.

Viola dared to believe she might be free. Then Ikârd's massive hand seized Viola's wrists and dragged her roughly down the stairs behind Sir Fenris and Councilor Erlichman.

The skirmish continued downstairs. The Howlers fought desperately to barricade the front door against a squad of the Northlanders. More voices called from the outside. Had they surrounded the entire cabin?

Sir Fenris's party passed down a long hallway and burst out the back door. Several horses stood tied to the railing of the back porch, including Councilor Erlichman's towering black festrier. The wind blew snow in snakelike wisps across the frozen lake. Sir Fenris and Councilor Erlichman untethered their horses while Ikârd kept hold of Viola.

What mad plan was this? An escape across the ice was precarious at best. Even if they kept to the more solid ice on the edge of the lake, they'd still have to escape down the treacherous mountain when they reached the other side, and Sir Fenris's diabolical log trap had cut off the only safe trail down.

Perhaps the threat of capture by the Poroo was enough to motivate such madness.

Councilor Erlichman leaped from a tall crate onto the black festrier, while Sir Fenris waved Ikârd toward a dapple-grey horse.

"Hoist her up," he said.

Ikârd grabbed for Viola's waist. She stomped on the big man's foot, balled her hands into fists, and swung at his face. His thick hand blocked her attack. He seized her waist and hefted her up onto the horse's saddle.

Viola tried to wriggle down, but Sir Fenris mounted the horse behind her, wrapped his arms around her, and grabbed the reins.

The Tsaftown soldiers were so close, but they would never make it in time. Not with Sir Fenris escaping on horseback.

"Over here!" Viola yelled. "In back—"

Sir Fenris clamped his hand over her mouth and spoke in her ear. "For the time being, you are still more valuable to me alive than otherwise. Don't do anything to make me reconsider."

As Ikârd reached for his own horse, a Poroo arrow struck his thigh. He stumbled and fell to one knee. Two Poroo hunters charged out the back door, screaming. Ikârd reached for his ax but found none. Fenris had left it in the lodge. Another arrow sank deep into Ikârd's chest, and the man collapsed on the deck.

"Hee yah!" Sir Fenris spurred his horse forward, right onto the frozen lake. Erlichman followed, leaving Ikârd to the gruesome mercy of the Poroo.

Viola's teeth rattled as the horse reached a full gallop on the unforgiving ice. If she could just get off the animal, then she could run to safety. A fall on the ice at this speed could be deadly, but was freezing to death as Sir Fenris's hostage any better?

They neared the middle of the lake. Viola's stomach sank as she realized that in his haste to escape the lodge, Sir Fenris and Erlichman were riding across the weakest part of the ice.

"Stop!" Viola yelled. "The ice won't hold! Head toward the shore!"

The men ignored her. Could she be wrong? Perhaps the elevation had given the center of the lake time to freeze solid. But two riders? With a festrier?

"Turn back!" She fought in vain to steal the reins out of Sir Fenris's hands.

A loud crack rose up from the lake. The festrier stumbled and slammed into the surface at full speed, knocking Councilor Erlichman off the saddle. With the impact, the ice shattered beneath the animal, creating a gaping hole. The horse went under the water for a moment, then reemerged, thrashing its front legs.

Sir Fenris's horse reared up, desperate to avoid the icy pit that had just opened up. Sir Fenris cursed. Viola grasped for the saddle horn but lost hold. She slammed back into Sir Fenris, and they fell from the horse.

Viola's head smacked against Sir Fenris's face. Her head rang. She rolled off him directly onto the ice. While her head spun, her fall had been far gentler than she could have possibly hoped. Sir Fenris had taken the worst of the impact, and he lay in a daze beside her, clutching his head.

Sir Fenris's dapple-grey horse bolted back toward the safety of the shore. Erlichman's festrier still thrashed in the water. The poor animal fought to gain some sort of purchase on the edge of the hole, but the ice continued to shatter under the animal's weight. With every kick, the horse widened the break farther and weakened the surrounding ice.

On the far side of the broken ice lay a limp body. Viola shuddered as she recognized Councilor Erlichman. A crimson streak ran across the ice to the spot where his head had come to rest.

Viola's head throbbed, but she needed to get off the ice before it gave out underneath her. Eric had come for her. His men were here. She was nearly rescued. If only she could reach the shore, then this nightmare would be over.

She slowly pushed to her hands and knees. The ice beneath her creaked like a hungry beast ready to swallow her alive. She crawled slowly, moving one agonizing bit at a time.

Another fracture formed beneath her, trapping her in place.

Storms. Viola had been so close to freedom. To returning home and holding her daughter. Sir Fenris and Councilor Erlichman lay incapacitated. Nothing stood between Viola and the lodge.

Yet the ice would not let her go. Now all she could do was wait to see when the freezing waters would sentence her to a bitter cold demise.

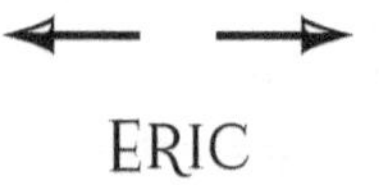

ERIC

The last stretch of the trail seemed like the longest portion of the entire mountain. The trees had only narrowly saved them from the avalanche. Torin Oxbow had been slammed into a tree and was slow to get up. Clave had survived, saved by Eric's quick thinking, but the lad had taken a nasty gash to his head. And poor Derby had been buried upside down in the snow, leaving Wroxton and Gedmund to dig him out.

Eric and Dunn left the men to tend to the wounded and gather the horses while they rallied up the last of the trail. The dimming orange light of sunset revealed a full battle in progress at the lodge. Captain Demry and his team had completely encircled Fenris's hideout. Within a day, the combined team of Northlanders and Poroo warriors had performed the legendary feat of scaling the sheer cliff on the far side of the mountain, then had immediately laid siege to the enemy. Their exploits deserved Eric's highest commendations. Perhaps he could commission Jeffrey to write an entire saga in their honor.

Eric and Dunn had nearly reached the battle when they saw two horses ride away from the back of the lodge and onto the frozen lake. One black festrier. And one horse carrying a man and a woman. Even in the fading light, he knew the woman had to be Viola.

"Secure the lodge!" Eric yelled as he turned toward the lake.

Dunn grabbed Eric's shoulder. "My lord, you can't go alone."

"More men will only weaken the ice further." Eric pulled out of Dunn's grip. "Go help Captain Demry. That's an order."

Before Dunn could protest again, Eric sprinted out onto the lake.

It was folly to ride horses on the ice at this time of year. It was equally foolish to think one could catch up to horses on foot. Eric had no other choice. He would not let them get away.

He kept his eyes on the pair of horses and pushed himself harder. He ignored the frozen daggers that stabbed his lungs with each breath. Ignored his burning legs and the stitch in his side that threatened to turn into a cramp. Ignored the ever-growing distance between himself and his quarry. Any hesitation meant he would lose them in the woods and Viola would be gone forever.

"Viola!" He yelled her name repeatedly, but each cry lost more of his voice until nothing came out but a raspy wheeze. The cold numbed his face, and his lips refused to shape words.

A sickening crack split the air, followed by a deafening splash. Thrashing silhouettes appeared in the distance, obscured by the dimming light. The smaller, grey horse ran toward Eric, its saddle empty. Eric slowed until the animal safely passed him on its way back to the lodge.

Up ahead, a massive shape bobbed in the water. The black festrier Erlichman had been so proud of. The creature had broken through.

Three bodies lay on the ice, and two were directly in front of the hole.

Eric was close enough now to see Viola on her hands and knees, her dress draped around her like a tent.

"Viola!" he cried.

Eric slowed to a trot, not wanting to slide into her. She held her position two or three horse lengths away from the gaping maw in the ice. Fenris lay sprawled out behind her, not moving but close enough to grab her ankle if he came to his senses.

Behind them, the festrier flailed violently in the water, its hooves scrabbling against the slick, jagged edges of the ice.

Viola looked up at Eric. "Eric, stop! The ice!"

He halted, spying a dark fracture directly beneath her. "Can you move to me?" he asked.

Viola shook her head. "It breaks more every time I move."

Eric's gut churned. With the horse trying to get out, the ice grew weaker by the moment. For Viola, falling through might not be a death sentence, but it would put her in range of the drowning horse. Plus her heavy woolen dress would soak up the water and pull her down.

Eric cast aside his sword and belt and slid down onto his belly, distributing his weight evenly across the cold surface. "I'm here. Lie down flat. Then come forward a little at a time."

Viola did as Eric said, mimicking his prostrate pose and pushing herself forward, bit by bit. Eric dared to inch closer and managed to brush the tips of her fingers.

Then Fenris stood, his form silhouetted against the orange sunset. He groaned and hunched to one side. Drew his sword and shuffled forward.

"Fenris, don't." Eric delicately pushed up to one knee. "The ice is giving way."

Fenris continued toward Viola, his sword gripped limply at his side.

"Stop, Fenris!" Eric yelled. "You'll go through the ice."

"Think I have much to live for at this point, Little Eric?" Fenris took another step, now dragging the tip of his sword along the ice.

Eric didn't know what to do. Even with Fenris wounded, Viola was nearly within striking range of his blade.

"Perhaps you've won at last," Fenris said. The sword's tip scraped across the frozen surface. "But if I must lose, then perhaps vengeance will be victory enough." He hefted his sword with both hands and raised it above his head, preparing to stab Viola.

Eric pushed to his feet and leaped over Viola. He seized Fenris by the wrists, and the two struggled for control of the blade. Their momentum brought them toward the broken edge of the ice. The horse's nostrils flared as its front legs thrashed, spraying ice water over Eric and Fenris.

The ice groaned under their feet. The battle for the sword threatened to send all three of them under. Eric couldn't let that happen. Regardless of any risk to himself, he needed to keep Viola safe.

The horse kicked furiously in Eric's peripheral vision, its powerful legs cutting through the frigid water in frantic attempts to find solid ground. He and Fenris were one ill-placed step away from the edge. The ice cracked under their combined weight, and the fractures ran out from under them like skeletal fingers, reaching toward Viola. She screamed.

In a breath, Eric made his decision. He hooked his arm around Fenris's shoulder, threw all his weight backward, and dragged them both into the freezing water.

The chill hit Eric like a thousand needles piercing his skin. Darkness swirled around him. His chest trembled, and he fought to keep breath in his lungs. Fenris's sword slipped from both men's grasps and disappeared into the black water. Eric and Fenris tumbled end over end through the water and traded blind punches back and forth as their limbs tangled.

Eric lost all sense of direction in the murky water. A faint flicker of light appeared to his left. He tried to disengage with Fenris and swim toward the brightness, but his arm caught in Fenris's cloak.

The cold leached more heat from his body. He tried to untangle his arm, but his limbs felt like they had been weighed down with stone, heavy and sluggish in the thick, biting water. His chest burned, but he fought the impulse to inhale.

Fenris's hands found Eric and slid around his throat. The two men twisted in the freezing abyss. Fenris was now in between Eric and the light. Eric struggled against Fenris's grip. The distorted silhouette of the festrier came into focus just before a massive hoof swung over top of them. Eric was running out of air, but so many obstacles stood between himself and the surface.

Desperate, he grabbed one of Fenris's injured fingers and wrenched it backward, breaking his grip, then he jabbed Fenris in the throat and pushed away, finally separating them.

Again the horse kicked overhead, and in one deadly motion, the festrier's hoof connected with the back of Fenris's skull. A dull thump carried through the water. Fenris went limp, and the momentum of the hoof's strike pushed his body away until it vanished in the shadows, leaving nothing but a trail of blood in his wake.

Eric could not linger. The overwhelming need for air consumed him, and salvation was directly above. He shed his waterlogged cloak and kicked upward. His vision blurred. He kicked and reached, kicked and kicked, each desperate attempt to move more sluggish than the last. The break in the ice was only a few strokes away, yet Eric's progress slowed.

A hand appeared in the opening, reaching down. Viola. Eric summoned one last push with his legs, then reached out and grabbed hold.

He burst out of the water. The frigid air stung his lungs as he sucked in several gasping breaths.

"Eric!" Viola cried.

She pulled on his wrist and tugged his arm over the surface of the ice. Eric kicked his legs up to the side and onto the ice. Then, with Viola's help, he crawled ever so slowly out of the hole.

The horse still struggled, but it had clearly lost strength. Its breath came in slow, desperate snorts, and steam rose from its back as its muscles strained with each futile attempt to climb back onto the ice.

Together, Eric and Viola eased away from the break until they were on solid ice. Then Eric collapsed into Viola's arms. The cold air stung the exposed skin on his face, and shivers racked his body. His vision blurred and the light seemed to fade. Was it getting darker?

"Eric, are you all right? I'm so sorry." Viola held him close and kissed him. Her warm lips pulled him from his frozen trance.

He reached up and caressed her face. "I found you."

Viola took his hand. "I thought I'd lost you."

She kissed him again. Eric savored her tender embrace. They had made it. Viola was safe. Fenris was gone. It was over.

Eric tried to speak again, but no words came. The frigid air threw him into a violent coughing fit. Viola peeled off her wool cloak and draped it over him, but he felt nothing.

"Hold on, Eric. Help is coming." She pressed her lips against his forehead.

Eric rested his head against the ice, his body drained of all strength. The cold surface burned his exposed skin, but all he could do was take one shuddering breath after another.

Men's voices carried across the lake.

"It's Lady Viola!"

"Is he injured?"

"Lord Livna needs help!" Viola yelled. "We need warm blankets. We need to get him out of these wet clothes."

Eric felt himself being dragged across the ice and lifted by several pairs of strong hands. He tried to move, but he could do nothing but watch breath escape in large clouds above him and the world fade away.

CHAPTER TWENTY-EIGHT
ERIC

THE RADIANT HEAT OF THE FIRE WARMED Eric's bones. Sitting in a comfortable chair in his study had never meant much, but it seemed the more he indulged in this leisure, the more he enjoyed it.

One day he would mount up Thunder again and go riding. Breathe in the crisp mountain air. Perhaps when spring finally arrived. Until then, he was content to indulge Master Rubart's prescribed bed rest as much as possible.

A month had passed since Viola's rescue, and still Eric's lungs hadn't fully cleared. He labored to breathe at times, and coughing fits took him at least once a day. His collection of cuts and bruises were nearly healed, though some scars lingered. Each one taken to protect his family and home. A worthy sacrifice.

Those thoughts, along with the fire, kept him very warm.

Eric's content musings were swiftly disrupted by the patter of little feet on the study floor.

"Papa!" Nevie scrambled up his chair and into his lap.

Close behind came Viola, a contented smile on her lips. Both mother and daughter were dressed for the cold. Viola wore a dark fur shawl and blue wool dress that complimented her figure despite the thick woolen layers. She planted a gentle kiss on Eric's cheek.

"Papa, it's Win'erstone day," Nevie said. "You gonna throw the big rock?" Her crooked grin warmed his heart, and he wrapped her in a tight hug.

"The biggest rock I can find." Eric tickled Nevie under her chin. She kicked and giggled.

Eric laughed with her until something in his chest caught and sent him into a coughing fit. Viola picked up Nevie and held Eric by the elbow, offering balance until the spasm passed.

"Has it been worse today?" she asked. "You needn't come to the ceremony if you don't feel well."

"It will...be fine." Eric spoke between coughs, trying to let his breathing settle.

"Eric?" She took his hand. They'd had this conversation many times.

"This is the first Winterstone Festival since the end of Darkness," Eric said. "I'll not cancel my appearance because of a cough." He might not partake in all the festivities, but he would do his one duty as lord of the city.

Viola offered a kind but pained smile. "As long as you're feeling up to it."

Eric raised an eyebrow. "Are *you* feeling up to it?"

She shifted Nevie to one hip and ran her free hand over her belly. "*We* are feeling fine today."

Eric laid his hand over hers. Viola's ruse about being pregnant had turned out to be prophetic. They'd kept the good news to themselves for now. There would be time later to share with family and the rest of the city. And come summer—the first Tsaftown would experience in over a decade—they would also celebrate the arrival of the newest member of House Livna.

No doubt many would speculate if Viola were going to have

a boy, finally giving House Livna an heir. Regardless, their new arrival, boy or girl, would be welcomed with loving, open arms.

Another coughing fit disrupted Eric's thoughts.

Viola rubbed his back. "Perhaps we'll have Rubart prepare another tonic for you."

Eric blanched at the mention of more tonic, though he knew it would be helpful. "Whatever the good healer thinks is best."

Viola's shoulders sank.

Eric reached back and took hold of her hand. "However long this lingers and however many bitter tonics I must drink, it was a worthwhile sacrifice to protect you."

She squeezed his hand. "You always say that."

"And I always will, my love." He kissed the back of her hand.

Viola's eyes brightened and she sighed. "I love you, Eric."

"I love you too." Eric's held her gaze, taking in her radiant beauty.

"We gonna go to the festival?" Nevie asked.

Eric and Viola exchanged smiles. The little one had been anticipating this day for weeks. It was time they got moving.

Eric stood up, and the three of them went down the stairs to the foyer. The rest of House Livna had gathered there and were chatting as they waited for Eric's arrival. Grandmother Merris hassled Lathia over her posture. The young woman had sulked on and off for the last month, still recovering from Clave's betrayal. Meanwhile, Eric's mother appeared to be having a pleasant conversation with the newest member of Tsaftown's ruling council.

"Councilor Blackburn, do you have an appointment?" Eric asked. "This is a day of celebration, and we'll be holding no official business."

"Bah." Walter waved his hand. "There will be none of that, my lord. Certainly you've better things to do than pester an old man."

Eric chuckled and the two men clasped hands. "Look at the cheek on this muskrat. Give him a fancy new position and all of a sudden he's drunk with power. Although I will say, you are certainly dressed for the part."

"I wish I could say the same for you," Walter said. "I would have had you wear the grey cloak today. You don't want to seem too fancy to the people."

Eric grinned. "Well, if the old man should find his duties on the council too strenuous, he is always welcome to take up his valet work again. My boots could use a good shining."

The two laughed so heartily that it sparked another of Eric's coughing fits. This one cleared quickly, though it was no more pleasant.

"If you two gentlemen are quite finished," Viola said, "the good people of Tsaftown are waiting for us."

With that, the seven of them made for the front doors. They were greeted by Captain Demry and the Fighting Fifteen in honor guard formation. It was more a sign of respect than force. The last of the Howlers had been rounded up weeks ago, removing the need for enhanced security. The members of House Livna were free to savor and enjoy this special day.

The group gathered on the front step, which had just been cleared of snow. At the bottom stood two teams of horses, each hitched to a sleigh built of beautifully crafted oak. The group divided themselves between the two sleighs, and Eric held Nevie on his lap.

The driver urged the team forward with his riding crop, and the horses trotted out of the courtyard while the Fighting Fifteen followed on horseback.

As they glided down the road from Lytton Hall toward the Dale, the rhythmic jingle of harness bells accompanied the clip-clop of horses' hooves. Nevie squealed as the sleigh picked up speed through the city streets. Several heavy storms had blown through in the last weeks, transforming all of Tsaftown into a sweeping landscape of snowdrifts. Yet as they made their way through the

Fisherman's Quarter, it was plain to see that the weather had not hindered citizens from coming out on this day of festivities. Most people wore at least three heavy layers to fight off the cold. In fact, some held to the Winterstone tradition of wearing as many layers as possible, even at the sacrifice of mobility.

When they finally reached the docks, the sleigh turned and glided down the bustling harbor road, the jingle of harness bells blending with the lively hum of voices. Musicians performed jaunty tunes, and groups of children gathered in loose dancing circles around the performers. The air was sharp with the scent of pine smoke and roasting meats from dozens of campfires where clusters of townsfolk huddled together, laughing and stamping their feet to keep warm as they awaited the official start of the Winterstone Festival.

Along the shore, piers jutted out onto the frozen harbor, each crowded with men readying their log ice-fishing houses on sleds or wagons, poised to rush onto the frosty expanse and claim their spots for the ice-fishing season.

Anticipation hung in the air as the sleigh came to a gentle stop in front of the raised viewing platform—the seat of honor for the lord of the city and his family. Draped in black-and-gold banners emblazoned with the dagfish sigil, the platform rose above the gathering like a ceremonial perch, positioned perfectly to overlook the main pier, a small stage, and the myriad of booths where vendors and performers had already set up.

Murmurs rippled through the crowd as the Livna family disembarked and climbed the steps to the platform, their breaths misting in the cold. Eric felt the weight of expectation on his shoulders as they all took their seats on the viewing platform to witness the launch of a prosperous ice-fishing season.

Eric had been to many Winterstone celebrations over the years, but none had ever lifted his heart like this. Derby and Walter started a fire in the wrought iron brazier that sat at the edge of the viewing platform. Once everyone had settled in and the fire started to crackle, Eric walked down to the main pier to meet the dockmaster.

On his way, he passed by several of the crews preparing to haul out the ice-fishing houses. Connor Clave stood among them, serving on one of the many teams that worked for Councilor Okerlund. Eric gave the newly minted fisherman a knowing nod. The lad had been surprisingly helpful in untangling the remaining inner workings of Fenris's group. In exchange for his cooperation, Eric had helped Clave get an honest job in hopes that working on one of Okerlund's crews would keep him on the straight and narrow.

Eric reached the end of the pier where Dockmaster Tahn, a squat, bearded man with a litany of tattoos on his exposed forearms, greeted him.

"Lord Livna, it is an honor to be here with you on this fine Winterstone day," he said gruffly.

Eric shook the dockmaster's calloused hand. "The honor is mine. The people look ready. Let's not keep them waiting."

Dockmaster Tahn grinned and handed Eric a smooth stone the size of a small melon. Eric walked slowly down the pier, turning the rock over and over in his hands. His father had performed this same ceremony countless times over the years. He wasn't merely retracing his father's footsteps, but dozens of his forefathers, going back to the founding of Tsaftown.

The story was that the first lord of the city had heaved a great boulder onto the ice to ensure it was strong enough to hold the weight of the fishing houses. No doubt the tale had been exaggerated over the generations, but the tradition of the Winterstone Festival had continued ever since.

And now the duty was his to perform.

How often over these months had Eric retraced his father's

steps? Yet today, for the first time, he felt as though he was not merely a soldier playing at lordship.

He was their lord.

The weight of that responsibility settled on his shoulders—their adoration and their fears—yet Eric felt newfound certainty in it as well. No matter what challenges faced him, this was where he belonged.

He hefted the stone again to get a sense of its weight, then he drew his arm back and hurled it with all his might.

The rock flew through the air, spiraling higher. The crowd held its collective breath as the rock reached its apex and arched back toward the ice.

When the stone struck the ice, a fine shower of frost sprayed up. The stone slid the distance of a dozen paces, rattling on the smooth surface before coming to a halt. The crowd cheered. Eric set his hands on his hips and turned to face the people, satisfied with his effort.

"Papa throwed the rock!" Nevie cried from the viewing platform.

This brought forth some laughter from the crowd.

Eager to complete his part in the ceremony, Eric shook the dockmaster's hand. "Master Tahn," he said, "the ice will hold."

Tahn raised his hands above his head and yelled, "The ice shall hold!"

Cheers erupted from the onlookers. Harsh calls bellowed out from the boat captains as the crewmen, who typically manned the sails of fishing boats, started hauling ice-fishing houses out over the frozen harbor. The pace was slow and methodical, yet enthralling as each crew headed for the spot they deemed the best fishing location for the season.

Eric shook hands with numerous citizens as he worked his way back to his family, who now stood around the brazier, enjoying the fire. Eric took his place beside Viola, who linked her arm with his.

"Well done," she said. "It almost seemed like you wanted to be there."

This earned a hearty chuckle from Walter.

Eric stretched his free hand toward the fire. "If all my public appearances are to involve feats of strength, then you shall find I'm very amenable to them."

Nevie tugged on Viola's skirt, whining that she wanted to go watch the men run on the ice.

"I will take you." Mother took the child by the hand and led her down the steps toward the piers.

The strum of a lute pulled Eric's attention to a small stage that stood just to the right of the Livna's viewing platform. A familiar, lithe figure leaped to the center front, which brought forth cheers from the crowd.

"Well, now that we are done throwing rocks," Jeffrey said, "I believe you people are in need of some true entertainment."

Those watching laughed and applauded. The bard had earned quite the following in the city.

"I must admit, I didn't understand why anyone would wish to live in a place such as this..." Jeffrey strummed a few chords. "And now that I've lived here these months...by the Three, I still have no clue why anyone likes it here. You people do realize there are warmer places to live, yes?"

His words drew jubilant laughter from the audience. Eric took his seat and leaned back, content to watch Jeffrey masterfully work the crowd.

Viola sat beside him and leaned over. Her warm breath tickled the inside of Eric's ear. "He certainly seems to be enjoying himself," she said. "If we're not careful, people are going to start begging that he be placed on the ruling council."

"That would be a sight to behold," Eric said.

Her grip on his arm tightened, and they both snuggled in to watch the performance.

Jeffrey strutted about the stage like a rooster and fingered a complex melody on his lute. "Yet here you are, the hardest-working folks in all Er'Rets. And not only do you survive the harsh temperatures up here, but you thrive in them. Everywhere else, they hide during winter, yet at the coldest time of year, the steadfast Northlanders hold a festival. You people are nothing short of an inspiration. That is why I have dedicated my latest song to the amazing people of Tsaftown!"

This brought out joyful applause. Two more musicians joined Jeffrey on stage, one holding a flute and the other a tambourine. The crowd hushed as the trio began to play. The newcomers started the song and wove their gentle tones into a rich melody. Then Jeffrey added his own voice to the performance.

> *"Far in the northern reaches,*
> *Lingers a land both cold and fierce.*
> *Yet the hearts of these stalwart people*
> *The bitter winds shall never pierce.*
>
> *"Their women lovely and wise*
> *Their men are strong and brave.*
> *In challenges great and small,*
> *There's no challenge they'll not stave."*

Jeffrey leaned his gaze very intentionally toward the platform where the members of House Livna sat, riffed with his lute for a moment, and winked at Eric.

> *"But among them is one,*
> *Whose will cannot be beat.*
> *He protects the land with sword and shield*
> *And sits in Lytton's highest seat.*

"Though ice and snow will rule the land,
And covers the world in frozen haze,
Yet through coldest day and darkest night,
The Lord of Winter reigns."

Eric eyed Jeffrey. Had this song been written as some sort of joke? Yet sincerity filled Jeffrey's tone. The honor struck Eric in the heart, and he felt a tear well in his eye.

The performance continued and eventually transitioned into a well-known dancing song. The flute rang out, and the tambourine player rattled her instrument joyously. Some of the spectators stepped out into the open yard in front of the stage and began to dance. Though not as many as Eric would have expected for a festival day. Typically the yard would be flooded with dancers, but only a few pockets of people danced on the fringes.

Lathia sighed, looking longingly at the happy faces that had gathered.

Eric stroked his beard. "Isn't it the city lord's role to initiate the dancing?"

Viola exchanged looks with Walter.

"That's the custom," she said. "But with your lungs still recovering, we thought it best to hold off this time."

Eric stood and offered his hand to Viola. "Nonsense. A lord has responsibilities. Come, let us dance."

Viola's brows lifted as she slowly rose. "Are you quite sure?"

"Is there something wrong with dancing?" Eric asked.

Viola accepted his hand. "It's just rather out of character for you, that's all."

Walter chuckled. "Yes. Out of character, indeed."

Eric narrowed his eyes at Walter. "Careful or I shall call Grandmother Merris and have her drag you out on the dance yard."

He led Viola toward the edge of the platform until Derby Wenk stepped up and partially blocked his way. "My lord, do you need my protection in the crowd?"

Eric's first instinct was to rebuff the young soldier. Then a better idea came to mind.

"Yes, I shall require you to follow us as we dance, but only if you have a partner." Eric nodded at Lathia, who still sat sulking on the far end of the platform. "My cousin looks as though she could go for a dance. Ask her."

Eric shoved Derby toward Lathia before escorting Viola down the steps into the yard. Eric gave his wife a playful twirl. No sooner had the lord and lady of Tsaftown begun dancing than throngs of couples filled the area. It seemed that many had been waiting to follow their lord's lead.

"You're feeling quite spry today," Viola said. "You've never once asked me to dance. Not unless protocol demanded it."

"It's a new day, my dear," Eric said. "Perhaps I've finally found my reason to dance."

Viola smiled and drew closer. "Truly?"

Eric kissed her hand. "Truly. I may not dance often, but when I do, you are my first and only choice."

Viola's smile warmed, and they danced among the people of Tsaftown.

Every so often, Eric's mind drifted to important matters that would soon demand his attention—echoes of what other dangers might linger over Er'Rets in a new world after Darkness, or what would happen if the legacy of Fenris hung over Tsaftown like a storm cloud.

But he pushed the thoughts aside and pulled Viola close.

Tomorrow would bring its own troubles, but today Eric chose to dance with his wife and savor the many blessings that Arman had bestowed on him and his family.

BONUS EPILOGUE

Thank you for reading *Lord of Winter*. We hope you loved the story. Find out what happens next with our Bonus Epilogue, a special gift, available only to our newsletter subscribers.

This Bonus Epilogue will not be released on any retailer platform, so scan our QR code to get your free gift. You acknowledge you are becoming a Sunrise Publishing, Andrew Swearingen, and Jill Williamson subscriber. Unsubscribe from any of the newsletters at any time.

The only man she loves is the one she can never have…

Lady Tara's dreams of marrying for love were shattered with her arranged marriage to the sickly Lord Gershom. Fine. She may not have love, but she has purpose—a position of power that lets her make a difference in the kingdom. At least her Carmack, her fiercely loyal shield, remains by her side, even if she must deny her heart.

Then Lord Gershom dies. And to her horror, Carmack is blamed. Branded a traitor, he flees, forcing Tara to choose between protecting the life she's built or following the man she loves.

Carmack Demry has secretly loved Lady Tara all his life, sworn to protect her at any cost—even if it meant watching her wed another man. But now, accused of a crime he didn't commit, he's on the run because staying away is the only way to keep her safe. Except Tara has other plans.

Determined to clear his name, she plunges into a web of treachery and deceit that reaches far beyond them both—one that threatens the very heart of the kingdom. Together, they must navigate a world of danger, unravel a conspiracy, and face a choice more perilous than any battlefield: deny their love or risk everything to claim it.

CHAPTER ONE
TARA

*T*HE FOOL WHO POKES A SLEEPING TAN-*niyn wakes more trouble than expected.*

Her mother's proverb sprang to mind as Lady Tara reached the heavy door separating her from her husband. She wanted her letter, but she hadn't the smallest interest in provoking a giant sea serpent, slumbering or otherwise. Perhaps she should wait for Carmack.

Tara glanced down the corridor toward the great hall where her Shield was meeting with the constable—something about a recent escape from Ice Island. Who knew how long the meeting would take, and Lord Gershom might rouse at any moment. Since his last bout of fever, the ancient man's only predictable habit was to destroy anything that confused him. Nothing was safe, not even Viola's letter lying harmlessly with Tara's sketchbook on the sofa. In his addled state, he would likely toss it into the fire or snatch it for use in the privy.

If only Tara had finished reading her letter during dinner, but as always, she was called away with great urgency, for the cantankerous lord of the house was not to be kept waiting.

Tara pressed her ear against the door. Lord Gershom's snoring easily penetrated the wood, so she nudged it open and peeked inside the solar. Though night blackened the windows, the timber clad walls glowed with candlelight behind the furniture huddled near the crackling fireplace. Lord Gershom slumped on the brown cushions of the far chair. The waning firelight cast deep shadows into his countless wrinkles, and his mouth hung open, a line of encrusted spittle stretching to his chin.

On the sofa cushion next to him lay Tara's belongings. She gripped the door handle. *Please, Arman, silence the hinges.* Though Tara pushed ever so gently, the iron hardware groaned. Gritting her teeth, she added the traitorous hinges to her lengthy list of unanswered prayers.

Gershom snored on. Tara slipped into the room and nearly choked on the old man's sour body odor. The jasmine-scented candles burning low in the sconces were no match for his poor hygiene, just as the valet was no match for his lord's combative refusal to bathe.

Tara tiptoed across every creaky knot in the hardwood floor, then slowly reached for her belongings on the sofa. Gershom's snoring hitched. She froze, her gaze locked on his chest until its shallow rise and fall resumed. Extending her fingers again, she took hold of the letter and sketchbook then headed for the door.

Snap!

Tara jumped. Only a cinder popping, but with her sudden movement, the letter slipped free and fluttered to the floor. Her skin crawled with the sensation of being watched. A glance over her shoulder confirmed Gershom's foggy eyes were fixed on her. She pivoted, her gaze darting to the side table. There, by the wine decanter, sat his tonics, including a sleeping draught. The lavender bottle seemed impossibly out of reach.

"Good evening, Lord Gershom." Tara curtsied low and scooped her letter from the floor. Slipping it into her sketchbook, she smiled as if welcoming a distinguished guest to Lytton Hall, her childhood home. "May I offer you some refreshment?"

Gershom's skeletal hands twitched. "Who are you?"

"Lady Tara, my lord. Your—" She paused. When she last reminded Gershom that she was his wife, he had thrown a pitcher that narrowly missed her head and hollered a slew of vulgarities about her four dead predecessors. "Your neighbor from Tsaftown."

"Neighbor. Bah!" He broke into a wheezing cough.

Tara rushed to the tray. She set her sketchbook aside and poured a generous dose of the sleeping draught into a glass goblet, then added wine to mask its fumes. She offered it to him. "Here, drink this."

His deathlike fingers tightened over her outstretched hand. Tara suppressed a shudder and guided the goblet to his mouth.

Not one drop of the ruby liquid crossed his lips before his hairy nostrils flared. "Poison!" He thrust the goblet away, sloshing its contents into Tara's face.

The liquid stung her eyes, and she rubbed them with her crimson sleeve. "What? No!"

In the blur, Gershom wrenched the goblet away and flung it to the floor, shards of glass pelting Tara's velvet gown. "Liar!" He grabbed hold of her wrists.

Tara lurched back, but he held tight, pulling himself out of his chair. "Lord Gershom, please let go."

"Who are you, trespasser?" he hissed.

Tara's stomach heaved at the stench of his tooth decay. "I'm Tara. Lord Edik Livna's daughter." Her late father's name barely escaped her quivering lips.

"Livna?" A flash of recognition smoothed the creases between Gershom's eyebrows, but suspicion quickly darkened his countenance again. "You are too old to be Livna's girl."

There was no point arguing. Gershom remembered the child

Tara once was, not the nineteen-year-old woman he'd married. His grip on her wrists tightened.

Feeling her bones about to break, Tara yelped. "You're hurting me."

He pushed her away, and she tipped sideways, her feet tangling in her skirt's heavy pleats. The floor knocked the breath from her lungs. Rather than fuel Gershom's anger, she lay still, peering under the sofa toward the door that led to the great hall and willing help to come.

Hinges creaked again, but the sound came from the wrong door—the corner servant's entrance. Rather than Carmack's black boots, two flour-dusted shoes stood rooted on the threshold.

Ghee, the cook.

"Where is my cane?" Gershom grabbed a fistful of Tara's hair and pulled her onto her knees. "You stole it, didn't you?"

"Ow! No, my lord."

The greasy-faced cook stuck his head into the room. "My lord?"

"Help," Tara whimpered, her eyes locked with Ghee's.

"Get out," Gershom snapped, "or I'll have you drawn and quartered."

"Yes, my lord." Ghee withdrew, shutting the door behind him.

Insufferable coward. "Carmack!" Tara's throat burned from the force of her scream.

"Quiet!" Gershom yanked her hair.

Tara clawed at his hands. Cursing, he released her and reached for the fireplace poker. She scrambled to her feet and lifted her hem to run when the iron shaft hit her shoulder, sending a crippling shock all the way to her fingertips. Gershom jerked the hook loose, snagging her sleeve and leaving a searing trail across her arm.

Suddenly, the main door burst open.

A whirl of muscle catapulted over the sofa with the ferocity of an attacking cham. Gershom let the poker fly again, but Carmack caught it mid-swing and filled the space between Tara and her attacker.

Gershom grunted, straining to free his weapon. "Let go, ruffian!"

With one jerk, Carmack claimed the poker and pointed at the sofa. "Sit!"

Tara's legs wobbled, and she peeked around his wide back. Gershom collapsed onto the sofa, clasping his chest and gasping.

Carmack tossed the poker aside and turned his attention on her. His ecru tunic, leather jerkin, and sable pants suited his dark hair and beard, but his thunderous expression darkened his mahogany eyes. "Are you all right?"

Too shaken to answer, Tara nodded.

Carmack's gaze shifted to her torn sleeve.

Half the length of her finger, the bleeding cut on her arm was the worst she'd ever suffered. If her mother were here, she'd be beside herself.

My dear, you are not allowed cuts, scrapes, or skinned knees like your brothers. Scars are repulsive, especially on a lady.

"You shouldn't be here with him," Carmack said, his deep voice gruffer than usual.

Behind him, Gershom sagged against the cushion, his jagged breaths quieted, and his eyes closed. Thank Arman for that. The ogre was falling back to sleep.

Carmack's gaze never left Tara's bloodied sleeve until he hung his head. How typically Carmack, blaming himself instead of her or even Gershom.

What would Mother say if she had caused a mess like this? Not that she ever would, but a saying popped into Tara's head anyway. *Keep conversations light, and your burdens out of sight.*

Tara gingerly pulled the ripped fabric over her wound. "Perhaps it can be mended with some ribbon?"

Carmack jerked his chin. "Ribbon?"

"No, you're right. Lace would be better."

"Lace? To stop the bleeding?"

"Gracious, no. For my dress."

Carmack pinched the bridge of his nose. "This once, might you forget about your finery long enough to notice you need stitching first?"

"Nonsense. It's naught but a hangnail." Tara waved her hand. With the movement, the cut proved a greater pain than the usual suffocating stays or jabbing hairpins. Unable to hold a steady smile, she brushed past Carmack toward her husband. "Now, help me settle—"

Lord Gershom was reclined at an awkward angle. His hands rested slack on his lap, not twitching. No wheezing rattled his lungs.

Tara's breath caught. The old man had turned positively gray. "My lord?"

Carmack stepped forward. "Lord Gershom?" He nudged Lord Gershom's shoulder, then leaned closer, pressing his fingers against his neck.

Why wouldn't the stubborn old goat answer?

"He's dead," Carmack said. "The fit must have finished him off."

She gasped. Dead? He couldn't be, not really. The old man looked like death on a good day, but Tara couldn't deny his pallor was worse now. And Carmack wouldn't mislead her about Lord Gershom dying. Tara's heart skipped a beat. Her husband *was* dead. Freedom.

Cruel heart, how could she be so unfeeling at a moment like this? But she couldn't help it. When she breathed again, it was as if it were for the first time since her father had announced her engagement.

The servant's door creaked open again. Ghee's gaping mouth betrayed his having eavesdropped. He skittered across the room to Lord Gershom's side. "My lord?" Ghee shouted into the dead man's ear. When no response came, he gave Tara a stilted bow. "Sympathies, my lady."

Sympathies was what one said to despairing widows at funerals, not her. Dizzied by her racing thoughts, Tara swayed.

Carmack steadied her, his strong arm around her waist, and she sagged against him, letting his warmth draw the chill from her bones. "Bring a litter to move Lord Gershom to his bedchamber."

"Aye." Ghee glanced at Carmack's hand upon Tara's waist, his eyes narrowing. "I'll help fer Lord Gershom's sake, but not on account of you asking. I know what you've done," he said and scurried out the servant's door.

The weight of Ghee's accusation sank in, and Tara pulled away from Carmack. "I fear what he will tell the others. What if they blame you for his lordship's death?"

Carmack shrugged. "Let them. The senile wheezer had no right to strike you."

"I am—*was* his wife, little more than his property." Tara swallowed the bitterness rising in her throat. "The men of Meribah Corner are loyal to Lord Gershom. Most have not seen how much his illness changed him in these last months." Worse were those who, like Ghee, had witnessed his outbursts and still revered him. "You saw how Ghee looked at us, what he said. He clearly drew the wrong conclusion. If he spins a tale about you attacking his lordship, you could be arrested or worse. You should return to Tsaftown."

He furrowed his brow. "Only if you go too."

"I can't leave, not with a funeral to plan."

"Then I stay." Carmack crossed his thick arms. "Besides, what excuse would I give Lady Revada for abandoning my post?"

"We both know why my mother sent you here." Tara glanced at the gruesome figure slouched on the sofa. Over the course of her marriage, Lord Gershom had kissed her exactly once, at the end of the wedding ceremony when Tara turned her face at the last second, allowing him to peck her cheek. Every other time her husband had looked her way with that detestable gleam in his eye, Carmack had stepped in, distracting his lordship so Tara could make her escape. "I am no longer in any danger of my husband's attentions."

"Gershom isn't the only monster in these woods."

"It's not monsters I fear but men fed lies and thirsty for vengeance. You have to leave. Let me manage this on my own."

Carmack uncrossed his arms, but instead of bowing, he closed the distance between them. "No, my lady. You need me here, now more than ever."

His tender address stunned Tara. When she stared into his eyes, the gathering storm seemed less ominous. Maybe no one would believe Ghee. Though well-known in Meribah Corner, he was only a cook. Perhaps she and Carmack could push through it. Together.

But she remembered Ghee's accusing gaze when he saw Carmack holding her. Saints, had the cook read something untoward into Carmack's simple gesture of support and mistaken it as motive for murder? Or had her own face betrayed her? While Carmack was always a model Shield, hiding her affection for him wasn't easy. Distance would help and was likely the only way to protect them both from scandal. But how to get Carmack to go?

Tara straightened her spine. She had to pull rank. "When my late father arranged my marriage, the only thought he seemingly gave to my future happiness was to ensure that on the day of Lord Gershom's death, I would inherit Meribah Corner."

Carmack scoffed. "Still a lopsided bargain in the elder's favor."

He had always been Tara's fiercest defender, but now was no time to stoke his protective nature, not when she meant to drive him away. Tara turned her voice to ice. "You miss my point. This estate is now mine, and the last thing I need is another man lording over me."

"I am not your lord, Tara. Or anyone's. Nor will I ever be." Carmack's cheeks reddened. "But as your friend—"

"Master Demry, you will call me Lady Gershom." Her heartbeat quickened in her ears, matching the tempo of the unseen mob advancing in her mind. She raised her chin, determined to see him safely away from those who might harm him. "I order you to leave."

Carmack shifted away from her, his eyes stormy and jaw clenched. "Don't do this. Don't ask me to run like a cowardly deserter."

The stricken look on his handsome face tore at Tara's heart. She hadn't considered how it might look if he left, only the danger of him staying. Ordering him to run was asking him to be less than he was, and Tara couldn't, no more than she could say he was wrong about her needing him, because she did. He'd been nothing less than her lifeline, a constant presence standing guard beside her.

But he couldn't stay beside her, not now. His freedom…nay, his very life might be at risk. Feeling her facade slip, Tara spun on her heel. "Fine, remain in Meribah Corner if you must, but stay away from me."

"If you wish it." His deep voice turned gruff. "Good night, my lady."

His parting footsteps faded, and the chill seeped back into Tara's bones until she felt no pain from her injuries. Through the leaded windowpanes, she watched Carmack cross the bailey to the gatehouse where he entered the constable's quarters. The mob Tara feared never came. Only Master Ulmer the steward, Constable Becker, and two guards.

After they carried Gershom's body away, Tara crouched to pick her letter and sketchbook from the floor. Haunted by Carmack's hurt expression, she numbly lifted Viola's letter and stood near the fireplace reading the blurry words through unshed tears. Somehow, a winter of trials had ushered in a season of domestic bliss for Tara's brother and his wife.

True love is possible, even for us...

For Viola, perhaps, but Tara would not fall prey to that dream again. She finished her letter and dropped the pages on the pile of dying embers, watching them shrivel in a satisfying flash of heat.

An icy draft whistled through the glass panes, and Tara returned to the window. Outside, the late winter wind whipped a dusting of fresh snow into drifts, erasing her Shield's footprints. The bitterly long season had saved its coldest night for last.

Acknowledgements

To my wife Mary, thank you for your love, encouragement, and (most of all) your patience with me as I've worked on this book. Lord of Winter would not have happened without you.

To my son Caleb, for being the reason I want to share my stories. I hope that Eric's story becomes one of the bricks that builds you into the man God has made you to be.

To Mom, for always loving me and nurturing my creative side (even when I decided to be a film major).

To Dad, for teaching me to love great stories, especially when the good guys win.

To Jason, for sharing many brilliant fantasy novels with me that I never would have found otherwise.

To Spencer, for letting me play with your G.I. Joes (and not being too mad when I buried them in the sand box). Those were some of the first stories I ever got to tell.

To Megan, for being the best big sister I could have ever asked for and for taking your dorky little brother to go see all those movies.

To Susan May Warren, for being an amazing teacher and motivator throughout this entire process. You truly are a marvel.

To Jill Williamson, for being an amazing friend, collaborator, and mentor. Who would have guessed when you signed my copy of By Darkness Hid in 2011 that we'd end up here? Thank you for trusting me to tell part of the story of Er'rets.

To my fellow draft authors, Kelly and Niki. I have been so blessed to go on this journey with you both. Writing our stories together has been a blast, and I can't wait to sit down and read your books.

To John Gund, I never could have imagined having a best friend like you. Thanks for all the proofreading as I submitted my first audition samples for this story. You saved my bacon from more horrible grammatical pitfalls than I care to mention.

To Sarah Gund, for being the first person to truly love one of my stories and beg for more. That encouragement kept me going during many, many long lonely writing sessions.

To my critique partners, Michala and Catherine. Thank you for reviewing my early submissions for this book and for always peppering me with questions that I couldn't quite answer yet.

To my Lord. You put the first stories in my heart when I was just a boy. And when I wanted to throw in the towel, You stuck your finger in my chest and said, "Don't you dare give up." This story and all the others were Your idea in the first place. All the glory belongs to You.

Andrew Swearingen is a science fiction and fantasy writer living in the beautiful forest kingdom of Southern Illinois.

He started writing fantasy adventure stories in middle school (usually when he was supposed to be taking notes in Math class) and is still on that journey today. Since that time, Andrew has published numerous short fiction stories in several magazines and podcasts.

In his non-writing time, Andrew enjoys hiking the trails of the Shawnee National Forest with his wife, playing Lego with his son, and searching for his next favorite nerdy board game.

Find out more at andrewswearingen.com.

Jill Williamson is a multi-passionate creative who loves the arts. She's written over two dozen books for readers of all ages and is best known for her Blood of Kings fantasy series, two of which won Christy Awards and made VOYA magazine's Best Science Fiction, Fantasy, and Horror list. She produces films with her husband and teaches about writing at conferences.

Visit her at www.jillwilliamson.com.

Love Romantic Suspense?

Try these amazing stories...

Available Now!

Do you love historical romance?
Try these...

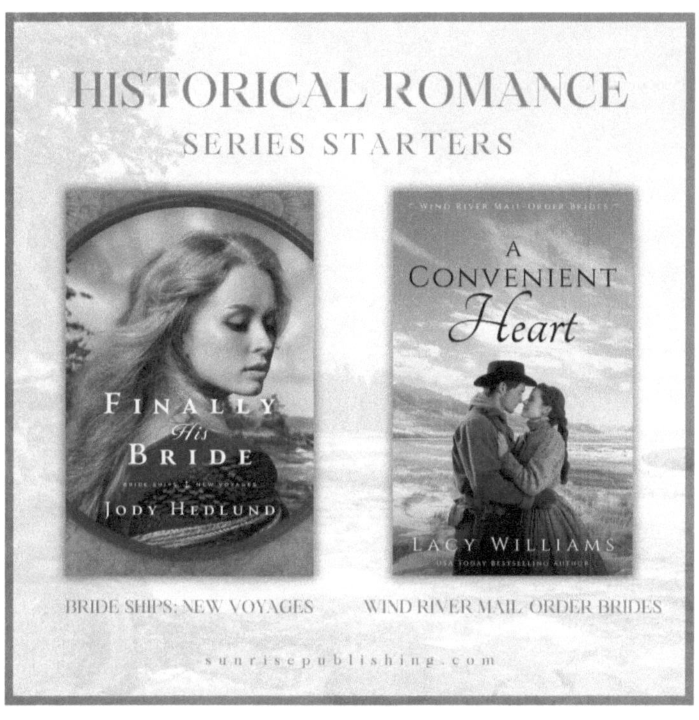

Jody Hedlund's Bride Ships: New Voyages and
Lacy Williams' Wind River Mail-Order Brides.
To view all our titles, visit our website
or scan our QR code below.

Connect With Sunrise

Thank you again for reading *Lord of Winter.* We hope you enjoyed the story. If you did, would you be willing to do us a favor and leave a review? It doesn't have to be long- just a few words to help other readers know what they're getting. (But no spoilers! We don't want to wreck the fun!) Thank you again for reading!

We'd love to hear from you- not only about this story, but about any characters or stories you'd like to read in the future. Contact us at www.sunrisepublishing.com/contact.

We also have a regular updates that contains sneak peeks, reviews, upcoming releases, and fun stuff for our reader friends. Sign up at www.sunrisepublishing.com or scan our QR code.

9 781963 372601